A PRINCESS IN TRAINING

"Do you still want me to show you what Nvengarians enjoy in bed?" Damien asked.

Penelope looked at him under her lashes, her cheeks flushed. "Yes."

He felt a tightening in his groin. "I am pleased to hear you say that."

She lifted her chin, though her eyes were wary. "I hardly want you to run off to another Nvengarian woman because you believe me too hesitant."

He traced his fingers along her cheek, turning her to face him. "Ah, Penelope. What I have to teach you will take many years to learn. I am patient enough to spend every day teaching you, if need be." He touched his mouth to Penelope's upper lip. She hungrily leaned into the kiss, but he pulled away. She sent him a look of frustrated need.

"We'll do this slowly," he said. "But do not worry. I will teach you everything…."

Penelope & Prince Charming

JENNIFER ASHLEY

LEISURE BOOKS NEW YORK CITY

For my own Prince Charming.

A LEISURE BOOK®

April 2006

Published by

Dorchester Publishing Co., Inc.
200 Madison Avenue
New York, NY 10016

ISBN 0-8439-5606-2

The name "Leisure Books" and the stylized "L" with design are trademarks of Dorchester Publishing Co., Inc.

Printed in the United States of America.

Visit us on the web at www.dorchesterpub.com.

Penelope &
Prince Charming

Prologue

December 1818

His full name was Prince Damien Augustus Frederic Michel of Nvengaria, a title that always caused mild panic. People were afraid they'd have to remember it.

"Call me Damien," he'd say. "It will save time."

Women called him *love* and *cherie* and *oh-please-don't-stop-doing-that* in whatever language they happened to speak.

He had black hair and the dark blue eyes of the people of Nvengaria, an athletic body and skin slightly darker than that of most Europeans. Nvengarian men were reputed to be devoted to the intense pleasure of the women in their beds, and ladies from Belgrade to Heidelberg to London were willing to find out whether this was true.

The woman in Damien's bed tonight was a Russian countess with blond hair, blue eyes, and a lush body that his own body was vastly enjoying.

His brain, on the other hand, was preoccupied. He had nearly died again this afternoon. But luckily he'd seen the assassin's knife a split second before it struck. His bodyguard had taken the would-be killer down, and Damien had walked on, pretending to the crowd on the Paris street that his heart wasn't screaming in his throat.

Hence, the countess.

Her gaze roved the knotted muscles of his biceps and shoulders in admiration. "My prince. My handsome prince."

Damien lowered himself to her and put his mouth against hers. "Hush."

She smiled eagerly and licked her lips, her tongue brushing his. "Make me."

He did. He slanted his mouth across hers, kissing her in burning strokes. His skin dripped sweat in the over-heated room, muscles contracting as he moved on her.

The wide mirror on the wall reflected her slender white body nearly hidden under his own bronzed nakedness, the round of his hips rising and falling. Candles blazed around the bed and throughout the sumptuous room, dozens of them, so that if a few burned out, Damien would not be left in the dark.

One candle guttered and smoked, making him want to sneeze. The countess's noises grew frantic. She tore her mouth from his. *"Damien."*

She lifted her hips, squeezing him hard. This was what he'd been waiting for—to lose himself in the mindlessness of it, to let her pressure on him erase all thought.

He gave a heartfelt groan, disappointment mixed with ecstasy. The intense, wild feeling boiling through him meant he would come down to earth in a second or two, and then it would be over.

He held on as long as he could. Too long, too long. *Damn.* He climaxed with one last thrust while she shrieked and moaned.

It was done. Damien withdrew and crashed onto the bed beside her. His arousal stood out in a sharp angle from his body, slick and wet from their lovemaking. He was already hardening again, nowhere near sated, but blessed, numbing sleep was coming to take him over.

The countess looked at him, smiling lazily. "Oh, my prince. That was the best I ever had."

He returned the smile, but didn't answer. She probably exaggerated. His body grew heavy, seeking sleep. Sweet, oblivious sleep.

Before he succumbed, he politely loosened the silk tethers that bound her wrists to the headboard.

She looked disappointed. He briefly kissed her lips, whispered, "Go to sleep," and then went there himself.

Damien awoke to a sharp knock on his chamber door. He dragged open his eyes and swore softly. By the bright candlelight, he saw that the clock had moved only an hour, and he was still exhausted.

He did not worry that a jealous lover had come calling for the countess. The only person allowed past the antechamber, the only one allowed to knock on the bedchamber door, was Petri, his valet.

If Petri knocked, he must have good reason. Maybe France had gone to war again, and the French king would once more flee into exile. That would make a good excuse for Damien to leave Paris, and he was looking for one.

Spain was nice this time of year. The Spanish court liked him. He could commission another painting from that retired court painter; Goya, that was his name. Damien liked his art. The man had a gift for seeing what was really there.

Or London. He grimaced. No, in London he'd have to visit the Prince Regent, and their last parting had been cool. During Damien's previous visit, the Regent had overheard someone say of Damien, "Now *he's* what a prince should be."

Damien rose from the bed. He absently brushed dried patches of cream from his skin and shrugged on his dressing gown. The countess slept on, her head pillowed on her arm, the blissful sleep of a woman with no conscience.

Damien silently opened the door and slipped into the antechamber.

Petri waited for him with six other men who'd crammed themselves into the little jewel box of a room. All except Petri were dressed in the full livery of the imperial princes of Nvengaria—bright blue coats, blue trousers, black boots, gold epaulettes, polished brass buttons, and medals.

Nvengaria liked to bestow medals. Damien doubted that rulers of other countries cut medals for rescuing the Imperial Prince's cat from a tree, but Damien's father had. Damien's father handed out medals for anything, pretending to be a benevolent man, though no one was foolish enough to believe he was.

Damien recognized the leader of the pack as Misk, the man the Imperial Prince sent to Damien when he had an important message for him, usually a death threat. Misk wore more medals than the other lackeys. Damien wondered how the man could stand up straight with all the metal hanging from his chest.

"Your Highness." Misk bowed low, medals clanking. "Terrible, grievous news I have."

Damien waited without alarm. Misk always had terrible, grievous news.

Misk removed a velvet drawstring bag from his pocket. Inside was a small box, inlaid in rosewood and teak in the designs of the imperial family crest.

The box was very old; the sides had been polished with time until the inlay was smooth, the lines of the design blurred.

Misk opened the box and handed it to Damien.

Inside lay a ring. A silver ring, thick and heavy, the flat head bearing the signet of the Imperial Prince of Nvengaria.

"That is my father's," Damien said.

"No, Imperial Highness. It is yours. Your father is dead."

Damien's heart missed a beat. The father who had imprisoned him, then thrown him into exile, threatening him with death if he so much as looked in Nvengaria's direction again. Dead and gone.

Damien drew out the ring, held it up to the candlelight. The silver, eight hundred years old, gleamed softly.

The men in the room dropped to their knees.

Damien looked over their bowed heads to the gilded vines lining the walls of the antechamber. He was now the Imperial Prince of Nvengaria.

For one moment, he said nothing. The men waited. He poised on the knife-edge of change—whatever decision he made here would seal his fate forever. No going back.

He closed his fist around the ring. "Petri," he said softly. "Pack my things."

Chapter One

England, May 23, 1819

Nothing out of the ordinary ever happened in Little Marching, Oxfordshire.

Ever.

"Where are you off to, darling?" Penelope's mother, Lady Trask, asked as Penelope and her friend Meagan donned bonnets in the high-ceiling hall of Ashborn Manor, the Trask country home.

Lady Trask stood at the large oval table in the middle of the hall, arranging flowers of varying shapes and clashing colors in a huge oriental vase. Lady Trask often arranged flowers. She also painted with watercolors. She did little else.

Penelope gave her mother a kiss. "To the village. To buy ribbons."

Lady Trask returned the kiss with a tiny one on Penelope's cheek, a long-stemmed, early rose in her hand.

"Take one of your books to Mrs. Swanson, dear. She likes your little stories."

Penelope had already put one of the collections of fairy tales into her basket. "Yes, Mama."

Lady Trask frowned at the rose. "You will not get white ribbons, will you? You are too old for white."

"Of course not, Mama," she said, tying the very brown ribbons of her small, flat bonnet. "I have not worn white in three seasons."

Lady Trask sighed. "A pity your father died. He could have found you such a rich husband, Penny, dear."

Penelope drew on her gloves, carefully fitting them over each finger. "You know I have decided not to marry, Mama."

Penelope's two betrothals had been disasters. Reuben White, a handsome man about town, had wanted a pliable wife who'd look the other way at his blatant affairs. Magnus Grady, whom she'd thought older, wiser, and safer, had turned out to want a pretty young girl to chase around the drawing room.

Penelope had cried off and been labeled a jilt, then a double-jilt. When her father died, his title and money had passed to her cousins, leaving her and her mother only a small jointure and allowance. Penelope's dowry had been drained to repay debt, rendering Penelope no longer a catch.

Lady Trask regarded her sorrowfully. "All girls wish to marry rich husbands."

"If I married, Mama, who would look after you?"

She considered. "Yes, that is a point. But Meagan's dear papa has been such a comfort."

That was an understatement. The two girls left the house before they could burst into giggles.

"They'll marry in a sixmonth, I'll have a wager on it," Meagan said as they strolled down the curving drive.

"I put it quicker than that." Penelope smiled.

They glanced back at the house. Meagan and her father, Michael Tavistock, had come from their home in the north of Oxfordshire to stay a time with the Trasks. Michael Tavistock had been strolling the garden while the two girls readied themselves to go to the village, "Waiting for us to clear out," Meagan had whispered.

"They've worn out one bedstead already," Meagan observed as they turned to the road that descended to the village. "I do wish they'd get on with it. I am tired of pretending to everyone that they are friends only because you and I are friends."

"It will be a rest, certainly," Penelope agreed. "But I believe they enjoy pretending to be illicit lovers."

"At their age." Meagan sighed with the wisdom of her nineteen years. "It gives them something to do, I suppose. Little Marching is so dull in the summer. Nothing ever happens here."

"I like nothing happening," Penelope replied with conviction. "It is restful. You know that each day will be quiet and slow, just like the one before."

Meagan snorted. "You say restful. I say dull. Dull, dull, dull. No balls, no soirees, no museums, just Little Marching and home."

"What you mean is, no men to flirt with."

"Well, no." Meagan opened her arms, gesturing to the rolling green hills that stretched to the hazy horizon. "Do you see any men here? None to dance with, to flirt with, to entice into corners—Ah, Penelope, they are fine creatures, men. A little patience, a little coaxing, and they can become quite civilized."

Penelope studied the white and yellow flowers by the side of the road. "So you say."

"Oh, come, come, Pen, even you cannot be immune. Tell me that a room full of trousers does not make you melt."

"Trousers with men in them, I suppose you mean?" She smiled.

Meagan looked dreamy. "Tight trousers. Tight coats on broad shoulders. Hair that makes you want to run wanton fingers through it. A handsome face, a wicked smile. Eyes that make you all shivery and warm at the same time."

Penelope came out of her doldrums to laugh. "I vow, Meagan, your papa had better get you married off quickly. You are going to burn into a little pile of ashes, and all will wonder at the sad end of poor man-mad Meagan Tavistock."

"Oh, piffle. I shall marry, but I shall only marry a very handsome gentleman who is madly in love with me."

"They do not exist, Meagan," Penelope said quietly. "We marry for money and property and to keep families together. When a gentleman wants love, he goes elsewhere."

Meagan looked remorseful. "Sorry, Pen. I forgot."

Penelope's heart gave a quick, painful beat. "You see, you should learn from my experience. Ladies of our station do not marry for love. It is convenience, that is all, no matter what pretty words they whisper into our ears."

Pretty words. Seductive murmurs. False, all of it. *Come to me, love, so that I can put an heir in my nursery, then run about with my favorite mistress and ignore you.* Thank heavens she'd found out the truth before the ring had been on her finger.

"Not all men are like Mr. White," Meagan said. "You were unlucky."

"But they are, my dear," Penelope answered. "Admire them all you want, but be aware of the truth. They want to marry for money and connections, nothing more. Handsome princes do not sweep in and take ordinary girls to their faraway kingdoms, except in stories. Real princes have double chins and marry for politics."

She closed her mouth, her tongue having flapped too long.

Meagan pursed her lips. She knew the story of Penelope's troubles, but Meagan insisted that both events had been aberrations. Young, pretty, red-haired Meagan had much to learn. Gentlemen just could not be trusted.

And so, Penelope was perfectly content to live out her life in Little Marching in the middle of Oxfordshire, where nothing remotely interesting ever happened.

Ever.

"Is this the village?"

His Imperial Highness, Prince Damien Augustus Frederic Michel of Nvengaria lifted the coach's curtain with a weary hand.

"Little Marching, Oxfordshire," the small, bearded man next to him said. "I am afraid it is, Your Highness."

Chapter Two

Damien studied the square church and cluster of white-washed, thatch-roofed houses before letting the velvet curtain fall. So this was Little Marching. After weeks of grueling travel, he had arrived at last.

"And she is here?" he asked.

"Yes," Sasha said. His former tutor touched his neatly trimmed beard as he always did when he was nervous. "Somewhere."

Damien instructed the coachman to halt in the village square. Rufus, one of the footmen, jerked open the door and made an exaggerated bow. Damien climbed down before the other footman, Miles, could whip the cushioned step stool under his feet. Both footmen shot Damien a disappointed look.

The village was silent as Damien strolled a little way along the cobbled square, past quiet houses with blank windows. He knew the villagers watched. How could they not? He was a stranger here, an object of interest.

And what an object. The hired chaise was painted a luxurious, shiny black, the spokes of its wheels picked out in red. The four horses were gray, perfectly matched, and sported purple plumes on their headstalls. The plumes drooped now from the long journey, but Sasha had insisted on plumes. Damien's own horse, midnight black and bred from the finest stock, was tethered behind the carriage.

Damien's tall footmen, Rufus and Miles, were Nvengarian to the hilt, with black hair, blue eyes, and bright blue, military-style livery. Sasha dressed in a Bond Street suit, over which he wore his red and gold sash of office as the prince's advisor.

For traveling, Damien had remained casual—a linen shirt and riding breeches with boots and a coat shrugged on over all. His black hair hung free, and like all Nvengarians, he did not wear a hat.

But even in subdued dress, his six-and-a-half-foot height and broad shoulders made people take a second look. He did not belong there, and the watching square made sure he knew that.

Damien glanced at a long, low building of crumbling stone on one side of the square. "Is that the tavern?" he asked his footmen in Nvengarian.

Rufus and Miles, the experts on country taverns, nodded.

Rufus and Miles had discovered that the best thing about world travel was beer. From Bucharest to Austria to the Low Countries to England, no matter what language the natives spoke, the two young men could make understood the words "tavern" and "beer."

Now they stood to attention on each side of the inn's door while Damien ducked inside. Sasha followed, then the two footmen brought up the rear.

Damien found a typical English tavern, low-ceilinged

with a smoking fireplace, settles along the walls, and tables bowed from years of use. On this warm afternoon, the room was mostly empty, as farmers were still in their fields and villagers worked at their trade.

The benches were half-filled with older men, grizzled-haired grandfathers taking refuge in a pint of ale and banter with friends. As Damien entered, every man lifted his head and stared.

Damien had been in English country taverns before. But on those journeys he'd been alone. The locals had looked him over, then stoically accepted him as another traveler. He'd never before entered a tavern with his entourage.

The patrons studied Rufus and Miles and Sasha and Damien. The silence grew hostile.

Sasha looked back at them, aghast. "On your feet," he cried, "for the most Imperial Prince Damien Augustus Frederic Michel of Nvengaria."

The landlord, who'd come forward at their entrance, stopped in his tracks. Someone snorted. Dark mutters began.

"Why do they not stand?" Sasha hissed to Damien in Nvengarian. "Why do these peasants not bow?"

Sasha liked people to bow. In palaces across Europe, Prince Damien was greeted with bows and curtsies and, at times, downright groveling. But then, Damien was handsome and rich and well liked. He was known for his generosity; plus, he was a crack shot, an athletic rider, and reputed to be one of the best lovers in Europe.

He was admired for his handsome body, his intelligence, his energy, and his interest in everything from new inventions to pretty tavern wenches. Good times were never far behind whenever Damien of Nvengaria visited.

But this time, once they'd reached England, Damien had traveled incognito, or as incognito as Sasha would let him. Sasha loved pageantry and was dismayed whenever people did not recognize Damien.

But then, poor Sasha had been locked in a dungeon for fifteen years. He'd dared to defend Damien once upon a time, and Damien's father hadn't liked that. Damien, who'd likewise been locked in a dungeon and knew how it felt, indulged Sasha whenever he could.

"They are not peasants," he told Sasha now. "If you call an English farmer a peasant, he will skewer your balls on his pitchfork."

The smaller man whitened. "Truly?"

Damien looked back at the hostile faces. He smiled. "Rufus, remind me of that magic phrase, will you?"

Rufus grinned. He drew himself up and said in his thickly accented English, "Drinks for everyone."

Men shifted. The air thawed. Damien announced to the landlord, "Your best ale for every man in the room."

He reached into his coat pocket and drew out a pouch that clinked. The landlord and patrons suddenly grinned.

An hour later, the place had been transformed. Rufus and Miles played a loud game of dice in the corner with three of the locals. Damien's coachman stood in the doorway, one eye on the carriage, one on the comely barmaid who brought him ale.

Sasha was immersed in a crowd of half-drunk listeners while he tried to explain in his accented English the entire history of Nvengaria.

Damien drew the largest group with his warm smile and store of off-color stories. The men of Little Marching laughed and slapped each other on their backs. The ale kept coming.

The commotion attracted the attention of the other villagers. The butcher and the blacksmith shed aprons and shut up shop to join the throng. A few farmers drifted in from their fields. Boys came to ogle Damien's coach and riding horse, and women peered into the tavern to ogle

Damien. The landlord's daughter gave him sly looks from under her lashes.

But Damien had not come for a dalliance. He had a task to complete before Midsummer's Day, or all would be lost. He turned to his fifteen new best friends and asked, "Tell me, is there a house called Ashborn Manor nearby?"

He got fifteen garbled answers, but most agreed that he should ride out of town to the north a mile or so.

He rose, remarkably steady on his feet, and made them all a courtly bow. The villagers scrambled to rise and bow back, with varying degrees of success.

Damien returned the bows and strolled out of the tavern. The villagers shouted their good-byes.

"Wait, my friends," Rufus slurred from inside the tavern. "Before I go, I teach you Nvengarian dance."

The tavern roared with laughter, then the clapping began.

The black horse shook its head and snorted as Damien approached.

"A little longer, my friend," Damien murmured, stroking him. "And you can go home." They both could.

Damien untied the stallion from the carriage, mounted, and rode off to the north.

"What on earth are they doing?" Meagan asked.

Meagan and Penelope paused on the road that wound down the hill and into the village. A strange carriage with horses sporting purple plumes stood in the street in front of the tavern below. A line of men were issuing from the door of the tavern, their hands on each others' waists. Occasionally, they'd wave their arms or kick their feet, making an odd chanting sound.

A few of the women who'd been peeking into the tavern were swept into the line. Other villagers, including the vicar, came out of their houses to watch.

"Should we go down?" Meagan asked worriedly.

"I am not certain."

They were distracted from the dancing villagers by the sound of hoofbeats on a curve of the road hidden by a stand of trees. A man on a black horse came suddenly around the curve, riding straight toward them.

The horse was one of the finest Penelope had ever seen. Her father's love of horses had taught her to appreciate good horseflesh. She saw that this one had every conformation point in balance, a sheen to its black coat, and a rippling midnight tail.

The man on its back was also the finest she'd ever seen. He was taller than any she knew, including Meagan's father. The stranger had wide shoulders and a broad chest, yet he rode well for a large man, moving in perfect time with his horse.

Tight trousers, Meagan had said. This man wore dun-colored breeches that molded to his limbs. Black boots hugged muscular calves, and his hair, black as his horse's, gleamed in the sunlight. His face was square, his skin bronzed. A black frock coat emphasized the powerful build of his shoulders and the tapered tautness of his abdomen, the tails sweeping back to reveal narrow hips.

"Oh, my," Meagan said. "Oh my, oh my, oh my."

Penelope's heart beat in strange, thick strokes, as though something had taken hold of her body and squeezed it tight. Time seemed to slow, sound and vision melting like hot glass.

The horse was upon them. Penelope knew she should move, but she was frozen in place. Meagan, timid of horses, lifted her skirts and scurried to the side of the road.

At the last minute, the man stopped the horse, pulling it to a skidding halt two steps from Penelope. A puff of dust rose from its hooves, and the horse tossed its head, bathing Penelope in a warm *whuff* of breath.

The man turned the beast, a movement that put his firm thigh and leather boot right in front of Penelope. She found her gaze riveted to the line of muscle of his bent knee, the supple folds of the boot around his ankle.

She forced her eyes upward. The man had a face of raw handsomeness, tanned as though he'd spent much time out of doors. It was a square face, cheekbones high and masculine, with a fine shadow of unshaven beard along his jaw. He wore gloves, expensive gloves, if she were any judge, over large and powerful hands.

She suddenly wondered what those hands would feel like on her body.

She went rigid with shock, wondering why she'd suddenly wondered such a thing. And yet . . .

The man looked down at her with eyes of intense blue, and smiled.

Penelope's knees went weak. This man knew how to smile. He did not merely lift his lips, he put every ounce of sincerity into it. He could make anyone on the receiving end of that smile happy she'd climbed out of bed in the morning. A girl would get up extra early if she thought she'd have a chance of seeing him smile like that.

Even better if he smiled from the pillow next to her.

Penelope jerked her thoughts from that treacherous place. The thoughts had come unbidden, and yet she could not stop them flooding her mind. His large hands in her hair, his smile as he leaned over her in the dark, his kisses on her lips, his voice whispering her name.

She shivered, hard, and the visions dissolved. But threads of them lingered, leaving her body hot and tight.

Meagan had crept forward to peer over Penelope's shoulder. "Who is he?"

Penelope had no idea. She'd spent three seasons in London and had never seen anything like him. She'd have remembered *him*.

And yet, she suddenly had the strangest feeling she did know him. Some thought deep inside her mind clicked, as though it were, well, *satisfied*.

The man bowed from the waist. "Good afternoon, ladies."

His voice was low and rich, his English just accented enough to send another shiver down Penelope's spine.

"Oh," Meagan breathed happily. "He's foreign."

"Meagan, do not be impolite," Penelope said, her own voice strangled.

" 'Tisn't impolite. It is a fact."

The man's smile widened. Both girls heaved a little sigh.

"Do you know a house called Ashborn Manor?" he asked.

"Of course we do," Meagan answered brightly. "We've just come from there." She pointed. "It is that way."

"Excellent." He sounded as though her answer was the most important news in the world to him. "Will you show me?"

Panic worked its way into Penelope's throat. "We do not know you, sir," she began, but at the same time Meagan said, "Of course."

He chuckled as they glared at each other. His laughter was a low, silken sound. "I wish to reach the house before my entourage finds me. Will you ride with me?"

He looked straight at Penelope. Or maybe he did not. Meagan was standing nearly on top of her.

"You must, Penelope." Meagan giggled. "I am afraid of horses."

Meagan stepped away, leaving Penelope alone in front of the large horse and the man's devastating smile.

He held out his hand. "Please. I would be most grateful."

He bent a little in the saddle, stretching his hand to her. *Ride away with me*, his eyes said. *Just for a little while.*

Against her wishes, Penelope imagined sitting on the horse with him, his strong arms surrounding her and keeping her safe. They would canter off to lands unknown, and he'd feed her strawberries, following them with kisses as gentle as snowflakes.

Her vision took them to a meadow, where she'd lie on the grass and he'd loosen her bodice, leaning to kiss her bared shoulder.

She gasped, stunned by the thoughts that kept invading her mind. His blue eyes twinkled as though he'd put the thoughts into her head himself, and knew what they did there.

Meagan was saying, "He is quite courteous. I vow, Pen, I do not know how you can refuse when he puts it so nicely."

"Because we do not know him," Penelope said weakly.

"Oh, Penny, where is the harm?"

Penelope took a deep breath. "I still don't think—"

Meagan grabbed her sleeve, dragged her a few steps away, and began whispering furiously. "If you do not wish to make his acquaintance, you are plain mad. He is the handsomest man I've ever seen in my life, and he's obviously rich—and foreign. We should show him that English people are hospitable, should we not?"

"Yes, but—"

Meagan did not give her a chance. "Think upon this, Pen. He's bent upon visiting the house. Right now. What do you think is happening up there? *Right now?*"

They shared a look.

As one, they turned back to the waiting man.

"Very well," Penelope answered, voice shaking. "I will ride with you."

"Excellent," he said again. When he said the word in that voice, she wanted to believe it.

She handed Meagan her basket, closed her fingers around his outstretched hand, and lifted her foot to rest on his boot. He pulled her upward, his strength taking all the strain. He settled her easily before him, and as in her fantasy, closed his arms around her.

"We shall see you there," the man called down to Meagan.

Meagan settled Penelope's basket, smiled, and waved good-bye, as the man turned the horse and started up the road for Ashborn Manor.

Treacherous girl.

Chapter Three

"How far is it?" he asked in Penelope's ear.

His breath was warm. He smelled of the outdoors and the tang of ale and a sharp, male scent. Strong arms encircled her, holding her steady at the same time he made her heart beat extra fast. She was also very aware that her buttocks and hips pressed firmly into the spread of his thighs.

"Half a mile by road," she stammered.

"Closer over the fields?"

"Um, yes."

"Excellent."

He liked the word. He spurred his horse into a canter and plunged off the road. The horse soared under them, then landed hard, but the man caught her before she could slide away.

"Do not worry," he said. "I will never let you go."

Her heart thrilled, though she knew he must not mean the words the way she wanted him to. His command of

English was not faultless; doubtless he only meant that he would hold her safely.

"I do not even know who you are," she said over the wind and thumping hoofbeats.

"Call me Damien," he said. "It is easier."

Easier than what? she wanted to ask, but she had to save her breath for the ride. She held double handfuls of the horse's silken mane, and Damien hung on to her.

She'd never been this close to a man before. Even dancing the waltz with Reuben had not brought her into this much contact with another man's body. Damien's broad chest was hard against her back, and he held the reins low, almost in her lap, gloved hands steady. The gloves were finely made, as she'd suspected, probably in Bond Street in London. They stretched over his fingers like a second skin, outlining the sinewy strength of them.

His skin was darker than an Englishman's, but tiny white patches creased the corners of his eyes, and fine lines brushed his skin there. He had a strong jaw and a square chin dusted with bristles, as though he'd not been able to shave that morning. His smile was warm, but he looked as though he could be fierce, and had been, when necessary.

He caught her scrutiny and his smile widened. "What is your name?"

For one awful moment, she could not remember.

"Penelope," she blurted.

"Penelope." He repeated it as though he liked the taste in his mouth. He lingered over each warm syllable. "*Penelope.* Like Odysseus's wife."

"Yes. Only I cannot weave."

He laughed. His eyes crinkled when he did, and her blood warmed to furnace temperatures.

"I should not have told you that," she said.

"That you cannot weave? Why should this trouble me?"

"I mean my name. We have not been introduced. You should not even know my Christian name, let alone speak it."

He chuckled, his chest rumbling. "But I am carrying you off. Why can I not speak your name?"

"Are you carrying me off?" she asked.

"Would you like me to? Where would you like to go, Penelope?"

"I thought you wanted to go to Ashborn Manor."

"I do. But my business there is dull. Perhaps I would like one more afternoon of happiness before I must attend to this business." He slowed the horse to a walk. They were far from the road, in a meadow of tall grass shielded by trees. "Would you like to make me happy, Penelope?"

Her heart thumped. "Are you flirting with me, sir?"

"No." His smile disappeared, and he looked down at her with darkened eyes. "I am—how do you say?— propositioning you."

Her cheeks flamed. He should not say that—not to her, not to the unmarried daughter of a baronet to whom he'd not been introduced. She must stop him, explain to him that perhaps where he came from such things were done, but not in England.

But her skin prickled with sudden and forbidden delight, and dark places inside stirred to life. A gentleman did not simply ride to Penelope Trask and say those words in a silken voice, with promise in his eyes.

She remembered Magnus, her second betrothed, and his drunken slurs that he wanted to grope her—she was going to be his wife after all, *what ails you, gel?*

This was not quite the same. This man was not drunk. His eyes were steady, his dark blue gaze holding something from her, she could not tell what. He smiled, but he was watchful.

"I think you are not familiar with English ways, sir," she managed.

"I have been to England before."

He halted the horse. They rested in the silence of the meadow, the quiet broken only by the drone of bees, and birds calling to one another in the sleepy heat.

"Penelope," he said softly. "Since I have left my home, I have not seen anyone like you." He touched his breastbone. "You have given me a pain, here."

She felt as though a fog were coming over her mind, as though he had cast a spell, like the magicians in her stories. "How could I? I am nothing remarkable."

"You are wrong." His breath touched her cheek. "All my life, Penelope, I have existed inside a fairy tale. I have lived an empty life and done empty things. Now, everything is real, and I must face it."

His eyes were not completely blue, as she'd thought, but flecked with black. They darkened further as he spoke, pressing back the flash of bleakness she had glimpsed before.

"Let me have one more page of the fairy tale, Penelope," he said. "Before I must close the book."

She could not imagine what he meant. She did know that if the gossipy ladies of the village learned that she'd come back here all alone with a handsome stranger, she'd be ruined.

A very naughty part of her, which had never spoken before, whispered, *Then why not enjoy it?*

Was she mad? He *must* have cast a spell on her. She thought of the villagers, dancing in a line down the high street. He must have done that, as well.

"What did you do to them?"

He looked momentarily puzzled. "Who?"

"The villagers."

"Ah." His smile returned. "I bought them ale. I made many friends."

Now for some reason, she wanted to laugh. "You must have." She looked at him in exasperation. "Really, who *are* you?"

"Just Damien. For now."

"Who will you be later?"

"I do not know." He looked off into the distance. "I do not know, Penelope. Someone you will not like, perhaps."

She gave a weak laugh. "I have known you ten minutes, and already you are the most baffling man of my entire acquaintance."

His gaze returned to her, a sharp focus like a wolf on a rabbit. "And you are the most beautiful woman of mine."

She so wanted the words to be true. Everything within herself wanted to be beautiful for this man, though deep inside, she knew she was plain Penelope, with wheat-colored hair and green eyes and a figure not willowy enough for London standards. This man likely had the pick of beauties wherever he went. He had to be flummoxing her.

"I cannot possibly be," she said.

"I am afraid you are. And I believe I have fallen in love with you."

"In ten minutes?" she asked, amazed.

"I think it would make no difference were it ten minutes, ten hours, or ten days. I am in love with you. Which makes what I must do very difficult."

"I think," Penelope said, "that you are completely mad."

"As do I."

He gently untied the ribbons of her small bonnet and pushed it from her head. She, the ninny, sat there and let him.

He brushed his gloved fingers over her hair. "It is like gold in the sunlight."

His touch was warm and gentle and started a shaking deep within her.

"I have read stories," he said, "in which a magician makes time stand still."

So had Penelope. She'd transcribed one such story in her book of fairy tales.

"Have you ever wished you could do so?" he asked.

She swallowed. "Yes."

He smiled, as though surprised she agreed. "I wish I could stop time now. I would stay here in this place forever, in the moment I fell in love with you."

"Too much sun," she murmured.

He looked perplexed. "What do you say?"

"Too much sun. It is a warm day. Your brains are addled."

He stared at her a minute, then burst out laughing. The horse, startled by the noise, danced sideways.

He calmed it with a touch. He swung from the saddle, then lifted Penelope down with him.

She grabbed her bonnet and jammed it back on her head. He removed it again, smiling as he did so. She reached for it, but he pulled it away, then tucked it into a bag strapped to the saddle.

She stared, baffled. "Now *my* brains will be addled."

"Will you kiss me, Penelope?"

His hands went to her waist. He stood over her, tall and strong, his hands warm through her cotton frock.

This could not be real. She'd landed in the pages of one of her own fairy tales. But no, such things did not happen in Little Marching. He'd kiss her, and she'd be labeled as fast, and people would say, "Poor, foolish Penelope, she let flattery go to her head. You see, my dears, why you should never trust a man?"

He lowered his eyes, black lashes hiding them. "I beg you."

She placed her hands on his arms. She meant to push him away, but she could only rest them there, feeling his strength. "I do not think—"

He touched his forehead to hers. "Please," he whispered. "Please kiss me, Penelope."

Without waiting for answer, he touched his lips to the side of her mouth, just barely, then drew back.

Warmth gathered at the base of her spine. She closed her hands over his arms, holding the rock-solid strength of them.

He touched kisses to her cheek, his lips smooth like warm satin, then moved to the curve of her neck, nuzzling the pulse points there. She let her head drop back, and he gently licked the hollow of her throat.

She closed her eyes. The join of her thighs felt hot and wet and strange. "Damien?" she whispered.

"I would like to see you bare." He slid his hands from her waist to cup just under her bosom. "I would like to see you in the sunshine, with your hair down, and your gown open."

Fire raced through every nerve. She was mad, she must be. And for this moment, strangely, she did not care.

"My brains *are* addled," she breathed.

"Will you do this for me, Penelope?"

His voice was dark, his body so warm against hers. His arousal touched her softly through his tight breeches; he made no pretense of hiding his desire.

No, this was nothing like Magnus. Damien smelled good; he was clean and strong.

"What do you want me to do?" she asked.

"Let me see you. Let me have that one little thing. Please."

His smiles had deserted him. His face was drawn, almost as though he were in pain. He asked it because he needed to.

"I cannot," she whispered.

He slid his palm over her breast, driving more fire through her. "Please, Penelope."

Tears stung her eyes. She shook her head.

He wiped the moisture from her eyelashes with his gloved finger, the leather cool and soft. "Do not cry."

Her decision should be so easy. She should either be frightened of him, or she should strike him and declare him not a gentleman and walk back to the road in a huff. But for some reason, it felt right to stand with him, to let him softly touch her face.

She reached up and rested her fingers on his cheek, and he turned his head and pressed a kiss into her palm.

Time *had* stopped. It froze into this moment when she looked at him and thought that maybe, just maybe, fairy tales could come true.

He kissed her brow, smoothed her eyelids with his lips. He kissed her mouth, coaxing it open, and to her shock, dipped his tongue inside. She tasted the bite of ale, and hot spice.

He tugged her lower lip between his teeth and gently sucked. Her knees would have buckled, but he slid his arm across her back and held her steady.

He drew away, his face an inch from hers. "Why did I meet you today? If I had waited a little longer in the tavern, we would not have passed. This is—"

He threaded his fingers through her hair, stroked his thumb over her temple. His eyes were downcast, brows drawn.

"Madness," he finished.

Madness, yes. It had to be. She was mad, and he was. Maybe the horse, who'd moved away to crop grass, was mad, too.

"Have you stopped time?" she asked him.

A smile tugged the corners of his mouth. "Do you want me to?"

"Yes."

She put her hands on his shoulders. His body was warm and hummed with strength.

"I will for you, if you want," he promised.

He kissed her again, his tongue sliding across her lips. He leaned and kissed her throat, and tugged at the top hook of her bodice with his teeth.

She tried to say "Damien," but nothing came out. Her throat was parched, and she could not swallow. She felt white heat in the depth of her belly, and her female juices wetting her legs.

She wanted to pull off her bodice and lie down for him, as he asked her to, while he sank to the ground beside her and covered her breast with his mouth. He'd suckle her, teeth scraping her aureole, while she'd rise to his touch.

She'd never, ever had such naughty thoughts in her life. She'd never known what fun they were. She smiled, and he caught the smile on his own lips.

Let this moment go on forever, she thought. No regrets, no remorse. Just this feeling of hot happiness in the middle of Holden's meadow, in the arms of a man called Damien.

She felt as though she belonged in his arms. Had always belonged, and would always. She wet her lips. "I like madness."

"Good." He pulled her close and kissed her again, lips against lips, the moisture of hers letting his slide easily across her mouth.

She was falling, down into the grass, where her vision would come true. He'd open her bodice and let his kisses fall on her bare flesh. She would not mind, no, not a bit. She'd thread her fingers under his long dark hair, and let him have anything he wanted. . . .

"Your Highness!"

The cry echoed from one end of the meadow to the other.

"Damn," Damien said without moving. "Damn it all."

Time started again. The horse lifted his head, turning curiously to watch a small, dark-haired man lope toward them from the trees.

Damien abruptly released her. Penelope drew in a long breath, like she'd not had air in several minutes.

"Er," she ventured. "Did he just say *Your Highness?*"

Damien took a step away from her, one of the hardest steps he'd ever taken in his life. The world came hurtling back at him in the form of Sasha, who sprinted toward them, holding his sash high out of the tall, damp grass.

His mission, the prophecy, Grand Duke Alexander, everything Damien had wanted to forget for a moment in this woman's arms, rushed at him again.

Let her go, his common sense told him. *She is only one woman.*

His heart told him differently. She was delectable and sweet, and he'd never tasted anything like her. Her golden hair was like summer wheat, strands of brown and gold rippling round one another. Her eyes were jade, light and translucent, with flecks of gold swimming in them. The top hook of her bodice was undone, drawing his eyes and making his fingers itch.

He could not have her, and he knew it. A dalliance, perhaps, but no more. He'd come here to find Lady Trask, to explain that she'd have to leave England and travel with him to Nvengaria to save his kingdom.

Because if he did not, Grand Duke Alexander would win, and Damien, in some grand, dramatic Nvengarian fashion, would die.

Penelope, standing next to him with her golden hair mussed and her chest rising against her loosened bodice, suddenly made all of it seem so trivial.

I need this, he'd thought. *I need it.*

"Your Highness," Sasha panted. "We thought you were lost."

He spoke Nvengarian, but his first cry had been in English, as though to warn the country girl in his arms that he was not for her.

"Here I am," Damien said in clipped tones.

Sasha looked confused. "I feared for you, Highness. Was that wrong?" He glanced at Penelope.

Damien relented. "No. Thank you for your concern." He put his hand on Penelope's shoulder. "But she is no assassin."

Sasha did not look so certain. "Who is she?"

Damien switched to English. "Penelope, this is Sasha, my royal advisor."

"Royal?" Her green eyes had lost their softness, returning to the wary light he'd seen there before.

"Your Highness," Sasha continued in Nvengarian, "you know she is not the one."

"Yes, I do know."

"Nedrak told you—"

"Nedrak is a charlatan," Damien said impatiently.

Sasha looked horrified. "He is a sage, and a great seer. He is never wrong."

"Well, he was wrong in this case." Nedrak, the highest of the Council of Mages, had told Damien that when he found the woman he was to marry, he'd fall in love with her. The prophecy was never wrong, he'd said.

The prophecy must be a bit off, because Damien had just met the woman he'd die for.

"Royal?" Penelope repeated. "Your Highness?"

Sasha bowed. "May I present his Imperial Highness, Prince Damien Augustus Frederic Michel of Nvengaria."

She stared at him, her well-kissed lips parting. "Prince—"

"Call me Damien," he said, his voice cool. "It will save time."

Chapter Four

In a daze Penelope led Damien and the little man called Sasha the rest of the way to Ashborn Manor. Damien guided the horse, the reins looped in confident hands, his movements as graceful and animallike as his horse's.

It was not often that a handsome prince popped out of nowhere and asked to kiss you, Penelope reflected. Never, in fact.

Even in her stories, the prince was preceded by fanfare and pageantry and the country girl he fell in love with turned out to be a long-lost princess anyway.

She'd read of Nvengaria, the tiny country hugging the western border of Moldova, near the Black Sea. It sat in a deep fold between mountain ranges, following a river gorge a few hundred miles long and not even a hundred miles wide. She had found this information in a book when researching Nvengarian folk tales. No one in England knew any tales from that country, it seemed, and she'd hoped to be the first to offer a collection.

But the books she'd read were sketchy; only one mentioned an obscure folk tale she hadn't understood, and that was all. She never met anyone from Nvengaria, nor known a person who'd gone there.

The likelihood that this man was its prince was remote. He must be a strolling player or similar kind of trickster, ready to prey on an unsuspecting spinster.

With kisses that took her breath away.

She glanced sideways at him, only to find him looking sideways at her. When their gazes met, he smiled.

It confused her, and frightened her, how hot she grew whenever he smiled.

They neared the house, a wide-winged Palladian mansion built a century earlier and then ruthlessly modernized by Penelope's mother. At the same time, the large carriage pulled by the gray horses with purple plumes turned onto the drive. Behind the carriage came several heavily laden carts.

Damien did not seem inclined to wait for them. He tossed his horse's reins to Sasha and strode toward the front door, which stood open to the summer air, without waiting for Penelope. The tails of his black coat parted as he walked, letting her see the lean muscle of his inner thighs, and how very tight his breeches truly were.

Sometimes Penelope and Meagan, while sitting as wallflowers in London ballrooms, played a naughty game of deciding which man in the room had the finest-fitted tight trousers. TTs, Meagan called them. If Damien appeared at a tonnish ball in the breeches he wore now, he would win hands down.

Damien disappeared into the shadow of the house. Penelope scuttled after him, breathless, pretending she could care less about his breeches.

Lady Trask and Michael Tavistock were nowhere in sight. The butler, Mathers, a man devoted to Lady Trask, stopped short in astonishment as Damien strode unimpeded into the hall. He seemed masterful in her own house, in a way her father never had been.

"Ah," Mathers dithered.

"I have come to see Lady Trask," Damien said. "Fetch her for me. I shall I wait in the drawing room."

Mathers gaped. "But . . ."

"It is all right, Mathers," Penelope said quickly, then wondered if everything really was all right. "Please take him to the drawing room and serve him tea. I will fetch Lady Trask."

Without waiting for reply, she turned away, heart thudding, and whisked toward the stairs.

She felt Damien's gaze on her as she swiftly ascended. His eyes held caution, but they also held warmth. He looked at her because he wanted to look at her. It made her uncertain and unsteady on her feet.

She reached the top of the staircase without falling, and hurried down the long hall to her mother's chamber.

The corridor outside Lady Trask's bedchamber door was deserted without a lookout. Penelope eased the door handle silently down and opened the door a crack.

She saw Michael Tavistock, naked, the sun shining on his dark red hair and muscular back as he faced the bed.

Swiftly, Penelope closed the door, her cheeks scalding. From inside, she heard her mother moan Michael's name, and Michael say, "I love you."

Penelope stopped, frozen, as his hoarse words caught in her throat.

I love you.

Michael Tavistock truly did love Lady Trask, Penelope knew that. She saw it in his eyes whenever he looked at her. For his own reasons, the handsome, forty-five-year-old man had become enchanted with Penelope's rather featherheaded mother. Penelope was glad, for her mother's sake as well as her own, because she very much liked Meagan's father. He was a kind man, and looked upon Penelope with as much protection and benevolence as he would his own daughter.

Now she felt a strange pain in her heart. Damien had kissed her, had told her, with that same catch in his voice, that he'd fallen in love with her. But he could not be real. None of this could be real.

Penelope went back down the hall, counted to twenty, then walked to her mother's bedchamber again, making as much noise as she could.

When she reached the door, all was quiet within. She knocked and said brightly, "Mama? Are you awake?"

After a time, the door opened a few inches. Michael stood behind it, in trousers and half-laced shirt, his hair mussed. "What do you need, Penelope?"

Michael had brown eyes and a strength and quietness that Penelope liked. His dark red hair had started graying at the temples, but still spilled from his forehead in thick waves. His face was not handsome like Damien's, but square and plain, the face of a man who knew what he looked like and was not bothered by it.

Michael had a commonsense wisdom that counteracted Penelope's mother's flightiness, and Penelope quite looked forward to the day he would become her stepfather. He and her mother had not mentioned marriage to either of the girls, but Penelope and Meagan had already decided upon the outcome of their affair.

"We have visitors," Penelope said, her mouth dry. "From Nvengaria."

Michael raised his brows.

"I know," Penelope said. "But I think it's true. And you are never going to believe this. . . ."

The drawing room was simply decorated and a bit drafty. Damien waited in it with Sasha as three people entered the room. The first was Penelope. Behind her came a woman of mature years but fresh beauty, whom he guessed was Lady Trask.

Last came a man slightly younger than Lady Trask, with red hair just going gray and an air of wise authority about him. Before the butler could close the door, the younger girl Damien had met on the road dashed into the room behind them, her face wreathed in smiles.

"Papa, you will never guess what happened." She stopped short when she saw Damien and Sasha. "Or, perhaps you would. Hello again." She waved at Damien.

The butler, looking harassed, leaned in the door. "Milady, there is a great lot of men and carts at the front door. Were we expecting visitors?"

"Ah," Sasha cried. "It is the prince's entourage and baggage, at last."

Sasha was never happy unless Damien surrounded himself with a dozen servants and six trunks full of clothes. If Sasha knew that Damien had once survived in the mountains of Nvengaria without a change of shirts or even any food and water, he'd faint dead away.

"What entourage?" Lady Trask asked, looking interested.

"What prince?" the man next to her demanded.

The younger girl—Meagan, that was her name—went to stand by them. The four faced him, a unit, together. The younger girl had the same brown eyes, dark red hair, and thoughtful brow as the man. Father and daughter.

The older woman and Penelope shared wide green eyes, golden hair and a certain set to their features. Mother and daughter.

Damien said to Sasha in Nvengarian, "No one told me the princess had a daughter."

Sasha spread his hands, palms upward. "Nothing mentioned a daughter. The ring passed to Lady Trask, no further."

The butler cleared his throat. "Milady, what shall I do with the, erm, entourage?"

"Put them upstairs, of course," Lady Trask said. "We have plenty of room. And prepare chambers for the prince." She stepped toward him, smile wide. "Are you truly a prince?"

Damien inclined his head. "I am Prince Damien of Nvengaria. You are Lady Trask?"

"Yes, indeed. Are we not introduced? Good heavens, Penelope, where are your manners? Make your curtsy, darling. He is a prince."

Penelope performed a model curtsy that would bring pride to any mother. Her expression, however, remained fixed, her eyes troubled.

"And Mr. Michael Tavistock, a—er—friend of the family. And his daughter, Miss Meagan Tavistock."

Tavistock bowed, as wary as Penelope. When he came back up, he took a step closer to Lady Trask so that he stood at her shoulder. *Ah.*

Tavistock was her lover. A man shared a certain close space with a woman after he'd bedded her. He did it unconsciously. Tavistock betrayed, by that slight possessive movement, what Lady Trask was to him.

That could be a problem.

Tavistock's daughter was a bit more enthusiastic. She curtsied, her young smile wide. "Pleased to meet you. The girls in London will be pea green when I tell them I met an honest-to-goodness prince."

The entourage was making much noise in the hallway. Over it rose the voice of the butler. "No, no, don't put that there. Bring it this way, man. *This way*, don't you understand English?"

Mr. Tavistock said quietly, "I think you had better explain yourself, sir."

Damien met his gaze. Here was the person who would oppose him if he could. This man was no fool.

"It is very simple," Damien answered. He snapped his fingers. "Sasha."

Sasha bowed and lifted a rosewood box he'd set on the table in preparation. Turning to the four watchers, Sasha reverently opened the lid. "From His Highness Prince Damien, to the most beautiful Simone Bradshaw, now Lady Trask, princess of Nvengaria."

Inside the box, on a lining of black velvet, lay a necklace of old, square-cut rubies. The center of the setting held a ruby the size of a robin's egg, polished and glinting dull red.

Lady Trask gaped. Her hand went to her bosom. "That is for me?"

"Lud," Meagan breathed. "Were I Catholic, I'd cross myself."

Penelope took a step back, putting herself behind the others, her eyes overly bright.

"Why did you call her a princess of Nvengaria?" Tavistock asked, brows lowered.

Sasha answered, "Because she is descended from his most divine majesty, Prince Augustus Adolphus Aurelius Laurent of Nvengaria."

Lady Trask blinked. "I am?"

"Did you not know?"

She laughed. "It is news to me."

"This is nonsense," Tavistock broke in.

"Oh, Michael, be a pet. I am enjoying myself. How do you know I am descended from this Prince Augustus Aur—whoever he is?"

"Because the lineage has been most carefully traced for eight hundred years," Sasha explained. "You are descended from the princess bound so fortunately in marriage to Prince Augustus of old. Your line is traced through the ladies of that house, while his Imperial Highness Prince Damien's is traced through the male line of his house."

"Are we cousins, then?" Lady Trask giggled. "Two hundred times removed? Fancy."

"No, not cousins," Sasha said quickly. "It all began in the year 1000, or the Year One of the most splendid reign of the two princes—"

"Sasha," Damien said. "Later."

Sasha did not deflate. "Yes, there will be plenty of time to tutor you in the glorious past of Nvengaria and its seventeen dialects. For now, do you have the ring?"

Lady Trask blinked. "Ring?"

"The one you wear on your middle finger," Damien said. He came forward, lifted Lady Trask's hand. "There."

It was the ring all right. Lady Trask stared at it like she'd never seen it before. It was silver, heavy and old, a thick band with a flat top. It had once held the crest of Prince Augustus the First, but time had worn down the etching.

Damien tugged off his glove. A twin of Lady Trask's ring encircled the forefinger of his right hand. Silversmiths had restored this ring every fifty years or so, so the crest of Damien's family was still quite plain.

He brought his own hand up to rest alongside Lady Trask's. Lady Trask said excitedly, "Look, Michael. They're the same."

"They were forged at the same time," Damien said. "Eight hundred years ago. They were a pledge, a bond of friendship. It is said that when the rings are brought together again, Nvengaria will prosper, as it did of old."

"Oh," Lady Trask said, green eyes starry. "My mother gave me this ring when she was dying. She said something about it being my destiny. I thought she was just senile."

"No, dear lady," Sasha said. He moved close to Damien and Lady Trask. "She was a most honored princess, pure of the line of Prince Augustus. As are you. And when you marry Prince Damien, you will bring together the lines of two dear friends to unite the kingdom."

"Marry?" Lady Trask breathed. "*Me?* Penny, dear, did

you hear that? A prince wants to marry your mama." She smiled at Sasha. "Do I get the rubies, too?"

"Of course," Sasha said. "They are the prince's betrothal gift to you."

"Fancy that, Penny. You'll be a princess, too, won't you? I wager Prince Damien will find a handsome duke for you."

Penelope was staring at Sasha, her look frozen, her thoughts obviously a little quicker than her mother's.

Meagan's expression had changed from excitement to confusion to hurt. "But, Lady Trask," she asked in a small voice. "What about Papa?"

Tavistock stood a few paces behind Lady Trask, his face as frozen as Penelope's.

Lady Trask's smile dimmed. She looked at the rubies. She looked at the ring. She looked at Damien.

Damien watched her consider going ahead and marrying Damien, then bringing her lover Michael along to Nvengaria, possibly as her "advisor" or some such thing. She searched his eyes, and obviously found that Damien would be wise to that and not allow it. She could not have it both ways.

She let out a long, heartfelt sigh. "You are awfully flattering, Your Highness, but I am afraid that I am already spoken for."

She gave the rubies in the box a long, wistful glance. Then she lowered her gaze, took a step back, and held her hand out to Tavistock. He took it without a word.

Damien began to admire her. He'd quickly grasped that Lady Trask was a silly, vain woman, whose head was easily turned by pretty jewelry. Most ladies of her ilk would have thrown over their plain gentlemen to marry Damien in a heartbeat.

But Lady Trask had decided that she wanted the man at her side more than she wanted to be a princess. More than she wanted the rubies. He must be a remarkable man.

Damien hoped that one day a lady would find him as remarkable.

Sasha looked crestfallen. "But she wears the ring. We cannot return to Nvengaria without it, without her. . . ."

"Never mind, Sasha," Damien said.

His gaze swiveled to where it had been drawn all this time. To Penelope, with her golden hair shining and her green eyes full of emotion.

Next to her, Meagan gasped and clapped her hands. "Oh, of course. Silly me, I never thought of it. Penelope must be a princess, too. He can marry Penelope!"

Damien's gaze locked with Penelope's. Her hair was still mussed from when he had stroked it, when he had kissed her.

She'd wanted to resist kissing him, he'd felt it in the stiffening of her body. But she'd kissed him back anyway, her lips innocent.

He'd felt something in his heart change, and he hadn't understood. But he understood now. Perhaps Nedrak wasn't such a charlatan after all.

"Yes," he said softly. "Penelope will do very well for me."

Penelope's green-gold eyes were wide, her face white with shock. "No," she said. She shook her head until her golden hair danced. "Oh, no, no, no, no, no."

"Do not be hasty, Penny, dear," her mother said. "Those rubies are awfully big."

Chapter Five

"I cannot marry him," Penelope said desperately.

Not when he looked at her like that. She saw danger, she smelled it. And so, like an animal, she scrambled to avoid it.

"Of course you can marry him," her mother prattled. "You certainly show no sign of marrying anyone else, not after you jilted two perfectly good gentlemen."

"Mama," Penelope began.

"You will not mind if I borrow the rubies from time to time, will you?" her mother went on. "And do say I can stay in your palace. Tuck me into a suite, nothing extravagant, just ten rooms or so. You won't even know I'm there."

"Mama!"

Prince Damien said nothing. He simply watched her, his gaze so intense it tingled the blood in her veins. Sasha, on the other hand, chewed his lip. "It is not that simple, Your Highness. She does not bear the ring."

"Oh, that is easy." Lady Trask tugged the silver ring from her finger, held it out to Penelope. "Here you are. I am leaving it to you in my will anyway. My mama told me to."

Sasha cringed. "No, no, you mustn't! It must be done with the proper ritual. If there is no ritual, the line is broken, and it means nothing."

"What is the ritual then? Let us get on with it. I want my daughter betrothed to a prince. Lady Matthews will be beside herself. Her daughters only married earls, and she does lord that over me something terrible."

"Oh, this is madness," Penelope cried.

"No, it isn't," Meagan said. "It's quite exciting. You're a princess. When Papa marries your mama, I'll be your stepsister, like in the story about Cinderella, except I won't be wicked or cut off bits of my feet or anything."

"Meagan, hush." Michael's deep voice cut through the shrill female ones, and everything went silent.

Michael had dressed hastily, and his coat was buttoned wrong, but his presence overpowered everyone in the room. Except Damien, of course.

Michael reached over and deliberately closed the lid on the rubies. He eyed Damien, face to face. "We have no idea who you are, sir. You could be a mountebank, a charlatan. I no more like this marriage idea when you offer it to Penelope as when you offered it to her mother. Unless you can convince me that you are other than a trickster, I will ask you to leave the house."

Damien inclined his head, but Sasha's jaw dropped. He glanced about as if expecting Michael to be struck by lightning. "How dare you speak so to His Imperial Highness?"

"Why the devil should a prince of Nvengaria come to Little Marching?" Michael asked. "Looking for a long-lost princess, no less? How foolish do you believe we are?"

Damien met his gaze, his expression as quiet as Michael's. *He knows who he must convince*, Penelope thought. *Not me, not my mother.*

Of course Damien was not worried about Penelope. Penelope had instantly succumbed, had melted in his arms and let him do what he wanted. He must believe he'd already won over Penelope.

She studied his upright figure, his powerful body, his still, steady gaze. He might not be wrong about having already won over Penelope.

"But, Papa," Meagan began, also sizing up Damien. "He *looks* like a prince."

"Penelope, please take Meagan to your room until we get this sorted out."

Meagan knew better than to argue when her father took that tone. She said, "Yes, Papa," and curtsied. Numbly Penelope allowed Meagan to tow her out. Michael followed them to the door, then closed it firmly behind them.

The hall was chaos. At least a dozen men in military-looking livery bolted up and down the stairs, while Mathers shouted at them all, and they blithely ignored him. Two tall footmen pointed and barked orders in Nvengarian.

The prince had brought at least forty trunks with him. They stood in a line by the stairs, ready to be hauled up one by one.

"No, no!" Mathers cried. "You cannot take them *all* up, there is no room. You, there, put that down!"

Mathers dashed after a lackey who had picked up one of Lady Trask's favorite statues and replaced it with a bust of the prince.

Meagan burst into giggles. "Oh, lud, Papa will have to believe him now. I'm going to write Katie Roper and tell her all about it. To think, she puts on airs because her sister married a baron. And you will marry a prince."

"I am not marrying anyone," Penelope tried to say.

No one paid attention. Meagan dashed up the stairs.

Mathers shouted. The lackeys shoved their trunks about with enthusiasm. Another bust of the prince came out.

Penelope fled the house.

She hurried down the path across the grounds to the folly nestled deep in the woods. The folly was a circular building with one side open and lined with Greek-style columns. The interior housed several statues of Greek philosophers in various poses of oration. Sayings of Aristotle, written in Greek, decorated the upper walls.

"Your grandfather's folly," her father always sneered. "A great eyesore, that's what it is."

Penelope liked the folly because no one ever came here. Also, the open side of the building afforded a view of the river rolling quietly at the bottom of the meadow. It was a peaceful place. Her place.

What had happened to the world today? She'd started a walk to the village with Meagan, and now everything had turned upside down.

She could not be a princess. How ridiculous! And yet, Damien believed it and that man with him, Sasha, believed it as well.

As soon as they had started talking about rings and tracing her mother's destiny, Penelope realized that she, too, was in the line of this ancient princess.

And then Damien had turned to her with those intense eyes and said that she would do for him.

Penelope sank to sit on the steps. She dropped her head back and let the wind ruffle her hair.

All the talk of falling in love with her had been flummery. Whether he was prince or trickster, whoever he was, Damien had come here to get himself a bride. His reasons for fixating on her were slightly more bizarre than the average gentleman's, but it made no difference.

A part of her had so wanted to believe him when he'd touched her face and said, "I've fallen in love with you."

All this couldn't be real. Her thoughts flew back to him standing with her in the meadow, his lips on her face and throat. *That* had been real.

She remembered the haze in her mind, how it had felt exactly right to let him cup her waist, bend to her, nuzzle her. She'd smelled the dust in his hair, tasted the sharp spice of his mouth.

She'd never let a man kiss her like that. Reuben had given her a chaste peck when she'd accepted his proposal. Magnus had tried to thrust his unpleasant tongue into her mouth, and she'd twisted away in disgust.

It had never occurred to her to flee Damien. She didn't *want* to flee Damien. She wanted his mouth on hers while she felt his hard muscles beneath her fingers. And yet, she did not believe herself a wanton. What she'd done had been . . . right.

When he'd flicked his gaze to her, knowing she was the inheritor of the ring, that too had felt right.

Nothing made sense.

Penelope tried to still her troubled thoughts, something she was generally good at, but they jumbled up on themselves.

"You are clearheaded, Penelope," her father would say. "Not like your mother, who is a flibberty-jibbet. That is why I love you."

He'd pat her fondly, eyes shining with pride.

In her childhood, Penelope had warmed to his praise. As she grew older, she'd noticed that his praise had a double edge—his words both commended Penelope and derided her mother.

Sir Hilton Trask had not liked his wife. "You are very beautiful, Penelope," he'd say. "Your mother, too, was once beautiful. But she has an empty head and frivolous emotions. She is nothing but a shell of a person. You, however, are thoughtful and smart. You outshine her in every way."

Penelope had thought her mother did not care what he

said. But then she'd catch her mother crying, when moments before she'd airily tossed off her husband's insults.

"Mama, he does not mean to be cruel," she'd say.

"Yes, he does," Lady Trask would sob. "He hates me and loves you. He always has. I do not understand what I did wrong."

Indeed, her father had once said to Penelope, "The only decent thing your mother ever did was give me you."

Her father had turned all his devotion to Penelope. If Penelope had been a shallow person, she'd have reveled in his attention, gloating over the fact that she'd edged out her mother. But Penelope was not shallow, and she could only be sorry that her father had dismissed Lady Trask as nothing. "Be kind to her, Papa," she'd beg him.

"I am kind. I give her as much money as she needs and all the gewgaws she wants. A woman like her is happy as soon as you dangle a trinket before her."

For some reason, this particular memory chose to haunt Penelope now. Tears welled up in her eyes and spilled down her face.

"I never meant to make you cry," Damien said behind her.

Penelope jerked her head up. He leaned against the column nearest her, his coat stirring in the breeze from the river. He was hatless, his dark hair black in the shadows of the folly. His boots were polished, buckles shined, the soles muddy from their walk through the meadow.

His kisses still burned on her mouth. He'd touched her with gentle hands and awakened a fire she'd never felt.

Desire, she thought in dismay. *I desire this man. Whether he be prince or liar.*

"I am not crying because of you," she said with difficulty.

He took two slow steps, then lowered himself to the stair next to her. "I am pleased."

He smelled of the outdoors and tobacco and a male

scent. His bulk shielded her from the breeze, warming her. His blue eyes swept to take in the view, his black hair brushing his shoulder as he turned his head.

"Does no one in Nvengaria wear hats?" she asked, sniffling.

"What?"

"Hats. You have not worn a hat, and neither have your men."

He turned his gaze to her, catching her once more like a moth entranced by a candle flame. If she moved too close, she'd incinerate.

"Hats never caught on as fashion in Nvengaria." A smile tugged the corners of his lips. "Too windy."

"What do you do in the winter?"

"We have fur things—*gzizbas*, they are called. They cover the head and ears. They look silly, but keep us remarkably warm."

She crossed her arms over her bent knees and laid her head on them. "You really are from Nvengaria."

"I know."

Her eyes stung, her cheeks wet. "I did not like the way you and your man so easily dismissed my mother in favor of me."

"She refused me. It was logical to next go to you."

"So I must be this princess? And marry you? You might have told me from the beginning and spared me your talk of love."

His thigh rested close to hers, muscles filling out his breeches. He was large and masculine, like no other man she'd met.

The silver ring clasped his forefinger. She looked at it, and saw what his gloves had hidden when she'd ridden with him, that his hands were callused and work-roughened. His strong, blunt fingers dwarfed hers as he lifted her hand.

"It is done, Penelope." His words were quiet, but final.

"I came here to find my bride, and you are she. I knew so when I first saw you, though I did not understand."

He was doing it again. His voice was smooth and low and wrapped her senses. She'd determined to be skeptical, but under the spell of his voice, she could only stammer.

"How could you know?"

He gave her his smile. "I told you I had fallen in love with you. In ten minutes. It was the prophecy, and my sage told me I would follow it, whether I willed it or not. I fell in love because I was destined to." He ran his thumb over the joint of her first finger. "Why I fell in love does not change the fact that I did so."

She pulled her gaze from his with difficulty. "You must be completely mad. Or I am. Princes of Nvengaria do not turn up in out-of-the-way villages and declare they want a bride."

"You know all about princes of Nvengaria, then?" he asked, humor in his tone.

"Well, not much. But Michael is right. You could be a charlatan. Most likely, you are. Nvengaria is a great long way away from here. Near Transylvania and Moldova and lands of the Ottoman Empire."

"You are well informed. Most English people have no knowledge of it."

"I know of it because I study fairy tales. I collect them into little books."

He looked interested. "You know Nvengarian fairy tales?"

"Only one," she said, trying to sound indifferent. "I found it in French. It was all about a fountain and a coin and an old woman and a goose. I could not understand it very well."

He nodded gravely. "I have heard that one. I do not understand it, either."

"I never found any about an eight-hundred-year-old ring and an English girl who should marry a prince."

His eyes twinkled. "That is because it is still being written."

She swallowed a lump in her throat. "I wish you would not look at me like that."

"Like what?"

He leaned forward, his dark hair brushing his shoulders, his eyes blue and intent upon her.

"Like you want to kiss me again," she said faintly.

"Would that be so bad?"

Yes. She was confused, and another dark kiss would confuse her more. "It would be very, very bad."

"I do not think so." He touched her hair.

"I think so," she said breathlessly. "Definitely, very bad."

He moved closer still, the heat of his body wrapping her like a blanket. "No, Penelope. With you it will always be good."

He leaned down and brushed her lips with a small, slow kiss.

Penelope drew a sharp breath. He smiled. His eyes went dark, flecks of black in the blue.

"Stop," she whispered.

"Why?" He caressed her lips again. "You will marry me. We may kiss as much as we please."

She drew back. "I have not said I would marry you."

"You will."

"You are arrogant."

"It is not arrogance. I know it will happen."

When he said it like that, she started to believe. She must be out of her mind. "What did Michael want to talk about?"

"Michael?"

"Mr. Tavistock. He sent Meagan and me out of the room so he could talk to you. It seems to have been a brief conversation."

He kissed the side of her mouth, his breath scalding her

cheek. "Mr. Tavistock and Sasha are having a merry argument. They will be finished by the time we return."

"Should you not have stayed and finished it yourself?"

He shrugged. "I have already told Sasha what to prepare. I was not fool enough to think you'd believe who I was when I sprang myself upon you. I have made many plans."

She swallowed. "Do you always do exactly what you want?"

"No." He brushed back the hair at her forehead. "I do what is best. Not what I want."

"And you think it best I marry you?"

"Penelope." He spoke like he savored her name. "The moment I realized you were the one I was to marry, I rejoiced. Not because I did not think your mother was worthy, but because I knew in my heart it was right." He cupped her cheek. "Rejoice with me, Penelope."

He kissed her. His broad fingers caressed her cheek, the silver ring cold against it, and his tongue flicked into her mouth, bringing sudden, hot spice.

She never thought she'd want a man to kiss her again. Not after Magnus. But he was Damien, and definitely not Magnus.

She dipped her own tongue inside his mouth. A strange sensation.

He smiled in response. She explored the taste of his lips, lightly licking them. She had no idea what she was doing, but she had the sudden urge to do so.

They played then, lips and tongues tangling. She held her hands balled in her lap, and he did not remove his from her cheek. Only their mouths met, seeking and exploring.

It grew hot. Or at least Penelope did. Fire pooled in her belly, her secret places damp and welcoming.

Damien made a noise in his throat. His fingers tightened.

If he laid her down, she'd let him. A light breeze touched her ankles, and she suddenly wanted to feel it the length of her legs. She wanted his warm hand behind her knee, spreading her thighs.

"I've never," she gasped, "wanted such things before."

He stroked his thumb over her cheekbone. "I am pleased that you want them."

"I do not know why I said that. You cannot know what I am thinking."

"I can know. I am thinking the same thing."

She rested her hand against his cheek, mirroring how he touched her. "I must stop before I do something foolish."

"Fall in love with me?" He kissed her swollen lips. "That is not foolish."

"Please."

She did not know whether she meant *please, stop* or *please, never stop.*

He brought her fingers to his lips. "I'll not push you, Penelope. I never will." He licked the tip of her middle finger. "But I'll kiss you while I'm waiting for you to make up your mind."

Why did she want to smile when he smiled? Touch him when he touched her?

She remembered when she'd been eighteen, three years ago, and had fallen in love with Reuben. She'd not been able to eat for three days or sleep for seven. She'd lain awake with her heart beating fast and her stomach aflutter and a smile on her face.

Infatuation, she'd realized later. Not love.

Now when Damien kissed her, she felt that long-forgotten flutter leap up and remind her what a fool she could be.

She should dismiss him and his silly offers of marriage and go about her business. Lock herself in her room and finish the new collection of tales she had begun translating this spring. Never see him again.

Instead, she sat here letting him kiss her. She wanted to kiss him.

It was happening all over again. Only this time, it would be much worse.

His mouth was a smooth line, pale red-brown. Her gaze fixed to it, to the way the right corner moved upward first when he smiled. His chin was blue with unshaven whiskers. For some reason, she wanted to lick his skin, to feel if it would be like sandpaper to her tongue.

"I know Nvengarian fairy tales," he was saying. "I will tell them to you."

Her interest stirred, in spite of herself. "Will you?"

"Yes." He gave her a wicked look. "While I lie next to you in our bed."

The heady vision of him lounging languidly on her pillows, his eyes heavy with passion while he related stories in his velvet voice, made her dizzy.

"Now you are trying to woo me with fairy tales."

"Why should I not?" He touched the tip of his tongue to her forefinger. "It is inevitable that we marry, Penelope. I say we do not fight it."

"You would marry me because an old prophecy says you must?"

"I always do what I am told."

She drew a shaking breath. "You do not. You do precisely as you please. You let everyone believe they are doing as they wish, but you direct everything without saying a word."

"Perhaps." He winked at her. "Do not tell on me."

When he did that, she could not help smiling in response. Drat him.

He let her look into his eyes for a few seconds. Then his smile faded, and he fixed his gaze on her hand. "You see through me well, Penelope. But do not try to see too much. You will not like what you find."

The glance he flashed at her was dark. It puzzled her.

She opened her mouth to ask more questions, but in that moment, Meagan appeared on the walk and called out to them.

"Are you finished kissing yet? I vow, I was hiding behind that tree for the longest time."

Penelope's face went hot. "Meagan, you ought to have announced yourself."

"I did announce myself," Meagan said as she stepped into the folly. "Just now. Did you say yes, Pen? You must have; you were certainly kissing him enough."

Damien grinned, the bleak look vanishing. "I am trying to convince her."

"You will," Meagan said with confidence. She flopped to the floor of the folly, her skirt rucking up her slender legs. "My best friend in the whole world is marrying a prince. I shall swoon. Someone fan me."

Damien obligingly waved his hand in front of Meagan's face. She giggled.

"Get up, you ninny," Penelope said, exasperated.

"A prince. Just fancy. Do they have many dukes in Nvengaria, Prince Damien? Could you make one marry me?"

"The dukes in Nvengaria are evil men," Damien said. "I will find you someone ten times better."

Meagan raised up on her elbows. "Ten times better than a duke? Oh, I'd like that."

Damien spoke in a teasing voice, but Penelope sensed he was not joking. Again she caught a flash of darkness in his eyes before he hid it.

"You must marry him, Penny," Meagan insisted, "so that I might have a man better than a duke. You would not deprive your soon-to-be stepsister, would you?"

Damien laced his fingers through Penelope's. The gesture was intimate and started the fluttering again.

"You see?" he said. "Your friend is on my side."

Penelope tried to look severe. "Her head is easily turned by handsome gentlemen."

"In tight trousers," Meagan finished.

"Ah," Damien said to Meagan, "Penelope believes I am handsome. That is a step."

"She likes kissing you, too," Meagan pointed out. "Two things in your favor."

Penelope jerked her hand from Damien's. "Honestly, the pair of you."

"Poor Penelope has been burned by love," Meagan said. "Twice. You must show her that true love is worth waiting for, Prince Damien."

"Excellently said," Damien agreed.

Penelope scrambled to her feet. Damien and Meagan looked up at her, not very alarmed. "I have not said I would marry him. And I will thank you, Meagan, to not takes sides against me. You are my friend."

Meagan remained, irritatingly, on the floor. "I know that. Friends do what's best for each other. And marrying Damien is best for you."

Penelope put her hands to her head, dazed. "He has cast a spell on you, too."

Damien rose. While Meagan sat up and watched with interest, Damien slid his hands around Penelope's waist. "I know this is troubling to you. I know I have frightened you. I, too, was hesitant—until I saw you. Then I knew that it was right."

His hands were strong on her back, resting lightly, but supporting her. "You will have time to get used to the idea. There are many preparations to make, many rituals to perform. I would rather simply get on with it, but they must be done. Sasha will insist on it."

Her mouth felt parched, and she barely heard his words. She heard only his voice, low and smooth. She saw only the blue of his eyes, felt only the warmth of his breath.

Meagan, untroubled by such things, chattered. "What sort of rituals?"

"All sorts," Damien answered. "We must pass the ring to Penelope officially, and then there will be festivals and entertainments and balls. We will have rituals for the betrothal, and then we will have a ritual for our first mating."

Penelope's eyes widened. Meagan grinned hugely. "Mating?" she chirped. "Did you just say *mating?*"

Chapter Six

Damien wanted to laugh at Meagan's delight, but the way Penelope watched him kept him sober. Meagan leapt to her feet, gathered her skirts, and danced about in a small circle.

If only Penelope would join her in rejoicing. They should link hands, dance all three together. They would not have much more time for joy. They should partake of it now.

Penelope had gone rigid under his hands. She'd softened to him while he kissed her, he'd felt that. But that progress had come to a painful and sudden halt.

He decided to play the fool. Prince Damien was good at playing the fool.

"This is the right word, is it not?" He tried a confused smile. "Mating? I know you English must have mating. There are so many of you."

"Oh, we know all about mating," Meagan said happily.

"Meagan," Penelope tried.

"You sound just like my papa. And you know that he and your mama know all about—"

"*Meagan.*"

Meagan snorted. "Do not become such a prude, Penelope. You will be betrothed, and my father will marry your mother, and it will all be in the family. Families are wonderful things. Do you not think so, Damien?"

Damien, who had never had a real family, could not say. He'd had a father, of course—the previous Imperial Prince, a tyrant who'd imprisoned Damien and tried to kill him on several occasions. Damien could not within any stretch of imagination call that family.

"Yes," he answered. "I would like to be in your family."

He suddenly wanted it with all his might. Selfish, perhaps, but so be it. If he must do this he would drag as much pleasure as he could from it.

"You see?" Meagan spread her hands, looked guilelessly at Penelope.

Penelope's bosom lifted against her gown. She was even more mussed now from his kissing, and even with Meagan nearby, that fact was making him rock hard. He wanted her alone, out here, where he could lay her down on one of these benches and muss her still more. He'd lay her back, unfasten her bodice one hook at a time, press it open, maybe with his tongue.

She firmly removed his hands from her waist. "We are not family."

She looked like she wanted to say more, but her words faded. They stood so close, despite her retreat, that her breath touched his skin.

She had lovely eyes, deep green, flecked with gold. Her eyes went with her golden hair, like sunshine captured.

One of the rituals involved bathing in a deep bath. He could already feel her slick skin under his hands as he washed her, purifying her for their first coupling. He'd slide fingers over her curves, finding the secret recesses of her.

That was one ritual Sasha was not going to supervise.

Yes, he would certainly drag every benefit out of this that he could.

He lowered his head, wanting to kiss her lips again, despite Meagan's interested gaze. Penelope tasted like a warm spring breeze. He wanted to taste her again. And again.

Stay with me, love.

Penelope broke away from him in a swirl of skirts. She glared at Meagan, then at Damien, then turned and ran from the folly. The wind lifted her dress, revealing a pair of plump calves and pretty ankles before the cloth swirled down again.

Her swaying backside held his gaze, too.

Damien let her go. She was too flustered, too frightened. He'd give her a chance to cool down, to regain her senses. And then he'd try again.

A part of him was glad she resisted. This woman would not meekly go where she was told. He liked a challenge, and he needed a woman who was up to it.

He needed a woman who would put her hands on her hips and face him down. A woman who could also face down his enemies. His heart beat faster. What a princess she'd make.

Meagan patted his shoulder in sympathy. "I said too much, didn't I?"

"I am afraid we both did."

Meagan kept her hand on Damien's shoulder. "She really was hurt before. Twice. Deeply. She is afraid to trust again."

Something darkened inside him. "Who would hurt her?"

"Stupid gentlemen with no sense of honor. Mr. White

was the worst. He made her believe he truly loved her, when, of course, he did not. Magnus Grady was just nasty." Her fingers dug a little through his coat. "I vow, Prince Damien, you are quite muscular. Does your prophecy say that you can marry the soon-to-be stepsister of the bride if she refuses?"

He looked into her impudent smile and grinned in response. "Alas, no."

"Well, that's all right." She let go of his arm. "I see the way you look at Penelope. You are far gone on her, are you not? I am pleased. She needs someone who will fall head over heels in love with her."

Damien *had* fallen head over heels in love with her, just like the damned prophecy had said he would.

He hadn't believed it. He'd never believed in magic before, thinking the Council of Mages a pack of charlatans who tailored their predictions to whatever the Imperial Prince or Duke Alexander wanted to hear.

But maybe, just maybe, they'd been right about this.

Damien also needed Penelope, and needed her for more than the reasons a man usually needed a woman. He wondered if that needing would in the end outweigh the love.

Penelope had disappeared through the trees, but her presence lingered. If he'd met her a year ago, he'd have lain her down and made sweet love to her right away.

No, probably not. He knew the difference between an untouched miss and the hungry married women who pursued him. He'd have looked at Penelope, had an erection-throbbing fantasy about her, but left her alone.

Now he wanted her, and he could have her. And he would have her. He'd change her *no* to a *yes*, and then they'd be betrothed, and, according to Nvengarian custom, they'd become lovers.

A betrothal was as legally binding as a marriage in

Nvengaria. Nvengarians did not consider a child conceived or even born before the wedding to be illegitimate, as long as the couple was legally betrothed.

He'd never given much thought to that custom before, but it pleased him now.

She'd say yes, and then he'd spend the rest of his time in bed with her, while Sasha carried on with the betrothal festivities.

What a lover Damien could teach her to be. Would teach her to be. His breeches tightened to the point of pain.

"I could imprison the gentlemen who broke Penelope's heart, if you like," he said. "I can tell Sasha to throw them into the deepest dungeons. Have them tortured even."

"Oooh, that sounds nice," Meagan said happily.

What Meagan did not understand was that Damien really could.

What Damien's father hadn't understood was that you were stronger if you did not.

Meagan suddenly cocked her head and put her hands on her hips. "My father is right about one thing. How do we know you are a real prince?"

Damien looked into surprisingly shrewd eyes in her pointed face. "I thought you were on my side."

"I am. But Penelope is my best friend. And soon to be stepsister. I want her to marry a prince, not a hoaxer."

"I quite understand." He descended the steps of the folly and politely held out his hand to help Meagan down. "But I will prove it."

"How?"

He gestured expansively. "I will hold a festival, in a week's time, for your family and friends. For your entire village. Sasha has already begun the arrangements. I invited many acquaintances from London, including a man whom you will believe when he tells you I am Prince Damien of Nvengaria."

Her eyes narrowed. "Oh, yes? And who is this man?"

"The Prince Regent."

"Oh." She looked thoughtful, then took Damien's arm as they began walking slowly back to the house. "That will work, I suppose. Providing, of course, that we believe he's really the Prince Regent."

Near midnight, Michael Tavistock entered Lady Trask's bedchamber and closed the door.

Lady Trask heard him, but she did not look 'round from brushing her hair. Her maid had undressed her, helped her into a dressing gown, then discreetly left the room.

Any minute now, Michael would cross to her, put his hands on her shoulders, tilt her head back and kiss her. Lady Trask waited in excited anticipation. Michael could kiss like fire.

He did no such thing. He remained by the door, his arms folded, watching her in the mirror.

Disappointment darted through her. The afternoon had been exhausting. Penelope had been most trying, completely ignoring Lady Trask's attempts to point out that she'd never get a better offer than from a *prince*, and what was the matter with her?

Michael, the exasperating man, took Penelope's side. He could not possibly know what it was like to have a daughter who'd jilted two perfectly good London gentlemen with money and connections. Granted, neither Mr. White nor that somewhat awful Magnus Grady had been as handsome and charming as Prince Damien, but really. To refuse a *prince*, it was too much.

Lady Trask had told her so. Michael had watched in silence.

Meagan, at least, had some sense. If Penelope was not careful, Meagan would snatch Damien out from under her friend's nose, never mind this prophecy business.

Prince Damien had not said much the rest of the afternoon and during dinner, but he'd watched Penelope. He was determined; that was a point. He'd not be put off by maidenly resistance.

Sasha had kept up a running commentary all afternoon and evening on the history of Nvengaria and the glory of Prince Damien until she'd wanted to scream. Michael's silence had unnerved her, as had the look in his dark eyes.

It unnerved her now.

She at last laid down her brush and gazed at him in the mirror. He remained rigidly on the other side of the room.

"Well, it has been an eventful day, has it not?" she began brightly.

"Simone," Michael said in a warning tone. "Don't."

His voice could always make her shiver.

"Don't what?" She rose from the dressing table and turned to him.

As usual, she was struck with how desperately she loved him. He was so handsome. So tall and strong and virile. And he didn't mind that she was fifty and past her first looks. Lady Trask slathered her face in buttermilk and lemon every night, and declared her skin as fresh as her daughter's. Michael seemed to like her skin. Liked touching it all over. Often with his tongue.

No man had ever excited her like he did.

And he was all hers. He was not poor, he could have his pick of any chit in London with skinny arms and a lisp, but he'd chosen *her*.

She crossed to him, put her hands on his shoulders. "Darling."

He did not move. His muscles were hard and still beneath her touch.

She grew worried. "Darling, what is the matter?"

He frowned at her. "You have been pretending that today is simply an amusing aberration. It is not. This is serious business."

"I know." Her eyes widened. "Imagine, a prince coming all this way to marry *me*. It was too droll."

Michael's eyes were cold. "Droll is not the word I thought of. You would have done it, wouldn't you?"

His look began to frighten her. "Of course I would not have. You know that. You heard me turn him down." She forced a laugh. "Michael, pet, you cannot think a box of rubies and a prince could sway me from your side." She leaned into his chest, rubbed her palms up and down his arms.

His heart beat slow and hard beneath her ear.

"But you were swayed," he said.

She looked up, her breath catching. "Michael . . ."

"I can never give you rubies, you know that. I cannot make pretty speeches and promise you a kingdom. You know what I have to offer, and it is not much. Not even as much as your husband gave you."

"I know, but I hated *him*." She seized upon this argument in her confusion. "I'd rather have the little bit you give me and be with you."

There, that should settle his pride. Men set such a store on how much they had or didn't have.

He still did not open his arms. She stepped back, put her hands on her hips. The movement opened her dressing gown a little. She hoped a glimpse of round flesh would make him come to her.

He did not move. Drat the man.

"Well, if you are going to be jealous," she tried, "you can just go."

His look grew more stern. "This man is prepared to marry your daughter and carry her off God knows where. And you stand here bleating about jealousy. Are you not the least bit concerned about Penelope?"

She grew offended. "Of course I am concerned! How can you say that? She is my daughter."

"All the man has done is wave around a box of rubies and go on about an old ring. Penelope at least has the sense to be skeptical. You seem to be willing to hand her over on very slender evidence."

Hurt welled up inside her. She remembered the day Sir Hilton Trask had stood at the top of the stairs in their London house and shouted, "Simone, you are the stupidest woman alive!"

She knew she wasn't smart like Penelope and didn't give a fig for what was in books. But she was smart in other ways, she knew she was. Her husband—and her daughter—simply never gave her a chance.

"Well, *you* are here, pet, to think of things like that, and make certain everything is all right." Flattering a man for his wisdom never hurt, either.

His voice was quiet. "I cannot help remembering how enthralled you were when you saw the rubies. I cannot help remembering that you forgot I was in the room until Meagan reminded you."

She stared at him. Was he mad? She could never forget Michael was in the room. His presence caught at her, making her heart beat fast as though she was a giddy girl. She'd simply wanted to see how far Prince Damien would go. Really.

She forced a laugh. "Oh, you are jealous, that is all. Do go away if you want to sulk."

She turned to the dressing table, loosening the gown as she went, to let it slide down and bare her shoulders.

He would come after her. He'd fold his arms around her waist, bury his lips in the curve of her neck and tell her how beautiful she was. Then he'd pull off the dressing gown and catch her breasts in his hands. He'd suckle them, and she'd run her hands through his unruly hair. The man made love with feral grace.

On the other side of the room, Michael said, "Yes, I

think it would be best if I go. I will stay until this business with Penelope and this man is settled, and then I shall take Meagan and go back home."

She spun around. "What are you talking about?"

He watched her for another quiet moment. "I said I would go. It is for the best. People are talking." He turned away. "Good night, Simone."

Before her stunned eyes, he opened the door and walked out of the room.

"Michael!" she cried.

The door clicked closed. "Michael, I didn't mean—"

His footsteps faded as he moved down the hall.

Raw pain washed over her. She couldn't lose him. She could not.

Lady Trask had never learned how to handle emotion with dignity. She'd never had to. She'd been spoiled as a girl, and her husband had ignored her. Her daughter treated her gently, but deep down, Lady Trask knew that Penelope did not really like her.

She burst into wild tears. She swung to the dressing table and swept bottles, brushes, cosmetics, and perfumes to the floor. Then she sank down amid the broken glass and stench of perfume and beat her fists on the carpet until her hands were cut and bloody.

Chapter Seven

Down the hall, Damien, sitting before the fire in pantaloons and lawn shirt open to the waist, heard the sudden commotion and Lady Trask's weeping.

Petri stepped to the door and looked out as hurried footsteps converged on Lady Trask's room. He watched a moment, then closed the door and returned to his task of carrying a glass of brandy to Damien. "Lady Trask, Highness," he said. "Upset at the loss of the rubies, no doubt."

"Mmmph, I do not think so." Damien took the brandy and cradled the goblet in his palm. He had heard the quiet opening and closing of the door beforehand and imagined that her lover Tavistock had gone to have a word with her. "I believe there is one thing more important to her than jewels."

Petri looked unconvinced.

Petri, Damien's valet, was only a few years older than Damien himself. The two men had been raised together, Damien to rule, Petri to serve. Petri had followed him into exile, finding a young Damien shivering and half-naked in the woods where the Imperial Prince's men had unceremoniously dumped him. Somehow Petri had gotten them over the pass and down into the Danube Valley before the wolves had found them. Damien knew he would have been dead many times over had it not been for Petri.

Despite their differences in station, Petri was closer to Damien than any brother could be. They could read each other's moods and almost knew what the other would say before he said it.

Petri pursued women with enthusiasm. Being valet to a prince gave him a certain cachet among the servants of the noble classes of Europe. While duchesses and countesses vied for Damien's notice, Petri busily seduced their maids.

"Behave yourself while you are here," Damien had told Petri when he'd arrived.

Petri had widened his blue eyes in innocence. "When have I ever not? Do I not know discretion?"

He did, Damien had to credit him with that. Damien never once had to extricate him from a delicate situation, not even when Petri involved himself with more than one woman at a time. He knew how to woo and seduce, and then withdraw with no anger on either side. Damien had to admire him.

As Damien sipped his brandy—purchased in Paris and lovingly carried by Petri the rest of the journey—he listened to the sounds of a household trying to control its weeping mistress. The walls were thick, but when doors opened and closed, voices drifted down the halls to him.

"My lady, my lady you must not—"

"She is hurt. She is bleeding!"

"Whatever is the matter?"

The last voice was Penelope's. Her gentle tones rose in exasperation, then the door closed, shutting out her words.

He smiled into his brandy. Penelope made his blood sing.

He wished she didn't. Damien had survived all this time by not letting himself feel. Flirt, yes. Seduce, yes. Feel, no.

Enchant a woman, enjoy every moment with her, cut the tie, was his rule. Most women with whom he had affairs—upper-class, nobly born widows and married women or high-class courtesans—did the same to him. They did not have the energy to waste letting Damien break their hearts, and he did not have time to cultivate an affair lasting more than a few days.

All that had changed with one smile from Penelope's lips.

After a time, he heard her leave her mother's room. "Good night, Mama," she said firmly, and shut the door behind her.

He grinned. The mother was weak and weeping, the daughter the pillar of strength. Penelope was strong and he liked that.

No, he *needed* that.

"Something funny, Highness?" Petri asked. The man refilled Damien's glass of brandy, poured one for himself, and sat down facing Damien, choosing a chair less comfortable than the prince's. Petri always reminded Damien that they came from different classes and always would.

"I am thinking of irony, Petri." Damien sipped the mellow brandy. "What did I expect to find here? I no longer remember."

"You expected a European princess with no chin, bad breath, and an irritating titter." Petri shrugged. "Or so you said."

"And I found a beautiful woman with a heart of steel." He stared moodily at his brandy. "I sound like a fool in a bad Nvengarian drama."

Petri grinned, his dark face creased. "I know what you need."

"A hearty kick with a thick boot?"

"A dose of what bit you, sir. You want this woman."

Damien snorted. "That is so. What betrays me?"

"Perhaps you should consider wearing looser trousers, Highness. At least until we're finished here."

"You are exceedingly amusing, my friend."

"You need a bit of relief, that is all."

Damien shook his head. He could not imagine going to any other woman now that he'd met Penelope. The women he'd had before, even bejeweled countesses and beautiful duchesses, paled beside this English girl with golden hair and green-gold eyes.

"I will not insult her by going to a courtesan to deflate myself. Besides, I do not think it would work."

"Of course not. I did not mean that. I meant her."

Damien had a sudden vision of Penelope beneath him on a bed, her hair loose on the pillow, her eyes heavy with passion. He would lick her swollen breasts as they rose to his mouth, take one taut peak in his teeth.

"'Tis tempting, Petri," he said. "But I cannot circumvent the rituals. The prophecy depends on them." And he would not break the prophecy, no matter what. "Besides, Sasha would kill me."

"When did you grow interested in following rules, Highness?" Petri asked. "And obeying Sasha's whims? He's gone a little mad over this prophecy, I think."

"He has," Damien agreed. "But he survived my father's dungeon by believing that magic would bring me back to him. I did return for him, and so now he is convinced that the prophecy made it happen. His entire life centers on this damned prophecy."

The prophecy said that Damien would marry the princess and bear a child who would be the glory of Nvengaria. Nvengaria would be united behind Damien and the princess, and the sorrows that had plagued the country under Damien's father would be erased.

If he sired the child before the betrothal, it would be illegitimate and not accepted as the next prince or princess, and the prophecy would be broken. He had been very close to laying Penelope down in that meadow today and taking her. He'd throbbed with need, and she'd not fought him.

Thank goodness Sasha had shouted at them just in time. Had Sasha planned that? Or was the prophecy working, putting Sasha in the right place at the right time to prevent the child from being sired too soon?

He was either growing as mad as Sasha, or . . .

Damien had never believed in magic, but his people did. Damien had arrived home months ago, after a long and treacherous journey, to a chilly welcome. Damien's father had been feared and hated; Nvengaria had suffered under his long reign. Grand Duke Alexander, head of the Council of Dukes, had ruled from behind the throne the year Damien's father spent dying. He had effectively taken over, dissolving the Imperial Prince's power.

Alexander, a man Damien's own age with cold blue eyes in a dark, handsome face, had calmly and ruthlessly blocked every one of Damien's attempts to step into his father's shoes. Alexander had said point-blank that he wished Damien to rule as a puppet prince to Alexander's dictation—or not at all.

The people of Nvengaria wanted a symbol to adore; very well, Damien could be it. Alexander and the Council would do everything else.

When Damien tried to have Alexander arrested for treason, however, the guards refused to obey him. Alexander had them in his hand. The palace guards and the military had loathed Damien's father and were as happy as Alexander to see the end of rule by Imperial Prince.

However, there was a prophecy, Alexander had said. His eyes had remained ice-cold, the ruby he wore in his ear winking like a drop of blood. A test of the prince's true right to rule. Fail that test, and. . . .

The prophecy of the Imperial Prince finding the long-lost princess descended from Prince Augustus of old, and reuniting the crown of Nvengaria was an ancient story that every child learned from the cradle. Nvengarians loved legends, the more ancient and ludicrous the better. They'd be ecstatic to learn that Damien would make it come true. And Nvengarians were just volatile enough that if he failed, they'd let their disappointment be known, violently.

Nedrak, head of the Council of Mages, said that the signs pointed to Damien as the prince to fulfill the prophecy. Nedrak was firmly under Alexander's thumb, but his eyes had glittered with eagerness. He believed in the magic, too.

Word that Damien would fulfill the ancient prophecy had quickly spread. A mob soon surrounded the castle, a peaceful one, come to encourage Damien to ride off on the insane quest. Alexander had not smiled, he never did, but he managed to look pleased. Damien could not refuse, and Alexander knew it.

So Damien made a fair speech to the multitude from the balcony of the Imperial Prince's castle, packed his bags, and traveled thousands of miles on the word of a nervous mage and a half-mad advisor to find the village of Little Marching, Oxfordshire.

He remembered the faces of his people when he had ridden out of Narato with his entourage, how the citizens had lined up to see him off in a fervor of cheering, their eyes shining with hope. Damien was the new Imperial Prince, he was following the prophecy, and everything would be put right again.

And so, he would do what Sasha told him and observe the rituals and pretend he believed it. He would drag Nvengaria out of the dust into which his father had ground it and save it from Alexander at any cost.

Neither he nor Alexander truly believed in the prophecy, but he had to admit that perhaps Sasha was not wrong about it. Events that had occurred since he'd left Nvengaria were nudging him toward belief. *Something* out there had pushed Damien unerringly to Penelope's doorstep. And he'd tumbled immediately into love.

He came out of his thoughts to find Petri grinning at him.

"What are you smiling about?" Damien asked irritably.

Petri's grin widened. He set down his glass and got to his feet. "I want to show you something."

He rose and walked to Damien's bed. As Damien watched, he moved the night table and swung open a door-sized panel in the wall beside it. "I found it when I checked the room. It is a passage behind the walls."

Petri always searched Damien's chambers even after the bodyguards did. Assassins liked to pop up and shoot things at Damien, so Petri went over every building carefully himself, not trusting anyone else to do the job properly. It was not a matter of *if*, but of *when* Alexander's assassins would strike.

Damien got to his feet. "Where does it lead?"

"Not far. It runs behind the corridor and opens to a bedchamber at the end."

Damien raised his brows. "Hmm, now, for what reason does a man build a house with a passage that leads secretly from one bedchamber to another?"

"I cannot imagine," Petri said, eyes twinkling.

"Penelope's great-grandfather must have been a rogue. To whose bedchamber does it lead?"

Petri grinned again. "Want to look?"

He held a candle at the ready. The black square tapering to darkness made something deep within Damien shudder, but he mastered himself.

Petri led him inside in silence, his lone candle making the passage bright. The low-ceilinged corridor ran straight, this wing of the house narrow and long.

A stone wall stopped their progress after about fifty feet, where the architect had decided to forget about the passage and get back to the business of building the house.

Petri gestured to their right, to wooden paneling that ran behind the chambers. A few feet above the floor was a small hinged panel, about six inches square.

In silence, Petri eased the panel open. Damien crouched down and put his eyes to it.

A night table half covered the hole, but he could see plenty. The room was a bedroom, a charming, girlish one. The bed had thin posts painted white, carving picked out in soft green, and was hung with green damask. A chair covered in the same fabric reposed by the fire, a comfortable seat for reading the stacks of books piled next to it, probably Penelope's collection of fairy tales.

A writing table stood nearby, papers stacked neatly, the chair square in front of it as though she lined it up precisely when she finished at the desk every day. The thought made him smile.

Penelope herself sat at a dressing table as neat as her desk on the opposite side of the room. Facing an oval mirror, she brushed out her long hair, which crackled and shone, beautiful, long, and golden. Damien had touched it when he'd kissed her in the folly, warm silk spreading under his fingers, soft and smelling of the lavender in which she must rinse it.

She stared at her reflection as she slowly pulled the brush through her hair, as though her mind were miles away. She wore only a dressing gown, presumably over her night rail, the gold and green brocade almost a match of the chair and bed hangings. Perhaps they were her favorite colors. Her hands were slim, holding the hairbrush gently, her movements graceful.

If Petri thought this would help ease Damien's arousal, he was very much mistaken.

With a quiet smile, Petri pointed to the hinges of a larger door, similar to the one in Damien's own room.

I ought to leave her alone, Damien thought. *Let her get used to me and what she must do.*

The trouble was, he had no time. If he'd had a year, he'd woo her gently, seducing her with words and gifts and small delights of kissing. Damien knew how to seduce. He'd become expert during his years of exile, when he'd learned to be the best player of all the games of the bedroom. He had learned that the only way to stay alive was to act the part of playboy prince, carefree and amusing, thinking of nothing more than the next woman in his bed.

Outwardly. Under the table, he had kept his hand in the affairs of European politics, forging ties toward the far-off day he would inherit his father's kingdom. That day had come sooner than he'd imagined, but the ties had been in place.

His father had expected him to die in obscure poverty, if the assassins did not kill him, perhaps in some poetically dingy room in Paris or Rome. Instead, Damien had returned with wealth and influence behind him, a result of canny investments and years of working his fingers to the bone. In the end, it had paid off, letting him live in comfortable style.

Damien had until Midsummer's Day to return to Nvengaria with Penelope. He did not have time for slow seduction; he had to be swift and sure, yet not let things happen too soon. It was enough to drive a grown prince mad.

The panel swung open into the passage. Damien moved the small piece of furniture and stepped around it into the room. Behind him, Petri obligingly closed the panel.

Penelope saw him in the mirror. The brush hesitated, hovering in the gold cloud of her hair. She did not cry out; she did not turn and demand to know what he thought he was doing. She simply watched him, her green eyes waiting.

Need sliced through him. Prophecy or no, this woman was beautiful. In dishabille, she was breathtaking. Her hair hung in a wave of dark gold, almost bronze-colored, to her hips. Lighter streaks roped through it, drawing his eye down its length.

He wanted to be naked and have that hair pouring over him. He wanted her to be naked and on top of him, the heat of her body blending with his as he made love to her in slow, sensual strokes. His breathing hurt him, and another part of him did, too.

Not yet, he admonished himself. *She will be in my bed soon enough. She will yield. And then . . .*

His mind whirled with *and then*.

She wanted him, too, he sensed that. She made none of the signals of the high-born women who'd wanted his seduction. No sly looks and come-hither smiles, no swish of hips or "accidental" lifting of skirts to bare silk-clad ankles.

Penelope simply wanted him with basic, primitive desire, the same that pounded through him. They were being pushed together by some invisible force, one that wanted them together no matter what. There was a mindlessness about the force—it did not care what else they felt, as long as they came together.

That mindless force made his feet move, taking him across the room to her, his hunger for her building in every step.

In the mirror, Penelope watched him come, her hairbrush still. He'd been handsome enough in his formal suit and cravat, she thought, but half-dressed, his shirt loose and open, he looked raw and barbaric. He might be a prince, but there was nothing civilized about him.

She sensed what she had when she'd seen him on horseback, a man in tune with wildness. Nvengarian rule was brutal, from what she'd read, much closer to England's own medieval times than the modern-day monarchs more interested in fashion than in ruling.

Political debates in Nvengaria could end in a duel to the death with swords, right in the council chambers. Men dueled in England, of course, but with rules and a gloss of respectability about it. Nvengarians went about armed and fought each other with vigor at the drop of a hat.

Watching Damien, his hair loose on his shoulders, his handsome, chiseled face so different from an Englishman's, she could well imagine him drawing a sword and plunging it into the chest of his enemy in the middle of the council hall.

He stopped behind her, tall in the mirror, the heat of his body brushing her back. The scent of brandy clung to him. Slowly, while she sat in mute contemplation, he gathered her hair in his hands, lifted it from her neck, and let it spill through his fingers.

Her hair falling on the back of her neck was cool and soft and erotic. He watched her in the mirror, his eyes intense.

He took the hairbrush from her and pulled it through her hair, watching the bristles furrow the gold. She closed her eyes, savoring the feeling as the brush moved from her scalp all the way to the ends of her hair.

He lifted her hair again, this time resting his hand on the nape of her neck, brushing the fine hairs there. Strong feeling shot through her. She felt her private places growing damp, and he'd only touched her neck, for heaven's sake.

"I regret," he said in a low voice, "that I caused you and your family pain. But my coming here was necessary."

"To find your princess," she murmured.

"To find you."

He pulled the brush through her hair again, then let his fingertips drift over her skin, a gentle touch from a powerful man.

"You should not be in my bedchamber," she pointed out.

He plied another stroke of the hairbrush, then leaned down and rested his cheek against hers. Unshaven bristles scraped her skin. "Tell me to go, then."

She opened her mouth to send him away, then closed it. All the resolve and resistance she'd felt in the folly had gone.

"You cannot ask me, can you?" he asked. He was serious, not mocking.

"No."

He set down the brush and slid his arms around her, palms resting just above her breasts. "It is the prophecy. It wants us to fall in love."

"A prophecy is a prediction," she said, puzzled. "It cannot want anything."

Can it? His hands were hot through her thin dressing gown and night rail. She had the sudden urge to move his palms down to cup her breasts. Her face heated, but the wanting did not cease.

"This prophecy is old magic," he said. "It was created hundreds of years ago when the line of Prince Augustus was lost. Maybe all that time changed it from mere words to something powerful. Perhaps it believes in itself so much that it forces us to believe in it."

She watched him, her green-gold gaze meeting his blue one in the mirror. "I would say that was ridiculous, if I did not feel . . ."

"I know what you feel." He glided his hands inside her dressing gown, smoothing the tops of her breasts beneath her night rail. "I feel the same. We need to be together. I do not believe the prophecy will let us turn aside."

She dropped her gaze. She loved his hands on her, wanted them all over her. No, she *needed* them to be all over her, needed it in a kind of mindless frenzy.

Damien smiled to himself. This was dangerous, but he knew how to hold back. He could have her, maybe make her taste what was to come, without taking her too soon and breaking Sasha's rules. He was adept; he could show her many things without being inside her.

His touch unnerved her, he saw, but she would not pull away and titter or pretend modesty. She had modesty, but not coyness. She'd kissed him well and good in the folly by the river, her mouth seeking, her desire strong.

He drew his fingers down the curve of her breast, feeling the nubs tighten and rise against the night rail. His blood stirred, the ferocity of his forefathers boiling to the surface. He wanted to drag her to the carpet and have at her. A ribbon trailing across her dressing table beckoned to him. A few games would not go amiss, either.

"I was betrothed twice," she was saying.

He leaned down and traced the shell of her ear with his tongue. "I know. Miss Tavistock told me." A protective fire kindled inside him. "If you let me, I will duel with these gentlemen and punish them for hurting you."

Her eyes widened, gold flecking the green. His ancestors raged some more within him, encouraging him to find these gentlemen and make them very, very sorry they'd made Penelope cry.

As though she sensed his violence stirring, she said quickly, "I cried off. I told them to go. They did not abandon me."

"If they had been good to you, there would have been no need to tell them to go."

She swallowed. "Mr. White—Reuben—I discovered by accident that he wanted a marriage of convenience. *His* convenience. I heard him speaking to his friend that with my dowry and family connections, he could pay his debts and set himself up well. Then he'd think nothing of returning to his mistresses. Both of them. The most beautiful women in London, he said. Nothing like his overly plump, dull-haired wife-to-be."

She drew a sharp breath as she finished, as though she'd never meant to say those words aloud.

"Hmm," he said. "I have changed my mind about sparing him, I think."

Any man who looked at this woman and thought *overly plump* and *dull-haired* was blind and a fool.

Sword fodder.

"Where can I find this Mr. Reuben White?" He kissed her cheek and quietly slid the tape of her night rail through its knot. "I will have Petri bring him here, and I will have a chat with him."

"Damien."

His temperature soared. He liked his name on her lips. He liked the way her tongue touched her teeth on the *D* and how her lips closed on the *M*.

Say it again, love.

"It no longer matters," she said. "What I meant to explain was that he wanted a marriage of convenience. Which is what you want."

The lacing of the night rail loosened and he slid his fingers inside, finding the bare flesh of her bosom. His arousal, which had been plenty hard since he'd entered the room, lengthened and tightened still further.

He felt his control slipping. He should go.

Not yet. Let me stay here a little longer.

He did not miss the way her gaze darted to the open V of his shirt and the naked muscle inside. She burned for him as much as he burned for her. Their first mating would be fierce and satisfying.

"I do not want convenience," he said, his mind conjuring images of the night of their betrothal. Yes, the ribbons would come in handy. Perhaps he'd start teaching her here, gently tying her wrists behind the back of the chair, pushing open her night rail, lowering his fingers between her legs. . . .

"What your prophecy wants, then," she said. "You must marry me to fulfill the prophecy and save your kingdom. I need a husband—at least my mother very much wants me to have one. She has a freehold of this house for her lifetime, but the keeping of me is dear."

He pressed a kiss to the crown of her head while his fingers discovered the delights of her. Her aureoles were tight, firm little peaks for his touch. He was beginning to lose the thread of the conversation. He knew English very well, but his brain started to revert to Nvengarian, and he had to think hard to translate. "You are not an object to be passed from hand to hand."

She smiled sadly. "I am well-versed in aristocratic marriages. The higher-born the family, the more a daughter becomes an object to be passed from hand to hand, as you say. Marriages aren't like in the fairy tales, where they fall in love and live happily ever after. It is *how much land do I get, and what alliances can I make, and how can her father influence my career in Commons?*"

He wanted to laugh, but he'd never dream of it while her eyes held so much sorrow. "What you say is true. I, too, know much about aristocratic marriages."

Indeed, not one duke or duchess or prince he knew had married for love. It had all been about connections and who was related to whom. The dukes kept mistresses, and their duchesses sought Damien. Marry for dynastic ambition, keep a lover for the tender side, were the unwritten rules of aristocratic marriage.

"But we have already fallen in love," he murmured. "Our fairy tale is real."

"What happens when the prophecy is fulfilled?" she asked, her voice unsteady. "Will we still be in love?"

He wanted to groan with the pleasure of touching her.

He brushed fingertips over the tight points of her nipples again, wanting to feel them against his chest. She must be wet and ready for him, he sensed it. All he had to do was coax her. "I hope so, my love. This feeling came unlooked-for, but I do not want it to go away."

She turned her head to look up at him, her red lips near his own. The scent of her made his already crazed brain madder still. "We fell in love for the prophecy's convenience," she said.

"Mayhap." He caught her nipple between his fingers, tugged it. She gave a little noise of pain, and he released her, but his hardness ached. "You admit we are in love, then?"

"I can find no other explanation for these feelings."

Her words were formal, but her voice shook. Her breath against his skin sent an explosive spark through his body. He wanted her with the mindlessness of an animal. Any longer in this room, and he wouldn't be able to stop himself. His control slipped again.

"This is dangerous," he said, almost to himself. "But I wanted to see you. No, I *needed* to see you, not just through the convenient peephole."

Her lips parted, showing him the waiting moisture inside. "Peephole?"

"In the panel. Do you not know of it?"

"Oh, behind the night table? I never pay it any mind."

"I will have Petri nail it shut. Else I might be tempted to kneel there all night." Watching her comb out her hair, braiding it, perhaps, to keep it neat in the night. Then to draw off her dressing gown and walk, bare under her night rail, to her bed. The cotton nightgown would cling to the curves of her body, sticking, perhaps, to any damp place.

She'd climb into her bed, lay her head on the pillow, and close her eyes, unaware that he watched, in pain and need, from behind the wall.

"Most definitely I will have him nail it shut. And have him prepare me a cold bath while he is at it."

She leaned her forehead against his cheek, her eyes half closed while she savored his touch on her bosom. Her breasts were heavy in his hands. He could pull the night rail down and suckle her, taste her until he was satisfied.

He did not believe a day would come when he was satisfied with her.

"I do not want you to leave," she breathed.

"I do not want to, either." He traced her cheek, his silver ring winking. "But mayhap I should."

"No." She slid her hand up the back of his arm, palm warm on his tricep. "Not yet. I need to touch you. I do not know why." Her fingers bit through his shirt, points of desperation.

"I know why. It is the same need I feel." He smiled into her skin. "We will burst into flames, I think, my Penelope."

"Perhaps we ought to." Her hands moved from his arms to his shoulders, then to his neck, touching the hollow of his bared throat. He imagined those interested hands roving the intimate places of his body, and he groaned softly, the pain in his groin rising.

She kissed the corner of his mouth. Her lips were innocent, wanting to learn. He slid his hands down her night rail and kissed her deeply.

He tasted sweet innocence experiencing the first longings of a woman. She swirled her tongue against his in an unpracticed manner, and the heat inside him began to beat. Blood lust soared, and his reason began to drain away.

Dear God, I am being punished for every sin I have ever committed.

He'd done them all, lechery, wrath, envy, gluttony, avarice, sloth, and most of all *pride.* His damned pride. The curse of Nvengarians, pride was.

He'd bedded some of the most beautiful women in the

world. He'd gambled on risky investments and won. He'd literally dodged assassins' bullets that missed him by hairs-breadths. Such attempts made him wilder than ever, as he celebrated in heady joy that he'd cheated death once again.

He'd once made love to a duchess on the parapet of a castle in Bohemia, while a river raged at the bottom of a seventy-foot drop, and her husband slept in the bedroom not ten feet away. An hour before, he'd thwarted another assassination attempt; this one, a man waiting in his bed-chamber with a loaded pistol. Damien had heard the click of the flint striking the pan just in time.

The assassin had been taken, and in his rush of height-ened elation and fear, Damien had gone to the duchess and dragged her out on the parapet, balancing between life and death while he ground himself into her.

The duchess had made certain all her friends knew, of course, and after that, Damien's reputation among women had soared. There was nothing, they said, *nothing* Prince Damien would not do.

Penelope's fingers tangled his hair. She played her lips over his, her eager kisses driving him wild.

Too soon, and the prophecy will be broken. The words pounded in his brain, as though someone else spoke them.

Why not have her? another, more treacherous voice sug-gested. Tip her to the floor, strip off the dressing gown, and have her right there. They would marry; what differ-ence did it make whether he took her now or later? The betrothal ceremony would be only a few days hence. Why wait?

It took the iron will that had seen him alive through the mountains of Nvengaria and into the Transylvanian Alps, alone with nothing but the rags on his back, to stop kiss-ing Penelope.

He slowly eased his mouth from hers, her little whimper of regret driving him wild. He took her hands in a firm grip and clasped them between his own.

"Penelope, this is the most difficult thing I have ever said in my life, but we must stop."

Chapter Eight

She gazed at him through half-closed eyes, her lips swollen and moist. She was ripe for bedding, and a so-convenient bed stood nearby.

"I do not want to stop," she said.

"I know, love. But if I lose this, if I lose this gamble . . ." He'd stand against a cold wall in Nvengaria with muskets aimed at him. Alexander would smile and take the first shot. And Damien would deserve it for not fulfilling his bargain to his people, for not being their hope.

He could have refused the ring and told Misk and his men to take themselves off when they'd found him in Paris. Instead, he'd realized that he had a chance to put right all that his father had destroyed. A fierce protectiveness had awoken inside him, which had only grown when he'd ridden at long last over the pass between the Carpathian and Nvengarian mountains and looked down to the lush river valley that was Nvengaria. His home.

"Gamble?" Penelope asked.

Damien drew a ragged breath. He had once taken refuge with Franciscan monks in Italy, and one of them had taught Damien how to clear the mind of thought and bodily desires. Damien had never mastered the art of meditation like the monk had, but he'd learned how to calm himself when the need arose.

The peace he'd found in the monastery eluded him here, but breathing gave him something to focus on besides Penelope's body.

"I will win," he said, teeth clenched. "We both will."

"You think the prophecy is making us want each other?" she asked. "That this is not natural?"

Damien raked his gaze to Penelope's open night rail and the shadow of her breasts within. "No, me wanting you is perfectly natural. You are a beautiful woman."

She blushed, suddenly shy. "You think me beautiful?"

He lifted her hand and licked her fingertip. "Your beauty is—how do you say?—a fact. Not my opinion."

"No one has ever expressed such an opinion."

She cast down her gaze, lashes shielding her eyes. Not maidenly bashfulness; she was embarrassed.

In London, young ladies tried to be thin sticks, starving themselves to look like narrow cylinders in their gowns. Pale hair, pale faces, pale lips, pale hands—this was the pinnacle of beauty, they thought. Walking marble statues, but they were nothing so lush as real Hellenistic statuary. The Greeks had known how to sculpt a woman.

In Nvengaria, the portrait of beauty was wildness. Black hair, blue eyes, high color, a ripe, womanly body. Nvengarians were a temperamental people. They lived at the extremes of anger, joy, love, fear, and elation. Not very restful, but they did not hide their feelings behind stilted conversation and rigid standards of acceptance.

If Damien took Penelope to Nvengaria, hordes of men would swarm about her, admiring her, wanting her. A primal protectiveness welled inside him. If he'd been an ordinary gentleman, he could count on fighting many duels for her. But he was the Imperial Prince, and she would be Imperial Princess. Touching Penelope without permission would be punishable by death.

So sorry, gentlemen. The lady is mine.

He wrapped his tongue about her middle finger and suckled it. His self-control had gone to hell, he who'd always prided himself on his control. He gave a woman pleasure and took pleasure for himself, but always it was controlled. He never engaged his heart, and neither did they. His feelings for Penelope made a mockery of all that.

Penelope's gaze riveted to his mouth around her finger, her eyes heavy. Knowing he could have her but *not yet* made his blood boil. She tasted so good. She was warm and salty, and he wanted to suck on her forever.

He deliberately removed her finger from his mouth. He couldn't resist licking his lips, though, scraping up all the taste of her he could.

"I need to leave you and walk to the passage and back to my room," he said.

She nodded. "That is probably best."

"The passage will be dark." He remained fixed in place. "After a year in a dungeon, I dislike dark, closed-in places."

"Take my candle," she said, then her brows drew together in concern. "How horrible. I did not even know dungeons still existed."

"They do in Nvengaria. My father threw me into one when I was a boy, beneath the castle at Narato. It is remote, damp, and nasty. His lackeys ripped me from bed in the middle of night, half suffocating me. The next thing I knew, I was in a cell with my wrists in chains and the door closing. It was dark." He drew a quick breath, age-old demons swooping at him from the past. "Penelope, I've never been anywhere so dark."

"How old were you?" she asked gently.

"Twelve."

"Why would he do such a thing?" she asked, angry.

"My father? I am surprised it took him twelve years to act against me." He toyed with her fingers while he answered. "A faction had gathered to overthrow him and put me on the throne. With their leader as regent, of course, and me to be their puppet. My father caught them and had them all executed in a gruesome manner. He could not prove I had any intention of going along with it, but to be safe, he locked me away. It took his Council of Dukes a year to convince him to let me out again. Public opinion was turning against him, and they feared an uprising. So my father set me free in a public ceremony—the prodigal son forgiven—then, in the middle of the night again, his men came for me and dragged me into the mountains and abandoned me. My father spun a yarn of sending me away to school in France, then later claimed that I'd run away on my own, because I hated Nvengaria. The truth was, he forbade me to come back. If I returned, it would be to face secret execution. Only the fact that the people of Nvengaria liked me and would never forgive my father if he got rid of me openly, kept him from giving the order to have me killed outright."

He stopped short, closing his mouth with effort, wondering where the flow of words had come from. He'd never told any living soul the truth of what had happened. Either they already knew, like Petri, or he had no wish to speak of it.

Penelope had done the same with her story of Reuben White's betrayal. Was the prophecy making them bare their souls to each other? Did it want them stripped naked before one another, and not only in the enjoyable way?

She laid a gentle hand on his arm. "I am sorry."

Candlelight gleamed on her tawny hair. He wrapped one glistening golden curl around his finger. "I survived.

Petri found me, and together, we swarmed across Europe and conquered it. To a boy, it was an adventure; do not feel too sorry for me."

"Was it?"

Truth snaked out of his mouth again. "No. I was damned terrified. I knew my father would send assassins after me, and he did. Petri and I lived hand to mouth, laboring in fields for food or a bed for the night, or we outright begged if we could not find work. I, the spoiled prince, was kicked in the face by burghers with nothing better to do."

He omitted the few who had wanted them for a different sort of labor, two handsome Nvengarian boys, and how they'd had to fight to get away.

She slid her palm across his lawn-clad forearm. "That is horrible."

Compassion rang in her voice. She cared. She was imagining that scared youth and wanting to comfort him. He'd left the boy behind years and years ago, but the tiny part of him who was still that child reached for her comfort.

Oh, no, no, no, he thought, wanting to laugh. *You tried to snare me with desire, now you are trying to snare me with her shining compassion.*

And I'm talking back to a stubborn, lust-driven prophecy.

"Penelope," he said. "I will take your candle and return to my room."

"Yes," she answered.

He remained on one knee before her, his fingers tangled in her hair, his gaze searching hers. "I cannot seem to move. Perhaps you should stand up and walk away from me."

"I will try," she said.

She drew her fingers down the inside of his arm. They played there, exploring muscle and sinew, while she flicked her gaze to his lips.

Damien said, " 'Tis not working."

"No," she answered.

"You could shout for Mr. Tavistock. I am certain he would haul me away, and possibly shoot me."

She smiled, her plump lips curving. "I cannot. I would be compromised."

He shared her smile. "I can think of far more entertaining ways to compromise you than being shot by your almost-steppapa."

"You should not think of them, then."

"True. These pantaloons are already extremely tight."

Her gaze dropped to the buttons of his pantaloons in a gratifying manner. He had a sudden vision of her snaking her delicate hands to his fly and popping open each button, releasing his arousal from its tight prison. It would tumble out, rock hard, and she would, with wonderment, trace it with her fingers.

He would teach her then, to lean forward and take it into her mouth.

"God and all his saints, help a sinner," he said huskily.

She raised her eyes. In them he read that she'd been envisioning the same thing. "What do we do?"

"I want you," he said. "I want to lay you down and come into you until you scream for me. Then I want you to beg for more. I want it so much I will say these crude things to a gently born lady and not care."

She looked at him with startled eyes and did not answer.

"I have offended you," he said. "Thank God. You will slap me and tell me I am a rake and a libertine and call for your servants to drag me away."

"No," she breathed. "I want you inside me."

He cupped her face. "Not good."

"I know. But I ache for you. I want you to touch me here. . . ." She slid her fingers down her body to where her dressing gown folded in her lap.

He caught her hand. "Do not show me. Else I'll never leave before tupping you in this chair."

She gave him a bemused look. "*Tupping.* A word I have never used."

"It masks another word I long to use. A good English word that is short and effective."

A mischievous gleam entered her eye. "I believe I know what the word is. Meagan told me. It is—"

He thrust his fingers across her lips. "Do not say it. Do not, for God's sake, Penelope." Or he'd ravish her. He knew it. He'd rip her flimsy nightclothes from her body and thrust himself straight into her.

A madness had entered him, making him feverish and randy and barbaric. He'd descended from mountain tribes that barely contained their violence to build a kingdom, and that feral violence lurked close to the surface.

If she said naughty words in his ear, the madman would fling aside the veneer of cultured prince and take her. And not feel guilty at all.

All humor fled him. His fingers still rested over her lips. With a crazed light in her eyes that matched his own, she touched her tongue to them.

"No," he growled. "We must stop. Do you understand me? Something is trying to break the prophecy."

"I thought you said the prophecy made us want each other," she said against his fingers.

He moved his hand. "So I thought when I first entered this room. But my prophecy wants everything to happen at the correct time. Sasha knows the prophecy inside and out. If he says we wait, we wait. Something is trying to make us move too soon."

"What is? More magic?"

"I do not know. Magic, from what Nedrak told me, works close to the bone. It stirs what is basic in us, underneath our reason."

She shivered. "I do not like it."

"There is joy in it. A release, rather like what we will feel when I finally take you." He broke off, watching her eager, uncomprehending gaze. "Never mind. I am dying to give in, which means we must fight it."

"How?" Her hands went to his chest.

"Think of something else. Ask me a question."

"Um." She drew a ragged breath, her fingers tracing the opening of his shirt. "Oh. Tell me a story."

His racing heartbeat slowed a fraction. "A story?"

"Yes, a Nvengarian fairy tale. You told me you knew them, and that you'd tell me . . ."

"In bed. I remember." His heartbeat increased again, imagining her lying on his pillow, her hair tangled with their lovemaking, while he murmured stories into her ear. "Yes, I will tell you stories. Let me think."

Shoving his mind down the road of childhood, to the tales his old governess had told him before the nursery fire, did lessen the pain somewhat.

He remembered the high room in the Imperial castle, where wind whipped at the eaves. He remembered his creaking old governess, chosen because she was elderly and alone and no threat to the Imperial Prince, spinning stories in her rasping voice. Sometimes the stories made no sense; sometimes she fell asleep in the middle of them, but he remembered how they'd enchanted him.

He sorted through the memories until he found something appropriate. He noted that his breathing had calmed somewhat.

Penelope gazed up at him, eyes heavy.

No, he still wanted her with mindless lust. But it felt more normal, the wanting of a strong man for a sweet, beautiful woman.

He leaned down, scooped her into his arms, sat himself on the chair, and settled her into his lap. "Once upon a time," he began. "There was a beautiful princess."

* * *

Penelope snuggled into him and laid her head on his shoulder. She felt heavy, as though she'd been held up by strings that had been suddenly released. His firm shoulder through his lawn shirt supported her, his arms kept her from falling. Safe, that was it, she felt safe.

The strong muscles of his thighs pressed her backside, and the scent of him was heady. But the madness had receded a little, settling down into warm, dreaming wanting.

He'd stopped shaking, as well. When she'd nearly said the naughty word that had sprung unbidden to her lips, his eyes had darkened with crazed intensity, and she realized he could take from her whatever he wanted. She would not be able to stop him from doing anything he pleased.

Had she been afraid like a sensible woman? No. She'd wanted to be compromised, wanted his hard weight on top of her, wanted his hands and mouth all over her body.

He mastered himself. She watched his control return, an iron will that told her better than his words, his jewels, and his entourage ever could, that he was a ruler. His ancestors had held Nvengaria against the outside world for eight centuries, and she'd seen in him tonight the strength that could do such things.

This amazing man now held her, plain Penelope Trask, on his knee, while he told her a story.

"What did the princess look like?" she interrupted.

He chuckled. She liked his laugh—his true laugh, the silken, warm one. She studied the gap in his shirt, enjoying the play of shadowed muscle beneath.

"She had long golden hair and beautiful green eyes," he purred, "And a body a man would die for."

He kept calling her beautiful. He said it like he believed it, his eyes dark and warm.

"What happened to this princess?"

"She was locked in a tower, far from civilization. 'Twas

a high tower, with no door and only one window. It was surrounded by a huge thicket in the middle of an impenetrable forest. The only person she ever saw was the hideous beast who guarded her."

"Why was she in the tower?" Penelope asked, growing curious. "What had she done?"

"Nothing. Her parents locked her there for her protection, along with boxes filled with treasure. Because she was so beautiful and so rich, you see, they feared that every man in the kingdom would try to snatch her away. So, she grew to womanhood there with the hideous beast to guard her."

"Until one day," Penelope prompted.

"Hush," he growled. "I am telling this story."

"I beg your pardon, Your Highness." She snuggled closer to him. "Please proceed."

"*Until one day*, a very handsome man approached. He had a long rope, which he tossed to the tower window. The princess looked out and asked what he was doing. 'Why, climbing the tower to rescue you,' he answered. She was delighted, knowing she would leave the tower at last. While she watched him struggle the very long way up, she asked him how he'd gotten through the impenetrable forest. 'Enchantment,' he answered. She asked how he'd gotten through the terrible thicket alive. 'Enchantment,' he answered. She asked how he'd gotten past the hideous beast."

" 'Enchantment,' " Penelope said with him.

He grinned. "Now, the princess worried that the beast had been hurt, because, although he was hideous, he'd always been kind to her. But she saw no blood on the handsome man's clothes, and concluded the beast must have been put to sleep or some such thing."

"Compassionate of her," Penelope murmured.

"The princess was indeed compassionate. And beautiful. And wise. She watched the handsome man climb the tower, and then she helped pull him inside. He was handsome indeed, tall and striking."

"Did he have black hair and blue eyes?"

"He was Nvengarian, so he must have. The princess was about to reward her rescuer with a kiss, a gift more precious than any jewel, when suddenly, he walked past her to the two huge boxes of treasure. He opened them and scooped out the coins and laughed. 'I'm rich,' said he."

"Oh," Penelope raised her head, indignant. "Then he only wanted the treasure? Not the princess? The nerve of him."

"Yes, he was not a prince, but a clever thief, helped by a wicked sorcerer. The sorcerer had given him magics to get through the forest and the thicket and to enchant the hideous beast, in return for a share of the profit. The princess was so angry that she went up to the man, while he was bent over the chests, and kicked him in the backside."

Penelope put her hand over her mouth, laughing. "Serves him right."

"Indeed. He turned around and looked at the princess, and then realized how extraordinarily beautiful she was. He went to her, took her in his arms, and kissed her. Rather like this."

Damien demonstrated, and Penelope met the kiss hungrily. The ferocious passion of a few minutes ago had gone, like a spell broken, but it still fired her.

His dark hair shadowed his face, and his eyes were still, the sophisticated Prince Damien again. She'd rather liked the glimpse of the other Damien, the one of raw emotion and intensity, the one who'd survived by his strength and his wits to make half the world eat out of his hand.

When the kiss ended, she asked, "Did the princess fall in love with him?"

"*He* fell in love with *her*. He said, 'If you help me get the treasure out, I will take you, too.' Well, the princess had long wanted to leave the tower, so she told the thief she would help him. He tied the rope around her waist and lowered her to the ground. Then he tied each of the two chests of treasure to the rope and lowered them as well. At last, he climbed down himself.

"The princess was quite excited to find herself at last out of the tower. But, as I said, the princess was very wise. She noticed at once that the thief had brought no cart or horse to help carry away the treasure. He had left his horse at the edge of the forest, he said. They would have to drag the treasure chests back through.

"The princess had a much better idea. At her waist hung a horn of silver, which she could use to summon the hideous beast if need be. She put it to her lips, and blew."

"Oh, dear," Penelope said.

"Soon they heard the hideous beast crashing toward them through the thicket. He emerged, huge and tall, with two great, bloodshot eyes and a horn on his head. He carried an axe, almost as big as the princess herself. He roared, furious, because he'd been in an enchanted sleep and the thief had gotten past him.

"The thief, terrified, tried to make the princess run away. But the princess turned to face the beast, unafraid. 'Beast,' she said. 'I have some heavy boxes. Can you carry them for me?' The beast at once hung his axe on his belt and picked up the treasure boxes, one under each great arm.

" 'Beast,' the princess said. 'I want to see the wide world. Will you show it to me and protect me from harm?' The beast nodded his great head. Happy, the princess took the beast's arm and told him to lead on through the thicket.

"The thief said, growing worried, 'What about me?'

"The princess gave him a dazzling smile. 'I thank you, sir, for helping me escape the tower with all my treasure. The beast has been my dear friend for many a long year, and I believe we will be very happy together. Good-bye.'

"The thief watched with his mouth open, as the beautiful princess and all that treasure went off with the beast into the forest. He knew he'd never, ever be able to fight off the hideous beast and he had no more enchantments. He had lost.

"The princess walked away with the beast, her hand on his strong arm. Together they discovered the wonders of the wide world, and lived happily ever after."

Penelope put her hand over her mouth, laughter burbling. "You made that up."

"No, indeed." His eyes sparkled. "My pledge to you, it is a Nvengarian fairy tale. I believe it is an admonishment to Nvengarians to not be so vain. Nvengarians are quite vain people."

She idly drew her slippered foot up Damien's calf. "I understand why. You are all so beautiful. Even your servants are strikingly handsome, like the two lads you have as footmen."

He grunted. "Rufus and Miles, aye, they are a pair. They rub it in anyone's faces that they were chosen to journey with their prince, not realizing it was a punishment."

Her foot stopped. "Punishment?"

His eyes cooled, shutting himself from her. "I have already said too much."

"Indeed, you have not. You've said entirely too little."

He brushed his fingers across her face, but the heat had gone, his storytelling having diminished the fierce fire between them. "You know what you need to know. There is a prophecy that I must fulfill by Midsummer's Day, to bring back with me the true Princess of Nvengaria. You are she. We will have our betrothal ritual here, and our wedding in Nvengaria. You should prepare for the journey, although any clothes and things you need will be provided for you as we go."

She slid from his enchanting lap and landed on her feet.

"Wait a moment, Your Arrogant Highness. I have not yet said I will marry you."

His eyes held wariness, but also a determination that nearly knocked her over. "You will."

"You are certain, are you?"

"Yes. You will come 'round."

"Why?"

He stood up. He was too tall, too masculine. In his open shirt, with his silver ring, he looked like a wild Magyar someone had convinced to wear civilized clothes.

His mouth moved into a smile, but the smile did not reach his eyes. "Because you are in love with me. The prophecy has made you so. You will come to me, and we will be joined."

For a moment, she wanted to melt at his feet and agree with every word he said. But Penelope had never been a compliant female. Had she been, she'd have married Reuben White several years ago and even now be living in misery. Instead, she'd lifted her chin, looked the handsome dandy in the eye, and told him the engagement was off. The consequences had been awful, the gossip vicious, but she'd done it.

"Oh, we will, will we?" she asked, her voice haughty.

The corners of his mouth creased. "You will make a fine princess."

He planted one hand on her waist, gave her a deep, breathtaking kiss, and strolled away to the panel in the wall.

She touched her fingers to her lips and willed her knees not to fail her. She'd not give him the satisfaction of falling to the floor and begging him to stay.

He swung the panel inward. A rectangle of cold darkness waited for him like a gaping mouth. She saw him flinch, then square his shoulders.

That tiny movement, the one acknowledgement that he

had not always been a pillar of strength, undid her like his kisses could not. She snatched up her candle in its holder and ran to him.

"Here, take it." She thrust the candlestick into his hand. He looked at her, the candle flame dancing warmth back into his eyes. "You should not suffer the dark because I am angry at you."

His cool reserve fled, and the barbarian prince returned. He slid his hand behind her neck and scooped her to him.

His kiss was hot, deep, his lips devouring. She tasted his spice and the hard thrust of his tongue.

Candle wax spattered to the floor, and he broke the kiss, slanting her a smile of hot promise. Then he ducked through the opening, and was gone.

As soon as he closed the panel, she let her legs bend. She went flat on her back on the floor, her arms outstretched, and sighed happily. "*What* a man."

Hers for the taking, she thought, and she shivered in excitement. That is, if she believed in magic.

Far, far away, across mountains and valleys, seas and rivers, in the deep gorge that was the country of Nvengaria, a man of about thirty-two sat, fingers steepled, and watched his mage peer into a sliver of crystal.

"Well?" Alexander asked, his deep voice tinged with impatience. "Did the spell work?"

Chapter Nine

The two men occupied a sumptuous room. Tapestries softened cold stone walls, and hangings of red and blue and gold adorned the doors. Alexander's chair was old, from three centuries previous, square and carved, strewn with cushions and cloths.

Alexander himself wore the softest of silk shirts, skintight buff breeches, boots of supple leather, and a military-style coat of best superfine. A blue sash woven with stiff threads of pure gold, the only one of its kind in all of Nvengaria, slashed from his right shoulder to left waist. The sash belonged to the Grand Duke, the highest of the Council of Dukes.

Gold encircled Alexander's fingers. On one ring, a ruby winked deep blood red. He wore another ruby stud in his ear, nearly hidden in his long dark hair.

The Grand Duke's full name was Alexander Octavien Laurent Maximilien. Where Prince Damien invited people to not bother remembering all his names, no one forgot Alexander's. He did not insist they remember, but people seemed to do so anyway.

Mostly people called Alexander *Your Grace*, that is, when they could gather the courage to speak to him at all.

Nedrak, the Grand Mage in the Council of Mages, found the man unnerving. Alexander would say nothing, but under his dark blue gaze, people found themselves stammering and sweating and wanting to tell him whatever he expected to hear.

Nedrak, alas, had to give him bad news.

He looked up from the scrying crystal to find those blue eyes on him, cold and intense. He swallowed. He tried to remember that he was as high born as Grand Duke Alexander, that he held a position almost as important as Alexander's, that Alexander was not yet supreme ruler of Nvengaria.

Didn't matter. The coil of panic would not go away. "The prince is strong, Your Grace," he said. "As is the girl."

"In other words, it did not work."

"No, Your Grace. I believe the spell was weakened by distance."

Alexander sat back, bringing his steepled fingers to his mouth. He did not believe in Nedrak's magic nor in the spell Nedrak claimed to have cast to force Prince Damien and his little princess to break the prophecy. He did not really believe in the scrying crystal, either, although Nedrak did seem to know what went on far away.

"Prince Damien's father nearly killed us all," he said softly. "Remember?"

"Too well, Your Grace." Nedrak nodded fervently, pleased he could agree with Alexander on something.

Alexander's thoughts moved from the burbling mage to the havoc Damien's demon of a father had wrought in Nvengaria. The former Imperial Prince had nearly broken the Council of Dukes with his idiotic schemes and had more or less ruled like a despot. He'd given away the gold on which Nvengaria had been founded to buy himself friends and pay tribute to the greedy Ottomans. Alexander and the Councils had fought hard to keep the Ottoman Empire from looking at them as a vassal state.

The result was that the stronger Russians, Prince Metternich and the Austrians, not to mention the Ottoman Empire, nearly rushed in and simply took what they wanted. Only luck and desperate diplomacy had kept them at bay.

Rumors had told of the Imperial Prince's depravity in private, of the women he'd ravished and ruined. Alexander never paid much attention to those rumors; a man could be dissipated and still be a good ruler. The Imperial Prince, unfortunately, had not been a good ruler.

The Imperial Prince had not liked it when Alexander's father, the previous Grand Duke, had disagreed with him. Alexander's father had been arrested, stood against a wall, and shot by three marksmen. The Imperial Prince had forced Alexander to watch the execution. He then expected Alexander to take up the mantel of Grand Duke, but only as the Imperial Prince's toady.

Alexander, though seething with the need for revenge, understood the folly of acting too openly against the Imperial Prince. So outwardly he'd stepped into his father's place as Grand Duke; inwardly he'd schemed and bided his time.

And now that monster's son, Damien, the libertine prince, beloved of monarchs across Europe, was ruler of Nvengaria.

Alexander had tried to stop the Council of Dukes from sending for Damien at the old prince's death. Nvengaria could do much better without the son of the idiot who'd ruined them, he'd argued. The Council could rule in the Imperial Prince's name while Damien continued entertaining countesses and fencing and being the life of royal parties.

They didn't need him.

But Misk, keeper of the Imperial ring, like all Nvengarians, liked tradition. The man was enslaved to tradition. So was the Council of Dukes.

Too much damned tradition in this country.

Misk had slipped out in the middle of the night, against orders, found Damien, and brought him home.

Alexander had looked into the eyes of the Imperial Prince's son and seen the same ruthlessness, the same uncontrolled will that had characterized the father. Alexander had decided then and there that he would not let Nvengaria fall a second time, and stirred the Council of Dukes and the Council of Mages to oppose Damien.

Damien had the love of the people—stupid people who saw only the pageantry of their prince—but Alexander controlled the army. And the treasury. And the Councils. Damien had popularity and tradition; Alexander had power and money.

Alexander knew he could save Nvengaria if Damien were made a puppet prince, a figurehead. Alexander would rule. Damien could ride his horse in parades and bow and be loved—and do exactly what Alexander told him to.

Damien, unfortunately, was as pigheaded as his father. He'd met Alexander's stare when he understood the scheme, and flatly refused.

When Damien understood that Alexander had the military behind him and could not be touched, he had backed off, and they'd come to an uneasy truce, but Alexander knew they'd soon fight to the death.

When the prophecy business had come up, when Nedrak announced that all the signs were right, Alexander felt fortune turn in his direction. The Nvengarian people loved prophecy and destiny and magic. They were all for

Damien going on a quest to find and restore the long-lost princess.

Damien hadn't believed the prophecy any more than Alexander had, but he knew the power of his people. If he'd refused, they'd have rioted. Nvengarians were not calm, rational people; they loved emotion and liked to bury themselves in it. Both Damien and Alexander knew that Damien had no choice but to go.

The prophecy said that Damien would return the princess by Midsummer's Day or die in the attempt. The Nvengarians liked that. Succeed or die. It touched their romantic souls.

Alexander did not trust that Nedrak's magic spells would force Damien to break the prophecy and thus sacrifice himself, but he did trust his hand-picked assassins.

Damien might succeed. But it was far more likely he'd die in the attempt.

Alexander smiled.

Nedrak nervously wet his lips. "What is it, Your Grace?"

"Nothing." Alexander rose, firelight catching in the bloodred jewel on his finger. "You may go if you like. I am finished here." He drew in a breath, preparing himself for what would come next.

"Are you?" Nedrak looked surprised. Duke Alexander rarely stopped working until well into the small hours of the morning.

"For now. I told my wife I would visit her tonight."

"Ah." Nedrak caught Alexander's cold eye and halted his sympathetic nod. "Please give Her Grace my very best wishes for her health."

"She is dying. It will do no good." Alexander pulled a watch from his pocket, checked it, then tucked it away as he walked to the door. "But I will tell her."

"Thank you, Your Grace," Nedrak said, and then decided it would be wise to close his mouth and say nothing more.

Alexander gave him a nod and quietly departed the room.

Nedrak waited until Alexander's footfalls had faded in the distance, then he sank into his chair, fanning his lined face in relief.

"I admire that man," he confided to his scrying crystal. "As I admired his father. A smart, capable man is the Grand Duke." He blew out his breath. "But he scares the *hell* out of me."

"The Prince Regent, here!" Lady Trask gasped, hands at her cheeks.

She'd known for two days the Prince Regent was coming, and yet Lady Trask found every opportunity to throw her hands in the air and cry that he'd never find her home acceptable and they'd never be ready in time.

Alongside her mother, Penelope worked through the chaos in a slight daze. She had not seen much of Damien since the night he'd come to her room, and he'd taken care not to be alone with her.

At first, Penelope thought him wise, because she'd nearly flung off her night rail and begged him to lie on top of her on the floor of her chamber. But as the hours, then the days, passed, she began craving him with mindless intensity.

She thought of the feeling of his hands on her breasts, his fingers manipulating her with skill. She relived the sensation over and over in her dreams and in her waking hours.

A man had touched her body and called her beautiful.

One kiss could not hurt, she'd think. Or one touch of his hand. Even a moment snatched with him so their gazes could meet and they could speak.

But Damien wrapped himself in preparations for the coming fête, and spent his time with Sasha or his valet,

Petri. He went to the village often, taking one or more of his huge footmen with him.

The footmen came home singing; Damien was always quiet and watchful.

Michael had decided to stay after all. He told Penelope he would not leave her and her mother until things were settled. He'd started to believe Damien's story, but was still wary.

"Damien is a personable fellow," he said to Penelope. "And if the Prince of Wales vouches for him, I shall believe him. But your mother grows too excited at the prospect of royalty near at hand."

"Please understand," Penelope appealed to him. "She adored being a baronet's wife and going to all the best balls and parties in London. She felt it keenly when all the income went to my cousin, and we could no longer live in Town."

"Penelope." Michael put his hand on her shoulder, his kind eyes still. "I know. But perhaps your mother cannot forgive me not giving her what her husband did."

"She loves you very much. Please give her a chance."

Michael promised, but evasively. Penelope worried—amid her worries of everything else. Her mother sometimes treated Michael poorly, but if he went, he would truly break her heart. Penelope could hardly run off with Damien and leave her all alone, in that case.

Then Damien would ride away, searching for another princess.

The thought of Damien taking another woman's hand and looking into her eyes and telling her the prophecy made him fall in love with her drove her wild. She could not face that possibility.

But the thought of leaving home and England for a remote land she knew little about terrified her.

It was not as though Damien lived in the next county or

even as far away as Northumberland. His kingdom was on the other side of the world, in a land of sharp mountains and cold winters and wild wolves.

She'd asked at supper one night how long the journey to Nvengaria would be. Sasha had answered at once. "A long and difficult road of many perils through many miles. There will be danger at every turn." His eyes glowed.

Damien had silenced him with a look but hadn't contradicted him.

Penelope knew that if she hadn't been so attracted to Damien, the choice would be easy. The sensible part of her told her to refuse Damien's suit, stay home to look after her mother, to try to reconcile Lady Trask and Michael so the two could make a happy marriage. Remain here as Michael's stepdaughter and Meagan's stepsister. That would be best for everyone.

But every time she pictured Damien riding away, never to return, her heart squeezed in pain. Losing Damien would hurt far worse than had crying off her engagements. The feelings did not even compare.

She had a thought—perhaps Reuben and Magnus had been so awful because she was meant to jilt them. Perhaps the prophecy had worked to make certain Penelope was free when Damien at last arrived.

Penelope turned the thought over in her mind, then impatiently dismissed it. She was getting as bad as Sasha.

On the Wednesday after Damien's arrival, Sasha had them gather in the large drawing room for the ritual of turning Lady Trask's ring over to Penelope.

Sasha wanted Lady Trask and Penelope to repeat their required phrases in Nvengarian.

"Oh, heavens, I never could," Lady Trask said, eyes wide. "Goodness, even my French master was that exasperated because during my lessons I kept calling the Queen of England a *putain*, which means whore, I believe. Goodness, I thought I was using a term of affection."

Meagan clapped her hand over her mouth, and her eyes grew moist. Penelope looked down in embarrassment.

"You see?" Lady Trask said. "I might blunder."

"She can say it in English," Damien broke in, his own Nvengarian accent strengthening with his impatience. "Your mother said the words in English when she gave you the ring."

"That is true," Lady Trask said.

"And yet the prophecy continues. Do not make them say the Nvengarian, Sasha. It is impossible."

Sasha opened his mouth to protest, but looked at Damien's face and shut it again. Penelope had come to learn that Sasha knew just how far he could push his prince.

And so Penelope stood in the late afternoon sunshine under the huge Palladian window that looked over the garden, and received the ancient silver ring from her mother.

"This ring I give you, of my own free will," Lady Trask said, "to hold and protect, until destiny draws it forth."

Lady Trask giggled a little over the words. Then, with Sasha hovering so close Penelope felt the man's breath on her shoulder, Lady Trask slid the ring onto Penelope's finger.

Penelope glanced at the card on which Sasha had carefully written her reply. "I accept this ring as the symbol of my lineage. I will safeguard it with pride, and carry it to my destiny."

Sasha's mouth moved along with Penelope's, and when Penelope let go of Lady Trask's hand, he gushed a sigh, "It is done."

The Nvengarian servants in the hall whooped in delight. Several of the English servants did as well. Mathers looked aggrieved, but the other Trask servants had decided that the Nvengarians' high spirits and habit of bringing forth ale or whiskey to celebrate just about anything were more to their taste than quiet soberness.

In the drawing room, Petri poured bloodred wine and handed it 'round. Penelope sipped hers, surprised at the thick, mellow taste. Meagan took a hearty swig, until Michael gave her the eye, and she innocently set the goblet on the table.

In the hall, one of Damien's footmen, Rufus or Miles—she could not tell them apart yet—shouted in heavily accented English, "All hail Princess Penelope!"

"All hail Princess Penelope!" came the returning cry, in English and in Nvengarian.

Lady Trask looked proud, Meagan, excited.

Damien was watching her. Penelope pretended not to notice, but the look in his eyes was dark and intense and satisfied.

Damien quit the house after the ritual, to avoid succumbing to temptation and dragging Penelope off to have his way with her. He'd wanted to drag her to him and kiss her and kiss her, savoring every inch of her.

The ring on her finger meant she accepted her lineage. That she was his for the taking. She'd looked up at him with confusion in her starry eyes, starting to believe in her fate and not certain she wanted to.

He wanted to take her to bed and show her everything her fate could be.

Best he leave the house before he swept her into his arms and ran upstairs with her, thus negating the prophecy, ruining his country, and playing into Alexander's hands.

To curb himself, he took Petri with him to the village to check on preparations there.

They found Little Marching teeming with activity.

Carts and wagons filled with lumber and canvas rumbled through the High Street. At the end of the High, in the village square, a platform had been built, the banner of the Imperial Princes—two snarling, golden wolves on a background of deep blue—already hanging from it. Awnings with the blue and gold of Nvengaria flapped from nearly every doorway and rose above the platform.

The tavern door stood open, and despite the work going on, plenty of men had found time to drop in for a pint.

As soon as Damien ducked through the doorway, a shout went up.

"Three cheers for Prince Damien!"

"Hip, hip, hooray!" Nvengarian flags came out and waved in fervor.

"Where did they get the flags?" Damien murmured to Petri in Nvengarian.

"Rufus and Miles," he answered.

"Ah." Damien called, in English, "Landlord, I will—what is the phrase?—I will stand the next round."

The cheering rose. Men working outside hurried in to partake. The landlord, smiling broadly, handed tankards to his barmaids as fast as he could.

The landlord's daughter flashed a hopeful smile at Damien as she brought him a tankard. Damien thanked her politely, then gave Petri a nod. Petri, taking the cue, slipped in beside her and easily diverted her attention. The village girls were finding Petri's warm smiles and faulty English quite enchanting.

Damien quietly sipped his ale, listening to the others talk and laugh. When he felt the time right—the patrons sufficiently benevolent toward all things Nvengarian—he stepped in front of the bar and raised his hands for silence.

It took a while, because every man in the place started shouting—"Quiet, the prince is about to speak!" "I am quiet—*you* get quiet." "If we all stop shouting, the man can talk!"

At last, Damien simply cut across their noise. "My friends." The chatter ceased as they turned to look at him. "I thank you for the warm welcome you have given me and my people. I have grown to love your little village in the few days I have been here."

This engendered more cheering. Damien knew it would. But Damien was used to waiting for crowds to quiet between sentences. In Nvengaria, one could never be certain what a speaker said to the masses, because he could never be heard over screaming of the crowd.

The English, at least, quieted a little in case he said something interesting.

"I have had word," Damien went on, "that the Prince of Wales will indeed be attending our fête."

More cheers. Englishmen, in general, rather despised the portly Prince Regent, but having royalty visit a village was reason for celebration. And another round of ale.

"You must do something for me," Damien said.

The hubbub died down again. Eager, somewhat glassy gazes fixed on Damien.

"You must show great honor to your prince," he said. "You must cheer mightily for him, and wave your English flags, and show your love of England to him. He will reward you well, I think."

The farmer in the back raised his flagon. "Long live Prince George!"

"Long live Prince George! God save the King!"

Damien waited, smiling gently. He wanted the villagers on his side in his quest to win Penelope, in case he had to recruit them to help spirit her away. As well, it was satisfying to gain the reputation of benevolence. Prince Damien had learned how to be welcome, even by people who instinctively disliked and mistrusted foreigners.

But he needed the Prince Regent on his side as well. The Prince was jealous of Damien, and he would be less than pleased to discover that Damien had walked into an English village and taken it over.

Damien hadn't really, he knew that. These men were salt of the earth who might grumble over the posh gents in London overtaxing their poor bit of land, but, by God, they were English posh gents, and English taxes and English bits of land. No foreigners would tell them what to do.

Damien also needed England to come in firmly on his side of the uneasiness in Nvengaria. He could not afford to let England back Alexander. Republics were fashionable these days, and Grand Duke Alexander had the Council of Dukes and the Council of Mages cowed. If Damien could keep England on his side by making Prince George believe he was the center of attention at this fête, then so be it.

"Thank you, my friends," he said to the assembly.

The same farmer shouted, "Long live Prince Damien!"

A huge cheer rattled the rafters. Damien bowed politely, smiled his thanks, and stepped away.

"I did not understand what you said," Petri remarked in Nvengarian as they strolled away, "but it sounded impressive."

Behind them, another man slurred, "Three cheers for Prince Damien!" His followers took up the call.

"Hip, hip, *horaaaaay!*"

To the same chant that had ushered them in, Petri and Damien ducked out of the tavern.

"They are good people," Damien answered his valet.

Petri shot him a look. "It is not simply their good nature. You are a natural ruler, sir. The peasants in Nvengaria do not bow simply because they have to. The peasants here do not have even that stricture upon them, and yet, they show their respect. And their liking."

"You exaggerate my virtues."

"No, you downplay them. Your father hated you for a

reason. The people loved you, and not him. Made him insane."

Damien growled, "No more of that, Petri."

Petri had known him forever and shrugged off reprimands. "You dislike hearing the truth, is all, sir. Look, here comes something that will cheer you."

Damien looked and forgot about Petri's too-shrewd digs.

At the other end of the High Street, Penelope was walking, basket on arm, with Meagan Tavistock. Meagan saw them and waved.

Damien lifted his hand. Penelope did not return the salute, but he felt her gaze rest on him, and his blood began to warm.

Sasha, still wearing his sash of office, trotted behind the ladies, followed by several Nvengarian servants. Good man, Sasha. He was carrying out Damien's orders to protect the princess at all times.

Men began pouring out of the tavern, singing a bawdy song about a lass and a man at her window. He would have to translate it for Petri, who would laugh.

Damien felt a heavy hand on his shoulder. His attention on Penelope, he assumed it a reveler wanting to thank him for his generosity.

Then Petri cried out and shoved Damien hard. Damien kept his balance and spun around to see a man with iron-gray hair and a wild look in his Nvengarian-blue eyes fight his way free of Petri. He lunged at Damien again, a hooked knife raised.

"Nvengaria!" he screamed.

Damien twisted out of the way as the knife came down. Petri grabbed the assassin from behind. The man fought ferociously, his expression insane but determined. He would kill Damien or die trying.

The men from the tavern caught on to the situation. They rushed to help, shouting, fists waving.

The assassin flailed his knife at Petri, who jumped out of reach with a curse. The villagers swarmed around the assassin, keeping him away from Damien, but they tangled up with each other, causing more chaos. In the milling confusion, the man squirmed away and hurtled down the High Street toward Penelope.

"Sasha!" Damien shouted.

Sasha looked up, alert, his mouth open, as the man ran at them, sprinting hard. Penelope and Meagan stopped, poised, not understanding.

Damien started running, knowing he'd never catch the man in time. The Nvengarian footmen, trained to protect their masters, rushed forward, but they were too far away. Mouth dry, he watched the assassin reach Sasha, who'd stepped in front of Penelope.

Meagan screamed and dashed behind the well at the end of the street. Sasha shoved Penelope against the wall of the well, shielding her body with his as the assassin sprang at her.

The assassin's knife came down, right into Sasha's back.

An instant later, the Nvengarian servants grabbed the man. The tavern-goers, shouting like Saxon warriors of old, pounded toward them.

The man jerked the knife from Sasha's body, the blade covered in blood. He screamed, "Nvengaria!" again, before plunging the knife into his own chest.

Sasha was sliding to the ground, Penelope trying to hold on to him. Blood blossomed on the back of his coat, too much blood.

Damien reached them, and caught the man as he fell. "Sasha."

Penelope knelt, her hand on Sasha's chest. Her green-gold eyes were anguished, her hand bloody where she'd scraped it against the stone well.

Damien's heart thumped until he was nauseated with

it. Damn, damn, *damn*. A Nvengarian assassin right here in this peaceful little village. And when he couldn't kill Damien, he'd gone straight for Penelope.

"Sasha," he breathed. *Don't be dead, God damn you.*

Sasha opened his eyes. His voice was weak. "Your Highness. I am not afraid to die for you."

"You will not die, old man, do you hear me?" Damien signaled to the servants. "Get him into the tavern and get his shirt off. Stop the bleeding."

The footmen, hand-picked by Damien for just these emergencies, moved into action. Rufus had a litter made and Sasha loaded onto it in minutes. Damien stood up as they lifted Sasha, who was bravely trying to keep quiet.

Penelope stood up with them, her hand on Sasha's shoulder. She had not said a word since Sasha's fall, but her eyes spoke volumes. She understood what had happened, what Sasha had done and why.

As soon as Rufus led off the train of servants bearing Sasha, Damien crushed Penelope in his arms. She landed against his chest, her soft hair brushing his chin. She smelled of sweet roses and sunshine.

He kissed her, a hard, brutal kiss that held his fear and his fury, never mind the damned villagers watching.

"Are you hurt?" he asked in a rough voice.

She shook her head mutely. Her ungloved hand rested on his chest, the silver ring shining softly in the sunlight.

The ring said she belonged to Nvengaria, and to him. He tightened his arms around her, kissing the silky press of her hair. He needed to touch her. He needed to spend three days in bed with her, his hands on her body, savoring every inch of her.

If Sasha died, Damien would take it out on every ounce of Alexander's hide.

If Penelope died, Damien knew he'd die himself. *After* he killed Alexander.

So this is what love does to you. It eats you from the inside out, and never lets you rest.

Prophecy or no prophecy, spell or no spell, he needed Penelope with him forever.

He cupped her face in his hands. "I couldn't reach you in time."

Her lips were bloodless, her eyes filled with the same stark worry he felt. "I saw him try to stab you. Why?"

Meagan's voice sounded beside them. "Oh, mercy, mercy, mercy. Does this happen to you all the time, Damien?"

She pushed her flyaway red hair from her face and gazed in horrified fascination at the would-be assassin on the cobbles. His eyes were wide in death, and a trickle of blood stained his mouth.

"More than I'd care for it to," Damien answered.

"He's dead, is he not?" Meagan pressed a hand to her throat. "How awful."

Penelope was looking at Damien, not the corpse. "It happens to you often?"

He shrugged slightly. "I am Imperial Prince of Nvengaria."

She wouldn't let him get away with merely that, he knew, but she could say nothing more in the middle of the crowd.

The men from the tavern and the Nvengarian servants who hadn't accompanied Rufus with Sasha stared down at the body. Damien did not recognize the man, but he was obviously Nvengarian. He had the eyes, the sculpted face, the bearing.

"What do we do with 'im?" a man asked.

Another, who proved to be the constable of the parish, scratched his head. "Well, we all watched him do himself in. Coroner might want an inquest, but there ain't much doubt. Foreign. Excitable. Tried to kill His Highness and offed himself when he couldn't. One of these radicals, no doubt."

"I want to see Sasha." Penelope tried to disentangle herself from Damien.

He nodded, understanding. He kissed her briefly and skimmed his hand down her back once more before he let her go. "Meagan," he said. "Go with her."

Meagan tore her gaze from the dead man as though she found it difficult to look away from him. Her eyes held stark horror, but her back was straight, and her concern was for Penelope as she took her hand.

Damien's estimation of Meagan rose. She was a staunch and steadfast friend. The two ladies walked toward the tavern, bodies close as though protecting each other from shock. Penelope's basket lay forgotten in the dirt, her shopping list ruffled by the slight breeze.

Once the ladies were out of earshot, the Nvengarian men let their emotions flow. One footman spit on the body.

"We will tear him apart," another said, his eyes blazing. "Nail bits of him to every tree as a warning to those who dare try to kill our prince."

"And our princess," another growled.

The others shouted assent.

They spoke in Nvengarian, but the Englishmen seemed to get the gist.

"Bloody upstart," one growled. "We should hang him from a gibbet."

More shouts.

"Now, gents," the constable interjected.

Damien said to his own men, "Let the English deal with this in their way."

The Nvengarians quieted a little, but their blood was up. They wanted something to fight.

"I will hunt that pig Duke Alexander and make him pay," the first one said.

"Steady, lad," Petri said, coming up beside Damien. "You wouldn't get closer than his fifth bodyguard."

"I will kill him and make him drink his own blood."

"I'd like to watch that." Petri grinned. "You know, Titus, these English lads here have never seen Nvengarian wrestling. Work off some steam and show them a thing or two."

Titus's young eyes gleamed. "Yes, sir." He switched to struggling English and pointed at the villagers. "You. Come. We show you fight."

"Do not kill anyone," Petri said mildly. "They're our allies."

Titus nodded gravely. "I will try to remember."

The footmen led the villagers off, save for the constable and a few men left to deal with the body.

Damien turned away. His blood was boiling as much as young Titus's. If Alexander chose to throw assassins at Damien, well and good. But not Penelope. Never Penelope.

He would have joined in the Nvengarian-style wrestling, which involved much kicking and punching and more resembled a free-for-all, if he weren't so concerned for Sasha.

"Titus is not wrong," Damien said as he and Petri made quickly for the tavern. "Alexander will answer for this."

"Are you sure it was the duke?" Petri asked. "Not very subtle for one of his assassins. In broad daylight and you surrounded by loyal men? He'd never hope to get away."

"He nearly succeeded," Damien pointed out. "If not for you, he would have. No, this is Alexander's work, Petri. He's found a way to rid Nvengaria of its dangerous radicals. 'Go hunt Prince Damien,' he's told them. And they have."

"Shit, sir."

"Exactly. I want Penelope protected. At all times. No one is to get near her. Ever. Do you hear me?"

"I understand."

Petri did. Damien knew the man would take care of things. They walked quickly to the tavern and ducked inside.

Chapter Ten

Penelope pressed the cloth to the wound in Sasha's back, her heart heavy. This man had saved her life. At the cost of his own?

She would never let that happen, she thought determinedly. The landlord had already sent a lad running for a surgeon, Mr. Phipps from Coombe Stepping, three miles away.

Sasha had bleated an embarrassed protest when they took off his coat and waistcoat and shirt, and had remained distressed until Meagan had consented to move off a little and turn her back.

On the other hand, he'd begged Penelope to stay. Held her hand tightly as though her very presence comforted him. She didn't have the heart to leave him.

He lay still now, face down, eyes closed, but he was awake and breathing normally, if heavily. Perhaps they might be lucky, and the wound would not be mortal.

Penelope replayed the scene over and over in her mind,

beginning with the man putting his hand on Damien's shoulder and aiming a knife straight at him. She had frozen, too far away to do anything, knowing at that moment she would watch Damien die.

Deep emotion she'd never known had rushed to her throat. Time had slowed, and she'd seen the knife flash with deadly accuracy toward Damien's heart.

When Petri pushed Damien aside, and the man had twisted away, Penelope had gone weak with relief. Even the sight of the crazed assassin running for her, the pain of the stones scraping her hands as Sasha pushed her against the well, had not scared her like seeing Damien nearly die.

She glanced at the ring on her finger, heavy and silver and old. She'd seen her mother wear it dozens of times, and her grandmother wear it before that. Did it have something to do with her strange need for Damien's well-being?

She sensed Damien enter the room. The men shifted as though his presence pushed them aside.

"Sasha, my old friend." Damien's voice held a note of gentleness she hadn't heard before. He placed his hand on Sasha's bare, rather plump shoulder. "For this service, I can never repay you. You will be honored in the city square of Narato. We will give you a parade."

This seemed to be the right thing to say. No thanks or sorrow or remonstrating for getting himself hurt.

Sasha brightened. "I only do my duty, Your Highness."

"True, but you could easily have stepped aside and let the bodyguards fight him off. It is their duty, not yours."

Sasha put out his hand. Damien clasped it. The older man clung to Damien's hand, seeming comforted by touching the silver Nvengarian ring. "The sacrifice is an honor."

"I'll not let you sacrifice your life. I need you still. A surgeon is coming. He'll stitch you up and have you organizing the rituals again in no time."

Damien spoke confidently, but he looked worried. The

wound might not have cut an organ, but it was deep and could so easily fester.

Sasha patted Damien's hand. "Do not worry, Highness. The princess is here. She will heal me."

Penelope looked up in surprise. Damien caught her eye, shook his head slightly. "You're not that far gone, Sasha. The surgeon will help."

"I need no surgeon if I have the princess." He spoke with happy certainty.

"Damien," Penelope whispered. "What does he mean?"

Sasha heard her. "The true princess of Nvengaria has the power to heal the sick and the injured."

Penelope's eyes widened. She opened her mouth to bleat a protest—she could certainly make a poultice and brew an herbal tea, but that did not mean she could close a man's wound or keep fever from entering his body.

Damien put his hand under her arm and pulled her to a corner. "Humor him, love. He needs you."

She stared. "Are you mad? When did you plan to mention this aspect of being the princess?"

"When it came up. Which it has."

"But I cannot heal him," she insisted. "What will happen when I cannot? Will he denounce me?"

"No, because you *will* heal him."

She studied his face, which was beautiful like a bright blade. "Damien, I cannot, truly."

"Wash his wound, rub his back, do something. Trust me."

His blue eyes were dark and warm. She wanted to trust him when he looked at her like that.

She needed to remember that this man was a leader who knew how to compel people to do what he wanted.

She closed her eyes and counted to ten. She truly needed to get Damien alone and make him tell her every last thing she needed to know about being a princess of Nvengaria. Of course, the last time they'd been alone, they'd almost broken the prophecy by making love on the chair at her dressing table.

The vivid sensations of that night returned to her. Desire coiled in her belly. He stood so close to her, his hand gripping her arm, his breath in her ear.

Their backs were to the rest of the room. She turned her head and brushed her lips lightly across his.

The contact nearly undid her. She wanted to fling herself into his arms and let him hold her and soothe her. The assassin had terrified her, and not because he'd tried to kill her, but because he'd tried to kill Damien.

She realized this had not been the first time he'd been so attacked. He'd implied as much to Meagan's hurried questions, and Sasha and Petri and his guards had known exactly what to do.

Her fright made her want to hold on to Damien and make sure he was all right. But Damien hadn't been hurt, and neither had she. Sasha had.

Damien's pupils widened, the black spreading through the blue. He wanted her.

She whispered against his mouth, "I will try, for you."

She turned, breaking the contact, and went back to Sasha. Meagan had turned around and was staring at her in trepidation. Meagan wanted to believe this all a fairy tale come true, but even she doubted.

Damien waited. Sasha waited. The men of the tavern waited.

Penelope swallowed, her throat dry.

"I will need a bowl of water, please," she said to the landlord, trying to keep her voice from shaking, "and some nettles to clean his blood, and lavender if you have it."

Penelope cured him. Or, at least, Sasha believed she did. Damien watched, both amused and proud, as Penelope washed and dressed Sasha's wound. She stroked her hands lightly over the man's back, without maidenly qualms.

Sasha had sighed happily and declared all the pain gone. He'd wanted to walk back to the house himself, but Damien had stopped him. Resting after battle, he said, was the better part of valor.

The landlord fixed Sasha with a room where he could recover. Sasha stayed without fuss, and when he felt better the next day, resumed planning the fete from there.

Damien had taken Penelope aside and kissed her to thank her. She'd looked serene, but also agitated. He didn't blame her. He'd meant to get her used to being Princess of Nvengaria little by little, but everything wanted to spring on her at once.

Events sprang on her at the fete, as well, until Damien would not have been surprised if she'd caught up a rapier and told him to go back to Nvengaria and leave her alone.

The first event was the Prince Regent.

He arrived in a royal coach, surrounded by at least two score Horse Guards, riding double file and carrying shining swords. He would stay at the Trask home, the largest house in the area, which meant that an entire wing had to be set aside for his use.

Fortunately, the family mostly used the east wing, so the west wing could be made over under Sasha's careful supervision into chambers fit for the stand-in monarch of England.

Penelope had no idea from where came Damien's resources, but they'd brought in a huge bed, wall hangings and paintings—some from Carleton House itself—soft chairs large enough to accommodate the prince's bulk, plates, candlesticks, draperies, footstools, tables, padded benches, dressing tables, and a Bath chair.

Meagan and Penelope watched the proceedings from afar, the Nvengarians letting neither of them get in the way.

"Oh, my," Meagan said. "Katie Roper never had the Prince Regent staying in her house. I shall be able to crow about this for the longest time."

Penelope was happy that someone, at least, was getting benefit out of all this mess. The rest of the household was in chaos, Sasha kept beaming at Penelope and coming to touch her hand, Lady Trask shuttled between excitement that royalty would stay in her home, and oh, dear, what about the state of the guest rooms that hadn't been used in a decade?

Damien's servants had taken over every aspect of the house, including the cooking, resulting in the old cook's giving notice. It took Damien to charm her into staying. He made her a sort of glorified chef who could sit on her backside and shout at people as much as she liked. Since most of the Nvengarian staff didn't speak English, she bellowed and they ignored her, thus maintaining mutual satisfaction.

"If I go to Nvengaria," Penelope said to Meagan as they awaited the Regent's coach, "would you come with me? If only for a little while? I would miss you so, and truth to tell, I cannot imagine going alone. Not even with Damien."

Meagan hesitated a long moment before answering. The approaching cloud of dust blurred the horizon, kicked up by horses and a breeze.

"I will understand if you do not want to," Penelope began around a lump in her throat. Meagan shook her head.

"Penelope, Damien says we cannot come with you. None of us."

She froze. "What?"

Meagan kept her eyes on the approaching coach, her cheeks pink. "I argued with him already. He says it is too dangerous for I or my father or your mother to come with you. That his enemies might use us to get to you or Damien. That he cannot spare the men to protect us all."

Penelope's mouth tightened. "Oh, did he?"

"Penny, I think he's right. I did not know what to do when that man ran at you with a knife. All I could think of was to dive behind the well. I couldn't even help you." She looked mournful. "What if I should be the cause of someone hurting you? Or Damien? I would die. That is, if the assassins left me alive long enough."

"But—"

"I brought forth every argument I could think of—that I am small and do not take much room, that I could look after you as well as myself, that I am a coward and would stay far away from any assassin—but he countered them all. He and his men can take care of you, Penelope. He is right. We'd only be in the way."

"You would not be in the way," Penelope protested, feeling desperate.

"Yes, we would, and you know it. We would not know what to do. Look how Sasha rushed to protect you."

"I would rather *not* think of it." She had relived the moment in her dreams over and over, Sasha shoving her hard against the stone well, his slight body covering her own, his sharp gasp as the knife slid into his back.

She also remembered how Sasha had relaxed and breathed out when she'd washed his wound in the tavern, happily declaring the pain gone.

Whether she truly did have healing magic, or whether Sasha only believed it so much that it worked, she did not know. But Sasha had recovered quickly from his wound with no ill effects. Damien's entourage, even the cynical valet, Petri, had begun to look at her with new respect.

Sasha stood not far from them, waiting stiffly, in full regalia. He'd put on a uniformlike suit that was even more military-looking than his previous suits. Medals dangled from his breast, and his sash of office shone like he'd polished it.

The other servants had spit and shined every piece of their livery as well. Those with more braid, lace, and medals strutted a bit cockier than those with less. Rufus and Miles stood with heads high, their chests covered with the most medals of all, their shoulders weighted with yards looped of braid.

In contrast, Damien wore a suit of almost drab plainness. It was obviously cut by an expensive Bond Street tailor, but it was severe black and brown, having none of the flash and color of the Nvengarian livery.

When the coach stopped and a dozen servants in the Regent's livery swarmed about the coach like bees on a hive, Penelope understood Damien's choice in clothing. Damien could have easily outshone the Prince Regent had he worn an elegant suit or Nvengarian finery. He had, for whatever reason, deliberately decided not to.

The footmen hauled the Regent from the coach and settled him in his Bath chair, taking care to balance his gouty foot. Damien bowed low before him, showing him every deference, then shook his hand like a friend. The Regent cast a jealous eye over Damien's athletic body, then assessed his clothes with a certain smugness.

Penelope pictured the thoughts in the Regent's head—Damien might be handsome and well-formed, but the Regent's own clothes were far more sumptuous. The prince of Nvengaria obviously had no idea how to dress.

Penelope saw Damien's face when the Regent was wheeled away to be greeted by an ecstatic Lady Trask. His expression held calm assurance that everything was going his way. He caught Penelope's eye, and winked.

She frowned back at him. The man knew exactly how to sweeten everyone to his will—Meagan, her mother, the villagers, and now the Prince Regent. Even Michael had thawed considerably toward him. Everyone did exactly what Damien wanted them to do, and fell all over themselves to do it.

Including herself.

He had convinced Meagan and her mother and

Michael to allow him to take Penelope away with him alone, leaving friends and family behind. He'd never consulted Penelope, or even mentioned it to her. He decided, then charmed others into going along with his decisions.

She scowled at him, earning herself a dazzling smile. It did not help that every time he smiled, she wanted to do every single thing he told her to.

She forced herself to frown again, then turned her back and went into the house.

The fete was the talk of society for years to come. Prince Damien had gotten it up in grand style, with banquet tents for the posh ladies and gents and tables outside for the villagers.

The villagers of Little Marching had privileged status at the food stalls and the games, which made them carry their heads a little higher. Nvengarian and British flags flew over everything, and every time a prince was spotted, a cheer went up. The Regent nodded and waved, reveling in his popularity.

There were races for ponies and men and children, archery competitions, a gypsy fortune-teller, games of chance, exhibitions in Nvengarian-style wrestling—which had become quite popular—fencing matches, country dances for the villagers, puppet theatre, and pantomimes.

Carriage after carriage arrived from London, guests filling the Trask home and neighboring houses and inns for miles. Ambassadors and other dignitaries visiting the Regent had been invited, along with his London set. Russian, French, and even Piedmontese noblemen met Penelope and declared her an unsullied beauty, and wasn't Damien lucky to find himself a fresh English rose? The Londoners peered at her avidly, then congratulated Damien, looking a bit puzzled, as though wondering *why* Damien would want such a fresh English rose.

No sophistication, she could almost hear them say. One

stooped, white-haired man bent to Damien, saying, "Innocence is lovely, Your Highness, but a short time at court will tarnish her. Ladies' heads are so easily turned by fashion and money." The man meant to say this in confidence, but he must have been hard of hearing, for his loud voice bellowed this proclamation over the crowd.

Damien, smooth as ever, only replied that Penelope was quite wise for her years, and she showed remarkable good sense. The white-haired man snorted in disbelief, and moved off.

Damien shot her a sly smile like it had been a good joke. Penelope said nothing, wondering if Damien truly thought that of her, or whether he'd been placating the white-haired London gentleman.

No matter what their reaction, Damien's betrothal to Penelope would be seen, witnessed, and remembered by people with connections all over Europe. The new Nvengaria ruler was taking a bride of both English and Nvengarian lineage to cement his position within and outside of Nvengaria.

He was busy turning the entire world up sweet.

Penelope bowed and shook hands and smiled until her face ached. Damien kept his hand on her arm or the small of her back, possessive, as he introduced her to his London friends and acquaintances. He made certain, somehow, that each person saw the silver rings on his finger and hers, the symbol that they belonged together.

Not until late afternoon could she snatch a moment to herself. When she saw her chance, she slipped away to the folly to rest in its cool shade and listen to the music of the river. She could not entirely shut out the noise of the fete, because the tents and stalls had encroached to within twenty feet of the folly. Only the woods around it had kept the tents out.

She sat on the steps, her back to a pillar, and stretched

her legs out in front of her. She removed her bonnet and ran her hands through her loosened hair.

So much had happened since she'd sat here the day Damien had arrived and told her he was in love with her. He'd inflamed her with kisses, convinced her she was a long-lost princess, enchanted the villagers, told her stories, given her healing powers, and brought the Prince Regent to visit.

It was all too much. He rushed through this, she knew, so that she'd grow bewildered and give in to what he wanted. Damien was a charmer, but a strong-arm charmer. He got his way in the end, even if he did it with a dazzling smile and a wink of his blue eye.

She felt the trap of it close around her, slowly, gently, but inexorably. Like a doe trusting an approaching hunter, she dazedly watched herself be pursued. If only the hunter were not Damien. He'd trapped her the moment he'd kissed her in Holden's meadow, and he knew it.

"He has certainly not lost his charm," said a haughty Englishwoman's voice, as though answering her thoughts.

Penelope froze. The most difficult thing about the fete had been meeting and speaking to the ladies of the *ton* and their foreign friends. They stared at her coldly, not hiding that they considered her an interloper. How dare she, a mere daughter of a baronet, try to rise above herself and marry a prince. Especially *that* prince? Damien was the most eligible bachelor in Europe, and this plain miss had snared him by trickery.

She remained still, praying the ladies would not see her. She could smile and make polite conversation with them when Damien stood next to her, but she had no wish to face them alone.

"Yes, a charmer, zat one," said a woman in a full-throated Russian accent. Penelope had met her, a Russian countess who fluttered her lashes at Damien and hung all over him. "Damien is zo handsome, zo—ah, I have no words to describe zis man, zis incredible man."

To Penelope's surprise, the other two ladies with the Russian countess dissolved into titters. "Oh, goodness," said the Englishwoman. "Do you think that poor mousy thing *knows?*"

"*Incredible* is a good word," a woman with a French accent said. "*Stamina*, this is another good word."

More titters. "Incalculable length, is what I say," the English one said.

The three ladies giggled, this time like they knew they were being naughty. "Eleven inches, would zis be not too far-fetched?" the Russian asked.

"No," said the lady with the French accent, and they laughed again.

Penelope's face scalded. Oh lord, if they saw her now! She remained rigid, her hands balling in her skirt, praying they would not notice her in the shadows of the folly.

"Do you know," the Russian countess went on. "I was wiz him when his man came knocking on ze door to tell him he was Imperial Prince. Ah, he was in zuch a state. Zo angry, and yet zo cold. Dangerous he was, in zat mood. I was zat afraid of him, and at ze same time—ah, glorious."

The other ladies agreed, sounding a bit jealous, that Damien unpredictable was quite exciting indeed.

"But what shall we do now?" the French lady asked. "He is marrying. We shall never see him again. Or his inches."

"Nonsense," the English lady said briskly. "He will deposit the chit in his castle, get a son on her, and forget about her. He will need to make state visits to England, and France, and Russia. And I imagine all that traveling will make him lonely. . . ." She trailed off suggestively.

The other two ladies were silent a moment, then they

burst out laughing, even more merrily than before. "I look forward to zis," the Russian countess gloated.

"The poor child will not know what to do with him, in any case," the Frenchwoman said. "She will hardly know the bed games Nvengarians like."

"Indeed." The Englishwoman put heavy emphasis on the word. "They are quite depraved, really quite depraved. She will be shocked out of her senses over what she is expected to do. One can almost feel sorry for her."

Did they know Penelope sat not five feet from them, hearing every word? Perhaps they did, and spoke so for her benefit. She remained still, smarting in rage and humiliation.

"Not quite," the Frenchwoman put in.

"Perhaps we ought to give her a book on *positions*," the English baroness suggested. "And explain to her about bed toys. Really, sending an untried miss into Nvengaria is a bit cruel."

"And ze little whips," the countess said eagerly. "Do not forget ze little whips."

Again they fell silent, and again, they burst into merry laughter. "Depend upon it," the Englishwoman said. "We will have our prince back."

"La, it is hot," the Frenchwoman complained when their laughter had worn down. "I must return to the house, although that simpering woman is all over me. It is more comfortable than the outdoors."

"Yes, what were they thinking, having a fete here, of all places?" The Englishwoman's voice grew fainter as she and the other two ladies began strolling away. "Damien could have asked *me* to host it in Hertfordshire. *We* have a proper house."

The other two murmured agreement and disappeared down the path.

Tears of fury fell from Penelope's eyes before she

dashed them away. How dare they sneer at her mother and the Trask home? How dare they flaunt that Damien had charmed every woman in Europe?

She got to her feet, glaring at the ring on her finger. She wanted more than anything to pull it off and fling it into the river. Her hand went to it.

She touched the cool band and stopped. The ring had belonged to her mother and her grandmother before her. It had nothing to do with Damien. Reluctantly, she breathed a sigh and let her hand drop.

Hugging her arms to her chest, she left the folly and strolled the path to the river. It was cooler here, with overhanging willows in the shallows. Not far along, the river gurgled into a deep pool, where Penelope and Meagan had swum as children.

She sat down on a log that formed a bench on the bank, stripped off her shoes and stockings and dabbled her feet in the soothing water. If Damien took her away, she could never come here again, to this place of her childhood where she'd found a modicum of peace. He'd take her away from her mother and Meagan and these woods and her fairy tales.

She clenched her hand. No, he would not. Just because he and Sasha had bounded here with stories of prophecies and princesses, and turned Ashborn Manor into a summer palace for their pleasure, she did not have to obey his commands.

Yes, he'd charmed her. Yes, she'd near fallen in love with him. But he could not take everything away from her.

"Penelope." His voice drifted down to her from the top of the hill, rich and deep, with his full-throated Nvengarian accent.

She heard him move through bracken down the hill from the path. She did not look up, keeping her eyes on the calm current of the river.

She saw his booted foot land on the log beside her, a

supple, now muddy boot that hugged the firm muscle of his calf and folded about his ankle.

His leg bent to show her a thigh in black breeches, his arm in a well-fitted brown coat resting on his knee.

" 'Tis not safe to wander here by yourself." He clasped a branch above him with a strong hand. "I do not trust Alexander to send only one assassin."

Penelope kept her eyes on the water. "I will be safe, Your Highness. I have decided not to be your princess, or marry you."

Chapter Eleven

He said nothing.

Penelope risked a glance at him. He was not looking at her, but staring across the river as though he studied something she could not see. The faint white patches in the corners of his eyes were pale against his darker skin.

"That will not keep you safe," he said after a time. "As long as someone believes you are a Nvengarian princess and precious to me, you are not safe."

Precious to me.

She tried to sound cold. "I do not want a marriage of convenience."

He turned to her, brushing his fingers over her hair. "I know that."

"And yet, that is what you try to rush me into."

His hand moved to the nape of her neck. "I hope it will be more than that to you."

"Is it more than that to you?"

He leaned down and buried his lips in her hair. "I believe I have more than demonstrated what this marriage will mean to me."

When he spoke in that tone, when he caressed her, it was so easy to believe he loved her. If only she hadn't heard those women—his mistresses—speaking of him as though they owned him, as though he'd run back to them as soon as they crooked their fingers.

What had he whispered to them in the night? Not words of love, or they'd have boasted of it. But he'd touched them with warm fingers and kissed their hair—

Penelope pulled away. "If not for the prophecy, you never would have come here. You never would have looked at me twice."

"You are half right." He did not reach for her again, but twined his strong fingers over his knee. "I would never have known that Little Marching existed if not for Sasha. But had I encountered you in London or elsewhere, I would have looked at you for a long, long time."

Eager need stirred in her, but she quickly suppressed it. "I am not fishing for flattery."

"I know." He glanced at her bare calves and feet in the water, his look appreciative. "I envy the fish come to nibble your toes."

Penelope resisted pulling her legs up and covering them with her dress. He grinned, the side of his mouth pulling.

"What I mean is, you never would have journeyed here and proposed to me if not for your prophecy," she said, a little shakily.

"Very likely not." He nodded once. "Although I like to believe that fate has been driving us together."

"That would indeed be a fairy story," she said. "The story you told me, the one about the princess in the tower—she ended not by running off with the handsome stranger from far away, but by staying with the true and trusted friend she'd known all her life. That is the moral of the story, is it not?"

He looked at her with a touch of bewilderment. "It is only a story, Penelope. It has no meaning."

"All tales have meaning. Usually, 'Be good and patient, and you shall be rewarded.'"

"In my experience, that never happens."

She glanced at him. "But it should be true. That is why people tell the stories."

He slid his hand under her hair again, teasing the curls at her nape. "When people tell our story, they will tell how I traveled many miles and through great peril to find you waiting for me at the end of the journey." His smile returned. "You made the peril worth every moment."

"You have a honeyed tongue."

The smiled turned wicked. "No, but you give me a good idea."

She blushed. He made his wanting for her so plain.

"We are talking about our marriage of convenience," she said.

"You like this word, *convenience.*" He sat down next to her and began to pull off his boots.

"I will be plainer, then. Mr. White wished me to marry him and have his children so that he could ignore me and do as he pleased. I would not do it for him, and I will not do it for you. I refuse to be a wife who is *convenient.*"

He pulled off his second boot and tossed it aside, then stripped off his stockings and dangled his feet in the pool.

His bare brown calves hung close to her slender ones, wiry black hair curling down his shins and onto his strong feet. They sat side by side, hips and shoulders touching.

It felt shockingly intimate, even more so than when he'd kissed her and touched her in her bedchamber. This was casual, an implication that he had every right to be casual with her.

"Penelope," he began, his voice holding a dangerous note. "For me to travel three thousand miles in search of a bride is not convenient. It is not convenient to leave my kingdom vulnerable to a scheming Grand Duke, nor is it convenient to scrape and bow to your joke of a Regent so that I may hold England's support." He slid his hand to her thigh. "And it is not convenient to find you here like this, knowing that if I take you the way I wish to, my very superstitious Nvengarians will declare the prophecy void, and I will have done all for nothing. No, I do not find this at all convenient."

She bit her lip. "I did not mean—"

"I will marry you, Penelope. I will do anything to fulfill the prophecy and save my kingdom. I want to do it with soft words, but if I have to throw you over the pommel of my saddle and gallop away with you, I will."

His hard expression told her he'd do it. When, like now, he dropped his suave and civilized facade, she saw the true man, the one who had survived hunger and pain and darkness and hatred. She had no doubt that if he wanted, he'd sweep her up and gallop away with her, like a nomad from a desert tribe.

"That would be a bit uncomfortable for a three-thousand-mile journey," she said in a small voice.

"Not for me, love. I could rest my hand on your very fine backside all the way."

She blushed. "You really should not say things like that."

"You must grow used to me complimenting your body. Your backside is fine, as are your breasts." He looked into the water. "And your toes are adorable."

"Now you have become Prince Charming again."

His look turned curious. "Is that how you think of me?"

"No, I think of you as exasperating. I do not know what to think of you."

He twined his bare foot, long and broad, around hers. "Fall in love with me, Penelope."

She quirked a brow. "Like every other woman across the breadth of Europe?"

His glance turned questioning, and Penelope wanted to slap her hand across her mouth. She'd not meant to admit that she'd heard the shameful conversation of his paramours. A well-bred woman never discussed such matters.

"Think you every woman in Europe in love with me?" he asked. "I assure you, that is not true. I believe my mother loved me, but she died when I was very small."

"Oh," she said, deflating. "I am sorry. About your mother, I mean."

"It was a tragedy. Also very dramatic, Nvengarian style. She climbed upon the gate tower of my father's castle and shot herself in the head."

Penelope stared at him in horror.

He glanced out over the water, his tone neutral. "It was her finest moment. My father was evil, but she got her revenge. Instead of quietly poisoning herself and letting the incident be swept under the carpets, she stood up on a moonlit night in full view of the city, and announced to the world exactly what my father had done to her. She showed the truth of what he was, a madman to fear and hate." He stirred the water with his foot. "At the time, I was very angry at her for leaving me alone, but I understand now that she had to do it. Her death was her only weapon against him, and she used it well." He fell silent a moment. "I do not know why I tell you these things. I never speak of them to anyone."

"Damien." Her voice held anguish.

He smiled. "Do not feel sorry for me, Penelope. My childhood is behind me. My life is much better now."

"With men trying to kill you right and left?"

"A few dodged knives is nothing compared to the barbs of my father, love."

He chuckled as though he'd told her a reassuring story. Penelope traced the sinews on the back of his hand. The scars that crisscrossed his skin spoke more clearly than words of the harshness of his life.

"It is better now," he repeated, "because I have found you."

Flattery again. His eyes had gone dark, and his head dipped toward hers as though he was ready to kiss her.

"You are asking me to leave behind everything I have ever known," she said desperately. "You wish me to ride off into the wilderness with you on the strength of a silver ring and Sasha's prophecy."

"I know." He smoothed her cheek. "And you are brave enough and strong enough to do it. You have the heart of a lion."

"I have not."

He nuzzled her, his breath warm on her skin. "You could face down the entire Council of Dukes and Alexander himself. You could have even faced down my father."

"The man who put you into a dungeon?" She stopped. "I am very angry at him for that, you know."

"You see? You have fight in you, Penelope. You will make a fine princess. Nvengarians love a woman with fight."

"I have never fought anyone in my life," she protested.

He shrugged. "I wonder what it must have been to jilt your Mr. Reuben White in the face of all the world. The English are not kind to a woman who decides to send a man away. They believe she should swallow what the gentleman does so that she may have a husband and a name. In Nvengaria, we admire a woman who takes a knife to a cheating betrothed."

She blanched. "I would never do that."

"No, you are civilized, and English. It took much courage for you to defy Mr. White and your mother and father, and the entire English *ton*, did it not?"

She nodded, remembering the pleading arguments from her mother, the cool anger of her father, the outrage of Reuben, who threatened to sue for breach of contract, the stares and whispers when she went out in public, the label of *jilt*.

But she could not have sold herself to a life of misery. She had dried her tears and gone on, pretending she was not in pain. Shortly afterward, her father had died, and the grief of that, coupled with the lack of funds to keep them in London, had forced her to think about other things.

"It was difficult," she said.

"You understate it, I believe. Yet, you did it. You defied them. A lesser woman would have accepted her lot and married him."

"You wish me to accept my lot with *you.*"

He chuckled, a warm sound. "Penelope, you are a fine one at debate. As I said, you will defy the Council of Dukes."

He slid off his coat and laid it carefully on the bank. Next he untied his cravat, unwound it from his neck, and folded it over his coat. He began to unbutton his waistcoat, tanned fingers deft and sure on the buttons.

Penelope's gaze riveted to him as he shrugged off the waistcoat. Beneath his London-tailored clothes, he had the body of a warrior. No wonder the Regent regarded him with jealousy.

He stripped off his shirt. His torso, brown with sun, was tight and strong, muscles moving under the skin with animal grace. Black curls dusted his chest, spreading across his pectorals, thinning where his flat, male nipples lay brown-red again his skin. His arms were large with muscle, round and hard biceps tapering to hollows on the insides of his elbows.

Black hair twined his broad forearms, his skin there even more tanned, the part of his body that saw the most sun. She had never seen a man completely bare-chested before, and she found that she wanted to look at him, to explore with her gaze what he was.

She wanted to touch, too. She imagined her pale fingers

on the brown flesh, tracing collarbone and hollow of throat, the damp skin over his Adam's apple. She'd move down to feather the indent between his pectorals, letting his dark curls of hair twist round her fingertips. Then to his brown nipples, drawing them lightly between her fingers, discovering whether they felt like her own or different.

She flicked her gaze to his face, knowing her eyes would betray her hunger, but not knowing how to hide it. She traced the sharp line of his jaw, the black curled hair that trailed behind his ears to his bare, strong neck. He smelled of sweat and salt, and she wondered if he'd taste of salt if she trailed her tongue across his throat.

He smiled at her, his lips moving slowly, as though he knew she wanted to taste him and liked it.

He lifted himself on the log, balancing on flat hands, arms tightening, and, before she could speak, he slid down into the water.

The pool was deep. Damien dove into the cool depths, the water heavenly after the warm summer sun.

His arousal was screaming at him. Damn, but he wanted her. Finding her here with her skirts rucked to her knees, her bare legs dangling, her toes tracing languid circles in the water, had made him hard as a rock.

He'd argued with her to keep his mind off her beddable body, but to no use. Thank God the water was cold.

He surfaced, and shook water from his hair. She was watching him, eyes round. "What are you doing?"

"Swimming."

"What about assassins?" She peered about her worriedly.

"I have men stationed along the hill and river to watch."

Penelope hastily pulled her dress over her legs. "Good heavens. You might have warned me."

"My men are trained to look without looking," he said. "Does it make sense in English?"

"I suppose," she said.

He laughed. She was so pretty with the sun on her hair, her lip drawn down in confusion. He wanted to kiss her and kiss her. He wanted to hold her against him in the water, to lift her dress and settle her on his very needy erection.

He swam across the pool, then dove again, reveling in the soothing water. He surfaced, right at her feet.

She looked at him in surprise. Slanting her a wicked grin, he lifted her bare, clean toes and drew one into his mouth.

He expected her to gasp and pull away, but she stretched out her foot, leaning back on her elbows, her eyelids heavy. She'd look so in bed, he imagined, lying back and waiting for him, lips parted.

He nibbled the toe, then suckled it, loving the taste of the water and her skin. Her posture pressed her breasts against her thin gown, her nipples tiny points against the fabric.

He'd never seen such a sensuous woman. Hers was a natural sensuality, free from the artifice of court women, closer to the wild beauty of the women of his own country.

He kissed her toes, one at a time, then lifted the other foot and did the same.

She watched him, smiling slightly, the hem of her dress dangling in the water. His hardness grew unbearably tight.

"I want to see you," he said.

He held each small foot in his palms. Gently he pulled her legs apart, the loose skirt sliding to her knees. Her chest rose with quickened breath.

He stepped between her legs, turning his head to lick droplets of water from her calf. The salt taste of her skin made his blood hotter still. He slid the skirt upward, dipping his tongue behind her knee.

She gasped. He expected her to pull away, perhaps to kick water into his face, but she remained still. The pulse in the fold of her knee beat faster.

"I want to see you," he said again.

She had every right to refuse him and send him away. They were not yet betrothed. Even in Nvengaria, an unmarried woman would admonish a man for making improper advances, unless she wanted them, of course.

Slowly Penelope reached down, and with slow fingers, drew her skirt up to bare her thighs.

Damien exhaled. Her lovely legs stretched to him, long and just a little plump. He kissed her thigh above her knee, and drew his tongue all the way along it to the shadow under her skirt.

She stiffened, but did not pull away. He spread her legs wider, palms resting on each thigh. He watched her fingers close on the cloth, and then, as his heartbeat soared, she pulled the skirt the rest of the way up.

A thread of sweet curls swirled over her mound and twisted along her opening. His arousal strained toward her, knowing where it wanted to go. He dragged in a breath.

"Penelope, I have not the words in English to say how beautiful you are."

She said nothing. Her face was rosy pink, her green-gold eyes fixed on him as though she worried what he thought of her.

He braced his hands on either side of her opening, and pushed her still wider. He let his thumbs come together in the middle, stroking down over her mound.

She gasped, eyes widening. He was, without a doubt, the first person to ever touch her there. Her honey flowed onto his hands, sweet and warm.

"Penelope, do you know what release is?"

"No," she whispered.

"You have never touched yourself? Felt the release of it?"

"Never."

Surprising. The ladies of London and Paris liked to tell him at length how much they enjoyed themselves alone in their beds. So much so that at times, he left them to it while he sought a tavern to enjoy ale and conversation.

From the look on Penelope's face, the thought had never occurred to her.

"I will teach you what it feels like," he said.

Her gaze locked with his, as though she was afraid to look away. Her lips parted, moist and red.

He could touch and taste her all he wanted, as long as he didn't ram his greedy hardness straight into her. Being inside her might negate the prophecy, but staying outside would not.

He rubbed her mound again, loving the hot folds that wanted to close over his thumbs. He lifted his hand and licked her moisture from it, spicy, salty desire.

She put out her hand in protest. "Damien, your bodyguards."

"Cannot see a thing."

They had been trained to look out for danger but to give him his privacy. Life did not go well for a bodyguard who did not. Some of them were left over from his father's rule, fanatically devoted to the Imperial Prince, whoever he happened to be. They would not ogle her; they'd be more worried about her trying to harm him.

They would have to learn that Penelope was on his side, an extension of him, not his enemy. She had been made for him. He tasted her on his skin and felt her become part of him.

He stroked her again, letting his fingers nudge a little inside of her. She closed her eyes, one hand threading his hair.

"That is the way, my love," he whispered. "Feel the joy of it."

She arched toward him, wanting him. He draped her legs over his shoulders, and lowered his mouth to her.

Sweet, hot, fiery taste. He loved her gasp of startled pleasure, and the deeper moan that followed it. Lovely innocent, feeling for the first time. She was his, and no other man's. The fervent possessiveness of his people welled up inside him, and he didn't bother to control it.

Her scent surrounded him, her taste drove him wild. He suckled her, earning small cries of pleasure while her hips rocked forward. She wanted him with the same mindlessness with which he wanted her.

Unlike when they'd been in her bedchamber, though, he knew he could control himself. For now. Then, a dark need had swept through him, as though a force from outside had taken over his thoughts. This time, he could fully enjoy her without the crazed clutch on his mind.

He flicked his tongue over her beautiful mound, faster and faster, smiling as she jerked and moaned. She twisted her hand in his hair, but he ignored the pain. She was ready, ripe for it. *Beautiful, beautiful woman.*

She dragged in a long breath, and then she came, her first surprised cries ringing out to the quiet rush of the river.

Damien grasped her hips and dragged her down into the water with him. His mouth landed hard on hers, taking her screams of delight into him. She instinctively wrapped her legs around him, clinging to him, positioning her needing opening directly over his arousal.

He rocked his hips, loving the friction, while he kissed her. He drove his tongue in deep, pressing her, making her taste him as much as he tasted her. Her nails bit his skin, sharp points digging into his back.

Eventually, her cries lessened, her frantic hands stilled, and at last, she eased her lips from his. She regarded him languidly, her lips swollen, a woman first awakened to the wild feelings inside her.

"Did I have a fit?" she asked, breathless.

He smoothed her hair and kissed the corner of her mouth. "That was release. Do you understand now why we crave it so?"

She nodded. "It was most strange."

"Would you like to do it again?"

Her eyes widened a little. "I can do that again?"

"As many times as you want, vixen."

"As many times?" She drew a breath. "I do not know if I can. I feel quite exhausted. And at the same time . . ."

"You feel, as you say, exhilarated?"

"Yes. Exhilarated." She lay her head on his shoulder. "Do you feel the same?"

"No."

"Oh." She sounded disappointed.

"I will feel it on our betrothal night. I will teach you how to bring me to release."

"I see." She looked shy and fetching.

"We will use that night to learn one another," he said, trying to stifle his anticipation. "That is what the betrothal ritual is for. To show the world that we will be bound in marriage, and to learn to pleasure each other's bodies. After that night, we will have no fear of the carnal pleasures we will seek in our marriage."

She smiled into his shoulder. "That sounds much different from English marriage."

"Nvengarian husbands enjoy making certain that their wives are pleased in bed, and they invent many and varied ways to do it. Do English husbands not do this?"

"I have not heard so. But my married acquaintances tell me very little." She sounded frustrated.

"Do not worry. I will tell you everything you need to know."

She lifted her head and smiled at him, eyes starry, then

she suddenly realized that he'd pulled her into the pool and they were up to their shoulders in water.

"Damien, my dress!" she gasped.

"Take it off." He scooped her against him and began unfastening the hooks in the back.

She did not protest much as he helped her untangle her arms from the gown and pull it from her legs. He lifted it from the water and laid it across the log, where it hung, deflated and wrinkled with water.

She wore no stays under the light summer gown. Her shift molded to her body, the tips of her breasts dark and large. The wet cotton clinging to her was almost more erotic than if she'd been bare.

He lifted her again, hands under her buttocks, the water making her buoyant. Her wet lips roved his as she wrapped her legs around him again; she was no longer shy about kissing him. "I love you," he said.

Her eyes were heavy, face flushed with heat. "Say it in Nvengarian. I want to learn."

He smiled. "We say *amor*. Like the French, you see? For *I love you*, it is *amor dem*."

She smoothed his wet hair from his forehead. "*Amor dem*."

He laughed. "No, that is for a woman. To say it to me, you would say *amor das*."

She wrinkled her nose. "I do so hate conjugation. My French tutor always laughed at me."

"It is English that is confusing. With no gender. Saying the same thing to a woman or to a man sounds very strange to us. As though you are hermaphrodites."

She laughed, a sound like sweet chimes. "I never thought of it like that."

He waited. Her laughter faded. She studied his face, as though memorizing it. "Damien." She brushed her finger down the bridge of his nose and over his lips. "*Amor das*."

"I love you, too, Penelope."

She did not ask again if he truly did. She traced the outline of his face, her eyes intent. "How do you say, *I want you?*"

He brought his lips close to hers. "You would say to a lover, *gushan das.*"

"Oh." She kissed him lightly.

He smiled. "Will you say it?"

"You already know I want you."

"Yes." He was going to take her to bed and love her for days.

She laid her head on his shoulder. "If I were cruel," she said softly, "I would ask you to make love to me now, and so break the prophecy." She lifted her head. "Then I would not have to go with you to Nvengaria."

He pretended to consider the strategy. "True. But it would not work."

"Why not?"

She sounded offended. He laughed. "Because I am in love with you. I will marry you and take you home with me, prophecy or no prophecy."

"You are giving me no choice."

"You have a choice." He tightened his arms around her. "Your choice is to come with me willingly, or to come with me unwillingly. I can imagine entertaining possibilities in both directions."

She looked puzzled. "Why would it entertain you if I was unwilling?"

His entire body throbbed. "Because then I could have the joy of taming you. If I must throw you over my pommel and ride off with you, you will learn my true nature. The one that tells me you are mine, and I will teach you to be so."

Her eyes widened. The idea frightened her, but not entirely.

He ran his fingertips down her spine. "I can think of

many ways to train you to be mine. In fact, I somewhat hope you will be unwilling."

"Ways?"

"Yes." He ran his hand up to encircle her wrist. "Bind your pretty hands. Not release you until you did my bidding."

She moved a little in his arms, brushing his aching groin. "How could I do your bidding with my hands tied?"

"Now that, my love, I will have to teach you when I have you in my bed."

She would be naked, her hair down, and she'd squirm against her bonds. She'd look up at him and ask him, in faint trepidation, what he wanted her to do.

The vision was compelling. He gritted his teeth. Penelope was driving him over the brink, but he was so enjoying the fall.

"You are a dangerous one," he said. "But remember, whether I compromise you too soon or no, I will take you home with me."

She opened her mouth to argue, but he kissed her before she could say a word. She got lost in the kiss, her body grasping what it was supposed to do.

He thought of the way she'd said in his own tongue that she loved him. He also liked the way her tongue moved in his mouth. He would teach her more Nvengarian, every naughty phrase she could repeat to him when they were in bed on long winter nights. And short summer nights. And all the nights in between.

He deepened the kiss, feeling her fingertips on the scratches she'd put on his back. Yes, this mating would be fierce indeed.

Up on the hill, three female figures emerged at the top of the path.

"It is the most cunning pool, Countess, my lady." Meagan Tavistock's voice floated to them.

He knew the women, one the Russian he'd been with when Misk had brought him his father's ring. The other was English, a baroness who had a fetish for sleeping with foreign nobility. She collected them, she bragged.

Penelope gasped. He thought she'd fling herself from his arms, but after one startled look upward, she suddenly pressed her mouth to his and kissed him with all her might.

He wanted to laugh, but he let her kiss him. He'd known that she'd discover things he'd done before he'd become the Imperial Prince. The ladies the Regent had brought with him were not known for keeping secrets.

This was her defiance, then. Let them see.

He held her tightly and kissed her back with enthusiasm.

He heard Meagan's gasp. "Oh, heavens. Oh, my. Oh, dear. I do believe it's Miss Trask and the prince."

More brush crackled as the three turned and hurried back to the path. Meagan's voice floated back to them, swelling with triumph. "Well, they *are* going to be married. A grand romance, is it not?"

Later, Penelope trotted downstairs in the house, her hand skimming the stair rail. She'd dried herself and changed her clothes, damp and refreshed from her impromptu swim with Damien. She'd put on a clean gown and brushed her hair, fastening it in a long tail to let it dry.

Damien had gotten Penelope back to the house, both of them sneaking in like naughty children in their wet clothes. She, who never giggled, hadn't been able to stop. Damien had had to kiss her to keep her quiet.

She felt strange, tired and yet rested, her body trying to grow used to the new feelings Damien had invoked. She'd never known, until he put his mouth on her, what wild thoughts could fly through her mind, and how excited and flushed and wonderful her body could feel.

When his tongue pressed into her, she'd thought madness had overtaken her.

The intensity of what her body could experience frightened her a little, but at the same time, she longed to feel it again.

As she stepped off the last stair, her thoughts still far away, Petri, Damien's valet, emerged from the sitting room and stopped in front of her.

"Highness," Petri said. "I speak to you, yes?"

Petri did not know as much English as Damien or Sasha, or even the footmen Rufus and Miles. His lack of English had not stopped him from making conquests of several of the Trask maids, if all she heard was correct. She hadn't the heart to scold the girls since Petri's master was busy weaving his spell around Penelope.

"Yes," Penelope said to Petri, nodding. "I mean, of course."

"Please to come," he said, bowing and gesturing to the sitting room.

The chamber was mercifully empty, the guests still reveling at the fete. They would be for most of the night, Damien having promised a feast, a bonfire, and fireworks.

Petri waited patiently in the middle of the room. A tray with a coffeepot, cup, and honey waited on a table, as though he'd prepared carefully for this conversation.

The enigmatic valet complemented Damien well. They were the same age and possessed roughly the same looks. Petri had black hair, clear blue eyes, and a brutal handsomeness that was wreaking havoc below stairs. Damien had the same brutal handsomeness, but one controlled and contained, like a honed sword, to serve his needs.

Petri's attractiveness was unstudied and raw. He had no need to be cultivated, unlike his master.

He gestured Penelope to a chair, and she sat. Like the good valet he was, he fetched her a footstool, then carefully poured coffee and added the exact amount of honey Penelope liked.

"Thank you." She accepted the cup and sipped. He nodded and gave a grunt, as though he did not know the words for "you're welcome."

She politely gestured to the chair facing her, but he refused it, and stood, his hands behind his back in a military stance. "My English," he said, "is not so good, I am sorry."

"That is all right," Penelope said. "Take your time."

Petri studied her coffee cup and then the tray, then drew a breath as though what he had to say would condemn him, but he had to say it anyway.

"You marry Damien, yes?"

She shook her head slightly. "I have not decided."

He leaned forward, his blue eyes piercing. "No. You marry him."

"Petri . . ."

He held up his hands, made a curt gesture. "You marry him. If no, die."

She started. Did he mean to make a threat, or was he simply struggling with English? "What do you mean?"

He frowned in frustration. "I have not the way to say."

"We can send for Sasha if you like. He speaks English well."

"No," Petri said harshly. She thumped back into the chair. "No Sasha."

"Oh." She grew nervous. Violence lingered close to the surface in all of Damien's Nvengarians. She'd witnessed that in their exhibitions of wrestling and sword play. She'd seen that Damien trusted Petri more than he'd trust a brother, but would Petri have the same loyalty to her?

Petri motioned for her to stay in the chair, nodding as though to reassure her. He crossed to the door, opened it, and called out into the hall, "Rufus!"

After a few moments, one of the tall footmen who followed Damien about like dogs appeared. He and Petri spoke rapidly and quietly in Nvengarian. Rufus looked past Petri at Penelope waiting, then he came into the room. Petri closed the door.

Rufus bowed to her. "I help Petri speak English." He looked proud and slightly superior that Petri needed his help.

Petri said something else in Nvengarian. Rufus bowed at Penelope again. "He says he wants you to know. If you do not marry Prince Damien, he will die."

Something jumped inside her, as though he told her something she'd already been aware of but had refused to acknowledge. "What?"

"It is the prophecy," Rufus said apologetically. "The prince must fulfill it or die. So if you do not marry, if you do not become the princess . . ." He trailed off, giving a little shrug as though he could not help what happened next.

Penelope's mouth went dry. "It is only a prophecy. Just words."

Rufus and Petri looked at each other. Rufus said a few words in Nvengarian, and Petri shook his head. "You understand not," Petri said.

"I know that you and Sasha believe in the prophecy," she tried, "and Damien believes in it, too, even though he claims he does not."

Rufus scratched his head as he translated for Petri. Petri gave a harsh laugh.

It was frustrating having a conversation in this fashion. She waited impatiently for the two to talk and for Rufus to translate back into English.

"Petri does not believe in prophecies, or magic, either," Rufus said at last. "I do, but Petri has had harsh life. No, he says the prophecy does not kill Damien. The Grand Duke does."

She gripped the arms of the chair. "Who?"

"Grand Duke Alexander Octavien Laurent Maximilien, head of Council of Dukes."

She remembered Damien mentioning the name *Alexander*, though she hadn't been certain who he meant. "This grand duke sent the assassin?"

Rufus nodded. He snarled something in Nvengarian, then said, "He is evil man."

Petri agreed, his scowl dark.

Rufus said, "If Prince Damien returns without princess, then no prophecy. No prophecy, then . . ." He broke off as though groping for a word.

"What?" Penelope put her hand to her throat. Damien had said nothing of this. He'd gone on about rings and love and being drawn together, and said nothing about dying if he did not bring her to Nvengaria.

Rufus beckoned to Petri. "Like this," Rufus said.

Rufus mimed tying a blindfold around Petri's eyes, then stood him against a wall. Petri waited, calm and still. Rufus picked up a tall silver candlestick and shouldered it like a rifle.

He grunted as he jerked into the perfect mime of *ready, aim, fire*. An explosive sound came from his mouth as his imaginary gun went off, right at Petri's chest.

Penelope rose from her chair, hands to her face. "Dear God. You mean he will be executed."

Rufus brightened. "Yes, that is word. Executed."

Chapter Twelve

Penelope froze in place while the room whirled around her. She saw not Petri against the wall, but Damien, waiting stoically while blue-coated Nvengarian soldiers raised rifles and fired a volley of bullets into his body.

She heard the roar of the guns and smelled the acrid stink of gunpowder and the iron bite of blood. Damien's blood.

Her knees gave. The floor rushed up at her, and then she suddenly found herself supported by the strong arms of a concerned Petri, who barked an order at Rufus. Rufus, alarmed, got rid of the candlestick and found brandy.

Petri made her drink it, pressing the glass to her lips himself. His handsome face, faintly scarred, hovering close to hers, held worry.

The bite of the brandy made the room stop spinning. Penelope drew a long breath. "Thank you for telling me, Petri," she whispered.

Rufus translated, though Petri had gotten the gist. He grunted.

His blue eyes held relief but also grim determination. He was a servant, but he cared for Damien, she could see that. He'd do anything, she sensed, to save his master's life, including tie her up and drag her to Nvengaria to marry his prince if he had to.

They heard a step, and all three looked up as Damien entered the room.

Damien's light mood evaporated when he saw Penelope surrounded by Petri and Rufus, who seemed to be ministering to her. Penelope's face was white, her eyes enormous. Ringlets of damp hair straggled across her face, making his blood burn.

He regarded the tableau with narrowed eyes. Rufus looked guilt-stricken, Petri defiant. Penelope rose slowly, never taking her gaze from him. She moved to him as though dazed, and not until she put her fingers out to touch his arm did she blink.

"Damien," she breathed.

They'd told her.

"Petri," he growled in Nvengarian, "I will boil you in your own blood for this."

"She deserved to know, sir." Petri's back was straight, his eyes steady. "She needs to marry you. I know you will go back with or without her, and I can't let you go back without her."

"Do not blame him," Penelope said quickly. "I do not know what he is saying, but it is not his fault. It is yours for not telling me the truth." She glared, her beautiful eyes shining with anger.

"Do not defend him," Damien said. "I told him to keep his mouth shut."

Out of the corner of his eye, Damien saw Rufus trying to sidle away. He pointed at him. "I will deal with you later." To Penelope he said, "I want your decision to be a true one. I want you to marry me because it is your choice."

Her cheeks grew pink. "You said you'd carry me off if I said no."

"Still I might," he said. "But I wish it to be a true choice from you. Your decision should not be based on a threat to my life."

"Damien, I cannot let you die." Her eyes flashed again, her face still more beautiful for her anger. "How did you think I'd feel when I learned that my decision sent you to your death? That I'd condemned you because I worried that you will ignore me after we marry? No matter how much you ignore me, I will not let this Grand Duke execute you."

"How could I ignore you?" Damien asked, incredulous. "I have thought of nothing but you since I arrived, and I will likely do so for the rest of my life."

He would likely be permanently aroused with her. Even now, thoughts rose unbidden of Penelope in the river with her wet chemise clinging to her body, her dark aureoles pressing the fabric, every curve of her outlined for his hands.

Her hair was still damp from their encounter, and this fact was incredibly erotic, especially when he remembered tasting her. *Sweet, sweet woman, all honey and cream and all for me.* If he didn't have her soon, he'd explode.

"You are changing the subject," she said.

"You *are* this subject, love. I will not ignore you or allow Alexander to kill me. If you believe he will embrace me tenderly when I return to fulfill the prophecy, you are wrong. He will still try to kill me, whether I fulfill the prophecy or no."

"But if I understand right, if you arrive with me, your people will believe in you. They believe in the prophecy, like Sasha. They would help you defeat this Alexander. Without me, they will lose faith in you."

Damien said nothing, because she was right. Having the people of Nvengaria on his side would give him more power than Alexander, despite his control of the military. The Nvengarians would also embrace Penelope whole-heartedly, and not just for Damien's sake.

She was beautiful and spirited. They would adore her.

She would marry him and go home with him. He saw that in her eyes. She was willing to risk all the danger for his sake. He knew that if he tried to leave her behind now, she would smuggle herself along in the baggage, no doubt aided by Petri, Sasha, Rufus, and all the other servants. They already adored her.

He reached out and traced a curl on her cheek. "I suppose I will have to live with having an astonishing woman in my life," he said with a lightness he did not feel.

"You ought to have told me," she said stubbornly.

"I ought to do so many things. I am not one for obedience."

She watched him, agitated, her green-gold eyes filled with fear and anger and worry. Worry for *him*. Women in the past had chased him and desired him and threatened suicide when he left them, but not one had ever worried about him.

She grew more astonishing every day. He tilted her chin with his fingers, brushed a kiss to her mouth. " 'Tis done, love," he said, his groin tightening in anticipation. "I will tell Sasha to begin the betrothal rituals."

"You seem preoccupied," Grand Duchess Sephronia said.

Alexander came out of his reverie at the sound of his wife's voice. Sephronia lay on a scroll-backed chaise, plumped on pillows. The beribboned peignoir she wore and the cashmere blanket over her legs could not disguise her extreme thinness.

Her beauty had gone, her once-vivacious face now

sunken, her skin stretched over her skull. Her luxurious black hair had been shaved for her fever, and what little had grown back consisted of thin black wisps on her head.

She no longer allowed anyone into her rooms, except her maids and Alexander. She would have kept Alexander out if she could, but he insisted on visiting her every day. He had never been in love with her—she had been too frivolous for deeper emotion—but she was his wife, and he would not allow her to die alone and forgotten.

He stirred now and answered her question. "My sources inform me that Damien has found his princess, and she has agreed to marry him. Also that more than one assassination attempt has failed."

"Oh, dear." Sephronia bit her lip. She did not really understand the prophecy business, but she knew that Alexander wanted Damien dead.

"One tried to stab him in broad daylight and was thwarted by his bodyguards," Alexander went on. "The other tried to shoot him as he frolicked with his princess in a river and was frightened off by another young lady and guests at the house." He shook his head. "These hotheads want glory in killing the Imperial Prince, but what they mostly do is make fools of themselves. One might find luck and kill him, I suppose, but I will simply have to deal with Damien when he reaches Nvengaria."

"Poor Alexander." Sephronia gave him a weak smile. "Prince Damien is a headache, isn't he?"

"He is like his father. Has his father's luck. But I will snip this sapling of the family tree and be rid of him." Alexander scissored his first two fingers. "No more Imperial Princes. Nvengaria can emerge into the modern world. We are four centuries behind, at least."

"What about the princess?" she asked. "Will you snip her, too?"

He smiled a little. "No need to be so barbaric. She is an

Englishwoman with no knowledge of Nvengarian non-sense. I will send her back home. She is an imposter, in any case."

"Your subjects might not think so," she pointed out.

Sephronia could sometimes see to the heart of a matter. If the romantic Nvengarian people wanted to see a long-lost princess, they'd convince themselves she was a long-lost princess. "I have the proof," he said, thinking of the papers hidden away in his chamber. "They dislike being duped, and will not accept her."

"The people might not believe you. Of course," she said slowly, "you could always marry her yourself."

She sounded wistful. Sephronia had never been in love with Alexander, but she had loved being Grand Duchess, loved dressing in finery, loved playing hostess, loved setting fashion for Nvengaria and countries around them. Even Parisian ladies looked to see what Sephronia wore in any given season. Her greatest regret was that her illness no longer allowed her to assume her duties.

"I will not marry again," Alexander said. Courtship and marriage were the last things on his mind. "I have no need. I have a son, and he is enough for me."

"Yes," Sephronia said proudly. She'd never taken much notice of their small son, now five, but she prided herself on having given Alexander a robust male heir. "You are a handsome man, Alexander. You will need a woman."

He shook his head. "Not a wife. Nor a mistress. I have no need to slake my lust every night."

"You are so strong." She reached out a wasted hand and touched his knee. "I wish I could have been strong, like you."

He covered her hand with his own, her fingers like bare sticks. Sephronia had slaked her own lusts in wild affairs with dandies and roués pleased to bed the wife of one of the most powerful men in Nvengaria. She was always discreet, bringing no open shame on Alexander, but he knew about every single one of her lovers. He kept his eye on them, in case they were scoundrels trying to use her to get to him. She had been very careful, he granted her that.

"You were strong enough," he said.

She gave him a tender look. "Did you ever take lovers? I never knew."

"One or two."

"Good. I am glad you were not alone."

Her concern amused him. Alexander had never been one for sentiment and romance. He enjoyed his pleasure with women, but did not lose his heart. He admired and delighted in beautiful women, but he did not need a female to make his life complete. His marriage to Sephronia had been political, and both of them had known that.

Her eyes took on a faraway look. "We were beautiful together, weren't we, Alexander? Me on your arm at every ball and soiree and every gathering at court. You, the most handsome man in Nvengaria, and I the most beautiful woman. Everyone envied us."

"Yes," he said.

He remembered her black hair shining with pearls, her gowns cut to show her slim shoulders and elegant breasts, the lift of her head on her long neck. He'd escorted her in his Nvengarian regalia and sash of office, the most powerful couple in the kingdom.

They'd been invited everywhere; hostesses were known to lock themselves into their chambers for days and not come out if Alexander or Sephronia turned down an invitation. Sephronia had danced and laughed and flirted and wooed and been the toast of the town. Had Alexander ever had the opportunity to take her to Paris or Rome or London, she would have forced society there to eat from her hand.

Even her pregnancy had been celebrated. She'd set fashion again by having her dressmaker create clever gowns to hide her swelling figure.

She'd always been careful in her love affairs never to conceive a child that was not Alexander's. She knew that putting another man's son in Alexander's nursery would not only be embarrassing, but dangerous. The father might use the child to gain power or to manipulate Alexander. Politics in Nvengaria always balanced on a knife's edge.

She sighed. "I know balls and soirees are not as important to you, but they were my life. They were my triumph."

He squeezed her hand. "I was always proud of you, Sephronia."

Tears shone in her eyes. "Where are they all now? All those men who declared they loved me and threatened to shoot themselves if I did not abandon you for them. Since I fell ill, not one of them has tried to see me. Not one. Only you."

"I am your husband," he said simply.

She gave a little laugh. "No one would blame you for deserting me. You are kindhearted."

"I believe you are the only person in the world who calls me kindhearted."

"You *are* kind. Deep down inside. I've seen it in you." She gave his hand a weak squeeze. "What I would like you to do is find someone to make you happy. Not for politics or power, but just happiness. I could never give you that."

"I am happy enough." He had Nvengaria to rule, and that took all his time and attention. "I do not think rulers have time for happiness. We rule, and this matters."

"I know, but you deserve someone to love you." She withdrew her hand, resting it on her chest. "That is what I wish for you. And you will best Damien. I know you will."

Alexander rose. He'd learned to sense when she was too tired to continue talking, and rather than embarrass her by letting her fall asleep, he'd rise and say a formal goodnight.

Tonight, for some reason, he had the compulsion to lean over her and press a kiss to her forehead. "Sleep well, Your Grace."

She touched his face. "You as well, Your Grace."

Alexander left her without another word. He closed the door, his heart heavy. She would die soon. He'd provided the best in care for her, but nothing could cure her. She would have the most elegant monument in the country, but that hardly compensated.

"Papa."

He heard his son's voice calling from the upper balconies of the prince's palace. He took the steps two at a time and caught up with his wandering son. "What are you doing out of bed, pup? It's past midnight."

"I could not sleep, Papa. I managed to slip past my nurse before she awoke."

Alexander suppressed a grin at his choice of words. Little Alex already loved intrigue and covert meetings. He'd make an excellent Grand Duke.

"Let us return before she misses you." With his son perched on his shoulder, Alexander climbed into the dark reaches of the castle. He liked that Alex did not flinch from the shadows. The old prince had died when Alex was young enough not to remember the horrors of him. With any luck, Alexander would banish every horror the old man had perpetrated, so that his son grew up in a new world with nothing to fear.

"I will go riding tomorrow," Alex announced. "Mama is too ill to ride, isn't she?"

"Yes," he answered.

"My nurse says she will die soon. Is that true?"

"I am afraid so." Alexander saw no reason to hide the truth from the boy. He'd learn of it soon enough.

"Poor Mama."

"Yes."

There had never been any intimacy between Sephronia and Alex. He knew her for his mother, but he watched her from afar and knew very little about her.

"Are you going to kill Prince Damien, Papa?" Alex asked.

Alexander shifted the boy's weight on his shoulder. Alex was growing, getting heavier. "If I must."

"Is he a very bad man?"

"He is."

"Nurse says his father used to eat little boys for breakfast. Is that true?"

Alexander saw that he'd have to have a word with Nurse. Telling Alex the truth was one thing; embellishing tales was another.

"He was a bad man, but not a cannibal."

"Oh." Alex sounded a bit disappointed. "Is Prince Damien a cannibal?"

"I don't know. When he returns, we will ask him."

"And then you will kill him?"

Alex sounded interested, just like his mother. "Yes," Alexander answered. "I will kill him."

The ritual bonding of the bride- and groom-to-be commenced at the end of the week.

"About time," Damien muttered as Petri dressed him in his most formal of uniforms.

"You are keen, sir." Petri smirked. "I've never seen you so keen for a lady."

"This is a very special lady. You ought to be congratulating me, not laughing at me."

"I do congratulate you, sir." Petri tugged the cravat tight. "She is a most entrancing young lady, and she will make a regal princess. I feel great happiness for you."

"You also look forward to me slaking myself so I will stop grumbling."

Petri's blue eyes twinkled. "When the royal rod feels the taste of her flesh, the ache will ease up, sir."

"I doubt it, Petri. I doubt it. I will not be sated with her until I'm old and gray and half dead."

"You do have it bad, Your Highness." The valet hid his grin, not very successfully.

Penelope had won over Sasha with her healing powers and now Petri with her understanding and concern. He had no doubt she could walk into Nvengaria and win over the Council of Dukes, the Council of Mages, and Alexander himself in the space of an hour. That is, if she got the chance. Alexander would not give up without a bloody and vicious fight.

Petri eased Damien's tight-cut coat over his shoulders. For this ritual, Damien wore the military-style clothing of the rulers of Nvengaria, a dark blue coat hung with too many medals, military breeches and boots. Last, Petri settled a sash of gold cloth over Damien's right shoulder and fastened it at his left hip.

"You are every inch the Imperial Prince, sir."

Damien glanced at himself in the mirror. His hair curled from his forehead to his collar, and his blue eyes were dark with anticipation. He looked well enough, but the uniform also brought out the resemblance to his father.

"Let us get on with it," he said, turning from his reflection.

"Right, sir. Sasha is in ecstasy downstairs. He's been dying for this day forever."

"Well, he deserves ecstasy. He's worked hard."

"He so much needs a woman," Petri muttered. "Preferably two."

"You could always spare him one of yours."

Petri grinned. "Charity is not my strong point, sir. But I'll find him a lass. I imagine after today, ladies around here will go for anything Nvengarian."

As long as Penelope did, Damien did not care.

He had already endured several days of Sasha's rituals, which had only heightened his need for Penelope. He'd spent a long dull night in a chapel, to cleanse him of sin. Then he and Penelope had attended no fewer than three feasts, where they served each other traditional Nvengarian fare—venison, hare, fish, and wine. Especially the wine. Sasha had brought crates of the stuff, thick and red from the vineyards of Nvengaria's finest wine-makers. Each ritual needed a different wine, and the guests partook, enjoying the discovery that Nvengarian wine was twice as heady as what they were used to imbibing.

The rituals were highly enjoyed by all but Damien. He'd not been able to touch Penelope, because the first round of rituals called for the couple to be celibate. No slaking needs on each other, no slaking them on anyone else.

But tonight was the bonding ritual, in which the couple would, in front of witnesses, agree to be bound to each other, by blood, forever. At the end of the ritual they'd be officially betrothed, and afterward they could slake all those needs that had built in the interim.

Damien growled in anticipation. What to do first? Strip her right away, or make her remove her clothes bit by bit while he watched? He could position her in front of a mirror while he stood behind her, still dressed, and taught her about her body. He let this enjoyable vision thread his mind.

Or should he take her fully, on the bed, all at once, and when he was sated, teach her the myriad ways of pleasure? Or should he slowly build, starting at her fingertips, until their lovemaking was explosive for both of them?

Petri, as if knowing his thoughts, clapped him on the shoulders. "Time to go, sir."

"Thank God. Let us get me betrothed."

Petri grinned again, and the two of them left the room and headed downstairs.

At the bottom of the staircase paced a man dressed in a kilt with a white lawn shirt and a stiff black coat. He had dark hair tied back at the nape of his neck, with one escaped lock cascading over his cheek. He had a military bearing, and he walked restlessly, his hands behind him, holding himself apart from the murmuring guests in the ballroom.

When he heard Damien on the stairs, he looked up. He had a square, hard face, the face of a man who'd seen too much. But the hard face suddenly creased in an infectious grin, and the man's restlessness vanished.

"Damien, you wild dog, why didn't you tell me you were getting married?"

Damien came off the last step and clasped the man's hand in a firm grip. The Scotsman thumped him on the shoulder, grinning hugely.

"What are you doing here, Egan?" Damien demanded. "I thought you had gone to chase bears in Russia."

Egan McDonald laughed out loud. "Too many husbands after my Scottish blood. Thought it best to beat a retreat. Then I stroll through London and read that my old friend Damien of Nvengaria is sticking his head in the noose. How'd she catch you?"

"You have not met her yet, it is apparent."

Egan raised his brows. "Oh-ho, you are well and truly snared. I see it in your eyes." He turned to Petri and said in perfect Nvengarian, "You let him fall into the trap? I'm surprised at you, Petri. You're supposed to protect him."

Egan McDonald was one of the few friends Damien had made during his long years in exile. He'd met Egan in Rome, a few months after Waterloo. Egan, a captain in a Highland regiment, had gone to Vienna after the British victory, then had traveled to Rome, wanting to explore that city.

He'd met Damien late one night in a passage at a hotel, and they discovered they'd both been enticed to meet the same woman. When Egan understood that Damien was Nvengarian, he'd suggested, in that language, that they leave the duplicitous lady and share a bottle of brandy instead.

Surprised at Egan's command of Nvengarian, Damien had agreed, and they'd adjourned to a tavern. Egan had then told Damien an extraordinary story. While wandering the wilds of Europe some years before, he'd been waylaid by robbers, beaten, and left for dead by the side of the road. He admitted he was drunk and had little wherewithal to fight. He would have died, but for the kindness of a Nvengarian girl named Zarabeth, who had found him and convinced her mother and father to take him home with them. The family had nursed him back to health—"sobered me up," he said—and he'd stayed with them until he healed.

The girl, Zarabeth, turned out to be Damien's distant cousin.

Egan and Damien had become friends over the tale and the brandy. Damien liked finding a European who was neither fascinated nor awed by the fact that he was a Nvengarian prince. Egan, though son of a Scottish laird himself, had an easy way about him and cared nothing for a man's rank, only his worth. This philosophy did not make him particularly popular with snobbish courtiers, but Damien enjoyed his egalitarian ways and found his good humor infectious. Egan could also let his brogue ebb and flow—when he found an Englishman annoying, Egan's accent became so thick it could barely be deciphered, but in the next instant, he could speak in the clipped, clear tones of any high-born Englishman. The brogue slipped in again when he was drunk or angry, but when sober, he had the ability to turn it on and off at will.

Whereas Damien had acquired a reputation as a charming seducer, Egan had acquired one for being wild and reckless. He made love to women with the same enthusiasm that he lost thousands on a roll of dice or proposed duels to defend a lady's honor. He won at cards with the same recklessness, and would be one day flush with money, the next day destitute. He cared nothing for either state, living through it all with high good humor and an indifference that Damien admired.

Egan had commanded his troops on the Peninsula with careful efficiency. "Fine for me to walk the edge of the cliff," he'd say in explanation, "but not for me to drag a hundred men with me." He'd taken care of his lads so well that soldiers far and wide nearly worshipped him. They lauded his bravery and his wisdom and his ability to use gutter language like the lowest of them.

Even the French he'd defeated had known of Egan McDonald, the Mad Highlander, and vied to introduce themselves to him when he captured them. In London, former soldiers inevitably came up to him in the street to shake his hand. "Now that's a *real* officer," they'd say to their companions.

Egan took his celebrity like he took anything else, with a shrug and good-natured indifference.

Even with Egan's easy friendliness, however, Damien sensed he'd never gotten to know the true man. Egan kept something buried within him that he showed no one. It swam to the surface sometimes when Damien and he talked about Nvengaria, but just when Damien thought he'd at last broken through the Mad Highlander facade, Egan would change the subject.

Damien saw a glimpse of the real Egan now as Egan asked, "And how is your wee cousin Zarabeth? Remember me to her, and tell her I am bad at writing letters."

"My 'wee' cousin is a grown woman and married to a duke. One of the damned Council."

Egan stopped, his mouth opening. He looked almost comical in his surprise. "Married?"

"Three years now. An arrangement between her parents

and his family. I do not like the man, but I was not there to prevent it, unfortunately."

"But good lord, she's just a bit of a thing. She can't be after being married yet."

"She is, I believe, twenty-two."

Egan's brows furrowed as though trying to reconcile the loss of time. "You say you don't like him?"

"No, but no need to bring your claymore. He has given her a huge estate of her own and plenty of money and jewels. She is the toast of the town, much admired by one and all."

His harsh face took on a faraway expression. "Little Zarabeth. She was always so quiet and kind."

"Quiet? Zarabeth? She was a wild hellion. But tenderhearted."

"She was kind to me." Egan stopped and pulled his face back into its usual carefree lines. "Does she ever mention me?"

Damien shook his head. "I've not had opportunity to speak with her much of late."

"Damn," Egan said softly. He stood a moment, lost in thought, then seemed to remember their present situation. He straightened up and clapped Damien on the shoulder. "Come on, old man. Time for you to lose your freedom."

The moved together toward the ballroom. "I take it you have never thought of marrying?" Damien asked, although he knew the answer already. Egan had very strong ideas about marriage—the English expression was "over my dead body."

"Not me," Egan replied fervently. "A carefree bachelor to the end of my days."

"You might change your mind when you see my lady. But if you do, remember she is already taken, and that I am a dead shot."

"No fear," said Egan, then they entered the ballroom, and the Highlander's words died on his lips.

Damien wanted to stop in stunned admiration as well. He had not much paid attention to the London seamstresses who had swarmed the house, but now he saw the results of their labors.

Penelope was resplendent in a gown of cream silk that gathered under her breasts and fell in a smooth line to the floor. Seed pearls decorated the bodice, which bared a hint of bosom. Lace draped her upper arms, leaving her lower arms bare. Her honey-colored hair was gathered in ropy curls and wound about her head. Pearls glistened against her locks, and a single curl artfully escaped and dangled to her shoulder.

At least a hundred people stood in the room, most between her and him, and yet, her gaze went immediately to him and stayed there. Her red lips, lush and ripe, parted as he approached.

The guests moved aside for him, growing silent as he crossed the room, like a breeze rippling through wheat. He never noticed them. He saw only Penelope and her gold-green eyes and her sweet body in its glorious dress that he wanted to rip from her body.

Sasha stood next to Penelope, waiting like a father about to give away the bride. He smiled benevolently as Damien stopped before Penelope.

Damien looked down at her, scarcely able to believe that in the space of a few minutes, he would be betrothed to this incredible young woman. He felt the corners of his mouth pulling upward in a grin. Penelope, on the other hand, did not smile. She watched him, her eyes shining— *with tears of joy?* he wondered.

"Honored guests," Sasha said. "Let us begin."

Every person in the room had already riveted attention on Penelope and Damien. Sasha beckoned to Petri, who stepped forward bearing a tray. On the tray lay a small, clean, sharp knife and a piece of rope. That was all. Penelope's brows twitched as she regarded the tray; they had not told her beforehand what the ritual would entail.

It would be barbaric, as all things Nvengarian were—barbarism covered with a thin veil of civilized behavior. But then, Damien had once witnessed the marriage ceremony for the English. The woman promised to submit herself body and soul to her husband, something no Nvengarian woman would promise, and the man vowed to worship her with his body. Even the ring put on the woman's finger was a symbol of bondage.

The Nvengarians went about it more blatantly. The bondage in Nvengaria went both ways—man tied himself to woman and woman to man, usually literally.

Sasha beamed and began. "I will say the words in Nvengarian and repeat them in English. That way, all may understand."

Closest to Penelope and Damien stood Lady Trask, handkerchief at the ready to catch her motherly tears, Meagan, smiling hugely, and Michael Tavistock standing quietly behind her. The Prince Regent sat in his Bath chair behind Sasha, enjoying the procedure and anticipating the newspaper articles that would describe how he'd attended the betrothal of the famous Prince Damien.

Egan McDonald stopped behind Damien, throwing Damien an envious grin. Damien and Egan had shared women in the past, *but not this time*, Damien promised. *The lady is mine.*

Mine. The word felt wonderful echoing in his head.

Sasha began. The ritual consisted of chants about how these two people had come together in love and would be bonded in love. He sensed Penelope's skeptical glance and looked at her.

Green-gold flecks swam in her eyes as she watched him. Warmth began in his belly as his gaze flicked to the soft cleavage between her breasts. He wanted to dip his tongue there, taste the salt of her skin. He imagined easing her bodice down to reveal the dark tips of her breasts, which were already pebbling under his scrutiny.

His gaze traveled upward, taking in her long, delicate throat, her lips, her beautiful eyes. He met her gaze, finding the sharpness softened. The prophecy was stirring them again. After this ritual, they would be betrothed, and then would come the mating. His blood stirred in anticipation. He wondered whether the prophecy would have the patience to wait through Sasha's chanting, because he certainly might not.

By the smirk on Petri's face, his valet sensed Damien's growing impatience. The man was positively gleeful. Damien had instructed him to have the bedchamber prepared and guarded, in case he had to rush with her there the moment Sasha finished.

Sasha droned on, the ceremony twice as long because Sasha stopped every few sentences to translate to English.

"Princess Penelope, do you agree to be bonded to Prince Damien, to share his bed, his troubles and his joys, his sorrows and his hopes, his children and his life?"

Penelope blushed. She glanced at Damien, and for one agonizing instant, he thought she would respond with a "No."

She swallowed, looked at her mother, who quickly sniffled into her handkerchief, then squared her shoulders and said, "I agree."

Sasha translated her answer to Nvengarian, and the room erupted in masculine cheers. The cheering went on and on, drowning out Sasha's identical question to Damien and his own, "I agree."

Sasha, his eyes wet with tears, took up the tray and offered its contents to Damien. Damien lifted the knife. "It will hurt only an instant," he murmured to Penelope. "I promise."

Her eyes widened. Gently Damien took her hand and turned it palm upward. Then, as quickly as he could, he slashed her palm straight across.

She winced, and he sensed Michael Tavistock start forward, to be blocked by Petri. Damien slashed his own palm, then clasped Penelope's hand and lifted it to head height between them.

Sasha took up the rope, looped it three times around their touching wrists and tied it securely. Damien and Penelope faced each other. Sasha reached up and closed his hand around theirs, and shouted in Nvengarian. "They are joined!"

The room erupted in cheers again, coupled with stamping and hooting. Damien felt Petri clap him on the back, and then Egan, grinning widely.

"What happens now?" Meagan asked, her tone excited.

"Now we dance," Sasha proclaimed, "and lead the couple forth to seal their betrothal in their first mating."

The English guests expressed either shock or delight, and the Nvengarians went on screaming. Circles formed for the dancing, Nvengarian hands dragging the London aristocrats into the dance. Rufus and Miles seized the handles of the Regent's Bath chair and swung him out to the middle of the floor.

Penelope and Damien were put into the middle circle, and married couples joined hands and danced around them. Outside the circle, the unmarried ladies and gentlemen danced. Men far outnumbered women in this group, thanks to all Damien's Nvengarians, and they vied with each other to grab the ladies' hands and twirl them about. Rufus and Miles had their eyes on a pair of giggling maids and showed off for them, dancing and leaping, Nvengarian style.

In the center of the circle, Penelope, still tied to Damien, held his hand and said very little. He moved with her slowly, letting the others wear themselves out in the frenzy of the dance. He wanted to save his energy for the long night to come.

The doors of the ballroom suddenly blasted open, and a icy wind slammed through the room. Shouts of dismay and surprise echoed. Penelope turned to Damien, a question on her lips, then Damien grabbed her shoulders and shoved her to the floor just as something small and fierce and dark hurtled past them and crashed into the far wall.

"What in God's name was that?" Egan cried. His hand dipped beneath his kilt and came up with a broad-bladed knife.

Penelope was trying to scramble up to look. Damien crouched protectively over her. "Stay down."

"What about you?" she panted.

"Never mind about me." The Nvengarian guards and servants had hurried to form a wall around Damien and Penelope, knives at the ready to face whatever it was that had hurtled into the room. Egan and Michael Tavistock joined them.

"Meagan," Michael ordered over the din. "Take Lady Trask out."

The Regent was whimpering with fear. He heard Meagan trying to coax Lady Trask away, but she was arguing, saying she'd never leave Michael.

"Perhaps it was just a large bat," Penelope whispered hopefully.

"No." Damien felt grim.

What had screamed past him, barely missing his head, had been a creature out of legend, a creature out of nightmares. *Logosh* were half demon, half human, changing from form to form at will. They dwelled in the Nvengarian mountains, cursed a thousand years ago, and lived high in cliffs, unseen by all but those unwary enough to stumble into their demesne.

Or at least, the legends claimed. No one had ever actually seen a logosh, and those who claimed to were usually drunk or known to be insane. Glancing over the shoulders of his men, Damien understood that seeing such a being could turn a man mad.

It was man-shaped, about the size of a boy, and clung to the wall like some strange reptile. It crouched, facing downward, with fangs protruding the sides of its mouth. It hissed, drool sizzling where it ran across the creature's chin.

"What on earth?" Penelope gasped.

It turned its head to follow her voice, then to Damien's alarm, it sprang at them.

Ladies screamed and shoved one another out the double doors. Damien whirled as the logosh sailed over heads toward Penelope. He caught up the small ritual knife and held it ready, the only weapon at hand. His left wrist and Penelope's right were still bound, but he dared not take the time to cut her free.

The creature soared overhead, lightning fast, and landed on first one wall, then the other. Sasha, white-faced, stared upward in amazement. "A logosh. God have mercy, he's sent a logosh."

Egan McDonald slapped him on the back. "Well, whatever it is, laddie, it'll taste the bite of Highland blade." He raised his dagger and shouted. "To me! The best Scots whiskey to the man who brings it down."

A dozen Nvengarian throats screamed a battle cry, and they launched themselves at the nightmare. The creature scuttled upward, and the men, sensing its wariness, surged forward, Egan running with them. "That's it, lads. It's no match for us."

No wonder they called him the Mad Highlander, Damien thought. *He'd fight the spawn of Satan himself.*

The logosh hurtled itself upward with astonishing speed. It clung to the ceiling for an instant and dropped to land an inch from Damien.

Damien roared and struck out with the tiny knife as he

tried to shove Penelope behind him. Petri had been borne away by those chasing the damn logosh across the room. Sasha stared, frozen. Michael Tavistock was protecting Lady Trask.

Damien kicked, catching the creature in the stomach. The thing shot upward again and dropped straight down, slashing at Damien's arm with its claws. Penelope tried to drag Damien from the thing's path. *She's trying to protect me, for God's sake,* he thought distractedly.

Then Meagan rose up behind it, a large candlestick gripped between her hands. She brought the candlestick down, *thump,* on the logosh's back. Or, the blow *would* have landed on its back had the confounded creature not twisted away. Meagan caught it on the shoulder, then all of a sudden, it was facing her.

Her pale face grew still. "Oh, dear."

Damien slashed down with the knife, but the blade was too small to do much damage. Then Egan McDonald appeared out of nowhere and plunged his dagger into the creature's shoulder. "Take that, hell-beastie."

The thing snarled and shrieked and shot straight upward again. But it was hurt. It scampered along the ceiling, the men chasing it. It launched itself from the ceiling through an arched window with a shattering of glass.

"After it," Egan shouted. "It's wounded. We'll hunt it 'til it's dead."

He hurtled out of the ballroom, the Nvengarians and more able-bodied Englishmen running pell-mell after him.

"I have not seen him that happy in a long time," Damien mused to Petri, who had come panting up.

"They'll get it for certain, sir. Jesus and Mary, was that truly a logosh? I thought they were make-believe, sir."

Sasha still stared out the broken window, his mouth hanging open.

Damien dropped the knife, stained with black blood, to the tray. "Penelope, love, are you all right?"

She gave him a shaky smile. "I believe so." She raised her hand, twining her fingers about his. "Look. We are still joined."

It happened then. Damien's control, held in check for weeks, snapped. "Petri," he said in a tight voice.

"The chamber is ready, sir. I will guard it myself."

Desire coursed through him, his veins raw with it. He closed his hand around Penelope's wrist. She looked startled, but he read the same hunger in her eyes. "Time to consummate this betrothal, love."

She could have asked many questions, beginning with "Now?" But she did not. Penelope, bless her, merely nodded.

He more or less dragged her out of the room, her slippers pattering on the floor as she strove to keep up with him. He passed the Regent, who was fanning himself with a large handkerchief, and Michael Tavistock, his arms full of a half-swooning Lady Trask. He swore Lady Trask had a calculating gleam in her eye.

Meagan had run to the window with the other ladies to cheer on the gentlemen. Sasha joined them, still in a daze, still bleating, "A logosh, by the saints."

No one was left to witness Damien scoop his mate into his arms and carry her away. Usually, a gentleman and his newly betrothed were followed to the bedchamber by their friends and servants, who shouted and sang and made ribald jokes.

But only Petri followed them, in silence, up the stairs. The rest of the Nvengarians were out chasing the damned logosh, which, Damien thought, was probably just as well.

Chapter Thirteen

Penelope had sensed the change in Damien as soon as he'd turned to help her to her feet in the ballroom. His eyes were wild, the darkest blue she'd ever seen them, his face hard and set.

He carried her all the way up the stairs, though she was quite capable of walking them. Or perhaps she was not. Her blood pounded, and she was almost dizzy with desire.

Damien had sliced one loop of the rope that bound their hands, and it had dropped away as he lifted her, but Petri had caught it up and now tossed it on the bed. Looking at the thin rope innocently lying there stirred something inside her. She was bound to him, that's what the ceremony said, and now she'd be bound to him on that bed.

Her hands went cold as she watched Petri deliberately remove Damien's sash of office. He helped ease the coat from his shoulders, the sleeve of it shredded where the creature had caught him. She swallowed.

When Petri reached for the cravat, Damien waved him away. She understood enough Nvengarian now to follow their exchange. "Out," Damien said.

Petri folded the coat over his arm and winked. "I'll be right outside, sir."

"Not too close."

"Of course not, sir."

With another knowing grin, Petri faded out the door and closed it softly.

"What if there is more than one?" Penelope asked, standing stiffly in the middle of the room."

Damien paused in the act of tugging his cravat knot free. "What?"

"What if there is more than one of those creatures? Whatever it was?"

He resumed untying the knot and pulled the folds of the cravat from his neck. His bare brown throat came into view. "There should not have even been one. It is a creature from myth."

"Another Nvengarian folk tale?"

He unbuttoned his waistcoat and untied the tapes of his lawn shirt. "The logosh. Legend has it that they were cursed a thousand years ago to live as half demon and half human, shunned by the rest of the world. But they are stories in books. They are not supposed to exist."

"One has just made a mess of my mother's ballroom." She tried to sound calm, a stoic Englishwoman who could face anything, but the shake in her voice betrayed her.

He threw aside his waistcoat, and closed the distance between them. "Jesus, Penelope," he breathed as he took her hands. "It could so easily have killed you."

"And you." She pushed at him. "It tore your arm." She fingered the slashes on his shirt, which were pink with blood.

"He barely opened the skin." Damien quickly slid out of his shirt, tossed it aside. She could feel the warmth he radiated, and wanted more than anything to place her palms on his chest, her fingers playing in his black hair.

She touched the wound instead. He was right; it consisted of little more than parallel streaks through his flesh, not very deep.

"Still, it might take infection. You should wash this, perhaps make a poultice."

She spoke distractedly. His broad chest covered hers as his hand slid behind her back. "Heal me, Penelope."

His sweaty, salty skin was an inch from her lips. She kissed the round of his shoulder, then daringly licked it.

He made a raw noise, his hand tightening on her back. "I will need water," she said.

She stepped away from his enticing body and went to his washbasin, where she found hot water waiting, probably ordered by the efficient Petri. A cloth hung nearby, which she wet and wrung out, and brought it back to him.

She had him sit while she washed his arm, drawing the wet cloth gently over the scratches. He watched her, closely scrutinizing with his blue, blue eyes, lashes flicking as he followed her movements.

"You understand what this bonding ceremony meant, did you not?" he asked in a quiet voice.

"Yes. We are betrothed, and now we may . . ." She broke off, face heating. She pretended to study his wound closely, rubbing away the already dried blood with her cloth.

"Not only that. We are joined as one. We are life mates. Bound to one another and responsible for one another."

She glanced up. "But we are not married yet. I thought the wedding would take place in Nvengaria itself."

"It will." He smiled. "The ceremony we just finished was the only one in the old days. The priests who wandered in to tame the barbarians imposed their own marriage ritual on top of ours, which is why we have two. The Catholic priests, not foolish, saw that our bonding ritual was important to us and agreed to let us keep it, as the betrothal ceremony before the Christian wedding. Of course, if they had not agreed to let Nvengarians keep their ceremonies, the priests would have been cut to pieces, and Nvengaria would still be pagan. The old ways are much revered."

She shot a startled glance at him as she finished wiping away the blood and laid the cloth on a table.

"That is why children conceived after betrothal are not illegitimate," he went on. "Because by Nvengarian custom, we are already married."

"Oh."

"But we are not married by English custom." He touched her cheek. "So if you wish to run away, Penelope, you still may."

She lifted her gaze. His eyes were dark, intense, waiting. "Do you wish me to?"

He stroked her lower lip with his thumb. "I need you. Not only for the prophecy, not only for Nvengaria."

"To prevent you being killed," she whispered.

"No, not even that. I need you for a far more basic reason than the one I came for."

"You need a princess." Her body swam with heat. "You came here to find a princess, any princess."

"Perhaps I believed so when I started out from Nvengaria. Perhaps I still believed so when I arrived in Little Marching. I believed it until I saw you and I kissed you." He cupped her cheek. "And then the world changed."

"That was the prophecy."

"I can blame many things on the prophecy. Sasha believes it guides the stars. I never meant for it to guide me. I never meant to love you." He gave a mock sigh. "But I do, and so be it."

"You always know the right words to say. You are always Prince Charming."

He grimaced. "I do not feel charming at this moment. I

GET UP TO 4 FREE BOOKS!

You can have the best romance delivered to your door for less than what you'd pay in a bookstore or online. Sign up for one of our book clubs today, and we'll send you **FREE* BOOKS** just for trying it out...**with no obligation to buy, ever!**

HISTORICAL ROMANCE BOOK CLUB

Travel from the Scottish Highlands to the American West, the decadent ballrooms of Regency England to Viking ships. Your shipments will include authors such as CONNIE MASON, CASSIE EDWARDS, LYNSAY SANDS, LEIGH GREENWOOD, and many, many more.

LOVE SPELL BOOK CLUB

Bring a little magic into your life with the romances of Love Spell—fun contemporaries, paranormals, time-travels, futuristics, and more. Your shipments will include authors such as KATIE MACALISTER, SUSAN GRANT, NINA BANGS, SANDRA HILL, and more.

As a book club member you also receive the following special benefits:

- **30% OFF all orders through our website & telecenter!**
  (Plus, you still get 1 book FREE for every 5 books you buy!)
- **Exclusive access to special discounts!**
- **Convenient home delivery and 10 days to return any books you don't want to keep.**

There is no minimum number of books to buy, and you may cancel membership at any time. See back to sign up!

*Please include $2.00 for shipping and handling.

YES! ☐

Sign me up for the **Historical Romance Book Club** and send my TWO FREE BOOKS! If I choose to stay in the club, I will pay only $8.50* each month, a savings of $5.48!

YES! ☐

Sign me up for the **Love Spell Book Club** and send my TWO FREE BOOKS! If I choose to stay in the club, I will pay only $8.50* each month, a savings of $5.48!

NAME: _____

ADDRESS: _____

_____

TELEPHONE: _____

E-MAIL: _____

☐ **I WANT TO PAY BY CREDIT CARD.**

☐ VISA   ☐ MasterCard   ☐ DISCOVER

ACCOUNT #: _____

EXPIRATION DATE: _____

SIGNATURE: _____

Send this card along with $2.00 shipping & handling for each club you wish to join, to:

**Romance Book Clubs
1 Mechanic Street
Norwalk, CT 06850-3431**

Or fax (must include credit card information!) to: 610.995.9274.
You can also sign up online at www.dorchesterpub.com.

*Plus $2.00 for shipping. Offer open to residents of the U.S. and Canada only. Canadian residents please call 1.800.481.9191 for pricing information.

If under 18, a parent or guardian must sign. Terms, prices and conditions subject to change. Subscription subject to acceptance. Dorchester Publishing reserves the right to reject any order or cancel any subscription.

JOIN NOW!

am insane with wanting you. Any pretty words are accident."

Her own blood felt hot, but she was suddenly shy. She
thought of the beautiful, golden-haired Russian countess
and the thin, Hellenistic baroness. "Why should you
want me? I am plain Penelope Trask."

He smiled. "Any man with eyes will want you. Seeing
the shock on Egan McDonald's face when he beheld you
was worth my journey. He looked as though, I believe the
English expression is, 'a ton of bricks had fallen on him.'"

Her blush spread. "Only two gentlemen asked to marry
me, and neither wanted me. Perhaps Magnus did, but in
an unsavory way. He did not want me in particular, any
young woman would have done."

"If I ever see this Magnus, I will skewer him," Damien
promised. "Perhaps only two men proposed to you, Penelope, but I wager many more wanted you. They said nothing because you were an unmarried miss, but they
wanted you. When they realize you are no longer an innocent, I will have to fight them off with a sharp sword."

She laughed. "You are very charming."

"I am not charming. I merely wish not to throw you on
the bed too quickly and take what I want. You deserve for
me to ravish you slowly."

"I do not want to be slow." She drew a breath. "I feel
quite urgent." She kissed his scraped flesh, which was
clean now, and damp.

"Urgent." His breath was hot on her temple. "A good
way of saying it."

She touched her tongue to the hard muscle of his arm.
"What do I do?"

"Unfasten your bodice." He threaded his fingers
through her hair, loosening it. "I want to look at you."

She obeyed. Her fingers were clumsy as she reached to
unhook the five clips that held the bodice together in the
back.

Damien tried to keep his impatience at bay. He should move slowly with her, introduce her to the world of pleasure at a gentle pace. But his arousal wasn't having any of it. He wanted to be inside her, and the wanting grew more frantic by the minute.

He reached around her and pulled the placket apart, hooks tearing from the threads that held them. She gasped in surprise, but the look in her eyes told him she was just as needy as he.

"Take off the dress," he said.

Obediently, she dropped the bodice from her shoulders, baring her arms and the half-stays that held her breasts snug, then slid the gown down her body, revealing a fine lawn underskirt. Quickly, she stepped out of the dress, then she shook it out and carefully laid it on a chair. He hid a grin at her practicality.

She returned to stand before him, lovely in her undress. The underskirt softly brushed her legs, revealing their outline, and her breasts lifted against the press of the stays.

"Would you like me to help you with your boots?" she asked.

His heart beat faster. Normally he did not consider removing boots to be erotic, but offered by his newly bound life mate, from lips full and red, it became suddenly desirable. For answer, he held out his left foot.

Penelope grasped his boot above his ankle. She bent, giving him a heady glimpse of the shadow between her breasts. Muscles in her slim arms worked as she tugged at the stubborn boot.

It came away all at once, and she staggered back a step and nearly sat down on the chair behind her. "Oops," she said.

"Are you all right?"

She straightened up, looked at the boot in her hand, looked at his stockinged foot, and began to laugh.

It was a merry sound, true laughter, with none of the

strain of the last weeks. Her eyes lit, her red mouth curved, and her body shook in a delightful way.

In two seconds, Damien had his other boot off and was seizing her by the arms. She still laughed, holding the boot between them, and he kissed and licked her lips, dragging that laughter into him.

He wanted to tell her he loved her, but need swallowed all words and all thought. He took the boot from her and dropped it on the floor, then crushed his hands through her hair and pulled her against him.

He kissed her lips, her nose, her temple, her hair tangling in his mouth. He bit her shoulder, catching the lace strap of her stays in his teeth. Her thin fingers rubbed his arms through his shirt with a desperation that matched his own.

He unhooked the stays and pulled them from her body, catching the weight of her breasts in his hands. The points hardened, the skin dark as he flicked his thumbs over them.

She gasped, her eyes going heavy.

His need wound into a wild frenzy, something inside him screaming *finish it!*

Damien lifted her and carried her to the bed. He laid her down, and she rose up on her elbows while he tore at the buttons of his trousers. He yanked the trousers off, then his stockings. He looked up to see her watching him with heavy-lidded eyes, her gaze traveling with interested thoroughness down his torso to his staff standing straight out, straining for her.

Her scrutiny would be flattering were he not so frantic. He climbed onto the bed, and she lay down, her hair fanning out against the pillows, her eyes dark under the canopy's shadow. Her hands rested on either side of her head, soft and limp, not fighting him.

He unfastened the tape that held her underskirt, and drew the skirt down her legs. She wriggled her hips, helping him draw it from under her bottom. She wore nothing beneath it. Her legs were shapely, thighs plump, rounded calves filling out her silk stockings, slender feet in beaded slippers.

The golden hair between her legs already glistened with moisture. He lowered his head and licked it.

She jumped, her gasp loud in the quiet. She tasted as heady as she had in the river a week ago, sweet and salty, honey with a bit of spice. He'd dreamed of her taste every night, wondering how he'd keep his hands off her until the ceremony.

Now she was his, to do with as he pleased. He smiled at the thought. He drank her, then he flicked his tongue over the hardening nub at the swell of her sex. She squirmed beneath him. She was wet now, oh so wet, her thighs parting of their own accord, her body arching to his mouth.

As he backed away, his hand fell on the discarded rope, the thin, silken strand Sasha had brought all the way from Nvengaria for the betrothal.

Quickly, Damien twined his left hand through Penelope's right one, and looped the rope tightly around joined wrists.

"We are one, we are bound." He said the words in Nvengarian, at the moment unable to translate to English. "I to you, and you to me. Forever."

She moved her fingers over his, caressing and slow, her eyes on the rope. Joined, bound, *one*.

"Will you join with me all the way, Penelope?"

So polite he sounded, when he was aroused too much to stop himself.

She flicked her gaze back to him, her face still. She still had the chance to refuse him, to remain a virgin and daughter to her mother. He saw the flicker of indecision and what it meant for her to make the choice.

"I want to join with you," she whispered.

His arousal throbbed once, wishing he'd get on with it.

"Excellent," he said, his voice as calm as if she'd agreed to take a stroll in the country with him.

She smiled a little. "You like that word."

"It expresses much. I will try not to hurt you."

She sobered, her eyes going quiet. "I have heard that it hurts much."

"It does not have to, if I take my time."

Every muscle in his body screamed with impatience. He did not want to take his time, he wanted to pound himself into her, *now.*

"Lift your hips a little," he said. He dragged a small pillow to him from the cushion-strewn headboard. "I will place this under you, so. It will help me go in a little easier."

She blushed, but let him arrange the pillow beneath her backside, tilting her hips upward, her knees a little apart.

Seeing her lying there, serenely waiting, her brow puckered with trepidation, wound his need to unbearable tightness. Her curls of hair were moist and ready, the petals of her parted, waiting.

He rubbed the folds gently, and their moistness increased, the scent of her heady.

"The beauty of you," he said softly. He licked his finger, wetting it, and drew it between her folds.

She writhed, her eyes going heavy, a woman drifting into arousal. He slid one finger inside, widening her.

She moaned softly. "Will it feel like that?"

"A bit." He slid in a second finger. He had no time to ready her for something as big as he was, but he could help her a little.

When he inserted a third finger, she made a soft noise and made to squeeze against him. He stroked the inside of her abdomen, slight pressure only, and her eyes widened.

"Damien?"

"Hush, love. Let me make you feel good."

She rose up on her elbows, her face flushed. "But I do not understand—"

He stroked, lightly again, and she began to come, jerking silently against his hand, her breath ragged. Quickly he slid his fingers out, positioned his tip at her opening, and slid himself all the way inside.

Penelope drew a sharp breath at the invasion. He was hard and thick and blunt and stretched her unbearably. It did hurt a little, but something within her wanted the hurt, wanted the joining.

She still throbbed from where he'd stroked his fingers inside her, which had sent her to strange and unbearable heights of pleasure. She did not know what he wanted, or what she wanted, or what her body wanted.

He lay on top of her, still, his weight warm. He squeezed his eyes shut, and the hand that was tied to hers clenched her fingers tight.

"Damien," she whispered.

He dragged his eyes open. "Shh, sweetheart."

His face was flushed, eyelids heavy, like he was drunk. She felt him full inside her, his arousal pulsing with his heartbeat.

"Is this lovemaking?" She smoothed his hair. "Is it over?"

"Do you want it to be over?"

"No. Not yet. Not for a while."

He gave her a lazy smile. "It will not be. We have a long way to go."

The idea both frightened her and entranced her. She lay back, holding the hand bound to hers, waiting for him to proceed. Sweat trickled from between their wrists, palms sealed together. The room was close and still, the windows shut against the summer's soft air. Petri, she knew, stood nearby, guarding them. She wondered about the passage that led from her room to

Damien's, but somehow she had a feeling that Damien had provided a guard for that, too. The Nvengarians were thorough.

And yet, the creature had gotten into the house, into the ballroom, and attacked Damien. She remembered its twisted face, its sunken eyes, though she sensed it was not old. And, if she had not imagined it, she thought that when the being took in the mass of people screaming and fighting it, and herself staring over Damien's shoulder, it had looked—confused.

The thought drifted in the very back of her mind, to be examined later. The front of her thoughts kissed Damien, loving the feel of him in her mouth, of him inside her.

He slowly drew himself out, then, just before the tip left her opening, he slid himself back inside, even farther this time.

Her sudden cry rang to the ceiling. He moved again, out, in, stroking her slowly. She dug her fingers into his back, as she had done in the river, but this time, she gripped so tight she felt her nails break his skin.

He made a soft noise of pain, but did not stop.

"Damien?" she asked, a frantic question. "Why do I—"

He could not answer her. He thrust into her again, deeper, the next one faster and harder. It hurt and it did not hurt, and she did not know what to do.

She lifted her hips to meet his, braced by the pillow. She kissed his cheek, feeling the burn of his whiskers on her lips. The feel of that, so masculine and warm, tipped her over some edge she'd been teetering upon.

Another cry burst from her lips. A dark wave swamped her, one flickering with the edges of fire. Damien braced himself on the bed, his bound hand pushing hers into the blankets, and thrust and thrust into her.

He gave a shout that ended in a growl, and his entire body ground into hers. "Penelope," he whispered. "Love you. Love . . ." He trailed off into a string of Nvengarian as he kissed her hot face, his own face wet, his lips warm and heavy.

She was not sure how they wound down from where they had been, but gradually, his thrusts quieted, and the pressure on her hand eased. His kisses became lighter, slower, his caresses more gentle, though he was still inside her.

She breathed out in a long sigh, her body loosening, limbs sinking into the featherbed. She closed her eyes.

She suddenly remembered the baroness at the fete, tittering with her friends about Nvengarians in general. "They are quite depraved, my dear, really quite depraved."

Penelope flushed guiltily and opened her eyes to look at Damien. If this was depravity, she liked it. Perhaps she was depraved, too. Perhaps because she had Nvengarian blood, however diluted.

He was smiling down at her, his hair tousled. "If ever I doubted the prophecy, I believe in it now. We fit together excellently well."

"Yes, it feels—excellent."

He was still pressed into her, erect and full. From what Katie Roper's sisters had told her, that was not supposed to happen. They tittered about a man's "limp bird" and a "cock that left its perch."

She touched his cheek. "Are you all right?"

"I believe this is the best I have felt in my entire life."

"But you are still rigid."

He chuckled. "That is your fault."

"Mine?"

"Mmm. For being the most beautiful and desirable woman I have ever seen."

She gave a short laugh. "I cannot be."

He looped a strand of her hair on the tip of his finger. "Why not?

She had no answer except that she'd always thought of herself as plain Penelope. "You make me feel beautiful."

"You *are* beautiful."

Her heart ached, and she did not understand why. "When the prophecy is fulfilled, will we still be in love?"

He kissed her, his smile wicked. "I cannot imagine feeling any other way about you."

"Nor I, you."

"In that case, I suggest we get as much loving as possible, to take advantage of our madness."

He tried to look so innocent and failed so miserably that Penelope burst out laughing. "You are trying to charm me again."

"Does it work?" His smile turned sly, and he leaned down to whisper in her ear. "What about this?" He said a few phrases in Nvengarian that she did not know.

She touched his hair. "I have a feeling I should not ask Sasha what those things mean."

"Ah, you misunderstand him. He would probably tell you most eagerly, happy that I am wooing you."

Her face heated. "Will you tell me?"

"Some of the phrases sound much cruder in English."

"I feel I should know what sweetnesses you are whispering into my ear."

"Not all of it is 'sweet,' as you say. Some of it you are not ready for."

"Tell me what I *am* ready for."

He considered, his blue eyes twinkling. "I am not certain what you are ready for. You are resilient, but I would like you to stay here with me for the rest of the afternoon and not scream and run away."

"You are making me crawl with curiosity. Tell me one thing at least."

His mouth twitched. "You are a brave woman. Very well, let me choose the most innocuous." The smile deepened. "I have it. There are certain places on your body that I would like to put my tongue." He leaned down and licked the curve of her ear. "This is but one of the places."

Her skin prickled. "You have already put it somewhere quite wicked."

"Yes, and I enjoyed tasting you again. I would like to tease your breasts with it. And lick your toes, which I have already done."

She blushed remembering the curling warmth inside her when he took her toes into his mouth. "And my fingers," she said. "And kissed me."

"And I would like to lick between the cleave of your breasts. And the cleave of your buttocks."

She stared, startled. "Goodness, why?"

His eyes darkened, and he suddenly withdrew from her, leaving her empty. "Turn over onto your front, and I will demonstrate why."

She hesitated. He watched her, likely deciding whether she was brave enough. She imagined his tongue tickling the base of her spine, and suddenly she realized very much indeed why she'd like it.

The loops of the silk rope had loosened; he hadn't tied them. She slipped her hand out of the bond and rolled over onto her stomach.

She glanced back over her shoulder at him. He knelt on the bed, his erection standing up from his body, curls of thick black hair at the base, the shaft slick and wet. His entire body was sculpted muscle and flesh, brown from the sun. All bits of him were bronzed, as though he let the sun kiss his entire naked body.

The thought made her gulp. Picturing Damien naked in the sun was not the fantasy of an innocent young lady. Although, she supposed she was no longer an innocent young lady.

When Damien touched his tongue to the hollow between her buttocks and spine, she gasped. The spark was even better than she'd imagined it would be.

He laid a soothing hand on her back. "Lie still."

His tongue slid further down, right between the cheeks of her backside. She dug her fingers into the coverlet, a moan escaping her lips.

He lifted his mouth. "I have barely done a thing, love."

Truly? She squeezed her eyes shut and held on tighter, as he bent his head again.

This time he licked all the way down, flicking his tongue over her backside, dipping between the cheeks, licking one side, then the other. Little cries escaped her, which she muffled in the bedclothes. She'd never felt anything like it, never imagined anything like it.

And then his fingers gently drew her apart, and his teasing tongue found her small hole.

She gave a little scream and crawled away from him, coming to rest on her hands and knees on the pillows, facing him. "Why did you do that?" she panted.

He sat back on his heels, his arousal not abating one bit. "If you do not like it, I will not do so again." His eyes were a mystery. "But you must tell me truthfully that you did not like it."

She opened her mouth to say so, then she closed it. A strange, hot sensation had covered her body. "I am not certain." She hesitated. "Am I depraved?"

"Depraved?" He laughed. "Why should you think you are?"

She drew a ragged breath. "Because I might have liked it."

Damien covered his face with his hands, and his shoulders shook. "I assure you, Penelope, that for a Nvengarian, I am almost tame."

"What about for an Englishman?"

"That I do not know. I have met Englishmen whose

tastes would make the most healthy Nvengarian cringe, and I have met Englishmen who do not seem to know or care what a woman is for. I suppose I am somewhere in between."

"I think that I am not supposed to be discussing this with my husband. My betrothed, I mean."

His smile vanished. "With whom did you propose to discuss it?"

"No one, of course."

He looked perplexed. "Why should I not talk about bed things with the woman I love?" He reached for her, closed his hand around her wrist, and drew her toward him. "I want to know everything you like and everything you do not. I want to touch every place that makes you scream, I want you to tell me to put my tongue where you want it and where I want it, and I want to teach you to do the same to me." He cupped her cheek. "I want to give you as much pleasure as a man can give a woman, and I need you to guide me, so it will be the best I can make it."

Her heartbeat speeded. If this was depravity, she rather liked it. She might be ashamed of herself later, but for now, she was quite enjoying it.

"Lie down," he said.

She took his hand and brushed a kiss to his palm before she obeyed. "What are you going to do now?"

"Wash you," he said unexpectedly. "You bled a little."

Surprised, she raised her head and looked down at herself. She remembered a fearful debutant whispering to her about the knifelike pain a woman must endure when her husband broke her maidenhead, and the gush of blood that would follow.

Penelope had felt a full ache, rather than bright sharpness, and she saw only a few smudges of already dried blood on her thighs.

He took up the cloth she had used to dab his wounds, rinsed it in the basin, then brought it back to the bed. It dripped a bit on the coverlet, leaving round, dark spots that thinned as they spread.

Gently, Damien smoothed the cloth over the inside of her thigh, wiping away the stain that meant she was no longer an innocent.

So many debutants fretted over the transition between maidenhood and womanhood, fearing it would hurt, knowing people would *know*, wondering how profound that night would be that changed them.

Penelope had missed the change; she had been so caught up in holding Damien and kissing him and feeling him fill her. She supposed that was the change—from blushing girl to a woman unashamedly embracing the man she loved. This was a change now, as well, she lying on her back with her legs spread, while he knelt, naked, next to her, and bathed her with the cloth.

It felt the most natural thing in the world to lie here with him, neither of them worrying about their state of undress and what each looked like to the other. A happiness seeped into her bones and for some reason made her want to wriggle her toes.

"I love you, Damien," she said softly.

Chapter Fourteen

He smiled down at her, lashes sweeping to hide his eyes, but she saw the flicker of triumph in them. "Good."

He drew the cloth over her thighs again, although she reasoned she must be clean. The cloth left a dampness behind that air touched and made cool.

"I cannot tell you it will be easy," he said. "I wish that I could."

"Because Grand Duke Alexander is trying to kill you?"

"More than that." His look turned serious. "My father nearly destroyed Nvengaria. It needs something to bring it back to its feet, something to believe in. They want the princess even more than they want the Imperial Prince. That is why they cheered me as I rode from the gates, because I would bring you back with me."

"Oh." She closed her eyes, liking the feel of the cloth moving in little circles on her skin. "What do they want me to do?"

"I do not believe they wish you to *do* anything. They simply want you to *be*."

"That does not sound very difficult."

"It will be. They will want to love you, body and soul. They already do love you, the princess who will restore Nvengaria."

"Oh." Trepidation fluttered through her heart. "What if they are disappointed?" She opened her eyes. "Your people are rather volatile, Damien. What if they decide not to accept me?"

She imagined herself being chased through the gates of a mountain town, people driving her forth with pitchforks and swords.

He chuckled, as though reading her thoughts. "You have seen how Sasha and my entourage view you. They have already decided you are the perfect princess and will do anything for you. Even Petri, the most skeptical of men, has embraced you, so to speak. He is enormously pleased that we will marry."

Penelope knew this responsibility he was thrusting upon her should worry her. She was not a princess; she was plain Penelope Trask, twice a jilt with no prospects, with no idea how to be an important woman, wife to a prince. But somehow, in the afterglow of her first joining with a man, the danger and difficulty seemed far away and unreal.

Perhaps it was the prophecy, willing her not to resist it. She had come to believe in this arcane magic after feeling herself change. A young miss such as herself should have swooned when Damien carried her off into the meadow and began to kiss her; she should have fought him hard, not succumbed. But at the time, there hadn't seemed to be a choice. It hadn't seemed wrong to let him kiss her and whisper to her what he wanted to do.

Likewise, it did not feel wrong to roll over and caress his

strong thigh and smile when he eased his hand through her hair. They were not married—at least, not by English standards—and yet she felt no shame lying here with him.

"Will you and Sasha tell me what to do when we get there?" She yawned. Strangely, the more she tried to focus on the daunting task, the more lethargic she became.

"We will not let you fall, Penelope."

She smiled, drowsing, imagining him holding her up in his powerful hands. Perhaps it would be all right. Perhaps the people of Nvengaria would ride out to meet her, banners waving, children shouting, men and women cheering and waving. They would be like Damien's Nvengarians, wild and strong, but fiercely loyal.

"Tell me a story," she said sleepily. She kissed his knee, inhaling his masculine scent. "About Nvengaria."

"Another fairy tale?" he murmured.

"Yes. You said you'd tell them to me in bed, 'member?"

"So I did." He set the cloth aside and laid down beside her. His large body, warm and long at her side, made her feel comforted and protected. "You rest, and I'll tell you about the princess and the logosh."

She shivered, but she no longer felt frightened of the logosh. "Does it have a happy ending?"

"It does."

"Tell it to me, then." She squirmed around until she could kiss his lips, then she snuggled down into the crook of his arm.

He smoothed his hand down her body. "Once upon a time," he murmured, "there was a beautiful princess."

And Penelope fell asleep.

Hours later, Damien jumped awake.

The room was still, the afternoon air hot. It was also silent. He heard no sound from the house, no sound from outside the windows. He wondered if the party goers, exhausted from the hunt and the heat, had returned to the house to sleep.

He'd smiled when Penelope had drifted off as he'd begun the story. He'd kissed her closed eyes, then lain down to wait for her to wake up.

He must have fallen asleep as well, tired by his frenzied lovemaking. Only it had not been very frenzied. Perhaps, he thought, his eyelids drooping again, he'd simply worn himself out from all the anticipation.

Being inside Penelope had been as fine as he'd expected. He smiled, remembering the brief pain of her nails, the heat of her frantic breath, how beautiful her face looked, twisted in passion, and the sweet cries of desire that she could not control.

His erection grew even as he started back to sleep. Later, he'd turn her gently onto her back and awaken her by sliding softly into her. Later . . .

He jerked awake again. Nothing had changed. Penelope slept on beside him, her naked body limp, her head pillowed on her bent arm.

His throat was parched. It was far too hot in the room; he had to open the window. Petri would not like it, but Petri was in the cool hall, not the stifling bedroom. Besides, Petri had made certain that Damien's bedchamber windows had a sheer drop to the back of the house, no overhanging trees or convenient ivy to climb.

A high blank wall would make no difference to a logosh, but Rufus and Miles must have caught the thing by now and sliced it to bits.

Damien unlatched and pushed open the casement, hinges creaking in the silence. He closed his eyes as a refreshing breeze touched his face, cool laced with damp. They might get rain this evening. It rained much in this country.

The silence outside matched the silence within. No servant plucked vegetables from the gardens for supper, no guests strolled the hedged walks. No aristocrats rode in the park, no grooms exercised horses in their master's stead. In short, no Englishmen, no Nvengarians, no one at all.

Damien quietly pulled trousers over his bare backside and exited the room. The hall was blissfully cool, and in a window seat near the end, Petri slept, his head thrown back, a soft snore coming from his throat.

Damien watched him in disquiet. Petri had never fallen asleep at his post in his life, no matter how tired he was.

"Petri." He shook the man's shoulder.

Petri's head lolled, but he did not awaken. Damien straightened up, grim. He wondered if the wine at the betrothal ceremony had been tampered with, the thick, bloodred wine that Sasha had carried so lovingly all the way to England. But in that case, why was Damien, who'd drunk far more of it than Petri, awake?

He'd heard of enchanted sleeps—in tales. But why not? A logosh had turned up and Damien was following a prophecy he did not understand. Why not an enchanted sleep as well?

He returned to the bedroom. Penelope slept on, her bare body relaxed and enticing. He wanted nothing more than to climb on the bed with her, drape himself over her, and drift blissfully to sleep himself.

He fought the urge. He pulled a fold of the rumpled coverlet over Penelope, who never moved, and leaned down and kissed her cheek. Then he rummaged in a drawer until he found a long, finely honed Nvengarian knife. Before he left the room, he closed the window again. A shame, because the weather had cooled, a few white clouds casting shadows over the heated afternoon. But he wanted no logosh or any other magical horror climbing in through the window while he was gone.

Petri snored in the hall. Damien left him there and ascended the stairs to the attic. The first servant's room he looked into held a mob-capped maid, fallen backward on her bed fully dressed, one foot dangling. She must have felt the lethargy, retired to her room, and was overcome with sleep before she could even lie down properly.

In another bedchamber, he found Rufus and Miles, or at least, he assumed it was his footmen in the tangle of at least eight bare legs, four ending in the dainty plump feet of English maids. He rolled his eyes and closed the door.

He left the servants' quarters and journeyed down-stairs. In the still house, he found sleeping guests and servants everywhere. The butler, Mathers, sprawled on a padded bench under the bust of Damien his footmen had erected, his hands resting on his ample belly.

He found Michael Tavistock in the sitting room with Lady Tavistock's head on his shoulder. Meagan was curled in a chair nearby, and Egan McDonald lay on the hearthrug, his kilt hiked above his brawny knees. He had a fine Highland snore.

"Damnation," Damien muttered, more to keep himself awake than for need of expression.

If the sleep were enchanted, why? Why would a mage go to the trouble of sending an entire household to sleep?

To kill Damien and Penelope in peace, of course.

Then where was the assassin, and why had he not struck? A trickle of sweat rolled between his shoulder blades. He softly left the ground-floor rooms, making for the stairs again.

Another question, who was the mage? No sorcerer was powerful enough to cast a spell all the way from Nvengaria, and he knew of no other sorcerers than Nvengarians. Oh, there were tricksters and women in villages and stargazers across Europe who called themselves sorcerers and witches, but in truth, they were not.

The thought that someone in his entourage was betraying him nauseated him. He'd been so careful, vetting the men and servants who'd volunteered to take this journey with him. He and Petri and Sasha had scrutinized every one of them, but he supposed Alexander would send only a very clever man.

And if it were Sasha . . .

No, he could not quite believe that. Sasha had been fiercely loyal since the day Damien had unlocked and opened the cell door of Sasha's prison with his own hand. Sasha, filthy and stinking and looking barely human, had heard Damien's voice and crawled to him, weeping. He'd clung to Damien's boot and said brokenly that he'd never given up faith that Damien would come for him. The guards had tried to pull Sasha away, but Damien had lifted the man, so emaciated he weighed next to nothing, and carried him out of the dungeon himself.

His old tutor was fanatically devoted to Damien. Sasha would have tried to stop any spell, not cast it himself.

Damien gained the upper hall again, where Petri slept on. As he reached to shake his valet again, he sensed another presence that he hadn't noticed before, a menace that tugged at his attention.

Slowly, he turned his gaze along the length of the hall, and then upward.

The logosh crouched on the wall in a shadowed corner. It was utterly still, its presence merely a darker blotch on the dark wall covering. Damien gripped his knife and walked toward it, making his footfalls noiseless.

The logosh never moved. It must have seen him coming; perhaps, it was readying itself to spring when Damien was in the choicest spot. Well, it would spring onto Damien's knife in that case. His pulse raced, his blood up, ready for a fight.

But the logosh remained unnaturally still. It could not

be dead, because surely it would lose its grip on the wall and fall. But what did Damien know about logosh? The fact that one lived at all was astonishing.

He stopped directly beneath it. He noticed then that its eyes were closed, and its ribs moved in and out in a deep, even rhythm.

Good God, the thing was asleep.

Damien smiled to himself without letting down his guard. Whoever had cast an enchantment over the house had caught the logosh in it, too. Perhaps the spell-caster was there, too, sound asleep.

These obstacles were beginning to annoy him. Time to clear them out.

"Starting with you, my friend," he murmured. He took another step and thrust his knife up into the sleeping logosh's ribs.

That was his intention, anyway. At the last moment, the logosh opened its wide, luminous eyes, shrieked, and sprang out of the way. The knife bit into its flesh, but not enough to kill it.

The logosh charged for the window. Damien leaped onto the sill, knife ready. Damned if he was letting it get away again, to heal itself and attack another time.

The logosh leapt at him, but its wound made it clumsy. Damien dragged the knife down its side, drawing black blood. The logosh jumped away, and Damien sprang from the windowsill and followed it. He struck again, but missed this time, the agile logosh managing to slither away.

Suddenly, he found himself slammed back into the wall, the logosh landing on his chest, its thin hand closing around Damien's throat. His head hit the wall and his breath deserted him.

He still had his knife, though. He brought it up and around to the logosh's body.

A door crashed open. "Damien!" Penelope cried, horrified.

The logosh glanced her way and froze. Damien used the distraction to jam his knife straight into the logosh's side.

The creature screamed. It half fell, half leapt from Damien, turned in a dizzy circle and crashed into the wall. Penelope, wrapped in the coverlet, scurried forward on bare feet, her eyes wide.

Damien held up his hand, arresting her movement. The logosh turned its gaze to her again, and he swore that its expression was pleading.

"Damn it, sir." Petri was awake and off the bench. He took in the wounded logosh, Damien panting and holding a blood-streaked knife, and Penelope wrapped in the coverlet. "I never meant—"

"Never mind, Petri. Help me finish it off."

He took a step toward the logosh. Suddenly the air around it shimmered, and then the logosh was gone, to be replaced by a small, very dirty boy, bleeding with knife cuts.

He heard Penelope gasp. The child could have been no more than ten, perhaps eleven, and he looked for all the world like any other Nvengarian boy Damien ever seen, the exception being that most Nvengarian children couldn't turn themselves into demons.

The boy pulled his arms and legs in on himself, hiding his nakedness, and began to cry, the small, terrified sobs of a child.

"Damien, don't," Penelope said.

Damien lowered his knife. It was one thing to carve up a demon, another to kill a child, even though that child had done its best to strangle him a moment ago.

"Holy Christ, sir," Petri breathed.

"I know."

"He's terrified," Penelope said. She sank to her knees.

"He's playing on your sympathy, love," Damien said quickly. "Once it heals, it will turn back to a deadly demon."

"I know, but . . ." She bit her lip. "Boy," she said in halting Nvengarian. "Do you understand me?"

The child-demon raised its head and stared at her. After a long pause, it nodded.

"Do you have a name?" she asked it.

Damien waited, poised to strike if the thing tried to attack her. He felt Petri tense on his other side.

The boy-logosh took a gulp of air and said, "Wulf."

Damien wondered if that was a name or simply a guttural sound in its throat. Penelope took it for a name. "Wulf."

The boy gave another nod. "Princess."

The word, in Nvengarian, was clear this time. Penelope pressed her hand to her chest, surprised. "Yes. Princess."

The boy held out his hand, fingers shaking. "Princess."

"He wants me to go to him," she said.

Damien gripped his knife. "And you will not."

"Princess," the boy repeated, his voice weaker, tears running down his cheeks to blend with the liquid from his nose.

"He's badly hurt," she said.

"He's a demon who tried to kill us." Damien spoke in Nvengarian so the boy would understand him as well.

Wulf shook his head, still staring at Penelope. "No. Princess."

"Were you trying to kill me, Wulf?" she asked him.

He shook his head. His face was white in the dim hall. "Help." His eyes rolled back, and he slumped against the wall.

Penelope got to her feet and started forward. Damien seized her in a firm grip. "No."

"He's a child, Damien. A hurt child."

"He is a demon."

"He has a name, and he said he was not trying to hurt me."

"Perhaps demons are liars, my love. Perhaps they simulate being a tearful child to lure their victims."

From the look on her face, she did not believe that, and neither did he. He felt both relieved and alarmed that the logosh was not an adult—as a child it was more vulnerable. But if he was a child, how large and strong were the adults of its kind? And, terrible thought, where was its mother?

"You started to tell me a story, remember, before I fell asleep?" Penelope said. "About a beautiful princess and a logosh? How did it end?"

"The princess healed the logosh after he was nearly killed by hunters. He turned into a handsome prince, and married the princess." He cast a glance at the half-conscious child. "He is a bit young for you, I think."

"Perhaps the story is true." She held up her hands as he started to argue. "I am certain it has been embellished in the folk tale, but perhaps a part of it is true—that a princess helped a logosh—and he remembers that. Perhaps they will not hurt a Nvengarian princess."

"They certainly have no compulsion about hurting a Nvengarian *prince*."

"But when he saw me behind you, in the ballroom, he turned away. And when I came out here, he stopped."

"Yes, I noticed."

Penelope's hair snaked about her in beautiful waves, her face flushed with their argument and her eyes bright with determination. The coverlet bared her shoulders and threatened to slide down her torso. She was almost edible, and damn enchanted sleeps and child logoshes that kept him from eating her up.

"He will die," she said.

"He came to kill me. When he is better, he will try again."

Penelope gave him a stubborn look. "If I can make him loyal to me, like in the story, he will not."

When they thought of all this again much later, each of them realized that neither had argued this logically or made a rational choice. But perhaps the prophecy was pushing them where it wanted to go. At least, Damien blamed it ever after for his decision.

He stepped aside. "Very well, love. But if you make a pet of him, he will *not* sleep on the bed with us."

Penelope smiled faintly at his joke and moved toward the boy.

"Sir, are you mad?" Petri asked.

"Very likely. But wait."

Penelope approached the child warily, not foolish enough to rush to it and embrace it. The boy began to shiver, whimpering in his half-dazed state. Penelope reached him. Damien moved closer, ready to drag her away if he suddenly became demon again, but Wulf did nothing.

She knelt beside him and gently pushed a lock of hair from his forehead, as tender as a mother.

The boy turned then, but only to fling his arms around her waist. Red blood, human blood, smeared the coverlet. Penelope, tentatively at first, then more firmly, gathered the child to her.

"It's all right," she crooned. He clung to her like any child hurt and frightened. Penelope rocked him and touched his matted hair, without betraying any sign of disgust. She looked at Damien over his head, her eyes so full of compassion that he knew he loved her all the way through and not because of a piece of ancient magic.

"I'll be damned," Petri whispered. "She's tamed a mother-loving logosh."

* * *

"Do not tell me," Alexander said as Nedrak looked up from his scrying stone with an anguished light in his eyes. "It did not work."

Nedrak gulped. "No, Your Grace. I am afraid not."

Chapter Fifteen

Alexander got impatiently to his feet and walked to the window. It was sunset, and the sky was streaked with crimson and gold. Mountains soared above the town, turning the view into a glorious landscape painting that no human's brush could ever match. The highest peaks were still tipped with snow, the slopes dark green with summer.

They were harsh mountains, without remorse, but their stark beauty, as always, pulled at his heart. If he could find a way to close the gate to Nvengaria, to keep the rest of the world out and save this pristine place forever, he would.

But he knew he could not. Nvengaria depended on trade with other nations, and no good came of complete isolation. He'd be damned, however, if he let Austria or Russia or far-off England swallow Nvengaria as part of some imperial conquest. Britannia could go rule somewhere else.

And there was Damien, hand in glove with the Prince Regent, winding the English aristocrats around his little finger. While Nedrak concentrated on the prophecy and nonsense magic, Alexander watched what Damien *did*.

What Damien had done was sweet-talk a girl into believing she was the long lost Nvengarian princess needed to save his kingdom, and buttered up the Regent and men in the cabinet and House of Lords so they'd come running to help at his call. England would sink its teeth into Nvengaria and never let go.

I will stop him.

"It is simply astonishing," Nedrak was bleating. "Astonishing. I wondered what the prophecy meant when it said the princess would tame wild things. I never dreamed it meant she'd befriend a logosh. And there is a mage there working spells, plain as day. That enchantment was not mine." He mused. "I wonder if *she* is the mage? She certainly is powerful."

His tone held admiration.

"Nedrak," Alexander said dryly. "You seem to be altering your loyalties."

The older man looked up with a start, sudden and abject panic on his face. "No, Your Grace. Never."

"If you help me break the prophecy, as you promised," he said, "you will be vastly rewarded. If you join Damien, you will die with him." Alexander leaned over the table. He was profoundly tired, and he could not say why. "You can, of course, decide to help neither of us. You may retire to the country with your grandchildren and leave politics behind. There are plenty willing to take your place."

Alexander saw the offer of retirement stir Nedrak's soul. Nedrak was always bleating about how heavenly it would be to sit with his daughter and son-in-law and five precious grandsons on the shores of the lake in the north.

But Nedrak was at heart a greedy and ambitious man. The thought that another mage would take his place ate at him. Besides, he did not trust Alexander not to send an assassin to the lovely house by the lake and to end Nedrak's life late one quiet night.

"No indeed, Your Grace," he said quickly. "I am your man. And your mage. Do not think for a moment that I would desert you."

Alexander let his features soften. "No, of course you would not."

He turned away, keeping his anger from his face. Nedrak was a fool and a romantic. Damien and his princess were more appealing to him than a stickler of a grand duke trying to pull Nvengaria from the mess Damien's father had made.

He couldn't understand why a man like that was alive when Sephronia . . .

Earlier that day, while the Nvengarian sun spilled through the valley, Grand Duchess Sephronia had been laid to rest. It was a bright day, a day for celebration and song, a day when Nvengarian maidens tossed blossoms at Nvengarian men in the town square, and the citizens strolled about in the warmth, smiling at neighbors, sipping coffee in cafés and enjoying respite from the harsh Nvengarian winter.

A mahogany casket, closed, had reposed at the gates to the marble mausoleum, the resting place of the Grand Dukes of Nvengaria and their families. Alexander, wearing formal military blue and a black band of mourning on his upper arm, kept his eyes on the blades of grass the casket had crushed as the priest droned on through the service. He held the hand of his son Alex, who clutched a small bunch of flowers, waiting for the moment when he was to lay them on his mother's casket.

The casket remained firmly closed. Sephronia had begged him not to let others see the wreck her body had become. Alexander had respected that wish and allowed no one to look at her as she lay in death. It was the least he could do for her after she'd endured seven years of marriage with him.

The coffin was carried through the gates of the mausoleum and lowered on lavish ropes into a stone tomb. Alexander led Alex by the hand to the square tomb, and lifted him into his arms. At his prompting, Alex leaned over and dropped his small garland of red flowers onto the polished coffin.

Alexander stepped back, still holding the boy, and waited for his men to close and seal the tomb. The scraping noise the carved stone cover made as they slid it into place was lonely and cold and empty.

As orchestrated, Alexander's men brought the huge mourning wreath of dark leaves and flowers and ribbons that Alexander had had made as soon as they'd brought news that Sephronia had died in her sleep. Setting Alex on his feet, he lifted the wreath himself and placed it carefully in front of the tomb. He stood a moment in silent contemplation, then turned and walked out.

Outside, in the summer air, the two dozen military color guards came to full attention. The captain saluted stiffly as Alexander passed them, leading little Alex by the hand.

As soon as Alexander had gone by, the captain gave a brusque order to the sergeant, who then bellowed out the order to raise arms and fire. The muskets cracked, fire spurting into the bright summer sunshine, signaling the end of Grand Duchess Sephronia.

The color guard lowered their weapons and stood once more to attention. Alexander nodded at the captain, implying thanks. Then he turned and led Alex to the black carriage and horses, and let it take him back to the palace.

Once there, he resumed his duties. His wife's death had barely caused a hiccup in the day-to-day routine of the palace. That angered him. The country should have frozen at least a day for her.

But he knew that ordering them to observe a day of

mourning would not have been popular. The people wanted to spend all their time preparing for bloody prince Damien and his long-lost princess. The newspapers tomorrow morning would have a precise engraving of Alexander placing the wreath on his wife's tomb, the entire first page devoted to a description of the ceremony and remembering the grand duchess's life. The people might worship Damien, but Alexander controlled the newspapers.

He had not been very surprised when Nedrak informed him that the ridiculous scheme of sending a logosh after Damien and Penelope had not worked. The fact had only increased the superstitious Nedrak's loyalty to the prince and the prophecy.

If the head of the Council of Mages turned on Alexander, he would pull many with him. Damn the man, and damn custom for giving an idiot so much power. Nedrak was left over from the dead Imperial Prince's rule; Alexander was determined to handpick the next one.

He turned back to Nedrak. "You have worked hard for me, Nedrak. Perhaps I have not seemed grateful, but I am worried."

Nedrak nodded, responding to the praise like a bird just thrown a crumb.

Alexander nodded thoughtfully. "Yes, I believe I will prepare a banquet in your honor, as a reward. I have been meaning to do so for some time."

Nedrak's eyes brightened, his pride stroked. "Why, thank you, Your Grace. I have, indeed, been working very hard to establish your right to rule Nvengaria." He paused. "I am sorry the logosh did not work. I was certain he would kill Prince Damien."

Alexander shrugged. "It was a good idea. It's just a shame the only creature you could capture was so young. Not your fault."

Nedrak preened, and Alexander barely hid his irritation. Fool. Nedrak liked romance and drama. Alexander saw things straight and clear. Damien would fail, and Alexander would make certain of it. In fact, Damien had already failed. A few more snares in place, and Damien would fall in the eyes of the Nvengarians, and that would be that.

Nedrak asked hesitantly, "Is there anything else you'd like me to do for you this afternoon?"

Alexander turned away, his hands behind his back. "No. You've done enough. Go about your business."

The dismissals always infuriated Nedrak—the two men should have been equals, after all. "Yes, Your Grace." He scuttled to the door, then paused. "May I express my deepest sympathies on the death of the Grand Duchess."

Alexander looked up. Nedrak shivered. He could feel the ice of those blue eyes all the way across the huge room.

"Thank you, Nedrak," Alexander said silkily. As the mage turned to leave, Alexander added, "And, Nedrak."

"Yes, Your Grace?"

"Do not speak of my wife again. Ever. Do you understand?"

Nedrak swallowed, his throat dry. "Yes, Your Grace."

Alexander looked away. It was like a gate clanging shut. Nedrak scurried into the hall. A stiff, silent attendant shut the door behind him.

"Cold-hearted bastard," Nedrak muttered as he made for the mage's council halls. Then he cast a swift glance around, fearing he'd been overheard, gathered up his starry robes, and ran. Alexander had spies everywhere.

Sasha was beside himself with excitement when he learned that Penelope had tamed the logosh. Not only had she tamed the boy, Wulf, she'd washed him and dressed his wounds, which were already closing and healing. Wulf, in turn, clung to her.

"It is in the prophecy, sir," Sasha prattled. " 'And the

princess will heal the sick and tame the beast.' I did not understand the part about the beast, sir; I thought it meant you." He flushed. "Oh, I did not mean . . ."

Damien smiled, but he felt grim. "My life was admittedly wild before my father died, but the prophecy seems to be amazingly literal."

"It is all coming true, Your Highness," Sasha said happily. "It is all coming true."

The household woke groggily from its enchanted sleep. Mathers, indignantly rousting servants from bedrooms, discovered Rufus and Miles with the two pretty maids and gave them all a good tongue-lashing. Rufus and Miles resumed their duties looking a bit sheepish and a lot smug.

Petri, on the other hand, sank into remorse. "I failed you," he said while he tried to straighten Damien's bedchamber, picking up things and absently setting them down again. "I have never, ever in my life fallen asleep while I guarded you, not even when we were lads begging for scraps. The logosh could have killed you while you slept, and I could not stay awake to prevent it." He squared his shoulders. "You may put me to the sword, sir. I will deserve it."

"For God's sake, Petri, we all succumbed to the damn spell. Do not turn dramatic on me, I beg you. You are my voice of reason in all this madness."

"You did not succumb."

"Yes, I did. I do not know what woke me, but I was sleeping as hard as anyone else. Penelope only woke when I smashed into the wall, and so did you."

He shook his head, his eyes haunted. "No, sir. I woke when the princess shouted. The logosh might have throttled you before I could reach you."

"Stop flagellating yourself. If you want to make recompense, find the mage who cast the spell. It had a decidedly Nvengarian feel to it, so it is one of us."

Petri's eyes flashed, anger replacing remorse. "I will flush him out, sir. And skin him alive."

"Now you sound like Titus. Before you skin him, bring him to me so that I can ask him a question or two."

"Yes, sir. I will not fail you."

"Good." Damien could bear no more of the man's guilt, and stalked out of the room.

He found Michael Tavistock in the lower hall. When Tavistock saw Damien descending the stairs, he swung to him and waited at the bottom. "A moment of your time, please," the Englishman said stiffly.

Damien nodded and gestured that they should talk in the sitting room. That room, however, proved to be full of giggling ladies who looked up eagerly when Damien walked into the room. "Good evening, Your Highness," they said collectively.

Damien stopped, controlling his impatience. "I beg your pardon," he said. He put his hand on his chest and made a deep bow. The giggling escalated, accompanied by fluttering fans and batting eyelashes.

Damien escaped, and Tavistock suggested they walk outside.

As usual, several footmen detached themselves from duties and followed, watchful and alert.

"When do you leave?" Tavistock asked him.

It was early evening, the long English summer day at last drawing to an end. The clouds he'd observed earlier had thinned, and only a few golden-streaked wisps adorned the horizon. Gentle swells of green hills flowed away from them and disappeared into haze where the sky met the ground.

A flat land, Damien thought, thinking of the razor-edged mountains of home. *Damn, but I miss it.*

He cleared his throat. "Immediately. Tomorrow. The last ritual is tonight. Penelope and I and a small part of my entourage will depart in the morning, with the rest following when they are ready. I realize they've become somewhat entrenched here."

He said it apologetically, trying his winsome smile. Not that it ever worked with the hardheaded Tavistock. Meagan had once claimed that her father was a cheerful and happy man, but Damien had never caught him at it.

"You and Penelope will marry in Nvengaria?" Tavistock asked.

"Yes. It will be the wedding of the year. She will be married in fine style, never fear."

"Will this be a Christian wedding? Performed in a chapel? Or another Nvengarian ritual?"

Damien kept his best Prince Charming smile in place. "In a cathedral, with a bishop."

Tavistock stopped walking. They stood a short distance from the house, halfway down the drive, at the top of a green hill that dropped down toward the village. "Penelope is an English girl, despite your tale of rings and lineage. I would rather see her married in an English chapel in a ceremony she understands."

The smile deserted him. "The ritual we performed this morning binds her to me as though she were my wife. The wedding in Nvengaria will only seal it. I assure you, this is no elaborate trick to gain a new mistress."

A spark of anger lit Tavistock's mild eyes. "So you say. I admit that I can imagine no man going to all this trouble to lure a young lady into his bed, but the point is, she has gone there. And you are *not* married. If you find a princess more to your taste on your way home, and abandon Penelope, she is unprotected and ruined."

"She is not ruined under the laws of my people," Damien said. "I assure you of this."

"But she is not of your people, Prince Damien. Nvengaria is a land far away and most people in Oxfordshire and even London have never heard of it. The English guests you invited are already inventing jokes about a maiden who cannot resist a prince. They wonder who you will charm into your bed next."

Damien felt the temper inherited from his father rise. "Who dares say these things?" He was surprised at how icy his voice had become.

"The Prince Regent for one. He wonders if Penelope is partial to all princes. Shall you challenge him to a duel?" Tavistock looked angry enough to do it himself, or maybe to challenge Damien.

"Damn," Damien said feelingly. He said a few more choice phrases in Nvengarian. His bodyguards glanced his way, wondering.

Tavistock went on. "I do not hold myself up as an example of excellent behavior. You know that Penelope's mother and I have been lovers. My only excuse is that we are older, Lady Trask is a widow, and I hope we were discreet. Penelope is a maiden, with much to lose."

"Do you think I would shame her?" Damien's accent became thick as his anger increased. "She will be Princess of Nvengaria, not the lover of a backstreet scoundrel."

"What I think is that you came from nowhere and have successfully enticed an innocent young woman into your bed."

Damien growled again, but he knew that from Tavistock's point of view, Damien's actions looked exactly as described. Tavistock might have come 'round to believing in Damien, but not everyone in England would, including, it seemed, the damned Regent.

He held on to his temper. "What would you have me do?"

"Marry her," Tavistock said. "Have an English wedding, here in the village."

"I do not have time. The days are marching and the road home is long."

Tavistock's dark eyes were steady. "There are plenty of powerful and influential men staying here. I am certain any of them can help you procure a special license. You need delay one or two days at most."

Damien balled his fists, but he made himself stay polite. He needed these people to like him, because he needed them to let him have Penelope, and not only because of the prophecy. He wanted her. He was painfully aware of how much he wanted her.

"I will speak to Egan McDonald," he said. "He will be able to obtain a special license from whoever gives them in your country. Everyone admires Egan."

"Good." The brown eyes, flinty hard, did not soften.

Damien understood. "You are waiting for me to tell you that I will keep myself away from Penelope until then. That she will sleep alone."

"It would be best."

He sighed. "That is a cruel, cruel thing to ask a man, Tavistock, whether he be Nvengarian or English."

Tavistock shrugged. "I care very much for the Trask family. I do not want to see them compromised or slandered in any way."

"Neither do I. Very well, you have won. I will marry Penelope in your English chapel with your English license. By the time the poor girl is finished, she will have married me three times over."

"It will still the wagging tongues."

Damien thought of the ritual that was to have been tonight, and closed his eyes in painful longing. The bathing ritual, in which the bride and groom were cleansed and then brought together to wash each other.

Sasha had supervised the building of a special bath in a ground-floor chamber. Traditionally, the ritual was attended by a crowd of the bride's and groom's families and friends, who drank wine and cheered them on. Damien had gotten Sasha to pare the number down to himself and Penelope's mother and Meagan, to spare Penelope embarrassment.

He had been looking forward for a long time to standing behind Penelope in the deep water, drawing the ritual sponge over her neck and shoulders. Her hair would curl in the damp, strands clinging to bare skin flushed from the heat of the bath. He'd rinse her with a trickle of water, then follow the trickle with his tongue. His hand would come up to cover her breast, to pinch the tip into a firm peak, and she'd arch back against him in longing.

He willed his imagination to still, and opened his eyes. Tavistock was watching him narrowly.

Damien made a conceding gesture, as though it made no difference to him. "Very well," he said with difficulty. "I will inform Sasha that the ritual is to be postponed."

"Oh, Penelope, just fancy, I'll be your bridesmaid after all."

In the garden at the Trask home, Meagan threw her arms around Penelope's waist. Penelope hugged her friend back, then released her without a word. Not far from them, Wulf sat in an unused flower bed, digging to his heart's content.

He loved to dig, much like any boy his age, making little trenches and strange forts out of the rich earth. His wounds had healed with alarming speed, an event which both Sasha and Wulf attributed to the healing powers of the true princess.

No one in the house was particularly happy to hear that the logosh, albeit turned to a small boy, was staying.

"Penny, dear," her mother had said as she entered the small servants' room to which Penelope had carried Wulf. Wulf had lain under a pile of blankets, his pale face bruised and scratched, his hand firmly closed around Penelope's.

Lady Trask hovered in the doorway, her hands fluttering nervously. "What if he turns into a demon again and tries to eat us all?"

"He will not," Penelope said. She did not know how she knew this, but she knew it with all her heart. "He will not turn into his other form unless I tell him to."

Lady Trask shot Wulf a last look around the door. "Well, please be certain not to tell him to, there's a good girl."

They had discovered this morning that Wulf liked sugar very much, after he'd eaten an entire bowlful in the kitchen. He'd showed no ill effects, and Penelope had soothed the cook's temper and dragged the boy away. He also liked carrots, and happily munched through the bunch that Penelope gave him.

Penelope watched him dig and burrow, getting himself filthy, but humming a happy tune while he did it.

She herself was beyond frustration. Last evening, Damien had appeared at supper and made the abrupt announcement that he would be marrying Penelope by special license in the village chapel tomorrow or the day after that, as soon as he could arrange it.

Everyone had stared in surprise, except Michael Tavistock, who looked satisfied, and Sasha, who looked unhappy. Penelope understood his unhappiness when Damien went on to say that the rest of the Nvengarian rituals would be postponed until he and Penelope were properly married.

The supper guests had clapped happily and said their congratulations. Damien had warmed them with his benevolent smile and raised his glass to Penelope.

Penelope had sat in stunned silence, wondering what on earth had just happened. But she had no opportunity to speak to Damien or argue with him or even look at him. He had disappeared after supper, and she had not seen him since.

"I wish I had time to get a proper dress made, but there it is," Meagan was saying. "You are so lucky, Penelope. A handsome prince riding out of nowhere, sweeping you off your feet, and marrying you. It is too romantic."

"It is, rather," Penelope said colorlessly.

"Please remind him, when you reach Nvengaria, that he has promised me someone ten times better than a duke." She tilted her head to one side. "I wonder what he means by that?"

Penelope shook her head. It was another fine day, and the sun shone hot. Her parasol cast a blue shade over her, while Meagan's sent a yellowish glow over her face.

"I've been hoping to get you alone," Meagan said, a little pink creeping into her cheeks. "Yesterday, when we were all running after Wulf and then falling asleep, did you . . ." She waggled her brows. "You know."

Penelope had tried to put it from her mind, but in a rush, she remembered the heavy weight of Damien's body on hers, the feeling of being stretched and opened, and the strange fullness of his length inside her.

She remembered it vividly, as though her body transported itself back to the hot room with him for a time, then was deposited again in the garden with a crash. She drew a breath and opened her eyes. "Yes," she said.

Meagan squeezed the handle of her parasol. "Oh, my dear friend, how wonderful for you. Was it—I mean, did it hurt?"

"Not really. Not as much as I'd feared." Penelope was blushing, too, and she looked over at Wulf to distract herself. He was getting dirtier by the minute.

"Goodness, I am relieved to hear that. Maddie Roper said she screamed aloud when she was first—well. She also said her husband did nothing but grunt, rather like a pig. I hope Damien said sweet nothings instead."

Penelope remembered him whispering under the shadow of the canopy while he kissed her with hot thoroughness. "He said things in Nvengarian."

"Ah. Well, when you learn more Nvengarian, you will

understand them. That would make me wish to study harder."

Penelope looked at Meagan's eager, teasing face, and dissolved into laughter. "You always make me feel better."

"Why should you not? I am pleased he is such a good husband already. I will bless your good fortune and hope to be wed myself to a gentleman with tight trousers who does not grunt in bed. That is as much as an old maid like myself can wish for."

She sounded mournful, but her eyes danced.

"Do not let your father hear you speak so," Penelope admonished.

Meagan deflated. "Poor Father. When we woke yesterday, he was holding your mama, and I so hoped that things were settled between them. But I am afraid not. Papa is being uncommonly stubborn."

Penelope bit her lip. She'd not had the chance to speak to Michael during the whirlwind preparations and rituals that Sasha insisted on. Her mother seemed resigned that Michael would leave her. When Lady Trask no longer had the heart to have hysterics, Penelope knew that she was truly suffering.

"Damien has overturned all of our lives," she said.

"That is true," Meagan agreed. "I vow, I never dreamed I'd be chasing fairy-tale monsters and chatting with the Prince Regent and being a bridesmaid for my dearest friend who is marrying a prince."

Penelope smiled. "You like the world upside-down, do you?"

"You must admit, Pen, that life was becoming deadly dull. Damien arrived just in time to save us from a summer of hideous ennui." She sighed. "I did hope that I would be engaged myself to one of these Mayfair gentlemen before you left, but it is not to be."

Penelope raised her brows. "I have seen you dancing with Mr. McDonald more than once. He is handsome enough, even if he wears kilts instead of tight trousers. Have you not tried to gain his admiration?"

"Do not tease me, my darling friend. There is nothing wrong with kilts, especially when you wonder, you know, what is under them. No, the Mad Highlander is handsome and gallant, but he loves another."

"Who?" Penelope said, interested in spite of herself.

"I have no idea. But I see it in his eyes. That faraway look, you know, as though he is wishing he could be with his beloved, though he knows he never can. It is terribly romantic."

Meagan was not smitten, then, if she could look upon the roguish, teasing Highlander and weave a tragic tale about him.

"You are inventing things," Penelope chided.

"No. It is there if you look for it. I know about people."

Penelope had to concede that Meagan did. She acted like a silly young miss, but mature wisdom lurked behind her shrewd eyes. If she claimed that Egan McDonald was pining for love, he likely was. Penelope's mother, too, was pining for love, though she did not hide it as well as Mr. McDonald.

"You have given me an idea," Penelope said, her spirits picking up. "I believe I can resolve things between my mother and your father."

"Truly? May I help?"

"I *believe* I can," Penelope repeated. "Depending upon how stubborn the pair of them remain. The problem is that your father does not believe my mother loves him. At least, not enough."

"Yes," Meagan said. "What he fears is that he is not good enough for her, and that she will throw him over the moment she finds a gentleman wealthier or more handsome."

Penelope began to answer, then stared at her friend in surprise. "You agree with him."

Meagan shrugged, her face going pink. "She did get very excited when she saw Damien's rubies."

"That is simply her way, Meagan. She learned to be silly and frivolous because it kept her from being hurt. People *expect* her to be silly. But she loves your father very much, and I will prove it."

"I hope that you can," Meagan said, her eyes serious. "Father is near to brokenhearted."

"I will prove it right away." She folded her parasol with a determined jerk. "Can you watch Wulf for a moment?"

"No," Meagan answered at once. She held her hands palms out as though trying to stop a runaway horse. "I love you, Pen, but no."

Penelope glanced at the boy. "He is awfully dirty. He will have to bathe again or Mathers will scold something awful. Mathers hates dirt on the carpets."

Fortunately, Wulf seemed to enjoy baths. He liked to splash water everywhere and dive below the surface, coming up spluttering. For all Penelope could see, he was enjoying being a little boy.

"Wulf," she said.

The effect was instantaneous. Wulf dropped the piece of wood he was using to dig, leapt to his feet, and ran to Penelope's side.

They'd given him clothes from one of the groom's sons, serviceable breeches, shirt, and shoes. In them he looked like a normal ten-year-old boy. His eyes were a bit large in his small face, but other than that, he looked in no way out of place.

He stood before Penelope, smeared with dirt but peering avidly at her, as though he hung on her every word. He might look like a child, but he behaved almost like a feral dog, one who loved one master and one master only. He understood Nvengarian, but he spoke little, save for a few words at a time. Since Penelope only knew a little of the language herself, their conversations were brief and halting.

"We must wash you," she told him.

Wulf's face brightened. "Bath," he said, and grinned.

He grabbed Penelope's hand and started hurriedly for the house, as though fearing she'd change her mind.

"Pen," Meagan said, panting behind them. "How can you be so certain he will not hurt you?"

"I just know," Penelope said over her shoulder. She could not explain the conviction, and she did not want to examine it too closely herself. "He will not hurt me."

"What about the rest of us?"

"Nor you," Penelope said. "I *know*, Meagan."

Meagan made a skeptical sound. "Well, I suppose it's no more bizarre than a prince and a prophecy. I used to say that nothing remotely interesting ever happened in Little Marching."

As they emerged from the gardens, two horses and riders, followed at a little distance by liveried Nvengarians, came up the long drive to the house. One was dressed in a Nvengarian-style uniform, the other wore a kilt—Egan and Damien returning from their visit to the Bishop of Bessborough and the quest for the special license.

Chapter Sixteen

Horses did not like Wulf. They knew good and well that he was a demon, and sought to put as much distance as they could between themselves and him.

Egan and Damien dismounted as soon as Penelope and Wulf entered the drive, tossing their reins to grooms. The horses hurriedly followed the grooms, snorting and looking nervously over their shoulders.

Penelope stopped, remembering her first encounter with Damien, when he'd looked down at her from atop the midnight-black horse. His smile, that lazy smile that promised a lady so much, had made her bones melt.

Nothing had changed. He walked to her, the sinful, promising smile in place.

He and Egan were handsome in different ways. Damien's polished sophistication overlaid strong control, a veneer of manners over the tumultuous emotions he inherited from his people. Egan had little polish, his kilt and boots and coat made for riding and fighting, not sitting in drawing rooms. He had raw strength, a man who would be equally at home sleeping in the heather and fishing for his dinner as dining in a castle.

Both were tall, broad-shouldered, handsome specimens. No wonder the gazes of the ladies present followed them wherever they went.

Damien put his fist under her chin and bent to kiss her briefly. He had not spoken to her or been alone with her since they'd found Wulf. His announcement that they'd marry in the village had caught her unawares, and she wanted to be angry with him for not consulting her in this matter.

But as their lips met, she momentarily forgot her anger. Without realizing she did it, she hungrily took his mouth, seeking him with her tongue. Smiling into the kiss, he slid his hand behind her head and drew her closer.

Egan laughed from two feet away. "Make an honest woman out of her first, lad."

Face heating, Penelope broke from him. Egan was grinning, Meagan giggling. Wulf stared at them intently, as though not knowing what to make of them.

Damien teased the curls at the nape of Penelope's neck. "I will as soon as I find the vicar. Thanks to Egan, who commanded the bishop's son on the Peninsula, I have the license, and tomorrow, you and I will become husband and wife." His eyes glittered. "Under English law, that is. Now, everyone will be happy."

He gave her another smile, this one of satisfaction. Once again, Prince Charming had arranged everything to his liking.

Penelope could have walked off in a huff, reminding the prince he had never bothered asking her, and perhaps making him look a bit of a fool. Polite Penelope Trask would never do such a thing, of course, but it was tempting to think of it.

Damien destroyed even the thought by lifting her hand

and kissing it, then tucking it through his arm and strolling with her back to the house. The smile Damien slanted down at her promised wickedness once they were fully married, and that she would enjoy wickedness with him very, very much.

Later that evening, while Lady Trask played hostess in the card room, Penelope entered her mother's bedchamber, found what she wanted, tucked it under her arm, and made her way to Michael Tavistock's chambers.

The house was quiet, most of the guests playing cards or billiards or strolling the gardens under the light of paper lanterns. Wulf had gone to sleep in his small bedroom in the attic with as much enthusiasm as he played in the dirt or ate or took baths. The boy seemed to attack the basics of life with a gusto that made Penelope slightly ashamed at how much she took them for granted.

Because it was quiet, she was able to hear Damien and Michael speaking in Michael's chamber as she approached the door.

"By tonight it will all be over," Damien rumbled. "We will be married, and the betrothal rituals finished. A relief, I will confess."

Penelope froze, her hand on the door handle.

"For Penelope, too, I imagine," Michael's dry voice answered. "You have put her through much."

"Indeed, she has borne it well." There was a pause, then when Damien spoke again, his voice sounded more distant, as though he'd strolled to look out the window. "We will have the marriage tomorrow and leave the next day."

"You are rushing her a bit, aren't you? Let the poor girl adjust to being your wife for a day or two, first."

"But I do not have a day or two. I must present Penelope in the Imperial Prince's castle on Midsummer's Day, and time marches swiftly. I have had to waste much time convincing her and you and everyone in the household that I am serious in this venture. I have reasons for my hurry."

Michael answered thoughtfully, "I understand them. This Alexander does not sound like he will give you a second chance to win over your people. But can you not give her a day to ready herself, to say her good-byes?"

Damien answered something, but Penelope missed it because a step behind her, either of a guest or a servant, startled her. She could hardly be found listening at a door, so she rapped on the wood and entered without waiting to be invited.

Michael looked up in surprise, then relaxed when he saw it was Penelope. Damien turned from the window. His blue eyes met hers, strong and steady, and he looked in no way ashamed that he'd been caught speaking about her.

She closed the door behind her. "I hope you will at least let me pack a valise," she said crisply. "I will need a change of clothing."

Damien remained where he was, answering her as though she had not spoken in irritation. "We will take as much as we can carry easily, then Sasha and the rest of the entourage will follow with a baggage train. They will move slowly, and you and I and Petri will ride ahead in carriages and on horseback. Wulf, too, I imagine, since he will not let you out of his sight."

"You have planned well," Penelope said, a little out of breath. "And so far in advance."

His eyes were still. "Believe me that I would love to linger and enjoy the hospitality here for days to come, but I have no choice."

She did not want to soften. She tried to stand resolute, then a spark flickered in his eyes, recalling the desire of the previous afternoon, when she lay in warmth with him, their bodies damp, skin on skin.

The dratted man could always melt her bones. "I know

you are not marrying to please me," she said. "But to save your throne."

A slow smile spread across his face. "I would not say there is no pleasure in it."

Her face heated until she was certain she was red as a poppy. How he could insinuate these things in front of Michael was beyond her comprehension.

"I will pack," she said hastily. Face still scalding, she approached Michael and held out the book under her arm. "Read the passages I have marked," she said. "Please read them before you decide to go."

Michael accepted the book mutely, brows raised in curiosity. Penelope spun away from him, shot Damien a glance, then, when he gave her another lazy smile, she turned abruptly and scuttled out of the room.

At seven the next evening, a bemused Damien found himself in front of the lily-bedecked altar in the chapel at Little Marching, saying the English vows while he pushed a gold ring onto Penelope's finger.

Behind him, Nvengarian uniforms filled the chapel, as did the finery of the ladies and gentlemen of Mayfair, including the Prince Regent in his Bath chair.

"With this ring, I thee wed," Damien said in clear, rolling tones. "With my body, I thee worship."

Penelope looked up at him, her eyes serene. She'd been angry as anything, he knew, when she'd interrupted his conversation with Tavistock, in which he'd implied that he was happy all the nonsense was over. Her eyes had flashed, beautiful as always, when she'd loftily demanded whether he'd give her time to pack.

Fool, he chided himself. *How charming to tell a woman she is a piece of necessary baggage.* His frustration was making him imprudent.

He would make it up to her. After this ceremony they

would have supper, and then the bathing ritual would commence. The idea of the ritual was to metaphorically cleanse the bride and groom of their life beforehand, all their sins, all their mistakes, so that they could start afresh with each other. A nice idea, and it involved running his hands over Penelope's slick, naked body.

She made the correct responses to the service in a clear voice, neither missish nor shy. She was marrying him in the eyes of her people, in the eyes of English law, and she would hold her head high.

The villagers and Londoners hastily prepared to enjoy themselves, and the Nvengarians, never willing to be left out of a celebration, joined in. As Penelope and Damien left the chapel, the collected group cheered madly, voices raised in joy, albeit rather slurred with the quantities of wine already drunk.

Flower petals littered the air, fluttering like pieces of brilliantly colored silk, then drifted to cling to his coat and Penelope's gown and shining hair.

Back at the house, they had to sit through a long supper punctuated by endless toasts. Damien held Penelope's hand under the table, but that was the only contact he had with her. He knew very well that this was only the beginning of such celebrations, which would become much more elaborate when they reached Nvengaria, if Sasha had his way. Sasha had already begun daily lessons with Penelope, trying to hammer into the girl the complex Nvengarian language. Damien thought Penelope would be up to the strain. She was resilient, his princess.

Even so, he planned to have plenty of private time with her. Part of Petri's job was to see that Damien would be left alone when he needed to be. No one got past Petri. He was a steadfast servant and a loyal friend.

He wondered again about the enchanted sleep that had struck the entire household. It had not gotten as far as the village, inquiries had proven. Only the Trask house and the people in it had been affected. Sasha was busily trying to ferret out the mage who'd cast the spell, and so was Petri, but so far, they had not been successful.

As long as no one enchanted him and Penelope in their ritual bath, he thought. Sasha had given Damien a few charms, mostly twists of feathers and bone in colored wire, that he said would stave off spells. To please him, Damien had tucked the bizarre-looking things under his pillow and in a corner of the bathing room, though he did not have much faith in them. But one never knew.

At long last, Egan stood up, clad in his best kilt, shirt and formal coat, the plaid of the McDonalds wrapped about his shoulders. "My friends," he said, swaying slightly. He had brought out his wedding gift to Damien, a few bottles of richly amber Scots whiskey, and one, of course, for himself. "I give you a good man and an excellent prince, a man who will always be rich in charm and friendship." He hesitated, then grinned. "Who is too damn good-looking for his own good, and who's snared himself the most courageous, the most beautiful woman to grace the soil of England. I give you, Penelope and Prince Charming."

"Penelope and Prince Charming!" Light glinted off glasses as they rose into the air.

Egan thumped his glass back to the table. "And now, let the poor couple do what they're dying to do, enjoy their nuptial duty."

The gentlemen, led by the Prince Regent, roared with laughter. Penelope went bright pink. The ladies laughed, too, Meagan giggling and the Russian countess sending Egan a hopeful look.

Damien stood up, raising his own glass, and the table quieted. "I thank my friend Egan for his generous words. Egan is eager to finish this ceremony so he may continue his search for the fabled dram of Nvengarian whiskey, the most potent liquid in all the world. It exists only in legend, but Egan is willing to brave that the legend is true. 'Tis his lifelong ambition."

Laughter echoed around the table. Egan grinned, not looking offended, knowing Damien needed the attention from him for a few minutes. "A sip to any who help me find the wee thing," he announced. More laughter from the gentlemen.

When they quieted, Damien said, "My bride and I must start for home tomorrow, and so we will say our good-byes." Those who hadn't known this expressed dismay. Meagan's happy expression became tinged with tears. "You have kindly welcomed me and my people. You will never be forgotten." He lifted his glass. "The front gate of our castle will always be open to you."

That brought another burst of laughter, and some applause.

"You have proved good and loyal friends, and I will reward you," Damien continued. "Sasha has prepared gifts, which he will give you tonight." He gave them a sly look. "I will be busy."

His audience roared with laughter, gentlemen and ladies both. "You are very naughty, Prince Damien," Lady Trask said, covering her mouth. Michael Tavistock even smiled, appeased by Damien's capitulation to the wedding ceremony.

Yes, all were happy with Prince Damien this night. And yet, the person he most wanted to be happy with him, Penelope, sat quietly at his side, smiling a little, but saying nothing. He sensed a few sparks kindling behind her eyes. They were not sparks of love. She wanted to argue about something.

But Penelope knew how to behave in front of a crowd. She rose with him and went around the room, saying her good-byes to those who had traveled to see her. The Regent even kissed her hand, giving her a lecherous look over it.

She would part with her family tomorrow, but they

would not see the guests formally again. It took a long time before Damien could extract himself and Penelope from the room, but finally, he led her out the door to more applause. Sasha swept among the guests then, Rufus and Miles and Titus following with heaping baskets, to bestow gifts and give each guest a speech. That should keep them occupied for a while.

At the foot of the stairs, Damien gathered Penelope to him and kissed her, not giving her time to begin whatever argument brewed in her head. She wanted him, that was plain, the tips of her breasts pressing sharply against the bodice of her yellow silk bridal gown.

He wanted to slowly tear the dress from her body in long, leisurely rips, watching each piece fall to the floor in a yellow puddle. He wanted to be inside her, buried deep, wanted it with mindless brutality. *My woman, my princess, my wife.*

Rituals first. He broke the kiss. "Ready yourself," he said in a low voice. "I will come to you."

Penelope looked up at him, startled. She nodded once and turned away, apparently forgetting what she wanted to argue about.

As she hastened to the stairs, he gave her a little push on her backside. That earned him a glare, but he saw the need building in her eyes. This ritual would be sweet.

Hot water slid down Penelope's back where Meagan poured it from the pitcher. The pitcher slipped and a cascade hit the floor, splashing all over Penelope, Meagan, and Penelope's mother. Penelope expected Lady Trask to shriek about her ruined dress, but she'd had plenty of champagne, and like Meagan, she dissolved into giggles.

All very well for them, Penelope thought. They were not standing stark naked in the middle of the antechamber on a piece of oilcloth, shivering while soapsuds and sloshes of water dripped from her body. The bath that

Sasha had commanded to be built steamed gently nearby. Not long from now, Damien would come in and the ritual would commence.

"Do hurry," she said.

"Penny, dear, this is no time for maidenly vapors," Lady Trask said. "You have already been in his bed, why are you suddenly shy?"

"It is different, somehow. It is more . . ."

"Official?" Meagan suggested. "Whereas a few days ago, you were only being naughty."

Penelope's face heated. "Everyone knows what we are going to do. I feel them waiting out there. The other day it was private. Now I am on display."

"At least Damien did away with having a crowd watch you bathe each other," Meagan pointed out. "Good heavens, Sasha wanted to invite twenty people, and seemed most puzzled when Damien objected."

"Sasha is a strange man," Lady Trask agreed. She absently squished a sponge against Penelope's shoulder. "He does love his rituals."

"He's harmless," Meagan proclaimed. "Damien says he went a bit crazy being in a dungeon so long. Goodness, I would too." She suddenly looked mournful. "After tomorrow, I'll never see you again, Penny."

"Do not say that," Penelope said, her jaw hardening. "You will come to Nvengaria. I will visit England. I've said so."

"It is such a long way away," Lady Trask said sadly.

"Mama, you are getting water all over your frock. Now do not start crying, because I will, and we do not have time. Sasha said Damien would enter at nine o'clock precisely."

For some reason, she did not want to be standing upright, nude and wet, when Damien walked in the doors. She wanted to be in the bath, seated, the water up to her neck. She felt somehow that she could face him like that, not exposed, shivering, and vulnerable.

Lady Trask nodded, letting tears flow. "You are my daughter, Penelope. Of course I must grieve you leaving me behind, even though I am so happy you have made such a match. I never would have thought you'd catch a prince."

"Mama."

Lady Trask threw her arms around Penelope, soap and water and all. "Oh, my darling, I do love you so. I am so happy."

"So am I," Meagan said. She burst into tears and flung her arms around Penelope from the other side.

They cried and hugged each other, until all three ended up as wet as could be.

Out in the hall, the tall case clock struck nine, echoing and sonorous. They broke apart, panic taking over.

"Wait, you're still soapy," Meagan cried. She threw water from an ewer at Penelope as she ran for the bath. The water arced through the air, half of it splashing Penelope, the other half soaking the blue silk wall covering.

Penelope stared in dismay, but Lady Trask burst into giggles. "Excellent, Meagan. I always hated that wallpaper. Penelope's father picked it out."

Penelope climbed the two stairs to the platform and lowered herself to the marble bench inside the bathtub, water sloshing.

Just in time. At the same moment, the door pushed open, and Damien, clad from neck to ankles in a sumptuous dressing gown, crossed the threshold. Sasha stood behind him, his hand over his eyes.

Damien's dark blue gaze took in the two dripping, smiling women, then moved to Penelope waiting in the bath, her arms crossed modestly over her breasts. She sensed his body tighten, though he made no perceptible move.

He slowly approached the bath and stepped up to the platform. Penelope fastened her attention on the brocade slippers covering his feet. His strong ankles showed below the hem of the dressing gown, just touched with dark, wiry hair.

"Lady Trask, Miss Tavistock," he said in his deep voice. "You may go."

Meagan and Penelope's mother clung to each other, giggling. "Au revoir, Penelope," Meagan said, then the two of them hastened from the room, holding each other as they went. Their high-pitched laughter echoed through the hall.

Damien kept his gaze on Penelope, but his eyes were amused. "I can do this alone, Sasha," he said in Nvengarian.

Sasha peeked through his fingers. "But the ritual must be followed precisely, Your Highness. I must ensure—"

"Penelope understands it. She will make sure I do it correctly."

Sasha glanced quickly at Penelope, head and neck alone visible above the lip of the bath, and nodded in relief. "That is so. Yes, the princess will know how to do it."

He bowed low and marched smartly out of the room, banging the door behind him. After a moment came the sound of a key in the lock.

"You see," Damien said, "already they have decided who is the stronger in this marriage. The fair Penelope, not the Imperial Prince."

"I am certain he did not mean that," Penelope said.

"I am certain he did."

He let his gaze rove her, from her pinned-up hair to her bare throat to her body under the steaming water. "Penelope, you are the most beautiful woman I have ever beheld in my life."

Penelope did not answer. She could not believe the truth of this, and concluded the prophecy must be working through him.

His eyes darkened. "I have been going mad with wanting you."

She pointed with a dripping finger at the side of the

tub. A huge bath sponge sat on a tray next to a dark bottle of Nvengarian wine and two goblets. "We must do the ritual. With the sponges and the wine and everything."

"Have no fear, I will do Sasha's ritual." The glint in his eyes turned wicked. "But I imagine it will be much more pleasant without anyone watching."

She shivered. "Does the betrothed couple truly have to bathe in front of their families and friends? Sasha seemed surprised you did not want to follow the tradition."

Damien loosened the first fastening from his dressing gown, baring his column of throat. "The bathing ritual is ancient, not always observed these days. But ours is a royal wedding, and so we must do the most arcane, bizarre rituals historians like Sasha can find. We are special, and we must suffer for it."

She let her gaze linger on the hollow of his throat, which was damp with perspiration and the steam of the bath. "It must seem strange to you, as well," she said. "You grew up in the courts of Europe, not Nvengaria."

He unhooked the next fastening, baring the line of his collarbone and the hollow between his pectorals. "The courts of Europe have strange rituals all their own, which I am happy to abandon."

"What sorts of rituals?" Penelope asked, more to keep her mouth moving than because of interest. Watching Damien slowly bare himself was far more intriguing than explanations about odd customs.

He pulled the next fastening apart to reveal his taut abdomen and the line of hair that pointed downward from it. She saw no waistline of breeches or linen band of underbreeches under the dressing gown, nothing but sundarkened skin that paled a little below his navel.

"None very interesting," he answered.

He unfastened two more silken ties, and the dressing gown fell all the way open. His legs were strong and straight and long, and his erection, dark and rampant, stood out from a circle of curled black hair between his legs.

Strange that simply seeing him erect for her brought such a flush of heat. She suddenly wanted to grasp the organ in her hand, to feel it warm and rigid against her palm.

She dragged her gaze away as Damien slid the dressing gown from his shoulders, letting it fall down the steps in a velvet wave.

"I do not mind that you like to look," he said. He carefully slid out of his slippers, his bare feet sinewy and strong. "Stand up."

Penelope lowered her arms from her breasts and rose on shaking legs, water cascading from her body in hot rivulets. When she stood upright, the water came to her hips, baring her navel and waist. She felt horribly exposed, and yet her skin prickled with excitement.

Damien took one step down to stand on the marble bench that a stonemason had constructed very quickly for a very high fee, which put Damien's lovely male organ more or less on Penelope's eye level.

She gazed at it in fascination. The tip was dark, the flange taut and flared, his entire length swollen as tight as could be. A bead of moisture rested in the tiny slit in the tip and she imagined his seed spilling inside her, as it had days before, when they had made love in the heat of the afternoon.

For some reason, she wanted to let his staff fill her mouth, to feel the rigid tip pressing the inside of her cheek. She wanted so much to understand what he was, even if she never understood why he fascinated her.

She ran dripping fingers lightly along his length, leaving a streak of water behind. He sucked in his breath, and she looked up at him. "I am not schooled," she murmured.

His eyes were heavy. "Do whatever you like."

Whatever she liked. Her mind filled with wicked imaginings, and she blushed.

She was happy that he'd showed her he was no stranger to wickedness, and liked wickedness in her. She remembered how he'd dipped the tip of his tongue between her buttocks, so briefly, and yet the feeling had sent her to heights she'd never imagined.

He would not be a conventional lover, and he would not expect her to be. Perhaps he did not know how to be. If the whispers she'd heard from the ladies at the fete, about Nvengarians and their lovemaking practices, were true, Damien would not expect propriety in their bedroom. Or their bathroom. She could be as daring as she wanted.

Her heart beating in strange, quick beats, she traced the flange of his arousal with one finger, then she leaned forward and kissed the tip.

"Taste me," he whispered, his voice husky. He touched her cheek, his fingers warm.

She wanted to, by all means. Quickly, before she could sway herself from it, she grasped him lightly with her fingers and pulled him gently into her mouth.

Chapter Seventeen

Heaven existed after all. It existed in the form of this exquisite woman taking him and teasing him with her hesitant, inexperienced tongue.

He let his head drop back, his eyes closing, hands curling to fists. *Love, love, I treasure you more than kingdoms.*

Her tongue moved, rubbing all over the sensitive place under his tip. He made himself hold still and let her play, even though he wanted to have her, have her. This was her first time; she did not need him to press into her mouth, much as he longed to.

Sweet woman, she opened her mouth wider and inched her lips down his length. His hand moved to her hair, curling in the silken strands, loosening the bindings that held it in its knot.

Damien knew the touch of women. He knew what they liked and what they wanted from him, and it varied little from country to country. Easy to remain in control of himself with a woman who knew exactly where and how long to stroke, how to press her fingers behind his scrotum to both arouse him and keep him from finishing too soon, how to know where he was least and most sensitive.

Penelope knew nothing. Her questing fingers brushed the stretched skin at the base of him, the tight hotness of his balls, the sensitive length of the underside of his shaft. Her tongue moved around the tip, exploring it, dipping behind the flange and back over the top. The occasional scrape of her sharp teeth was incredibly erotic.

He felt his seed start to build, wanting to spring out and flow into her mouth. Or, better, between the exquisite softness of her breasts.

Control, control. *The charming Prince Damien is ever in control.*

His body was not listening. It wanted the beautiful woman whose fingers and mouth quested, curious, his blushing bride learning what it was to be with a man. This daring woman he'd enticed into sin was catching on to what sin was very quickly.

"Penelope," he gasped, his voice hoarse. "Stop."

He spoke in Nvengarian, because he'd descended to a basic level where he could not think over words and what they meant. "Stop."

She drew back, removing the glorious touch of her lips, and turned pink. "I am sorry," she said in halting Nvengarian. "I do not know to make—pleasure to you."

The garbled grammar and her oh-so-sweet accent snapped the last of his control. He dropped from the marble seat, sending a wave of displaced water over the edges of the bath and down the steps to soak his dressing gown. He lifted her, the water giving her buoyancy, parting her legs so that her opening was pressed directly against his erection.

"Wrap your legs around me," he said.

Their hips were underwater. Holding her firmly, he guided her legs around his hips, then reached between them and opened her wide enough to slide his thick arousal inside. He took his fingers out of the way, clasped her buttocks, and pushed all the way in.

Her eyes widened. Water was not the best of lubricants; it dried delicate skin, and he had the sudden insane wish to be in a vat of scented oil with her. They'd slide together without friction, and he'd be in her tight and hard with no impediment. The lovemaking would be slippery and wild and they'd no doubt drown for their pains.

"Damien." Her chest pressed tight against his, droplets trapped between them, the tips of her breasts pebbling against his skin.

Inside her, God, tight and warm and pulling him into her. He was surrounded with her, skin and breath and scent. She pressed her cheek to his and wrapped her arms around his back, holding on.

He said breathlessly, "You are only allowed to speak Nvengarian when we make love."

She looked at him, perplexed. "I must have more lessons," she answered in that language.

He pressed deep inside her, fingers digging into the soft mounds of her buttocks. "Yes. Many, many lessons."

"You are . . ." She fumbled for the phrase. "You fill me."

He made a raw noise, unable to think anymore. He turned with her, setting her back against the lip of the bath. Her legs wound firmly about his hips, small feet pressed into his thighs. He wanted to stay inside her forever, to let this moment go on and on and on. But his body had other ideas.

Prince Damien's legendary control vanished. He kissed and bit her and thrust his tongue into her mouth, impatiently tasting, digging hard into mouth and between hips at the same time. The noises that came from his throat were animallike, and he could not stop them. Perhaps Nvengarians and logosh weren't so far removed from each other.

She made no noises at all, only silently rocked under him, her frantic fingers in his back letting him know that she felt the madness too.

"Ah, damn," he shouted as the first spurt of his seed shot into her. He clenched his muscles, trying to stop it, trying to stay locked with her longer. But his hips rocked in uncontrolled rhythm, his body doing what it was meant to do, pushing his seed from himself into her.

Blood roared in his ears, dimming the sounds of the sloshing water, her needy cries, his own hoarse moans. *Want you, want you, love you, love, love, love.* The words marked his thrusts. He wasn't certain if they came from his mouth or only whirled in his brain. *Love. You.*

One final, savage push, and suddenly everything finished. He held her as long as he could, his breathing hollow, his legs shaking. His cock was still rigid, still needy, but the fever had dwindled the slightest bit. His face was covered in sweat, droplets of sweat and steam rolling from his skin.

One by one, he released his fingers from her buttocks, smoothing the skin he'd likely bruised. Her legs still wrapped around him, his arousal firmly inside her, as though she couldn't let go.

He raised his head to kiss her and found her face wet with tears. They tumbled from her eyes, her lashes wet, her mouth twisted with weeping.

The sight smote him. "Penelope, God, did I hurt you?"

She hesitated a moment, then shook her head, moving her mouth in a little smile.

"I have never done that," he said. "I am strong, I meant to gentle it . . ."

She put her wet fingers to his lips. "You did not hurt me. Not like you mean. I am crying because you make me feel beautiful."

Tears spilled from her eyes. He kissed one away. "You are profoundly beautiful."

"I want you to think that without the influence of the prophecy."

"Scrag the prophecy. This feeling is deeper than magic."

She traced his cheek. "I never in my wildest dreams thought I could have a man like you."

He smiled. "Do not flatter me yet. You have not lived with me."

"I thought I was not the sort of woman a man could love. I broke my betrothals because I did not want to settle for someone who did not want *me*."

"I know." He regretfully slid out of her, his arousal still aching.

"And then I saw you. It might have been the magic, but I wanted you so much. I cried out for you, even though I tried to pretend to everyone, myself included, that I did not."

"Sweet love." He kissed her. "I made no secret that I wanted *you*."

"I craved you, and I want to be with you forever." She put her hands on each side of his face. "I still crave you, and I am jealous, and I *hate* those women who have been with you. I have become charged with emotion, wild with it, and I never was so before."

He trailed a lazy finger down her throat, the hot water making him languid. "Yes, you were, love. You locked it inside you, until a mad Nvengarian came to let it out."

"You have rearranged my entire life."

"I know." He kissed the line of her hair. "I know, my love."

"I fear I will make a terrible princess. I have no idea how to be a princess."

Her voice was tinged with panic. He smoothed his hand down her spine, trying to soothe her. "It does not matter. Sasha and I will guide you."

"The prophecy could make you find a girl with a silver ring, but that does not make me a good princess," she babbled. "Someone like the Russian countess or the English baroness would at least know how to give banquets and receive ambassadors. I was raised to be an English housewife."

"Penelope." He took a step back, slowly unwrapping her body from his. "The last thing I need is a woman with ideas of letting Russia get its great teeth into my little kingdom. Nor do I need an English aristocrat giving me his daughter for some kind of political gain. A simple English miss is exactly what I need, and you are the English miss I want."

"I know nothing of political intrigue."

"I know," he said fervently. "That is one of the reasons I want you."

Her eyes were a mystery. "If not for political intrigue, I would never have known you."

"That is likely so." He brushed a gentle hand across her skin. A woman did not want to hear that she was a safe bride. She wanted to hear that she was irresistible and maybe even forbidden, so that the gentleman risked much for her in the name of love.

The truth was, Damien had risked everything for her, including his life. "I need you," he said. "Not for Sasha's prophecy, not to be princess. I need you for myself." He leaned down and nuzzled her neck so he would not have to look at her while he spoke. "I need you to save my life."

"So that Alexander will not execute you?" she asked, puzzled.

"I do not mean that. I need you to keep me from becoming like my father. He was a monster; he destroyed everything he touched. He was so filled with hate and envy and anger that he could not let anyone love him." He raised his head, displaced water droplets spattering.

"Sometimes, when I am enraged, when I demand things to happen, I hear his voice in my mouth, I hear his words. From me, and I cannot believe it."

Her tone turned worried. "If you know, you can stop yourself."

"But what if I cannot? What if Alexander is right and the very worst thing that can happen to Nvengaria is to have me as prince? My father executed everyone who remotely disagreed with him. He ruled by absolute terror. He drove my mother to take her own life and executed his best friend, Alexander's father, the man who kept my father plied with drink the night I was born. He was godfather to me. And yet, the day of the execution, my father snatched the musket from one of the marksmen and fired the killing shot himself."

Her lips parted. "What had your godfather done?"

"Nothing at all, except remonstrate with him for how he treated my mother. My father, insanely jealous, accused the man of being her lover, then of plotting to assassinate him and take his place. Which was utter and absolute idiocy. He even made Alexander watch the execution, to learn what happened to a man who was not loyal. My father was a madman."

"But you are not."

"How do I know? Madness is inherited. How do I know I will not drive you to do what my mother did? Penelope, I do not know what I am."

The words ripped out of him. And why the hell was he busily telling her things that he'd never before told a mortal soul? Why was he constantly baring himself to her, prostrating himself before her and essentially saying, *Here is the wreck you have agreed to marry, God help you.*

"You are my love and my prince. That is all."

He held her, closing his eyes against the moisture in them. "No, he is here inside me like some damned ghost, like the demon your logosh turns himself into. That is why I am Prince Charming, as you call me, to hide the demon. I have been fighting him all my life."

She buried her face in his neck, her soft body and sweet scent penetrating the sharp fear. "You no longer have to fight him alone."

His arms tightened around her. Water trickled down his back as she soothed the hair at the nape of his neck. "I love you, Damien," she whispered.

It didn't reassure him, didn't make all his fears go away that she'd agreed to help him. But it would be so much easier facing them with her.

"I want to make love to you again," Damien said. "Right now."

She jerked her head up, startled. "What about the ritual?"

"Later." His arousal had sprung to life again, sorrow and fear giving way to hard need.

He turned her around and put his hands on her shoulders. "Get out of the bath and lie on the floor. Sasha left enough towels to cover a bed."

"But . . ."

He closed his hands on her skin, letting his fingers bite. "Your first lesson in becoming a princess is to obey your prince at all times and without question."

She sent him a skeptical look over her shoulder. "I am certain that is not a requirement. I will have to ask Sasha."

He let his eyes go wide in mock severity. "I am the Imperial Prince of Nvengaria."

"And I am Princess of Nvengaria, descended from one of the joint rulers. This makes me Imperial Princess, does it not? The equal of you?"

He wanted to laugh suddenly. She had spirit. "You question the will of your husband? English girls are raised to be obedient, are they not? And you just took a vow—before a vicar, no less—to obey me, did you not? Now get on the floor and make ready for me."

She turned around, smiling seductively, one hand out as though to stop him. "That is not very charming, my prince."

"I am tired of being Prince Charming. I wish to be the prince inside my wife."

She might be an innocent, she might know nothing about being a princess and a woman of the world, but she knew how to entice, whether she understood her power or not.

"My modesty, sir."

"You are naked in a bath with me," he pointed out.

"Only because of the ritual." Her smile widened. "Unless this is how all Nvengarians bathe?"

"It will be in our household. The Imperial Prince and Imperial Princess's bath chamber will be installed as soon as we reach home."

"Which we will never do if we do not complete the ritual."

He growled. The feral sound filled the room, and to his gratification, Penelope's eyes widened.

She tried to run. She made it up the step to the edge of the bath before he caught her. She stifled her squeals as he swept her up and carried her to the pile of towels that could have dried a household of ten, and laid her down.

She peered up at him under lashes lush and thick, smiling like she'd done something clever.

He could not resist. He flipped her over, earning another squeal, and slapped her backside gently once, twice, three times.

She shrieked and put her hands over her pink buttocks. "Why did you do that?"

"For disobedience, my naughty wife." He was so hard he knew he'd burst if he didn't make love to her immediately. He lowered himself to her and whispered into her ear, "Would you like me to do it again?"

She gulped, peering up at him from a very red face. "Yes," she said in a small voice.

He chuckled at the same time he wanted to groan. He was dying for her.

He got back to his knees and spanked her lightly five times more, until she was squirming and squealing, then he rolled her over, opened her legs, and took her again.

When Damien awoke, the room was pitch dark. Summer night air wafted through the open window, but it did little to cool the room still warm from the steaming bath. He and Penelope lay in a nest of towels to which they'd returned for more lovemaking after at last getting themselves through the ritual.

His hand tightened where it lay across Penelope's abdomen, but she did not wake. He recalled how she'd reached to rub the dripping sponge over his shoulders, stretching her arms overhead, her soft breasts brushing his chest as she murmured the words, "With this water, I cleanse you of past deeds, so that you may come clean to our marriage."

The English translation did not have the same weight as the Nvengarian words, but Sasha had made the words palatable for an English miss to say. He'd repeated the line in his native language as he'd slowly drawn the sponge across her shoulders and down her back. "With this washing, I clean you of any foulness of your past, making you spotless and shameless for my touch." Definitely not the same thing, but he hadn't wanted to shock Penelope.

Not that she'd been very shocked when he'd had his way with her after their bath the first time. She'd become loose and pliable, even begging for him. Her blushes when she'd snuggled into his arms and asked why she'd liked the spanking made him laugh.

They'd shared the thick, overly sweet wine, pouring each other's glass, then switching glasses several more times in a bizarre twist of the ritual that had them laughing.

"It is because the husband and wife might try to poison one another," Damien had explained. "What better way to assassinate but to send a beautiful daughter to wed a man, complete with vial of poison to pour into the wine during the betrothal rituals?"

Penelope blanched. "How awful."

"Times have not much changed, unfortunately."

"But you will put that all right."

"You have great faith in me," he remarked.

"You will." She gave him a look of confidence that dissolved into a smile. "I promise I have not put anything into your wine."

He gave her a wink. "Perhaps I have put an aphrodisiac in yours."

"I do not believe we need one," she said.

Her shy look, coupled with the brazen smile hovering about her mouth, had snapped his control a second time. He'd scooped her up, sending one of the goblets to fountain bloodred wine into the bath, carried her back to the towels and commenced another furious bout of lovemaking.

They'd taken each other to screaming climax, then drifted back down into soft, welcoming sleep, the towels draped across still-wet limbs. The candles around the bath had guttered and died, sending darkness over the room.

It took a few moments after Damien awoke again for him to realize he lay in complete darkness. The scent of Penelope filled his senses, and her firm back and buttocks nestled against his chest, his knee between her slender legs. The top of her head snuggled against his chin, her hair tickling his nose.

So this is contentment, he thought. He took a moment to

explore the unfamiliar feeling. His limbs were relaxed and limp, his mind at rest. He was not tired, yet not alert and watchful as he usually was when awake. He usually existed in two states: numbing sleep, which he only allowed himself while being guarded; and sharply awake, focused on the world around him.

He'd never lain in this quietness, happy to be exactly where he was and not wanting to be anywhere else.

It was dark, even oppressively so, because clouds obscured the moon and stars. And he did not care.

He smiled in the darkness, for the first time in his life welcoming it as a friend. It did not press him like a smothering blanket, as it had always done; it lay on him lightly, soft and kind.

He waited for the terror, for the vivid recollection of the dungeon below his father's castle, where he lay in a stupor, barely able to breathe, heavy irons weighing his wrists. He'd screamed for someone to let him out for God's sake, then lay in silent fear when no one came.

As a healthy boy, he'd soon become hungry, but he'd received no food until he'd been in the hole six days. By then, he'd been ravenous enough to simply grab the bread they tossed inside and stuff it into his mouth in gulps, like a starving dog.

Next time, he'd vowed to himself, he'd be too proud to accept it. He'd wait until they came in to try to force it on him, then he'd spring up, batter the guards, and make his escape. But his father knew all about torture. That bread was the last he got for another six days, and by that time, he was too weak to do more but cram it into his mouth again.

He'd been a child, too frightened at this change in his life to reason it out. He had simply existed down in that dungeon, careful not to soil the part of the cell where he lay to sleep, and eventually learning to make himself eat slowly so that his hunger would not return too soon.

He'd begged to be allowed to see his father, convinced that it had all been a mistake and that his father's enemies had shoved him down here. Eventually one of the guards had told him the truth, that his father had executed the men who'd wanted to raise Damien to the throne, and he would hold Damien in the dungeon until the world forgot all about him.

Damien lay next to Penelope now, memories drifting over him, but no longer shredding him.

He stroked the soft skin of her belly, wondering if their passion tonight had made her conceive. He hoped so. He'd like a little prince—or princess—to make him whole, to have a family bound by love, not wrenched apart with hatred.

The darkness soothed him, the soft breeze told him his thoughts were right. He kissed Penelope's hair again, letting himself enjoy this newfound contentment, until eventually he drifted to sleep.

Michael Tavistock settled into a chair in his bedchamber and idly opened the book Penelope had handed him the day before.

He froze when he saw, on the first page, the careless scrawl of Lady Trask, her handwriting as carefree as herself, with elongated vertical loops and fat, round o's. Simone's journal.

He quickly shut it before his eye could make sense of the words. He had no business reading her private thoughts, even if she, like many journal writers, wrote deliberately for posterity. She'd not given permission for him to read it, and he was certain that Penelope had not asked.

Read the passages I have marked, Penelope had said. *Read them before you decide to go.*

Three bookmarks made of jade satin ribbon marked

three separate instances in the book. Deciding to humor Penelope, he put his blunt finger on the first of the book-marks and opened to the page.

The most marvelous thing happened at Lady Marchmain's garden party today. Mr. Tavistock, the father of Penelope's charming little friend Meagan, showed great kindness to me. He escorted me about and brought me lemonade, and kept that horrible Lord Sweton away from me. The man is odious and fancies that I fancy him, ugh. In any case, Mr. Tavis-tock was a delight to talk to, because he would ex-plain what he meant when I did not understand, and when I said something stupid as usual, he would gloss over it and make me feel better. What *splendid* manners the man has!

To be honest, it was not simply his *manner* that caught my notice. I have always thought Mr. Tavis-tock handsome, and being able to observe him closely at the garden party only firmed my opinion. His body is *quite* muscled, and I took any excuse to lay my hand on his arm; my heavens, the man is strong.

What I would like to observe is whether he is well-muscled all over, as I suspect him to be. He is forty-five, but where other men have let themselves grow portly, his stomach is flat as can be and his buttocks, firm and tight as I have ever seen.

Alas that I am a widow with a grown daughter. I can never hope to entice such a gentleman to remove his clothing for me so that I might study his muscula-ture. Perhaps I could offer to do a watercolor of him next time I see him, for Meagan of course. This will enable me to study him quite closely, even with his clothes still on him.

The entry ended. His skin heating a little, Michael flipped to the next marked page.

Is it possible for a woman of my age to fall in love? My darling Michael—Mr. Tavistock—came for a visit, bringing Meagan to see Penelope. I am fond of Meagan, who cheers Penelope up to no end. It lightens my heart to hear them laugh.

Mr. Tavistock and I walked in the garden after supper, while the girls giggled over something at the piano, and in the shadows of the house, Michael kissed me. I believe that I have never felt so alive until that moment; my entire body positively *hummed*. He did not say outright that he wanted to go to bed with me, but a woman *knows* by the way a man touches—so *possessive*—and the gentle but intimate way he kisses.

I did not answer his silent question, but when Penelope and Meagan retired to bed, still giggling—I wonder *what* girls find so amusing these days—I opened my bedchamber door and simply waited to see if he'd come. He did so, quietly, slipping down the hall and into my room. Before I could feel shy or awkward, he closed the door and kissed me, and then—

Well, my pen hesitates to describe every detail, but needless to say, I did discover that he is indeed quite well-muscled all over his body, and his buttocks are lovely and firm and well formed. Other bits of him are also well formed if one can write such things without blush.

In the morning, I thought he would pretend it had never happened—men enjoy casual encounters, leaving poor women to break their hearts—but to my joy he smiled at me and let me know by word and deed that he thought tenderly of me and enjoyed our little secret. I cannot write the joy I feel, it buoys my entire body until I think I am seventeen again. Good gracious, how I love him!

He walked with me into the breakfast room, where our daughters waited, *still* giggling, the silly girls. Then Michael began to blush, and I realized they were giggling over *us*. I thought to scold or be haughty, but alas, I thought of how Michael had rather *groaned* for me the night before, and I fell into a fit of giggles, too. Michael laughed, never minding, bless the man.

Michael smiled at the memory of leading Simone in to breakfast the morning after they'd become lovers, believing they'd been so clever and discreet. And there his daughter had sat, laughing at the absurdity of her elders, her eyes moist. Penelope had tried to shush her, not very successfully hiding her own mirth.

Michael turned to the last entry Penelope had marked for him, which was dated two days before Damien and his Nvengarians arrived.

I love him, I love him *desperately*. I never thought I'd come to such a pass, losing my heart so! But Michael is kind, bless him, never minding my featherheadedness, always knowing what to say or do when I blunder. He's said he loved me, and oh, what exquisite bliss to be loved by such a man!

He has spoken of marriage, but hesitates because he does not want to ruin Penelope's chances. A baronet's widow, you see, is a bit higher than a plain Mrs. Tavistock, even though my wretched husband left me next to nothing on which to exist. But Michael feels his status might impede things; sweet man, he is so humble.

I do believe my daughter longs to be a spinster,

which I try to explain is foolish, because no matter how miserable the marriage, the world takes much kinder to a married lady than it ever will to an unmarried miss.

But what would marriage be to Michael? Not a misery but unending joy, I think, every day a wonder. We are lovers now, but how exquisite to be with him as a wife! I could mend his shirts, even though I'm not much good at it, and kiss him when I came in for breakfast. I could wake up every morning by his side, and stretch out beside him every night, and not be miserable at all. Oh, for such a state!

It is already a joy to be his friend and lover, and I blush to think how shamelessly I touch his body. His—what shall I call it? Perhaps *rod* will do—in any case, it is the longest thing I've ever seen, and to have it hover near me sends me into transports of joy before he even touches me.

And when he does touch me . . .

Michael stopped reading. He shut the book and remained seated, pressing his thumbs into his forehead as he lost himself in thought.

Not long after, Lady Trask opened her bedroom door, a bit waspishly, assuming her very trying butler, Mathers, had come to complain again about the Nvengarians.

Her mouth popped open when she beheld Michael, coatless, his shirt unlaced, his hair hanging across his forehead in the fetching way it did. She stilled, her heart pounding.

"Michael," she said.

He held up a worn book that looked like her journal. Panic filled her when she realized that, oh dear, it *was* her journal.

She snatched it. "Good lord, whatever are you doing with that?"

"Penelope lent it to me."

"Penelope?" she gasped, not quite understanding. "Wretched girl, what on earth did she do that for?"

"Simone." His voice held warmth and a hint of amusement. He gently guided her into the room and followed her there. Hope bloomed in her heart.

"Michael?"

He smiled, his sweet brown eyes dancing with mirth. "Simone, you wrote about my *rod?*"

Her face scalded, and she hugged the journal to her chest. "You cannot blame me, Michael. It is so very intriguing, and quite adept."

He framed her face with his hands. "You beautiful, wonderful woman."

She gasped. "You have forgiven me?"

"I love you," he said. "Marry me."

She gave a squeal of joy and threw her arms around his neck. "Yes, yes, yes!"

He kissed her, delving the depths of her mouth—he had such skill in kissing. He held her close, his arms strong and caressing, then reached behind him and turned the key in the lock.

In the early hours of the morning, Damien awoke Penelope and whispered to her that they should adjourn upstairs to her chamber. If he knew his men, the Nvengarian entourage would gather outside the bath chamber door at morning light and lead rousing cheers when he and Penelope emerged. He should spare her that mortification.

He helped her into her dressing gown, kissing her deeply when he held it closed in front of her. He was in danger of tearing it off and devouring her again, and by the way she kissed him, she was ready for it as well.

He made himself back away, take her hand, and lead her to the door. It was still dark, and they had to fumble their way across the room, Penelope smothering giggles.

They found more light in the hall, sconces kept lit all night in case members of the household were restless.

The house was quiet, which suited him, most of his rambunctious footmen finally asleep, probably with whatever maids they'd enticed to their beds this time. He and Penelope had not been unguarded, however. Two Nvengarians were stationed at the end of the short hall, blocking any route to the door of the bath chamber.

They straightened and saluted when Damien brought Penelope by them. As soon as Penelope had gone past, they smirked knowingly at Damien.

As he and Penelope reached the first landing, a lugubrious lackey who had been half asleep on a cushioned bench sprang to his feet and plucked the sleeve of Damien's dressing gown. "The Regent requests a moment of your time, sir."

Damien recognized the man who hovered about to carry messages for the Regent. "He requests a moment, at this moment?" Damien asked. "He must know it is my wedding night."

"He does, Your Imperial Highness. He knows you leave in the morning and wishes to speak to you before then."

Damien chafed, ready to tell the lackey to push the Regent and his Bath chair into the nearest pond. Penelope, blushing beside him, murmured, "Perhaps you had better see what he wants."

"Damnation," he said, his contentment falling away. He needed to keep the Regent and the rest of England on his side, but hell, did he have to in the middle of the night with Penelope, tousled and sleepy-eyed, heading for her bedchamber?

She rose on tiptoe and kissed his cheek. "I'll wait for you," she whispered, then scurried up the stairs to the passage that would take her to her bedroom.

Damien cast her a regretful glance, knowing this would be the first of many times he would have to put politics before pleasure, then gestured for the lackey to lead him to the Regent.

The Prince of Wales sat in his Bath chair in a ground-floor room that had been refurbished for him. Once a lavish salon, it had been transformed into a bedchamber and sitting room for the prince.

"Ah, Damien." The prince climbed out of the Bath chair when Damien entered, the better for Damien to see his sumptuous brocade and velvet dressing gown.

Damien made a polite bow. "Wales," he said. If the prince could not be bothered with formalities, neither would he.

The prince preened, as though pleased to be on such an intimate basis with the most fascinating royal in Europe. They were not exactly private; six footmen and a valet scuttled about the room in various duties, none of them trying very hard not to eavesdrop.

"My felicitations," the prince went on. He held out a pudgy hand.

Damien shook it. "Thank you."

He wanted the prince to get on with it, but the Regent called for brandy, and one of the lackeys broke away to fetch a cut crystal decanter and glasses.

"I did not intend to linger," Damien said.

The Regent gave him a knowing look. "She's a comely lass, eh? Of course you want to go back to it." He winked and chuckled, his chins wobbling.

Damien pasted a smile on his face, remaining polite.

"Truth is, Damien, we have much to discuss." The prince waved his hand, loaded with rings, at a nearby chair and himself sank back into his wheeled conveyance with a grunt. "I'd rather discuss it, don't you know, at Carleton House. You'll travel up with me in a few days, eh?"

"Actually, I am leaving tomorrow with the princess for Nvengaria."

The prince looked uninterested. "All you do is dash about, Damien. Hither and yon, up and down. 'Twill make you unpopular."

"I have an appointment," he said tightly. "On Midsummer's Day."

The prince waved that away. "Oodles of time, my boy. You are quite famous and you've just gotten married, and I want you at Carleton House first, before you go off wooing the crowned heads with your beautiful bride. You're mine, Damien." Steel entered the watery blue eyes turned toward him.

"Nvengaria is always grateful for the friendship of the English monarch," Damien said neutrally.

"I *am* the English monarch," he snapped, then softened his tone. "Or will be very, very soon, and not before time. You need me, or your pocket-sized kingdom will crumple into dust. Already you are beset by internal strife, are you not?"

Damien accepted the glass of brandy that the very interested footman handed him, and regarded the prince coolly. "And who has told you this?"

"Common knowledge. Common knowledge." He drank his brandy, evading the question. "Your father tore Nvengaria apart and you need more than a little princess to put it back together." He tried to look wise, but his face had always been rather round and foolish, and the expression failed.

"What precisely are you offering me?"

"Not here." The prince looked about hastily. "At Carleton House. Where we may talk freely with all my advisors." He beamed. "And I will host several grand balls to celebrate your nuptials. People will talk of the celebrations for years."

Damien caught on. The prince's advisors had told the Regent to get Damien there at all costs so they could make all kinds of binding treaties with Nvengaria.

Damien knew the Regent was right about one thing. Nvengaria was weak and divided, with Russia nibbling on one end and Austria nibbling on the other, and the Ottoman Turks watching like a vulture, waiting to pounce on the carcass. An alliance with England might keep the two powers at bay, but Damien had observed that the English often "helped" by walking into a country and taking over, even if only temporarily. He wanted to be no pawn of Englishmen.

He would have to walk a delicate balance, be every inch Prince Charming.

Inwardly, he rolled his eyes; outwardly, he smiled and said, in the thickest accent he could muster, "But of course. My bride will have pleasure at your gatherings. We look forward to this very much."

Chapter Eighteen

Late the next afternoon, Penelope rode toward St. James's Palace in the opulent coach Damien had hired. She'd traveled the distance to St. James Street from Little Marching alone in the carriage, accompanied only by Wulf, who'd promptly curled up on the seat opposite and fallen asleep, and her maid, Hilliard, an Oxfordshire woman of about thirty whom Damien had hired to look after Penelope until other servants could be arranged. Hilliard had never been to London before and was quite nervous.

Both the Regent and Sasha wanted Penelope and Damien to enter London in a landau, the top pulled back so that they could wave at the people. Damien and Petri said no, too much risk. The matter was settled by the rain that had begun to pelt in earnest at Maidenhead and showed no signs of slacking.

Damien had been a bit distant with her ever since she'd risen early this morning, alone, said her good-byes to her mother and Michael and Meagan, and entered the coach.

Meagan and Lady Trask had wept copiously, and Michael had hugged Penelope hard and said "Be well, Penny," and "Thank you." Before the coach pulled away, she saw him slide his arm around Lady Trask's waist and hold her close. That, at least, had gone well.

Hilliard craned her head to look at the approaching palace in awe. "Oh, miss—I mean madam, I'll get lost in there, surely I will. And likely the royal servants are too hoity-toity to point me right."

"We are not staying in St. James's," Penelope said, her own stomach beginning to flutter. "We are staying at Carleton House."

"What is Carleton House? I thought we were to lodge with the Prince Regent and all the royalty."

"Carleton House is the Regent's own house not far away. We'll be right at the park, where you can stroll to your heart's content. It will be quite beautiful."

She spoke reassuringly, but she far from felt it. This was Penelope's first foray into Damien's world, the world of princes and kings, palaces and royal estates. Her mouth was dry and her fingers frozen.

It was one thing to promise to be his bride and his princess while safe in her father's house in Little Marching. Now she truly had to be a princess, and she hadn't the remotest idea how to go about it.

I will be fine. Sasha will help me. He must have memorized every protocol in the world.

But Sasha, too, was used to the royal way of life. To Damien and Sasha and Petri, Penelope's corner of Little Marching had been the odd place; places like Carleton House and St. James's and Kensington Palace were common and everyday. The inhabitants would know her for a country girl, and she'd embarrass herself and Damien.

No, she was panicking. Damien would help her, he'd said so. And Egan McDonald, Damien's friend, had come along, riding lazily in a linen shirt and old kilt, nothing hoity-toity about him.

"They like the antics of the Mad Highlander at Carleton House," he'd said, winking at her as they prepared to leave. "They'll likely ask me to toss the caber in the ballroom or play the pipes, maybe dance a Scots reel. What they don't know is I think tossing logs about is boring, the pipes give me a headache, and I can't dance worth a damn."

He'd made her laugh, no doubt his intention, because her tears threatened to pour like the rain banging on the carriage roof.

When they rolled in through the ornate gates of Carleton House, Hilliard gave a groan of despair. "This is even worse, madam. I should have stayed at home, like me dad told me. 'No good comes of getting above yourself, girl,' he said, and he's right, most like."

"Most like," Penelope echoed faintly. She gazed at the opulent house that rose at the end of the drive, and knew that she'd gotten above herself with a vengeance.

Three nights later, she descended a wide flight of sweeping marble stairs on her way to the public rooms, dressed in the finest ball gown she'd ever owned.

Her transformation from plain Penelope Trask to Princess of Nvengaria had happened astonishingly fast. Because Midsummer's Day was only two and a half weeks away, Damien had insisted to the Regent that any celebrations or soirees in their honor had to be given immediately. The Regent blustered, but Damien was firm. Penelope knew time was running out for the two of them to reach Nvengaria by Midsummer's Day, though the Regent seemed obtuse about their need for urgency.

That meant Penelope needed new gowns, fast. The dressmakers summoned to Little Marching had already given her a fine wardrobe for traveling with Damien, but the three modistes and their flurry of assistants, who had flocked to Carleton House on their arrival, alarmed her.

They'd sewn 'round the clock. The modistes, at first painfully polite to each other, fell to screaming obscenities like fishwives by day two, while their assistants bowed their heads and sewed like mad.

The results of this temperamental trio were incredible. Tonight Penelope wore a gown of shimmering rust-colored satin, decorated with darker rust braid and bronze-colored lace at the hem. The décolletage skimmed her shoulders and bared more of her bosom than she cared to, but Madame Gautier, who had created the gown, assured her, "Zis is ze best for you—your shoulders zo lovely, your breasts zo creamy white. You will draw attention of every man in the room."

Penelope knew that Madame was not really French; when screeching at her rival modistes she'd lapsed into the almost unintelligible accent of Manchester. Penelope was not certain she wanted the attention of every man, or woman, in the room, but she knew it was inevitable, no matter what she wore.

The tale of her marriage to Damien had drawn the attention of the world. Every newspaper she saw bore an account of Damien's search for his bride, describing how he'd found an unspoiled English rose buried in the country of Oxfordshire, how he'd fallen on his knees and begged her to marry him.

The writers, often proclaiming that they had witnessed the events, described in luxury of detail, entirely made up, the wedding ceremony in the "rustic country chapel" of Little Marching and the elaborate betrothal ceremony in Lady Trask's ballroom. They went on for pages about Damien, Imperial Prince of Nvengaria, bringing out anecdotes of whatever charming or outrageous things he'd done in his past.

Other papers went on and on about Nvengaria itself, with descriptions of its soaring mountains, deep river valley, and castle-dotted slopes. "Picturesque," most newspapers called it. "A charming, pocket-sized, fairy-tale kingdom" another noted.

Penelope read every story about Nvengaria, knowing in the back of her mind that many were made up, but at the same time, wanting to know whatever she could. Sasha's lessons tended to be political, rather than about the people and the landscape, but the newspapers lavished attention to the fashions, castles, city squares, palaces, forests, and craggy mountains of the country.

A few did dwell on the political situation, speculating that Damien would find difficult opposition from Grand Duke Alexander and the Council of Dukes.

One article focused on Alexander himself, going on at length about how the Grand Duke's father had been executed by the old Imperial Prince and that Alexander's wife, the Grand Duchess, had recently died of a wasting disease. Now he was a grieving widower with a small son. A drawing of him, a fierce-looking man of Damien's age with a handsome Nvengarian face, broad shoulders, and sharp eyes, peered out at her from the pages of the story.

Penelope looked back at him, realizing that here was a man who would not simply bow out and let Damien walk to his throne unmolested. What would Duke Alexander make of Penelope, the simple English girl who claimed to be Princess of Nvengaria? She saw no sympathy in that gaze, only ruthlessness.

She had no chance to discuss these newspaper stories with Damien because neither of them had a moment to spend alone together. Damien had been pulled off almost immediately behind tall, gilded doors to mysterious meetings, and Penelope had been pushed and pulled by dressmakers, and given more hasty lessons in Nvengarian by Sasha.

Not to mention looking after Wulf. The boy wanted to explore every cranny of the gaudy palace, and saw no reason not to change into his demon form to climb to the lofty ceilings and examine paintings there.

"If we take him to Westminster Abbey," Egan McDonald said on one occasion when Penelope had to coax him down, while the terrified staff looked on, "mebbe he could be a gargoyle."

She thanked heaven for Egan's presence every day. While Damien wooed ministers and ambassadors, Egan remained at Penelope's elbow, escorting her through the palace and relieving tension when she was scrutinized by the Prince Regent's many guests, including the beautiful countess and baroness whom she'd overheard talking about Damien at the fete. She was not certain she could have survived the first days without Egan.

Egan even now met her on the wide landing, resplendent in crisp plaids and lawn shirt, and led her down to the ballroom for the first of the Regent's planned extravaganzas.

"Don't look so disappointed to see me, lass," Egan said, grinning. "You hurt a man's feelings."

She smiled, contrite. "I'd hoped Damien would be able to escort me tonight." She rubbed her cold fingers together, absently noting the new diamond-studded band next to her silver Nvengarian ring.

Damien had given her the diamond ring the day they'd reached London, having sent for it from Bond Street jewelers. "The first of many such things I will give you," he'd murmured as he slid it on her finger. He'd kissed her with promise, his blue eyes dark, then disappeared to meet with the Regent.

"He's being pulled this way and that, poor lad," Egan

said as Penelope slipped her hand in the crook of his arm. "Everyone wants a piece of the Imperial Prince, and he's trying to run through them quickly so you can leave for Nvengaria in time for the Midsummer festival. The Regent, now, he doesn't understand the hurry." He winked. "Why rush away when you can linger over fine wine, lavish entertainment, and beautiful women?"

"There are many beautiful women about, aren't there?" she said glumly.

Egan lifted his brows. "Now, then, Miss Princess, none of that. Damien has eyes only for you. I've never seen him look at a woman the way he looks at you. Like he wants to eat you up."

She felt herself blush. "But this is their world. The ladies here are sophisticated and know all the rules. I blunder and never realize it. I am the simple country fool who caught the prince's eye, and they wait eagerly for him to turn his eyes elsewhere."

"Which he'll never do." Egan pressed her hand. "I know Damien. He's loyal and true when he believes in someone, and he believes in you."

"And that plunges me into abject terror," she said. "What if I disappoint him? What if I cannot be the princess he needs me to be?"

"My dear, you need some Egan McDonald wisdom." He grinned. "You said they know all the rules and you don't. Well, then you make up your own rules. If they want a charming country lass; be a charming country lass, don't try to be one of them. When they look at me, they see the Mad Highlander, so the Mad Highlander I become. I can do and say what I like, and no one says the worse of me, because I'm the Mad Highlander. Do you see?"

"It is a bit easier for you," she pointed out. "You are a war hero."

"And you are the Imperial Princess of Nvengaria.

They've never met an Imperial Princess, so you can be Imperial Princess any way you like. They believe everyone from Nvengaria is half-mad anyway, which is true."

"You are saying I should be eccentric?"

"With you, lass, you be just as you are, and you'll wrap these posh ladies and gents around your little finger, just like you've done me and all the Nvengarians."

She took his arm again. "You are very flattering."

"I'm only truthful. Come on, then, let's join the queue. Think of it this way—the Regent spent a fortune on this knees-up. The food and drink should be palatable."

She laughed, knowing that he was trying to make her laugh, and let him lead her through wide halls to the crowd gathering at the top of the ballroom stairs.

When it was their turn to enter, the major domo straightened to his full height and bellowed: "Lord Egan McDonald and her Imperial Highness, Princess Penelope of Nvengaria."

All faces turned upward as Egan led Penelope down the grand stairs. She felt every gaze in the ballroom rivet to her, curious, or hostile, or excited. But her eyes were only for Damien, who had just slipped through a door on the other side of the ballroom, one that led to the Regent's chambers, where they'd presumably been meeting.

He looked every inch a Nvengarian in severe military-style suit, with his rows of medals dangling from his chest, his gold sash of office a bright slash from shoulder to waist. Gone was the casual man who'd ridden across Holden's meadow with her weeks ago, who'd kissed her in the tall grass. Gone was the man who'd tossed his clothes from his body and slid into the river to suckle her toes. In his place was the Imperial Prince, his stance straight, his face severe. Only his blue eyes glittered as he took her in, his bride, his princess, his showpiece.

She lifted her chin, knowing that diamonds sparkled

in her hair and that her gown was a masterwork. The lines about his mouth softened a little, the corners tilting upward.

The guests at the bottom of the stairs crushed forward, each wanting the privilege of being the first to meet the new princess.

"Ah, McDonald," said a gentleman lucky enough to be at the forefront. "Introduce me, there's a good chap."

He held out a pudgy, beringed hand to Penelope, bowing and grinning and taking in every inch of her apparel. He turned out to be an earl, the men with him, a baron and a general. Their wives nearly shoved themselves across the ballroom to take advantage of their husbands' "in," and Penelope faced their smiling, eager faces with a demure smile of her own.

When Egan led her away, her legs were shaking, and her smile felt stretched. "Nicely done," he murmured in her ear.

"Thank you, may I retire to the privy now?"

He chuckled. "No, lass, you're doing fine."

He led her in Damien's general direction, but so many people shoved themselves in front of them, all thrusting hands to her and demanding introduction, that it took the better part of an hour to get through them all. Not only did she have to greet them, she also had to spend a few moments conversing on all sorts of subjects—they wanted her opinion on everything from the latest fashion in riding boots to the King of France's restoration.

Penelope, who had never been asked her opinion on anything before, except by her father, answered the best she could and hoped she did not sound like a fool.

"You come from Oxfordshire," one gentleman who smelled of port remarked. "What effect do you think enclosure has had there?"

"What think you of the idea of steam engines, Your

Highness? Is it the fantasy of a madman, or the future of England?"

"Do they have plays in Nvengaria? Like our Sheridan and Shakespeare?"

"What sort of flowers did you have when you married the prince? What did your dress look like? I saw a drawing in the newspaper, but it did not resemble you in the least."

Penelope thanked heaven she'd listened for years to her mother make small talk about nothing. She was able to make replies that did not sound too insipid, and even had her own opinions about things such as enclosures and steam, thanks to her father.

By the time Egan and she made it through the crowd, she was already exhausted. They found Damien speaking at some length to a tall woman in a simple but elegant ensemble of deep blue, which offset her glossy brown hair. She was older than Penelope, probably Damien's own age of thirty, with a lovely face and chocolate-brown eyes framed with lush black lashes. She wore only a circlet of pearls on her perfect white throat, and Penelope at once felt overdressed and over-glittering.

"Ah," Egan said in a loud voice. "The lovely Anastasia. My dear, it has been too long." He made a deep bow with a flourish, his McDonald plaids whirling.

"Do I behold Egan McDonald?" the creature said, her voice dusky and low, with hints of sultriness. "I last saw you chatting up lasses in Paris, drunk as a lord."

"Or drunk as a laird," Egan said cheerfully. "You are as beautiful as ever, my darling Anastasia."

"You are as flattering as ever." Her gaze moved to Penelope, but she would not speak until introduced.

Damien, whose dark gaze had landed and lingered on Penelope's bared shoulders, said, "Penelope, may I present Anastasia Dimitri, Countess of Nvengaria. Anastasia, my wife, Her Imperial Highness, Princess Penelope."

Anastasia curtsied as the other women had, but the look she cast over Penelope was more thorough, more careful. She laid her hand on Damien's arm.

"Oh, Damien," she breathed. "Yes, she'll do."

"You are Nvengarian?" Penelope asked politely, her heart thumping.

"Austrian," Damien answered. "She married a Nvengarian count."

Anastasia's dark eyes flickered. "And I became more Nvengarian than the Nvengarians, Your Highness. If I may say so, you will make a splendid princess."

She did not remove her hand from Damien's arm. Damien did not seem to notice this. Egan did but said nothing. Anastasia continued to study Penelope, something behind her neutral expression that Penelope could not read.

Penelope's throat felt tight, and she struggled to keep the inane smile on her face. "Thank you, Countess."

"Anastasia is on our side," Damien said in a low voice.

Anastasia sent him a sharp look. "Of course, I do believe some of Alexander's reforms to be necessary. Some of them are overdue."

"I do not deny that he is an intelligent man with excellent ideas," Damien answered. "But his methods are to gut everything completely and start again, which is foolish."

"If he could be put to use heading reforms, he would be a formidable ally."

"That is, if he can take the time from attempting to murder me," Damien said.

"True, but—"

To Penelope, it sounded like the two of them had argued the point countless times. Many arguments, many conversations, when Damien had barely spoken of Alexander to Penelope.

There is no reason I should be jealous, she scolded herself.

And whyever not? said the part of her that saw the world

very clearly. The two had obviously been friends, perhaps more than that. Damien had not seen his way to mentioning her before. Had they been lovers? Were they still?

"Are we to speak of wretched politics all night?" Egan broke in. "The pair of you would bore a tortoise. This is a ball; I say we join the dancing."

The musicians were warming up in the gallery, the opulent ballroom clearing so that dancing could commence.

Anastasia squeezed Damien's arm. "They will love to see you lead your bride out in the first minuet."

"I intend to." Damien's eyes warmed, and he held out his gloved hand to Penelope. "My love?"

She put her hand into his strong one, trying to suppress the shiver that flowed through her. She had not slept with him since their wedding night, and her body craved him.

The other two noticed their attention on each other, because Egan snickered and Anastasia's smile grew wide.

Damien bent them a severe look. "Mind your own business. Egan, take the countess out."

"The minuet is a bloody silly dance," Egan said. "All that hopping and bobbing and bowing in place."

Anastasia snaked her elegant arm around Egan's. "Lead me out, McDonald. You can do a Highland sword dance for all I care, but I need people to see me enjoying myself in a frivolous fashion."

Egan looked aggrieved. "Aye, it's work, work, work for poor old Egan. Use him and discard him, he doesn't care." His grin fixed in place, he tucked her hand under his arm and strode smoothly to the forming squares.

Damien led Penelope a little way behind them, his arm bent formally at the elbow, her hand on his.

"Is she Egan's long-lost love?" she asked. She remembered Meagan stating that she believed Egan had a secret sorrow, a love unrequited. Anastasia was certainly beautiful enough for any number of men to fall in love with.

Damien looked puzzled. "What are you saying?"

"Never mind. I thought perhaps the two of them—"

"Egan and Anastasia?" He looked so astonished that Penelope wished she'd said nothing. "No, Anastasia had one love, and that was her husband."

"Was?"

He leaned close to her, his warm breath tickling her ear. "He was killed in the Peninsular War at Vitoria. He fought in an Austrian regiment, whose commander more or less abandoned his soldiers in an outcropping far from the town. The were pinned down by the French, and not one of them survived."

Penelope looked up at him, startled. "Good heavens."

"Yes. I can say no more at present."

Penelope wondered what more there could be to the story, but they walked surrounded by glittering couples heading to begin the dance, all of whom eagerly watched the prince and princess. Nothing private could be said here.

It was the last moment alone Penelope had with Damien the entire night. They opened the dancing in the head square in the place of honor, the entire ballroom applauding when they appeared. Damien kissed Penelope's hand before he released her so she could take her place, which engendered more applause.

The minuet began. Penelope had not seen Damien dance before. He moved with exquisite grace and animallike precision, his body moving in fluid time with the music. No hopping and bobbing, as Egan called it. She noted other ladies in the room turning heads to watch him, eyes sliding to Penelope in envy.

She caught sight of Egan from the corner of her eye. He bounced up and down, exaggerating the steps and hops, letting his kilt flap like a wild flag. But she saw that he, too, moved with feral grace, though he tried to hide it.

Damien noticed her watching him. "He plays the clown," he breathed as they drew close.

Penelope wanted to lean to him, wanting him with a mindlessness that alarmed her. His medals clanged softly as he bowed and straightened. His eye caught hers, the spark in them telling her he sensed her longing.

"He distracts people," she said softly in return.

His brows quirked at her perceptiveness. "He makes them forget what they want to pay attention to."

They parted then, before he could elaborate on the cryptic statement. Penelope smiled at the other gentleman in the square, to whom the dance had her turn and curtsy.

When she and her husband drew together again, her need swamped her, and she gazed hungrily at him. One wisp of his hair fell to his brow, just above his heart-stopping blue eyes.

"Damien," she murmured.

His hand tightened on hers. "I know."

The pressure of his fingers told her. He wanted her, had for all the tedious time they'd spent in the Prince Regent's overly elaborate palace.

She had a sudden vision of him closing his fingers hard over her wrists and dragging her through the crowd, out the ballroom doors, and up the many staircases to his high-ceilinged chamber and his huge curtained bed. She wanted it so much it put a sharp taste in her mouth.

His fingers slipped from hers, and he shook his head once, ever so slightly.

Disappointment cut her. She curtsied and stepped back to her place, trying to keep the hurt from her face.

This is what it is to be a princess, she thought. Not spun-sugar castles and happily ever after, but endless ceremony and parading before others when the heart longs only to be with the beloved.

She squared her shoulders. She could do it. She was made of stern stuff. She'd gone into this knowing she married Damien to save him, to fulfill his quest so his people would rally to him as prince. She loved him enough to want to save his life, even at the expense of her own happiness.

No matter that she was a drooling pool of lust. She hadn't slept with him or even kissed him in days. Would this be their life? Coming together once a fortnight for hastened greetings before being whisked off to other duties?

Well, she would not let that happen. Saving Damien and Nvengaria was important, but once that was finished, she would insist on having a marriage. Certainly they could be prince and princess during the day, but at night, when the servants were gone and the candles lit, they would be husband and wife, in all ways.

She sent Damien a determined glance. He caught it and gave her a faint lift of brows in return.

The dance ended. She curtsied to the other gentleman, then the lady. They were high-placed diplomats from Prussia, she remembered, and she said her thanks in German, what little she knew of it. The husband and wife, both white-haired and looking vastly experienced with the diplomatic life, smiled and pronounced her charming.

Damien's fingers locked about her elbow as he led her away, burning her skin through his gloves. She was very aware of his powerful body close to hers, his heat against her side. He leaned down, his breath warming her ear. "Not long, love."

She looked quickly up at him, hoping to catch the desire in his eyes, but some other diplomat was already sliding to them. Damien pasted a neutral smile on his lips and turned away to greet him.

Chapter Nineteen

Penelope did not dance with Damien again the rest of the night. She became separated from him quickly, but she was never alone.

The Regent himself claimed her attention and introduced her to ambassadors and diplomats, dukes and generals, and other fine people at his ball. He showed her off like a proud papa, and started putting out the story that he'd been instrumental in Penelope and Prince Charming coming together. Most people knew of the Regent's propensity to exaggerate, and ignored him.

Penelope danced with dukes and foreign counts, ambassadors and emissaries. Each of her partners passed her to the next in a smooth exchange, and she was led into the supper room by a man called the Duke of St. Clair, who was young, handsome, and charming in his own way. He did something high-placed in the Admiralty, she gathered, though he was no naval man.

She caught sight of Damien escorting a middle-aged

duchess to a place somewhere down the long table, turning to charm her. Penelope could always tell when he slid into the role of Prince Charming. His smile became secretive, his movements more foreign, as though he struggled with the customs of the country and was making the best of it. His accent would become more pronounced, and he'd smile apologetically for his blunders while the woman he charmed melted under his serene blue gaze.

Penelope sent him an ironic smile when he caught her gaze on him. He used her attention to point her out to the duchess, smiling an almost bashful smile that caused the duchess to tap him with her fan and give him a "naughty boy" look.

Penelope restrained herself from rolling her eyes, and Damien gave her a surreptitious wink.

After supper, the dancing began again and became interminable. Penelope lost track of all the people she'd met and their names and faces, though of course, they all expected her to remember *them*. Egan, thank heavens, saved her more than once, rudely claiming a dance with her, rushing her off to the floor like a jealous suitor.

When she tried to thank him for the reprieve, he merely bowed and said, "At your service, Princess."

It was Egan who led her out of the ballroom at last, when the crowd began to grow restless. Egan told her that they'd stay until the last trump unless she left first.

She had to go around the entire ballroom and say her good nights. She did not see Damien at all and wondered where he was, but no one else seemed to miss him.

Her feet aching, her face almost numb from smiling, she let Egan lead her out the doors, up the stairs, and through another door into the private halls and stairways of the palace.

They reached a deserted staircase, a silent sweep of

marble that led to the opulent private chambers. Penelope collapsed to a step with a heartfelt sigh. "Is it all over?"

Egan laughed as he plopped to the step next to her and leaned back on his elbows. He stretched out his legs, his kilt spilling over brawny thighs. "Must have drunk a vat of champagne tonight. My head's spinning 'round and 'round. What is that woman doing up there?"

Penelope craned her head to look at the fat goddesses parading across the ceiling far above them. Most of them were overly plump and quite naked, and looked a bit silly.

She turned to make a quip to Egan and was startled to see his cheeks wet. She sat up. "Are you all right?"

"Aye," he said, not moving. "I was remembering looking at paintings like these with a lass once, and what she said about them. She had a sharp wit, she did. I fell in love with her that day, I think."

His eyes held vast sadness. Penelope put her hand on his shoulder. "And you lost her?" she asked.

He stared at her blankly, then blinked, as though he'd not meant to say the words out loud. He made a brushing-aside gesture. "Don't listen to me, Princess. I'm bloody drroonk."

"Do not begin the Scottish burr with me, Egan. Tell me about this woman."

He made a face. "'Tis nothing, lass. She married another. I'm man enough to get over it."

Penelope gave him a skeptical look. Egan scrubbed his face with a sinewy, callused hand. "All right, she was a wee lass called Zarabeth. She saved my life; I fell in love with her. And if I weren't so bloody stupid, I'd have snatched her up, instead of wandering the world drowning myself in malt whiskey. She made me promise to give it up. I didn't. We quarreled. I left. That was years ago, and now she's married some duke. End of story."

He said the words in a hard voice, as though it was something he never thought about anymore.

Penelope knew better. "I am sorry."

He pointed a thick finger at her. "Don't you dare tell a soul. I don't want to read stories in the newspaper about the Mad Highlander and his broken heart."

"I'd never betray a confidence, Egan."

The finger wavered. "Sorry, Princess, I didn't mean to doubt you." He put his hand to his head. "Och, teach me to drink champagne. Damn bubbly froth with no body. Nvengarian whiskey, now that stuff will give you balls of brass."

Penelope laughed. Egan glanced at her as though he'd forgotten who he was speaking to. "Ignore my manners. I'm only the Mad Highlander."

She opened her mouth to tell him she liked him the way he was, but she saw Damien below, walking swiftly through the open and deserted hall. Anastasia was by his side, her arm locked through his, the train of her skirt a silken ripple on the marble.

Penelope rose, ready to go down to them. At that moment, Damien turned and pressed Anastasia against the wall, putting his large body over hers.

Penelope heard nothing over the rushing in her ears, could see nothing but her husband leaning close to Anastasia, resting his weight on his arm above her head, her white hands pressing back into the marble wall.

Two lackeys in the Regent's livery clattered past the couple below, thankfully not looking up to spy Penelope, rigid and openmouthed on the stairs. The lackeys skirted Damien and Anastasia, pretending not to see them, and hurried through another door on whatever errand they pursued.

Damien took a step back from Anastasia, but she remained against the wall, looking up at him with her sculpted face.

Penelope became aware of Egan's fingers heavy on her elbow, his voice in her ear devoid of its Scots accent and champagne-drenched slur. "It's not what it looks like, lass."

Her cold fingers closed on her skirts. She wanted to run, to flee the palace, flee London, run all the way back to the safety of Oxfordshire. Her throat felt tight, her legs weak.

"What is it, then?" she asked stiffly.

"Damien will have to tell you that. An open stairwell is no place for it."

He made her proceed with him up the stairs. Penelope turned her head to stare down at Damien, who'd leaned toward Anastasia again.

The catty part of her wanted to race down the stairs, yank Damien away, and tell the fair Anastasia to stay away from her husband. *Like a fishwife,* she thought, cringing. *Perhaps I'd strike her, too, maybe rake my claws across her face.*

Then she'd die of mortification. A lady never twitted her husband about his mistresses. She looked the other way and pretended they did not exist. That was the only way husband and wife could live in harmony.

Gentlemen took mistresses. It was the way of things. Her father never had because he'd had no use for women at all, but he'd never had much use for his wife, either. However, she knew good and well that most gentlemen of the *ton* gave their wives one house and tucked ladybirds into another.

She bit her lip and turned away, hoping Egan was right about it not being what it looked like, and then hoping she was not being too dreadfully naive.

Damien shed his tight coat like an unwanted skin, and Petri caught it in waiting hands. "Thank God that pantomime is over," he said.

Damien was used to being an object of fascination at

European courts, but tonight, he'd been fawned over and followed and teased and bantered with like never before. The elusive, charming bachelor Prince Damien had caught himself a beautiful bride.

"But you ought to have seen her, Petri," he said as he unbuttoned his waistcoat. "She makes an astonishing princess. She knows how to talk to people, how to say what they want to hear, how to be charming and pretty and yet not so pretty and charming that people envy her. They *like* her."

Petri gave him a grin as he folded away the Imperial Prince's sash. "I'm sure she was a paragon, sir."

"This was thrust upon her before she had time to prepare, and she rose to the occasion. I thought we'd go straight to Nvengaria, where she'd have training and polishing before we ventured to entertain crowned heads. She is amazing."

"A true princess, sir."

"Cease your laughter, Petri. A man can be proud of his wife and still be a man."

"Perhaps you should tell her this yourself, sir."

Damien shot him a glance as Petri pulled off his silk waistcoat. "I intend to. And so much more than that."

Petri chuckled. "I like you being in love, sir. It makes you—exuberant."

"It maddens me. I want to snatch her away and spend a week in bed with her, but I have to woo the Regent and fight Alexander, instead. I want her in the sheets, with you occasionally pushing food under the door to us when we get hungry."

"Happy to oblige, sir."

Damien began unwinding his neckcloth, relieved to rid himself of the strangling folds. At the same time, someone tapped on the door, and Petri strolled to answer it.

A lackey announced, "The Princess Penelope," and Penelope followed him in, agitation in every step.

She still wore her ball gown, cut to reveal her lovely shoulders, long neck, and beautiful breasts. The skirt brushed her hips and legs, reminding him of what they looked like bare.

Her face was flushed, her eyes sparkling, gold and green, like amber and jade. Diamonds flashed in her hair, a fine net of them draped over a simple braid coiled on the crown of her head. He'd noted other ladies gazing over her coiffure with interest and predicted that "the Penelope" would soon become all the rage.

She was the most beautiful thing he'd ever seen. He slid his cravat from his neck and held the slithering linen folds to his manservant. "Petri," he said.

Petri knew exactly what he meant. He caught the neck-cloth before it dropped, took up the coat and sash, and discreetly faded into the next room.

Damien loosened the tapes that held his shirt closed, while he indulged himself in gazing at her. "Penelope, love," he said, savoring the words. "What is the matter?"

She opened and closed her hands, took a step forward, then halted, as though not trusting herself to go too near him.

"I want you to teach me, Damien," she said, her voice breathless. "I want you to teach me to do everything a Nvengarian woman would."

He stilled, his body tightening. "Are you certain?"

"Yes."

"Be certain," he repeated. "I do not want to hurt you, or shock you, or frighten you."

She lifted her chin. "If Lady Anastasia of Austria can weather a Nvengarian marriage, then I can. I am of hearty English stock. I want you to have me do—whatever you would ask Lady Anastasia to do."

He grinned suddenly. "Spy on the Austrians?"

She stopped, lips parting. "Spy?"

He drifted toward the huge, much-draperied bed that the Regent had assigned him and leaned against a post, hoping Penelope would take the hint and follow. "Anastasia is better than any intelligence officer you will ever meet. She keeps me informed, in detail, of what Prince Metternich is up to. He likes to cast his eye on Nvengaria, and I do not wish him to. He adores Anastasia, and tells her everything. He believes he keeps *her* spying on me."

"And is she? Spying on you, I mean?"

She began to walk toward the bed, to his delight. "Anastasia blames the Austrian army for her husband's death," he said. "The Nvengarian contingent volunteered to follow them against Napoleon when Metternich entered the war. We little wanted him marching his forces in our direction. Only our mountains had stopped him from flushing us out, but that would not last forever. The Austrians had no compunction about using Nvengarians to decoy the French forces, were not interested in those men's lives. Anastasia has never forgiven the generals or the entire Hapsburg empire. She will do anything to work to Austria's detriment."

"Oh." She looked down, some of her bravado fading. "Egan told me you had her working for you. I assume that you embraced her in the hall for the benefit of the servants who walked by."

So she had seen that. He'd thought her safely upstairs where his actions would not hurt her. Damn Egan McDonald for not whisking her out of sight.

"You assume correctly." When he had leaned against the wall, pressing Anastasia against it, she had kept up a snarling diatribe under her breath about the Regent, his servants, his house. The Austrian ambassador was trying to interest the Regent in a bite of Nvengaria, although the Regent exuded confidence that Damien would let him have more in return for a stand against such a thing. Anastasia promised to bring Damien more exact intelligence before he left for home.

"You were lovers?" Penelope asked. Then she looked horrified and pressed her hand to her mouth.

Damien wanted to smile. The small spurt of possessiveness pleased him. It meant she wanted him and was not simply marrying him to save his life.

"Damien, I am sorry," she breathed. "I do not know why I asked that. It is none of my business."

He held out his hand, inviting her to step into the circle of his arm. "Come here, Penelope."

Looking embarrassed, she glided across the room until she came to rest beside him. He slid his arm around her waist, cupping the curve between breasts and hips.

"It is your business, and I wish you to know," he said. "I was her lover, but very briefly, years ago. When Anastasia's husband was killed, she came to me. I was in France—Nvengaria was not officially at war with France, and I was in exile. I enjoyed staying at Napoleon's court and watching what the bumptious little man and his hoi-polloi family got up to. The English enjoyed my secret reports as well." He smiled, remembering the vast pleasure he'd gotten by playing spy. Frivolous Prince Damien had never been suspected of sending secrets to King George's generals.

"Anastasia was grieving. I have never seen a woman so devastated by grief. She was ready to destroy all of France for killing her husband and all of Austria for causing it to happen. She loved Dimitri more than her own life." His voice softened. "I tried to comfort her, but she wanted Dimitri, not me. She had so much passion and so much rage, so I told her to channel this rage into working for me and Nvengaria, to keep the huge empires and kingdoms from using us. She accepted and began at once." He paused. "She does not simply report to me, she talks to Alexander as well, knowing he is a formidable power in Nvengaria. I think she does not care who rules, me or Alexander; she cares only for punishing Austria and keeping Nvengaria far from its reach."

Penelope looked up at him. "She does care for you, very much."

"She is grateful to me," he corrected her. He kissed her hair, diamonds scraping his lips. "She would have gone mad if I hadn't recruited her, and she knows it."

"It was kind of you."

"Partly kind. Partly ruthless, because I saw what a good tool she could be."

She kissed the line of his jaw. "You are not a monster, Damien, no matter what you try to tell me."

He closed his other arm around her, basking in her scent and her softness.

"Now that I have told you the story," he asked, "do you still want me to show you what Nvengarians enjoy in bed?"

She looked at him from under her lashes, her cheeks flushed. "Yes."

He felt a tightening in his groin. "I am pleased you say that."

"I do want to know." She lifted her chin, though her eyes were wary. "I hardly want you to run off to another Nvengarian woman because you believe me too hesitant."

He traced his fingers along her cheek, turning her face to him. "Ah, Penelope. What I have to teach you will take many years to learn. I am patient enough to spend every day teaching you, if need be."

Her flush deepened. "Where I come from, a man does not ask his wife for carnal things; he slakes his need on a mistress."

Damien felt a sting of disgust for English husbands. "Not, it pleases me, where I come from."

He touched his mouth to Penelope's upper lip. She hungrily leaned into the kiss, but he pulled away. She sent him a look of frustrated need.

"We'll do this slowly," he said. "But do not worry. I will teach you everything."

"Including . . ." She broke off and bit her lip. "The little whips?"

He stared at her, his already hard arousal springing to full length. "Little whips?"

Her face was crimson. "Yes, she—I heard that you liked—" Her voice lowered to a near whisper. "I am willing to try."

"God in heaven." Damien drew a long breath, trying to still the vision of a naked Penelope, tethered facedown to his bed, writhing in pleasure while he stretched next to her and tapped her buttocks with a strip of leather. His muscles were tight, sweat beading on his brow. "Is that what you want? I do not have such a thing with me, but I can arrange . . ."

"I do not know what I want." She touched the opening of his shirt. "I want you."

"Penelope, you play with fire."

The look she slanted him told him she did not care.

"Hell." He stood up and took her hands, raising her to her feet. "Make certain, love. I do not want to frighten you."

She gazed up at him, resolute, though her fingers trembled. "I am certain."

He framed her face with his hands and kissed her, hard, then he released her, and said, "Stay there."

In the outer chamber, Petri had busied himself with the task of unpinning and shining each of the medals attached to Damien's coat. Damien hadn't earned all of them. Ten he'd inherited at his father's death, and six had been bestowed on him for the simple act of returning to

Nvengaria to become Imperial Prince. Once he brought Penelope home, his coat would likely sport so many medals he'd barely be able to wear it.

He said in Nvengarian, "No one is to come in, Petri. No one. Do you understand?"

"Perfectly, sir." Petri's eyes twinkled. "What if the house is burning down?"

Damien considered. "Only if these chambers are in any danger."

"Yes, sir."

"Good night, Petri."

"Night, sir." Petri grinned and returned to his task, taking a moment to turn the key in the lock of the outer door.

Inside the bedchamber, Penelope stood where Damien had left her, her expression both excited and wary. He moved to her and gently turned her to face away from him. "I will play lady's maid and undress you."

"Hilliard will be furious," she said, her voice shaking.

"I will make it up to her." Gently he untied the silken ribbon that kept the bodice closed, then slowly unhooked the tiny fabric clasps down its back. Her sleeves, mere wisps of silk, loosened and dropped.

He took a moment to trace the curve of her shoulder blade. Her skin was hot and slightly damp, and the flesh rose where he touched it.

I do not deserve her, he thought, as he followed his touch with his tongue. *But lord, how I want her.*

He unfastened the hooks that closed the waistband, and the entire dress loosened, letting him easily skim it down her hips and legs.

Penelope made a futile grab at it. "I should not leave it on the floor. It was so costly."

"You are Princess of Nvengaria," he said. "You may have a dozen."

"I will not win the love of your people if I am frivolous about dresses."

He pretended to bow to her wisdom. "You may have a point, my dear. Step out."

She moved her silk-clad feet outside the circle of the gown. Damien lifted the dress with reverence and laid it carefully over a long sofa on the other side of the room. He turned back. "Better?"

She faced him, clad in stockings, slippers, chemise and stays. She looked less like a regal princess and more like a dairy maid, except for the diamonds in her hair.

He gazed at her in pure hunger, loving the way she looked, enticing himself by not allowing himself to touch her.

She waited under his gaze, clearly wondering, until she asked, "Are you not going to be lady's maid any longer?"

He put his fingers to his lips, as though pondering the matter. "I have a better idea. Undress for me, Penelope. Let me watch you."

He drew forward a gaudy, straight-backed chair with a leopard-print cushion and positioned it about five feet from her. He sat down, stretched out his legs, crossing one foot over the other, and waved his hand. "Proceed."

Instead of obeying, she giggled. "You look like a sheik, waiting for his harem ladies to dance for him."

He contrived to look stern. "There is a bit of Turk in the Nvengarians as well as wild Magyar, so I suppose it is natural." He gestured again. "Undress, my harem lady."

She began to frantically tug at the hooks that held her stays closed. He held up his hand. "Slowly. Make me anticipate."

She stared a moment, as though wondering why he would want that, then she made her hand still. Slowly, she unhooked the top clasp of her stays, waited, then unhooked the next one. He watched, savoring, as her breasts loosened beneath.

She unfastened the last hook and drew the stays from

her body. She looked at them for a moment, then walked to the sofa and laid them reverently next to the dress.

He stifled his laughter as she moved back to the precise point on the carpet she'd stood before, and untied the tapes in the front of her chemise. The short-sleeved garment bared her elbows and clung to her plump breasts and hips. He blessed whoever had invented it: though meant for modesty, it revealed much.

Penelope pulled a ribbon slowly out of its knot, dangling the tie as long as she could before moving to the next one. He forced himself to keep still, not letting his smile crease his lips. She had no idea how to move like a courtesan, and her attempts were charming and quite enticing.

She ran out of ribbons to untie, and stood looking at him shyly. Then, very slowly, she dropped the chemise from her shoulders and let it slither to her feet.

His heartbeat shot skyward. Dear God, the woman was beautiful. He curled his left fist in his lap, wanting both to bear her to the ground, animallike, and to sit still and slide his gaze over her lush body.

Her breasts, a firm rise of flesh with dusky tips, rose with her breath; her slender waist tapered to sweet hips. Though her thighs probably were plumper than she liked, they deliciously framed the golden hair and the treasure within that he'd kissed and licked and loved.

Gold lace garters were tied just above her knees, and her white silk stockings smoothed over her lower legs to her silk slippers. She looked at him, her fingers curling at her sides.

She reached for the garter binding her right leg.

"No," he said swiftly. She looked up, wondering. "Leave the garters and stockings on. And your slippers."

She raised her brows in question, but stood up slowly, obeying.

He drew in a breath. "In the cupboard, on the bottom shelf, is a glass bottle. Bring it to me."

She bit her lip, as though about to protest him ordering her like a servant, then seemed to decide it was part of the game. She walked to the cupboard, Damien admiring her elegant backside all the way, and pulled open the door.

The huge gilded mirror that stood next to the wardrobe let him watch both her back and her front as she leaned down and extracted the bottle of scented oil he'd purchased in a rather exotic shop in the Strand.

She straightened and held out the bottle. "This one?"

"Yes." He rose and set a narrow table with a round top next to the chair. "Bring it," he said, sitting down again. "Be careful."

He did not think the oil could possibly mar the room's loud red and gold carpet if it spilled, but he'd hate to waste it. He'd bought it after much thought, carefully inhaling each sample the proprietor brought out to him. He'd decided on one that put him in mind of Penelope, a delicate sandalwood with the barest hint of roses. He'd paid an exorbitant price for it, the proprietor cannily gauging that Damien could afford it, but simply watching her carry the bottle to him in both hands made it worth it.

"Set it down here," he said, patting the table.

Penelope placed the bottle carefully on the table, her small breasts curving forward.

"Now," he said, unable to keep the hunger from his voice. "Come here."

She stood before him, and he touched his palm to her belly, stroking a little while he breathed her scent.

"What do you wish me to do?" she asked.

"Come to me, love." He slid his hands to her hips and tugged her forward, nudging his knees between hers. He lifted her, hands under her thighs, and pulled her down to straddle him.

Delicious, he thought, and began to kiss her.

Chapter Twenty

Penelope shivered with sensations. The hot wet of his tongue on her mouth, his strong fingers on her thighs, the cool of his rings on her flesh. Her legs were spread wide, the feel of his lawn shirt and cashmere trousers strange against her bare body.

She rubbed herself a little against the fabric, liking the friction against her sensitive skin, liking that behind the cashmere, he was desperately hard. Damien pressed his teeth into Penelope's lower lip, the scrape complementing the burn of his shirt on her breasts.

His eyes darkened as he skimmed his hands up her back, and down again to rest against her buttocks.

"Penelope, love, you make me want . . ." he trailed off into Nvengarian, muttering words in a husky voice.

She moved her hand up his tricep, firm behind the fine lawn. "What is the bottle for?"

"For my pleasure," he answered, his voice still low. "And yours."

With one hand, he pulled off the glass stopper. The mellow scent of sandalwood floated to her, laced with the rich scent of roses. He brought the bottle between them, and spilled a stream of oil onto his fingers.

Her eyes widened. "You'll get it on your shirt."

He gave her a hot look. "It will be worth the sacrifice."

He set the bottle on the table, then rubbed his hands together, his fingers growing shiny with the scented oil.

He placed his palms on Penelope's waist and began to massage her there, stroking fingers and thumbs over her sides and ribs, below her breasts. She closed her eyes, letting his touch soothe her.

More oil splashed to his hands, and he moved to her breasts. He cupped them in his palms and lavished attention on the tips, circling his slick thumbs over her aureoles. He leaned down and kissed her neck, bared by the upward sweep of her coiffure.

He slid his hands to her back, pulling her closer, and she snuggled against his warm shirt, ignoring the streaks of oil she left on it.

He roved his hands up and down, sculpting her shoulder blades and waist, kneading her neck, skimming oil down her spine. He replenished the oil and stroked it over her buttocks, circling each with his palm, drawing his hands under them and to the underside of her thighs.

He dribbled oil to his fingers, letting her see, watching her with an unreadable gaze. "When you no longer like it," he said, "you tell me to stop."

She nodded, but could not fathom why she would want him to stop. Having his gentle hands warm her skin with oil was most pleasant, even if a bit naughty. But they were married, and a husband could smooth oil onto his wife without censure.

Damien slid his hands, fingers spread, to her buttocks again. He kneaded each one, pulling her hips the slightest bit apart. He leaned forward slightly and slid one oiled finger, just barely, into the small hole between her buttocks.

She gasped aloud. Hot dark sensation flooded her body, and her skin rippled with fire. She opened her eyes wide, wondering if the sensation hurt or if it were simply unbearable pleasure.

"Penelope."

Penelope dragged her gaze to his. He watched her, eyes intent. "You tell me," he said. "You tell me whether to stop or to go on."

She swallowed, nodding. "Go on," she whispered.

"You are certain?"

"Yes." She barely heard the word.

"If I hurt you, you tell me."

"Yes."

He cupped her cheek with one hand, and with the other, slid his finger in, ever so gently, another fraction of an inch.

She cried out, letting her head drop back. "Damien, please."

"Please stop?" he asked, voice hard. "Or please go."

"Go," she said wretchedly. "More."

Very carefully, he pushed his finger farther, another inch. She cried out again, squeezing her thighs, wanting to draw him all the way in and wanting him out of her at the same time. Tears gathered in the corners of her eyes.

His other hand moved, slick with oil, down her front, to slide between her thighs. His fingers moved to the folds of her opening, teasing them, parting them.

"Damien," she cried. She moved her hips forward, wanting to drive herself onto him. She pulled at his finger behind her, and that hurt a little. She froze.

"Shh," he soothed. He played his thumb across the sensitive button above her opening, moving the sheath, circling it with his touch. The heat inside her grew unbearable. She whimpered. He played still more, moving the fingers of both hands inside her. His thumb on her nub burned and ached.

When he kissed her, she closed her lips around his tongue, suckling mindlessly, wanting to and not knowing why.

He pinched her sensitive nub with his thumb, his nail just barely scraping her, perhaps unintentionally. The sensation triggered her. She dropped her head back, tears dripping from her eyes, and screamed her climax at the overly gilded and ornate ceiling.

Damien played with her further, his hands points of wild, raw pleasure. This was what he meant when he said his people were uncivilized, they let themselves be stripped of modesty and propriety to revel in this carnal, beautiful feeling.

"Damien," she sobbed.

"Yes, love. Let it have you."

She screamed again, writhing against his hands and his chest, feeling his teeth close on the skin of her neck. She bucked and arched, wanting every bit of the pleasure inside her. She'd never imagined feelings like this existed; she wondered how she'd lived her entire life without them.

She spiraled on the sensations, having no idea what words she cried, nor how long she'd kissed him, nor that she'd bitten him until she saw the teeth marks in his neck. When at last the feeling broke, and she tumbled back to herself again, she found her face wet with tears.

Slowly and gently, Damien withdrew his hands, sliding them out as carefully as he'd slid them in.

He made love to her after that, still in the gaudy chair. "We must get as much use as we can out of the ugly thing," he said.

He rid himself of his clothes, then had her turn about.

He grasped her hips in his hands, still slippery with oil, and entered her while he sat in the chair. She arched against him, her back to his broad chest, closing her eyes to the feeling of him stiff and upright inside her.

He'd stationed the chair so the gilded mirror reflected their nude bodies locked together. Her white legs twined his strong brown ones. Her legs were open, his thick stem pressed up into her.

One of his sinewy hands rested on her white abdomen, while he slid his fingers through her wiry curls, teasing her until she felt like fire. When she came this time, he was inside her, heavy and wide, and she screamed for the joy of it.

He pumped into her, groaning wordless sounds into her ear, as she writhed on him. When he climaxed, he closed his eyes tight, pulling in a long breath and letting it out as one long "aahhhh."

Then he licked and nipped her neck and lobe and cheek, as though tasting her was the most heady thing he'd ever done.

"I love you," he whispered hoarsely as they both wound down, melding together in the chair. "I love you, sweet Penelope."

They touched and kissed one another for a long time after that, eventually using the oil again, sliding it over each other's bodies. Penelope giggled as they slithered from the chair, too slick to remain in it, and Damien's warm chuckle answered her.

On the carpet, he made love to her again, this time pinning her hands above her head and riding her in slow, long strokes.

He was still inside her when she fell asleep, exhausted, on the carpet, but awoke again to find him carrying her to the bed. He laid her in the middle of the huge mattress, then climbed beside her and arranged the bedding around them, like a warm, comfortable nest. She smiled as she drifted to sleep again, spooning against his broad body, his warmth a satisfying blanket. She'd never felt so safe.

Damien opened his eyes to find Petri standing above him, a worried look in his blue eyes. "Sir."

He spoke softly, but Damien put his finger to his lips. Penelope slept beside him under the sheets, her face relaxed, her body limp.

"I'd not wake you were it trivial," Petri said. The candle he held wavered, splashing hot wax to the coverlet.

"I know." Damien could not slide from the bed without waking Penelope, they were so twined together, so he nodded at Petri to tell him.

"Do you remember, sir, the man called Everard Felsan?"

Damien felt a qualm of disquiet. "The Prussian pugilist turned mercenary?" he asked. "The man who will do any deed, including murder, for the right amount of gold?"

"That is precisely the man, sir."

"What about him?" Damien continued, though he knew good and well what Petri was about to say.

"Young Titus came to me swearing he'd spotted Felsan in a tavern near Charing Cross."

"Young Titus likes to drink and tell dramatic tales."

Petri nodded. "I would have said the same, if Rufus and Miles hadn't rushed in not a quarter hour later with the same news." He looked grim. "Felsan is in London, in this corner of it. I'd wager even money that I know the name of the man he was sent to kill."

"Or the woman," Damien said softly, looking down at sweetly sleeping Penelope. "God damn it all, we must not let Felsan near her." He drew in a breath, his mind spinning plan after plan, until he settled on one. "All right, Petri, here is what I want you to do."

In the weak light just before dawn, Penelope followed Damien from the servants' door of Carleton House and joined a crowd walking to the markets for the morning. Carleton House employed a large staff and the Regent liked to hold lavish entertainments, so shopping for household stuffs took many hours and many hands.

Petri and Titus walked nearby, dressed as English servants. Petri wore his breeches and red coat negligently, but Titus looked aggrieved. He was proud to wear the Imperial Prince's livery, and looked upon English clothes as second class. Even so, he did not look too out of place.

The only incongruous one was Sasha. Petri had wanted to leave him behind with the rest of the entourage.

"He'll slow us down," she'd heard Petri argue as she'd hastily dressed in the next room. She'd learned enough Nvengarian now, thanks to Sasha, that she could understand most of Damien's and Petri's conversations. "He'll never pass for English, and he never shuts up about you and the princess. Not that you're not worth adoration, sir, but he puts you in danger."

"He is an old man," Damien said in a quiet but firm voice. "I will not risk that Felsan will not try to kill him if he's left behind, or somehow use him to get to me. I promised to protect him."

"Easier if you and me slip away on our own. We know how to do it. We draw Felsan after us and lose him. That way the princess and Sasha will be safe."

"No." Penelope had burst out of the dressing room, hastily hooking up the bodice of the old gown Petri had brought her. "I'll not sit here in this birdcage of a palace while an assassin chases you."

"We all go," Damien said. "Petri, you and me, Penelope and Sasha, and Titus and Egan McDonald."

"And Wulf," Penelope said.

"And Wulf, since he will not leave your side. Felsan no doubt has hired several colleagues to help him, and drawing his attention would do no good if he is targeting Penelope rather than me. We all go, we slip away, and get ourselves to Nvengaria as quickly as possible."

He spoke tightly, and Penelope knew he was worried, not only about the assassin, but about making the long journey in time. Midsummer's Day was fast approaching; Damien had hoped to be well on the way by now.

They told only a few others of the plan. Rufus and Miles were devastated to be left behind, but they brightened when Damien told them what he wanted them to do. Under the cover of darkness, a sumptuous carriage, muffled and heavily curtained, rattled from the gates of the palace and hastily turned east, heading for the Dover road.

Petri said he saw several shadows detach themselves from the surrounding streets and follow the coach. If they caught it, they'd find Rufus and Miles inside, looking innocent and drunk.

Damien did not believe the decoy would draw Felsan for long, but it would give him and Penelope time to leave the palace and begin their journey.

Penelope wore a scarf over her golden hair and a flat hat over that. A brown gown and apron like any kitchen maid's completed her costume. Damien wore the garb of a stable hand, loose shirt and coat, breeches, and scuffed boots.

He in no way looked odd in these clothes, though they were a far cry from his fine suits and Nvengarian prince's regalia. She remembered his stories of how he and Petri had worked like farm laborers for years, struggling to survive, and realized he had grown up in clothes like these. He was probably more used to them than the trappings of princes and aristocrats.

Wulf dressed like an errand boy, looking the most comfortable of the lot in his shabby clothes. He clung to Penelope's hand and stared about in wonder, rather ruining the disguise, but the people of London seemed to ignore small boys by habit.

They walked and rode in carts through Charing Cross and the Strand to the markets at Covent Garden. There, they filled baskets and sacks with food and drink, then broke from the English servants and continued quietly along the Strand toward the city, still looking like nothing more than servants running morning errands for their masters.

At the water stairs near Somerset House, Damien led them down to the Thames, where Egan waited in a small barge. He helped Penelope over the gunwale and down into the cabin that lay below the flat deck.

"I was army, not navy," he said to Damien. "And I'm already seasick. Why am in I in charge of watercraft?"

"If anyone could procure a boat for a song, it would be you," Damien replied.

Egan grinned, mollified. They pushed off from the stairs, Penelope peering from a gritty window in the bows as the bank of the Thames flowed by. She thought she saw a gray shadow at the top of the stairs, and she drew a breath to tell Damien.

"I saw him," he breathed in her ear. He laced his arms around her waist, drawing him back against her. "He's watching, but has not signaled or made to follow. Soon we will be lost in the crowd hurrying to the sea."

She leaned against him, closing her eyes. Visions of the previous night swam through her head, his warm body pressing hers to the carpet, the tickle of wool on her back, the hot stroke of his tongue on her lips.

"You will be safe," he murmured. "I promise I will keep you safe."

"But will you be safe?" she asked.

"No." He nibbled her ear. "I am the Imperial Prince of Nvengaria. I have not been safe since the day I was born, and I never will be. If I keep ahead of those trying to kill me, I think that is enough." He smiled into her skin. "Life is exciting this way. You never live one moment without appreciating it, and every joy that comes your way is that much sweeter. You learn to savor the beauty. Like you."

She turned in his arms and kissed him, then held him tight against her. Savoring, yes, she had learned to savor what he gave her.

It was there, in the dingy cabin smelling of old potatoes and the brackish mud of the Thames, that she first realized what she had pledged herself to do. She'd given up a peaceful life of spinsterhood in her mother's house, writing books of folk tales in her plain hand, for a life of tumultuous love and danger. Her days had been lonely, perhaps, but filled with sweet, simple joys, the sort that Damien longed to savor.

She would give him that, she vowed to herself. She would give him sweet simplicity, a respite from his life of fear and tension, a place he could lay his head on her bosom and sleep, free of care.

She would do this for him, she thought, as she lifted her face to his and kissed him, if it took all her resources and all her strength.

"They seem to be on water," Nedrak said. He held his scrying stone between his fingers and peered into it short-sightedly. "With sails. A ship. Hmm. The captain looks like a veritable pirate. Perhaps they have been captured."

Alexander turned from the window. The people of the city were beginning to prepare for the Midsummer festival, which would fall on the summer solstice. The festival was usually one of the most frenzied of the year, with the exception of Yule; pagan holidays were soundly embraced in Nvengaria. Things had only now died down from the fertility festivals of May Day, which always meant a fine crop of children at New Year's.

For Midsummer, there would be fireworks, flotillas on

the river, feasting and music, and this year, Prince Damien returning with his new princess, restored from the line of Prince Augustus of old.

The Council of Dukes expected Alexander to banish the entire festival, but Alexander smiled and said it could continue as planned. "The disappointment when Prince Damien fails to arrive will be more exquisite," he said smoothly.

The Council nodded, some pleased, some troubled.

"Your assassin seems to have let them get away," Nedrak said.

"No, he has not," Alexander replied. "He will hunt them until he succeeds."

"The prophecy, Your Grace, is strong. It protects him. And her."

"Nedrak."

Nedrak closed his mouth as Alexander leaned over him. "No more scrying," Alexander said. "No more magic. All your magic hasn't done a damn thing to help me. All the fanatics have only succeeded in killing themselves. It is not magic that will solve this, it is money. I hired the very best, and he will not stop until Damien is dead." He leaned closer. Nedrak's eyes were wide. "All your chanting and predicting did not save Nvengaria from near ruin. It will not put it back together. I will." Alexander struck his chest with his finger. "*I* will."

"The Council of Mages . . ."

"The Council of Mages is a pack of fools. This is a new world, Nedrak, one of steam and rifles and fast ships. There are medicines now that keep away smallpox—think of it Nedrak, no one need die of that disease again—and ways to pump clean water to keep away the cholera. Those are ten times better than all your magic, do you not think? I watched hundreds die of smallpox while the old prince refused to let my father send for the vaccine. He believed in the chanting of his mages, and when they could not help, he had them put to death. You remember that, do you not?"

Nedrak, white-faced, nodded. "Yes, Your Grace. But perhaps Prince Damien will be amenable to new ideas."

Alexander straightened, and Nedrak sagged against the table. "Perhaps he will, Nedrak," he said softly. "And perhaps not. I looked into his eyes when Misk brought him back, and I saw the monster looking out. He might be filled with visions of the new Nvengaria at first. He might let the pretty princess ease his mind at first. But it will not last. The monster will win out. I will never let that happen."

Nedrak swallowed, his Adam's apple a sharp lump in his thin throat. "But what if your assassin fails, Your Grace? What will you do then?"

Alexander actually relaxed into a smile. "It does not matter. The entire prophecy is a sham. There is no Nvengarian princess. And when the people realize that, they'll tear him to pieces."

They landed in France after a run across the Channel on a ship called the *Majesty*, owned by a pirate turned viscount. Damien seemed to be old friends with him, a man with a thick mane of golden hair who gave his name as Grayson Finley. Finley's children, a twin boy and girl of seven and a boy of five, swarmed about deck, already competent sailors.

Another "old friend," a swarthy-skinned gypsy this time, met them on the road from La Havre with horses for them all.

Once on horseback, they made good time under fair weather, angling across France toward the German states. English people took this journey as part of their grand tour, to study art and architecture across Europe, but Damien led Penelope and his people at a brisk clip, avoiding cities and fine estates in favor of middling sized towns and tawdry inns.

One night put them far from any town, and they slept in a loft over an enclosed stable yard, breathing the odor of pungent hay and the horses below them. Petri brought them all a bite of bread and warm stew from the farmer's kitchen. Then they rolled into blankets and tried to sleep.

"Just like old times, sir," Petri said as he lay down next to Damien.

"Not quite," Damien rumbled. He put his arm around Penelope and drew her back against him, covering them with one blanket. "Life is much better now." He kissed her hair and soon fell asleep.

Penelope had little opportunity to lie with Damien as his wife on the hurried journey. The few times they found themselves alone together—and sometimes Petri would stand against the outside of the door to keep everyone out—Damien took full advantage, quickly shrugging off his clothes and taking Penelope fast and hard on whatever surface presented itself.

But there was no more lazing in bed together, no games, no wickedness, only basic, quick lovemaking, and endless roads with the saddle hard under her backside. Wulf rode on the saddle in front of her, much to her horse's distress, but the boy behaved himself.

They rode out of France, through Wurttemberg and into Bavaria, ever eastward, until they reached the waters of the Danube. In a little town with narrow houses pressed together into narrow streets, they traded the horses for a small watercraft and a man to guide them.

Penelope huddled in the stern of the boat as they pushed away from the banks and drifted between high-cut hills, bright green with summer. It seemed as though there was a castle around each narrow bend of the river. They came in the forms of a squat, square tower of an ancient fortress, now in ruins; the stern, upright walls of a later castle with round battlements; or a lacy palace glittering with windows, the summer home of some sprig of

German aristocracy. They had to stop interminable times for tolls, but Damien paid them without a word.

Penelope watched the world slide by without tiring of it. She had never been out of England, and around every corner was a new sight. Wulf gazed about with the same wonder, though the men, including Titus, slept against the gunwales as though uninterested in all this splendor.

Sasha, on the other hand, kept up a running monologue on the prophecy and the importance of arriving in Nvengaria at the precise moment, until Petri threatened to gag him. They were running behind already, and the atmosphere was tense.

The mountains rose, and Penelope bathed her senses in the beautiful, craggy hills that fell to the river. It was full summer, which meant that stiller parts of the river teemed with tiny flies, determined to make a meal of everyone in the boat. They passed a few miserable nights besieged by gnats, except Wulf, who happily ate them.

"Make him stop that," Egan complained.

Damien shrugged, swatting away the swarm about his face. "He is hungry. At least they are encouraged to look elsewhere for a meal."

Egan was white to the lips. "Have pity on me. I've not had a drop of whiskey in days."

"It will be good for your soul," Damien said.

"I haven't got a soul. Not anymore." He groaned and laid his arm over his eyes.

"Is he all right?" Penelope whispered later to Damien. "He looks in a bad way."

Damien leaned close to answer. "He has taken to a bottle more since the war ended. He feels useless. 'At a loose end,' as you English say."

"Perhaps he should marry."

Damien gave a soft snort of laughter. "Not he. He is in favor of marriage, but for everyone else, not himself."

"Very likely because the woman he loves is married to

another." Penelope sighed, both feeling sorry for Egan and liking a good romantic tale.

Damien gave her a puzzled look. "The woman he loves?"

"Someone called Zarabeth. He told me at the ball the Regent gave for us, the night that . . ." She broke off, blushing. She'd behaved shamelessly, and the trouble was, she was not ashamed.

He sent her a smile full of hot promise. "When we are off this boat and in a bed . . ." He pressed his lips to her temple. "I will show you so much more than I did that night."

She shivered. "There is more?"

"Oh, yes, Princess."

They said nothing for a time. As Penelope resumed her study of the mountains and other craft on the river, she asked, "Who is this Zarabeth?"

"My cousin. She has the title of 'princess' although her family is from a distant branch. I knew Egan was fond of her, but he never professed love."

"Perhaps not to you," she said. "But he loves her."

Damien looked thoughtful, but "Hmm," was all he would say.

They didn't see any sign of Felsan or other assassins. The river journey was uneventful.

"The mark of an excellent assassin," Petri said. "He'll find us, and at just the right moment, he'll pounce."

Petri's predictions did not make for a relaxing journey. They left the boat in Vienna, where the river clogged with huge barges and ships traveling east from Bavaria and west from as far away as Russia and the Black Sea.

They stayed the night at an inn, far from the fashionable world of opera and music and the brilliant Imperial Palace. There, Lady Anastasia found them. She met them in the private parlor Damien had taken and pushed back her cloak to reveal ballroom finery and diamonds in her hair.

"I will not offer you the inferior wine," Damien said. "You journeyed quickly."

"A fast carriage, frequent changes of horses, and a haughty manner works wonders," she said in her clear voice. She spoke English with little trace of accent, and Penelope knew she'd chosen English so Penelope could follow the conversation. "I was followed all the way. Alexander is taking no chances."

"And here?" Egan broke in.

"I was not followed," she said calmly. "But word was waiting for me. Alexander has dissolved the Council of Mages."

Sasha gave an anguished cry. "He cannot do such a thing. The Council, they have been formed for eight hundred years. They study and regulate magic and work for the good of Nvengaria."

Anastasia glanced at him with her lovely brown eyes. "Alexander has called them an annoying body of old mumblers."

"The people will never stand for it," Sasha declared. "They will rise up."

"I am afraid the people rather agree with him," she said. "They jeered Nedrak as he rode away to his daughter's house in the north. The only magic they want is the prince and princess."

Damien studied her a moment, then lifted his brows. "You agree?"

She flushed. "Nvengaria needs to be modernized," she said. "Without losing itself. That is what you must do. And I will do anything to help you."

Penelope remembered that Damien had said Anastasia worked for Nvengaria, not him. She would do what was best for Nvengaria. If Anastasia thought that meant ridding the country of Damien, she realized, the woman would work to do so.

"Go back to the palace and flirt with Metternich," Damien said. "Keep him busy while I put down this coup and restore the people's faith. Alexander always knows just how far he can push them."

"Alexander is not a bad ruler," Anastasia said, "if a trifle ruthless."

"I am Imperial Prince," Damien said. His eyes held a hint of ice, and the room grew chilly. "Nvengaria belongs to me."

Anastasia hesitated a long moment. She and Damien studied one another, then her flush deepened. "I beg your pardon, Your Highness." She dropped into a curtsy.

Damien's tone remained quiet for the remainder of the conversation, then Anastasia took her leave. He spoke as usual to the rest of them after her departure, but the atmosphere remained strained.

Chapter Twenty-one

The next day they took passage in a larger craft bound for Budapest. The water teemed with barges large and small, moving upstream and down. The going was slower, because as the river broadened, the number of towns with unloading barges and boats grew.

Penelope watched Damien's impatience grow; Midsummer's Day was now a scant week or so away. Damien planned to hug the river all the way beyond Transylvania, and in the cold mood he'd lapsed into after his conversation with Anastasia, no one argued with him.

He seemed to change as they moved eastward. The carefree prince dropped away, and he became more and more foreign—to Penelope at least—as he moved into the lands of his ancestors.

In Budapest, he left them behind at an inn while he met with a contact somewhere in the city. He refused to answer questions about it when Egan admonished him for going out alone.

"This city was my school," he said bluntly to the Scotsman. "I spent three years here learning how to move from mere survival to living on my own terms. I know every street intimately and slept in not a few of them."

"Weel, we don't know that, do we, laddie?" Egan said, his brogue going broad. "We don't know whether ye be dead by an assassin's blade or merely bein' intimate with the streets."

Damien only gave him a withering look and rang for a servant to bring dinner.

That night, since they had a bed alone, Damien made love to Penelope perfunctorily but swiftly, and then gathered her close, saying nothing, simply holding her.

From Budapest, the river ran straight south until Belgrade, where it turned abruptly east again, pulled toward the Black Sea. They plunged between the Carpathian mountains and lands to the south, the cliffs rising abruptly from the water. They drifted close to a cliff that had a small Roman tablet carved in it, to mark the spot where a Roman of old had crossed the river to conquer the barbaric peoples to the north.

Penelope let her fingers scrape the stone in wonder. She'd seen Roman ruins in Bath, but here in the middle of the wilderness, the lone marker that had stood for millennia struck her as lonely and powerful, silent and sad.

Not long after that, where narrow paths took them through cool mountain passes and soaring trees, Felsan struck.

Damien had sensed it coming, but he'd wished the man had waited until they were high in the mountains, Damien's own territory. He wanted to capture Felsan, truss him up, and deliver the Prussian facedown to Alexander in the throne room of the Imperial Castle.

How the devil the man had decided what route Damien would take, he did not know. One moment, they walked through cool woods; the next, Wulf gave a sudden whimper, and they were surrounded by men with drawn pistols.

"Hell and damnation," Egan said. He drew a long knife from his belt, and he and Petri and Titus formed a tight circle around Penelope and Sasha.

The leader of the mercenaries, a huge man with close-cropped blond hair and sunburned flesh, held his pistol on Damien. "Do not kill the woman," he told his men. He spoke in blunt, hard English. "Only the prince. If the others make it necessary, kill them as well. But not the woman."

Damien wondered why the declaration in English, when his men should already know their orders. He realized that Alexander wanted both Damien and Penelope to know that he would not order Penelope's death.

He must believe I will think better of him when I see him in hell.

"I commend you on your ability to track me," he said in German.

Felsan grinned and ran his tongue across the ball of his thumb. "The Austrian woman, she screams very hard."

Damien felt something evil tighten inside him. He went rigidly silent, but Egan growled like a bear. "You're dying for that, you mother-loving bastard."

"I left her alive. He said I was not to kill any of the women."

Damien heard Wulf whimper again, then the boy suddenly pushed his way between Titus and Petri and ran off into the woods. A mercenary raised his pistol, but Felsan signaled him to stop. "No women. No children. Only princes."

He smiled, showing crooked white teeth. "Step out and take it like a man, Your Highness," he said in Nvengarian. "Do not let one of these good servants leap in front of the bullet and sacrifice himself for you."

Titus snarled, his young face red with fury. "I would die a thousand deaths for him before I let you take him."

Felsan chuckled. "Only one death would be necessary."

"Titus," Damien said clearly, "shut up. I need you to take care of the princess. Do you understand? You guard her with everything you've got."

Titus went quiet, then gave a nod.

Damien looked at Felsan. "If you want me, I will step away. That way if you miss you will not hurt them."

Felsan's grin widened. "*Was ist das?* You will not try to pay me more money to be on your side?"

"You would take my money and shoot me anyway. A mercenary who gains the reputation of not staying bought is never again employed."

"A perceptive man you are. *Also, gut,* stand there." He pointed a thick finger at a tree to Damien's left.

"May I say my good-byes to my wife?"

"Yes. If she moves from the others."

Damien glanced at Penelope. "Love," he said softly. "Come here."

Penelope was white to the lips, and her beautiful eyes held great anger. He beckoned to her, and she stepped around Petri and walked slowly to him.

God damn Felsan. Damien had finally found what filled the empty places inside him, what ended the loneliness, what let him rest in darkness without fear. He'd found Penelope after a lifetime of searching, not even knowing he was searching. And he'd had no time, so very little time, to spend with her. Felsan deserved a special place in hell.

Damien reached for her, sliding his fingers through hers, and drew her close. She searched his face as he brushed his thumb across her cheek and leaned to kiss her.

He savored her mouth and the flash of her tongue against his. He knew she thought he had a brilliant plan that would save them all and destroy Felsan. He did have a plan, but it was far from brilliant and depended on much luck. Felsan was slowing him down and had very nearly wrecked what he had set up, the stupid man. Midsummer's Day was too close, only days away; he did not have time for this.

He eased the kiss to its end, their lips clinging a final moment, and touched her sweet face again. "You do what Egan and Petri tell you to, all right? Promise me."

Her gaze roved his face again. "Damien . . ."

"Promise me."

She watched him a moment longer, then wet her lips and nodded.

"Good." He brushed his lips to hers again, then peeled her hand from his. "Go stand with them."

She swallowed, nodded again, and turned to obey. She still thought he had a brilliant plan. He hoped she would not be too disappointed.

"No," Sasha screamed.

Felsan started. Petri swung around. "Shut up," he said frantically.

"No." Sasha fell to his knees in the dirt. He was weeping, tears running down his face. "You cannot kill him. Do you know what this man has done for me? He took me with his own hands and raised me up. He remembered me, he came for me. Any other man would have let me die, forgotten, but not Damien. He let me live. He is the true prince."

Felsan's men trained weapons on him, fingers nervous on triggers. "Shut him up," Felsan snapped.

"Sasha," Damien said warningly.

"Kill me, instead. I will die in his place. I am alive only because of him."

"Fine," Felsan said in a hard voice and aimed his pistol.

An unholy shriek echoed through the woods, a cry a

man might hear in a nightmare. Before any of Felsan's mercenaries had time to react, a black streak shot through the air and struck the startled Felsan.

Snarling and hissing, clawing and biting, Wulf, once more a demon, began to tear Felsan to pieces.

Felsan's pistol discharged. Damien dove for the ground, bearing Penelope beneath him. The mercenaries shot wildly, missing Wulf entirely. Egan tackled one of them, snatching the pistol from his grip and using it to shoot a mercenary who was aiming to kill Damien.

A few more pistols discharged. Blood blossomed on Egan's arm, but this only enraged him all the more. The Mad Highlander sprang, grabbed another mercenary in his brawny grip, and squeezed hard. With a crunch of bones, the man fell to the damp earth.

Wulf looked up and around, his face and sharp teeth red with blood, his lips drawn back in a snarl. Felsan was a silent and bloody mess beneath him.

The mercenaries who were still unhurt glanced at Wulf, glanced at each other, then turned as one and fled. One was kind enough to scoop up the man whose ribs Egan had broken, carrying him, groaning, over his shoulder.

Egan straightened up, his hand pressed to the bloody arm of his shirt. "God," he said, looking at the body of Felsan. "Now I truly will be sick."

They carried Felsan's body to the river and threw him in. He'd fetch up in a town downstream, where the priest could order him to be given a proper burial.

Penelope was silent as they walked on. She said not one word, not to ask if Damien were all right, or to lend sympathy to the frightened Sasha, or to Egan whose arm had been grazed, although she did help bind it.

"You can go back," Damien told Egan. "Catch a passing boat that will take you upriver, where you can have that properly seen to."

Egan gave him a look of disgust. "Abandon you because of a wound that couldn't slow down a rabbit? Don't bleat like an old woman."

Damien smiled to himself. Egan was fine.

Wulf, on the other hand, had disappeared. He had glared at their startled faces when they tried to move to Felsan's body, then with another shriek, he ran off into the woods. They had not seen him since.

"Do not worry about him." Damien tried to comfort Penelope. "These mountains are his home. He comes from here."

Petri added, "He probably went to see his mum."

Egan glanced about darkly. "So long as he doesn't bring her back for a visit."

They walked the rest of that day and on into evening. Penelope tired before long, and when Damien put a supporting arm around her, she looked up at him with dark eyes full of shock. She needed to rest, but he did not want to spend the night in the open. Some of the mercenaries might be courageous enough to try to murder them in the night, and they might not share Felsan's scruples about not killing them all.

Near sunset, a carter driving into the next village agreed to let Penelope ride on his load of turnips. Damien lifted her, unresisting, and laid her on the rough sacks. He made Sasha ride as well, even if the man insisted he was fine. As soon as Sasha climbed onto the wagon, he fell back onto the lumpy sacks, sound asleep.

Damien carried Penelope to the town's only inn, and bade the landlord get her a bath and a soft bed. The landlord and his wife looked closely at Damien, no doubt working out in their shrewd country minds exactly who he was. The pass to Nvengaria was not far from here, and the prince was expected with his princess any day.

Fortunately, they said nothing. The landlord's wife helped Penelope bathe, and tucked her into bed.

When Damien joined her much later in the night, he thought her asleep, but as soon as he stripped and climbed beneath the coarse blankets with her, she threw her arms around his neck, sobbing.

"Shh." With expert hands, he unwove the braid of her hair and smoothed it with his fingers. "It is over, love."

He eased his hand to the small of her back, kneading and massaging, while he drew her on top of him. He roved one hand to the nape of her neck and fit her mouth over his. He explored with his tongue, not forcing her to kiss him back, probing her mouth and the moisture behind her lower lip. He slid her legs apart as he kissed her, his erection swelling and stiff, and eased her down onto him.

His mind clouded as her hips began rocking against his, making love to him even as she wept. He scratched lightly across her back, raking his hand to her hips and thighs, tracing circles as he pushed up into her. The high bed creaked, a loose leg thumping against the boards of the floor, as he drove as hard and high into her as he could.

Her hair fell over him like a curtain. He caught strands in his teeth and tugged them. Her tears dropped to his face, hot like the rain that had begun outside the window, tears on the panes to match hers.

He rocked swiftly against the bed, scrape-*thump*, scrape-*thump*, scrape-*thump*. Black spots swirled before his eyes, tiny rivulets of sweat furrowing his skin.

Still crying softly, she lay down on him. Her back was slick with sweat, and their legs and bellies sealed together from the dampness. He moved his hands to her buttocks, but before he could go any further, she came, her climax uttered in gasps and moans.

"Penelope," he heard himself cry out. He squeezed his eyes shut as his climax took him, purple flickering on the edges of his vision. His seed poured out of him in violent shots, wanting her heat, her juices flowing back hot around him.

"Love you, love you." He thrust his tongue into her mouth, wanting to be inside her any way he could. "Love you," he said, his voice hoarse.

Her tears wet his chest. His climax wound down, though he was still stiff inside her.

"It's all right," he murmured. He heard himself speaking Nvengarian, but he was too exhausted to think in another language. "It is over, sweetheart. We are still here, still together. If he had not killed Felsan, I would be dead, and I would much rather be here in this bed with you."

She raised her head, her face twisted with weeping. "I was glad Wulf killed him," she said, her voice broken. "I was happy to see the blood, because he wanted to hurt you. I wanted to do what Wulf did. I felt it inside me, that insane rage. I wanted to tear him apart for trying to hurt you. I wanted to."

She squeezed her eyes shut, her sobs uncontrollable.

"Sweetheart." He gently pulled her down on him and held her close. "It does not matter, love. You were scared—and I did not particularly want to die."

She let out more hoarse sobs. "What is wrong with me?"

"Nothing, love." He smiled into her hair. "You are a Nvengarian, that is all."

Whether what he said comforted her or she had simply worn herself out with weeping, emotion, and lovemaking, her crying eventually wound down into little hiccups, and then she drew in long breaths, as though trying to still herself.

After a long time, he eased her from his body. Limp, she collapsed onto the pillows, and he curled around her and fell into a numb, oblivious sleep.

In the morning, Penelope felt a little better. She'd washed her tearstained face and dressed again in the frock she'd worn since London. The landlord's wife brought her breakfast of bread and creamy butter, ham, and eggs, and she ate them heartily.

She saw Damien through the tiny window, leading two horses back toward the inn. Egan and Petri waited for him in the inn yard. Of Wulf, there was still no sign.

She went downstairs to meet them, ready to press on-ward toward Nvengaria. She knew that the landlord's wife suspected who they were, and that everyone in the inn must have heard her and Damien's not very silent lovemaking the night before. Indeed, the landlord's wife had sent her a knowing smile, and when Penelope blushed, the woman's eyes danced in mirth.

The horses, Damien explained when Penelope reached the yard, were for her and Sasha. The others would walk, but they still had a long way to go.

Petri hoisted Sasha into the saddle. Sasha looked ill, white-faced and red-eyed, and he clung to the horse like a drowning man to an upturned boat. Damien seemed not to notice. He lifted Penelope into her saddle, laying a warm hand on Penelope's thigh.

The landlord's wife shuffled out with a packet of cakes that she passed up to Penelope, then squeezed Penelope's hand between both of hers and kissed it. She patted Pene-lope's foot and said something in a language Penelope did not understand.

"She wishes you to go with God," Sasha said, his voice strained. "And hopes God will bless your union with your husband and your kingdom. She knows who we are."

"She is a good woman; she will say nothing," Penelope said with conviction. She smiled her thanks at the woman, who took a step back and curtsied deeply.

"We need to move on," Damien said, paying no atten-tion. He scanned the little group gathered in the yard. "Where the devil is Titus?"

Egan looked about, as though just noticing the youth

missing. "Ah, well, he found a lass last night who responded to his winks. I am thinking he's still at it."

Petri chuckled, but Damien gave him a cold stare. "Find him."

He picked up the reins of Penelope's horse and led the beast out of the yard. Sasha directed his horse to follow. Behind them, she heard Petri shouting, "Titus, lad. Hurry yourself."

Damien and Penelope had made it all the way to the end of the quiet street before Titus burst out of the inn, trying to run and fasten his breeches at the same time.

Damien bent a glare on him when he reached them, and the young man flushed as he laced his shirt. "Sorry, Your Highness."

"What did you get up to last night, Petri?" Damien asked. "You are not so well yourself."

Petri looked slightly guilty, but Egan laughed. "Getting Sasha drunk, that's what we were up to. He needed it."

Sasha moaned just then and pressed his hand to his stomach. Damien turned abruptly and led Penelope's horse onward. They left the high street and passed out of the village, following the road as it climbed into the hills. About a mile from the village, Damien stopped.

"Egan," he said. "God damn you. This is far from over—do you think Alexander will stop because Felsan is dead? Was Penelope safe when you crawled into the whiskey bottle last night?"

"Hold steady, lad. We needed it after—that. And the whiskey was piss, so I paid for it."

"You celebrated by getting Sasha drunk, and finding Titus a skirt to lift."

Egan's eyes narrowed. "Ease off, Damien. He was only getting a bit of what you were having."

Damien slammed Egan into the nearest tree, holding a firm hand against his throat. "You speak of my wife like that again, and your claymore will be sheathed in your brain."

Egan looked slightly dazed and not a little sick from the bad whiskey, but he glared fire at Damien. "Let go of me."

Damien did not move. "We are not finished. We are not home. Alexander can strike at any moment. Penelope is not to be unprotected for one second, do you understand me?"

"I understand you fine," Egan said. One lock of brown hair fell across his face. "You take your hand off me throat, and I'll let you keep your fingers."

Damien released him, but not because of the threat. His face was granite hard, the look in his eye deadly. "You take care of her, or you go."

He turned around, lifted the reins of Penelope's horse, and led it onward. Egan and Petri exchanged a look. Titus looked sheepish and guilt-stricken.

"Damien," Penelope said softly. Damien glanced back at her, but his look was far from loving. "They did not have to come. And Egan was hurt."

He looked at her for a long time. Something flickered in his eyes, but she could not read it. Abruptly, he turned away and walked onward. They did not speak of the matter again.

The next afternoon, as they neared the crest of the mountains, it began to snow.

"What the devil?" Egan muttered as the first flakes fell.

"It happens in these mountains," Petri said laconically. "Late snowstorms, even in the middle of summer. Should be light."

Sasha raised his head. He felt better today, though he still moved carefully. "This is not natural."

"Magic, you mean?" Petri scoffed. "It snows here all the time. Won't be much more than a dusting."

Penelope felt the cold bite in the air and was not so certain. She recalled a winter she'd spent as a child in Scotland, at the country home of one of her father's friends. The air had held the same crisp note, the breeze slight but not brisk, and the snow had fallen in a dense cloud for hours.

A thick blanket of snow had coated the land the next day, a playground for a young girl. But whenever she grew too cold, she could run back into the house, where her father waited, and sit by a huge fire toasting chestnuts and drinking hot, cinnamon-laced tea.

Here there was no shelter in sight. They'd spent the night at the bottom of the pass in a tiny cluster of houses that huddled around a common area for pigs and sheep. There had barely been room for them all to crowd into a loft of one of the houses, and the people had had no extra food to share. Damien had left them coin.

The village, if it could be called that, was ten hours behind them. They'd climbed steadily into the mountains, the air cooling rapidly as they went.

Despite Petri's reassurances, the snow continued. At first it melted as it touched the ground, leaving barely a damp residue. Then the flakes fell faster, dusting the leaves and undergrowth with white powder. Imperceptibly, the snow began to stick to the ground, at first thin brushes of white against the dirt, and then Damien was leaving footprints as he walked.

An hour later, the snow flowed over the top of his boots. Penelope shivered, drawing her shawl tighter about her. Her gown was linen, not wool, garb for warm summer days. She twitched her toes in her boots, trying to keep the blood flowing.

Walking beside her, Egan rubbed his fingers together, then tucked his hands under his arms. "This cold gets right up me kilt."

Penelope tried to answer, but her lips trembled too much to form the words. Egan unwrapped the plaid from his body and draped it over her shoulders.

"Not much farther," Damien said. "The top of the pass is only a few hours away at most."

But after another hour, the air was thick and white, the sun gone behind the tall mountains. The wind sprang up, and before long, the squall had grown into a full blizzard.

"We have to stop, sir," Petri shouted.

Penelope could barely see Damien at the end of the reins that guided her horse. Egan bulked to her left, and Sasha's horse was a black smudge on her right. She could not see Titus, though she knew he walked on the far side of Sasha.

"Not much longer," Damien said without turning around.

Since they'd left the river, Damien had spoken only Nvengarian, as though he could not remember English words. Even when he talked alone with Penelope, he spoke his own language, expecting her to understand.

"You ought to have married Anastasia," she'd said softly the night before. She'd stumbled over the words, trying hard to make her Nvengarian smooth. "She knows all about Nvengaria and can turn diplomats up sweet."

"But she is not the prophesied princess," Damien said, then kissed her and lay down to sleep.

Tomorrow was Midsummer's Day. They had to be in Nvengaria tomorrow, to present themselves at the palace, to show Damien's people that the prophecy worked. If they stopped now, they would arrive too late.

"Sir," Petri said again.

Damien swung on him. "We are going on," he shouted over the wind. "When we descend we will get out of this." Petri stepped back, subdued.

The wind did not slacken. The ground continued to slope up and up and up. Damien had said it would flatten out, they'd ride along a ridge, and then take a steep, switchbacked path down the other side to Ovota, the first village on that side of the Nvengarian border.

But the path remained stubbornly rising, the wind in-

creased, and darkness descended. Penelope shivered un-
controllably, despite the warmth of the horse and Egan's
plaid. She could not imagine how Egan fared in only his
shirt and kilt and boots, but she could not bring herself to
unwrap the plaids and give them back to him.

She could no longer feel her fingers. When she put her
hand up to move the hair from her face, her glove came
away smeared with blood from where snow had scoured
the skin of her eyelids.

Egan saw. "Damien, damn it, man, we must have shelter."

"Not much farther," he insisted.

He might have encouraged them on into the wind if
Sasha had not fallen from his horse and lain senseless on
the ground.

Chapter Twenty-two

Egan and Damien found a woodcutter's hut at the end of a track, deserted and cold, but the absence of wind and snow felt heavenly to Penelope. They brought the horses inside, as well, and Egan dug up an armful of leafy branches for them to nibble on. The trees, in full leaf, were as confused by the storm as the travelers.

The warmth of the horses and six human bodies packed together on the other side of the room began to thaw Penelope. Her fingers and toes burned, blood painfully squeezing through them. They huddled together, Penelope and Sasha in the middle, Damien and Petri on either side of them, then Egan and Titus on the outside.

Sasha had awoken. He slumped against Penelope, still shivering, barely able to hold the flask of brandy Egan had pressed on him.

"I am sorry, Your Highness," he whispered. "I am a weak old man."

"You are fifty-two," Damien returned. "And we are all freezing."

Penelope sensed his deep anger, not at Sasha, but at the storm and Alexander and the prophecy. He'd been forced into this journey, into the task of finding his princess and returning her to sunshine on Midsummer's Day. He was angry at the time wasted at the Regent's palace, the delay in procuring the special license, the time taken to perform the rituals, and the time needed to convince Penelope to come with him at all.

Damien had wanted to sweep in, snatch up Penelope, present her to the Nvengarians, throw out Alexander, and get on with ruling. They all had delayed him, Sasha with his fanatic adherence to ritual, she with her bleating about marriages of convenience, the Regent and various ambassadors demanding their time with the prince.

Even with hard riding, they'd never make it to the capital city of Nvengaria to stand in the palace courtyard and declare themselves Imperial Prince and Princess of Nvengaria. They'd already lost.

She whispered to him, "We can go on, Damien, the two of us. We'll ride together. I can hold on."

The wind shrieked just then, and the roof rattled like it would fly off at any second. In the darkness, Damien said grimly, "No, it would kill you."

The blizzard howled, mocking them, and they sat in silence for most of the night.

Midsummer's Day dawned with the blizzard still howling. In the cold of the hut, they unwrapped their supplies of meat and bread and shared brandy and water. They had plenty of coffee, its rich smell leaching from the packet, but no way to heat water to brew it.

Damien and Egan groomed and tended to the horses. They were not elegant beasts, but sturdy, country stock, bred for stamina in the mountains. Neither Petri nor Titus would help in these chores, because, as they had reminded Damien from the first day, they were body servants, not horse servants, and wouldn't know one end of the animal from the other.

"I know which end we want facing the wall," Egan said, chuckling.

Horses, true to their natures, had rendered the air pungent, but no one wanted to venture outside to escape.

The day wore on. There was no sunlight, only a ghostly pale light that leaked around the door and through the cracks in the one window's shutters.

Evening saw no cease in the blizzard. It raged on, pressing at the walls, threatening to peel away the roof. Sasha sat with his knees drawn to his chest, silent tears running down his face. "The prophecy is broken," he whispered. "It is too late."

As night fell on Midsummer's Day, the day that was to seal Damien and Penelope together forever, she felt the prophecy ebb. The mindless need for Damien, the constant pull to him, began to dissolve.

She rose and went to him, where he stood peering through a slit in the shutter. What the prophecy made her feel was different from what nestled in her heart—caring for this man who'd risk anything to save his kingdom. But when the prophecy left him, he'd see in her only a plain English girl foolish enough to jilt gentlemen who condescended to ask her to marry them.

Fearing it would be for the last time, she slid her arms around his waist and rested her head against his shoulder.

He turned and gathered her against him. They swayed together in silence, arms locked around one another. She knew the others watched them, felt the sympathy in their gazes as Midsummer's Day slid away, and darkness filled the room.

The storm raged for three days. Then, as suddenly as it had sprung up, the wind died, the snow turned to rain, and then the clouds parted, revealing a half-melted world, filled with black, slick mud.

During those three days, they'd eaten and rested and kept each other warm without many words. Damien had spoken little to Penelope, and the morning the weather cleared, he did not even look at her.

Sasha looked the most brokenhearted of them all. As they walked outside, Penelope stretching out her arms and breathing the clear summer air, Sasha said, "Do not go on to Nvengaria, I beg you, Your Highness."

"And leave it to Alexander's mercy?" Damien demanded. "My place is there. I will not give it up to him."

"But he will execute you."

"Not without a fight, Sasha. I do not intend to meekly surrender to him."

"Sasha has a point," Egan broke in. He shook out his plaids and swirled them around his shoulders, a proud McDonald once more. "You can go back to England—or France or Rome or wherever the fancy takes you—and live on some estate with your wife and grow old and fat and happy. I have a fine house near Inverness, a bit drafty but lovely. You're welcome to stay there as long as you like, your servants and Sasha, too. There's some damn good fishing."

Damien smiled, but the smile did not reach his eyes. "It is generous of you, but no. What you can do for me is take Penelope back to England. She does not need to remain for this, and I have dragged her about long enough."

Egan hesitated, looking as though he wanted to argue, then he nodded once, strangely subdued. "I would be honored."

"Sasha, too. He deserves some rest and good fishing."

Egan nodded. Sasha jerked his head up, his eyes going round with hurt.

Penelope cleared her throat. "One moment, Your Imperial Highness."

For the first time in days, he sent his gaze directly to her. His eyes had gone chill and blue and hard. "Something displeases you?"

"We are married. Prophecy or no, I bound myself to you with vows and you signed a license. We are also betrothed in the Nvengarian fashion, which you said was as binding as marriage. That means we are married twice over, does it not?"

"Yes," he said, his voice neutral. "I will provide for you; you have no need of worry. Both now and after I am deceased. In fact, my London solicitors have begun to pay into an account for you ten thousand guineas per annum for you to use as you wish. It is bound in a trust so that any future husband would not be able to touch it. It is for your sole use."

Penelope stopped, her prepared speech dying in her throat. "Oh."

"You are a generous man, Damien," Egan observed. "Can I marry you?"

"I do not want it," Penelope choked out.

"You do," Damien said. "It is the least I can do for you agreeing to marry me. I apologize that it has not been a marriage worthy of you."

"Please cease speaking to me as though we have only just met," Penelope said. "I am a princess of Nvengaria and your wife. I am coming with you."

He did not look pleased. "I can face Alexander and his execution squad more easily if I do not have to watch out for you. I prefer to know that you are safely on your way to England and Little Marching."

"I do not wish to be shunted aside like an inconvenient wife," Penelope said. "Nvengaria is mine as well as yours now. I want to face Alexander, too."

Sasha clasped his hands. "Well said, Your Highness. I will go with you, to laud your name."

"No, you will not," Damien snapped.

"I believe we have you outnumbered, sir," Petri broke in. Titus stepped behind him, folding his arms to show his young muscles.

Damien swept his cold gaze over them. "The danger is not simply to me. Anyone who supports me will be suspect, and even if he does not kill you, you will live out your days in a dark cell. Egan he might escort to the border with an armed guard, but even he might be reported shot trying to help me escape."

"Have more faith in me," Egan said. "They'd not succeed, laddie."

"You have provided solutions for all of us," Penelope said crisply. "But what about our child?"

Damien stared at her. "What child? If you mean Wulf, he is not . . ." He broke off, going still.

"I mean the prince. Or princess." Penelope laid her hand across her abdomen. "I am not certain which, of course."

Damien was fixed in his place. His hair moved slightly in the summery breeze, but nothing else. He might have been a statue, carved and painted to stand there in the woods at the top of the pass, marking the road to Nvengaria.

Titus, catching on, whooped, his cry of joy echoing to the treetops. He threw up his hands and started moving his feet in a complicated Nvengarian jig.

Sasha's eyes shone. "Splendid, blessed news. Offspring of the joined lines of the princes of Nvengaria. The child of the prophecy."

"Congratulations, sir, ma'am," Petri said, his grin wide.

Egan laughed loud and long. "Now that's news that's perked me up." He removed a flask from his sporran. "A toast to Prince Damien and the Princess Penelope, and the fruit of their loins." He winked.

Titus let out another whoop, and Petri joined him. The two linked arms and started running in a circle, first one way, then the other, chanting and singing.

"His name," Sasha said, rubbing his hands, looking happier than he had in days. "The name is very important. I must do much research so we get it exactly right. And the rituals for the princess's lying-in and the christening. There is much to do, much to do."

"Hell," Damien said.

The procession crested the top of the pass not an hour after leaving the woodcutter's hut. Slick mud from the snowstorm slowed them at first, but as the day heated, the ground began to dry. When they reached the other side of the ridge, the path leading downward was completely dry, as though the storm had never touched it.

"Most definitely of magical origin," Sasha said.

Penelope secretly agreed with him. The storm had been too localized, too abrupt, too strange not to have been helped along. It had lasted just long enough to ensure they'd not make it to Nvengaria in time, and had dispersed before their food and water supplies ran out. The storm had been meant to discourage, not to kill.

At the top of the hill they came out of the trees, and Damien stopped. He drew Penelope's horse abreast of him, and said quietly, "Look."

The land dropped away in abrupt green waves, the folds thousands of feet deep. Pines thinned at the crest of the ridge, then grew dense and lush down the slopes, their heady scent thickening the air. Mountains rose stark on the other side of the huge valley, gray white cliffs jutting from the green cover of forest. A hawk soared just below Penelope down the hill, wings outstretched.

Far down in the valley, she saw the brief glitter of sunlight on water; farther north, she spied the spires of a castle gleaming in the sun among a fold of high hills.

Something stirred within Penelope, something deep inside her that had slumbered, she realized since the beginning of her days. It woke now, sending glorious emotion spinning through her, joy and excitement and wonder laced with a bit of fear and awe.

She drew a long breath, realizing that she smiled. Damien, watching her, caught the look.

"I feel as though . . ." She broke off groping for words. "Oh, Damien, I feel as though I am coming home."

Damien followed her gaze across the valley to the castle. "Yes," he said quietly. "I feel that, too."

He reached up and pulled her down from her horse. His arm warm about her waist, he led her under the trees, out of sight of the others, who seemed to have made a tacit agreement not to follow.

His hot, rough kiss took her by surprise. Penelope let her hat fall to the ground unheeded, as he raked his hands through her hair and kissed her with the wildness she'd always felt inside him.

"I will never regret finding you," he said. "Never regret marrying you."

For answer, she twined her arms around his neck. He lifted her in hard arms and held her against a tree. Knowing what he wanted, and wanting it, too, she scraped her skirt up her legs, baring her skin to the cool mountain breeze.

Damien peeled open his breeches, and his heavy arousal landed against her abdomen. He lifted her, arms cushioning her against the rough bark of the tree.

There was nothing gentle about the way he took her. It was raw coupling, needy and taking. She let him have her, digging her hands into his shoulders, the cries in her throat caught in his mouth.

He came very soon, and she did as well, her body frantic with need. She still loved him, even without the prophecy to force her, only now the thought was tinged with sadness.

At the bottom of the pass, as they neared the village of Ovota, two dozen of Alexander's military men on horseback surrounded them and told them to follow to the Imperial Prince's castle.

Damien had known they'd be there. Alexander would plan to the last detail, and every plan would have contingency plans, and contingency plans for those. If spells and assassins did not work, surrounding them with armed riders just might. At least the riders were leading them in the direction Damien wanted to go.

He knew the prophecy was broken. All Sasha's rituals had done was get him married to an innocent young woman who deserved a much better husband than himself. Even if he overthrew Alexander, life as Imperial Prince would be far from peaceful. Alexander was but one danger; Damien's life would be fraught with others.

Penelope should have married some minor baron or a peaceful gentleman whose idea of excitement was an especially long walk by the river. He imagined Penelope sitting before the fire in some comfortable country home, sewing her husband's shirts, smiling at him while he described the remarkable things he'd seen during his walk.

Lovely woman. Meant to be a housewife, not an exotic princess men like Alexander sent assassins to hunt.

He'd felt the frantic madness of the prophecy recede three days ago, while he'd held her during the storm. But now that the haze had receded, he realized how foolish and selfish it had been to bind this woman to him. He'd tried to make her go back home, but she'd lifted her chin and gave him that beautiful, stubborn look, then told him she'd follow him to destruction and beyond.

And by the by, Damien, I am carrying your child. The stun of that still had not left him.

He moved to Penelope protectively. "May we keep the pace slow, gentlemen?" he asked. "My wife tires easily."

She did not—she was the most resilient woman he'd met—but he did not want a frantic horseback ride to endanger her or their child. The captain of the troop, a tall man with coarse black hair, his Imperial Army uniform crisp and perfect, nodded.

Four horses were led forward for the others. Titus, lip curled, slid his hand toward the knife at his belt, but Damien glared him to obedience. The last thing he needed was Titus to start a bloodbath. The Nvengarian Army was disciplined, but they were Nvengarians.

They rode through a countryside quiet and still. Nearer the river, lush farms opened from villages clustered near the river's banks, but no farmers tilled the fields.

The River Nvengar was wide and flat, navigable, though shallow. Flat-bottomed barges usually filled the river, coupled with everything from the rowboats of peasant boys to the overly ornate watercraft of dukes. Today, the river remained strangely empty.

"Is it a holiday?" he asked the captain. "Or a funeral?"

The captain gave him a sideways look. "His Grace the Grand Duke ordered the folk to stay in their houses while the outlawed prince was captured."

"I see," Damien answered.

The road took them along the river, which was dappled with sunlight, a pleasant and beautiful ride on a summer's day. When they neared the first village, Damien said, "Petri."

Petri knew what he wanted. He dismounted, to the distress of the horsemen surrounding him, but they relaxed when he merely opened a pack and drew out a coat. He handed it to Damien, who drew it on as Petri mounted again.

The coat was part of Damien's Imperial Prince's uniform, a little wrinkled from being folded away. Petri had polished every medal until it glistened with its own light, and brushed the epaulets until the silken threads gleamed. Damien settled his gold sash of office over his shoulder and moved it into place.

The captain raised his brows, skeptical.

"They should know which of us is the outlaw prince," Damien explained. "To avoid confusion."

The captain did not answer, only giving the order to ride on. Damien saw Penelope smile at him. She knew, and understood.

The village square held signs of a Midsummer's Day festival abandoned. Colorful ribbons littered the streets, and blue and gold banners that read "Long Live Prince Damien" lay tattered and forgotten.

The doors were closed, the streets empty, but Damien sensed the villagers in their houses, no doubt glued to the windows, watching the procession go by. Damien glanced around as though he could see them, and he bowed, acknowledging them. Penelope, the wonderful woman, did the same.

They found similar silence and disarray in the next village, and the next. As the villages grew larger, the scattered and torn decorations grew larger, too, and more elaborate. In the town nearest the capital, a platform had been built with a painting of Prince Damien hanging at the rear. Alone, it swung with the light breeze, turning on its cord.

Damien sat straighter. He sensed the restlessness here, the building of tension that would explode soon. To bring the point home, he leaned over, lifted Penelope's hand, and kissed it.

They rode on. The city in mid-valley rose at the top of a hill, crowned by a castle and a thick wall, the fortification that had defended Nvengarian princes for eight centuries. Renovations through the years had graced a more elegant facade over the old fortress walls, until the castle glittered with glass windows and balconies and fantastic battlements that grew more ridiculous with each ruler.

The city below it contained the townhouses of the elite and the aristocrats, each vying for the most elaborate home. The results put Mayfair houses to shame. Hidden courtyards, ornate gates, fantastic gardens, cascading fountains, and variegated glass were the norm. The burghers, not to be outdone, did with paint and plaster what they could not afford to do with carving and gilding and glass.

Even the peasant class, the most numerous in the town, whitewashed their houses and filled window boxes with a riot of blooms. All blended into a charming, homey mess that Damien had missed with every breath he took.

Just before they rode through the city gates, which were unmanned, Petri said, "Sir," in a slightly worried voice.

Damien glanced over his shoulder. Petri was gazing behind them, across the narrow plain they'd just traversed. The Nvengarian soldiers looked, too, and stopped their horses. Penelope looked around, lips parting.

Behind them came a mass of humanity. They must have started at the first village, picking up people from the next one, and so on, following the entourage from town to town. They surged forward, not a mindless mob, but people walking purposefully, women holding the hands of children; farmers, peasants, and burghers; barons riding on horseback beside them.

Damien felt the people waiting for them in the city, the tension wound as high as it had been in the towns.

The captain signaled his men forward, and they rode beneath the arch of the city gate to a winding, cobbled street. "Bar the gates," the captain ordered.

"Bad idea, Captain," Damien said. "Gates can be ripped down, the iron bars used for weapons."

The captain looked uneasy. He'd probably helped defend Nvengaria against Russian forays in the north, but never dealt with the madness of an uprising. He gave Damien a nod. "Leave them open."

Penelope glanced sideways at Damien. He reached for

her hand, and she placed it in his without hesitation, their horses side by side.

Except for their worn appearance and the army men imprisoning them, this could have been a parade of the prince and princess riding among their people. Damien made damn certain it looked like it.

The mass of people who flowed into the city were joined by those already there, pouring out of houses and shops and inns to walk with the quiet and increasing crowd.

The captain led Damien and his party up the tight turns of the castle road, each turn overlooking a steep drop to the city. The crowd stopped at the castle gate, far below, looking uncertain as to whether they should proceed.

With a clatter of hooves, Titus broke away from the column and raced back toward them, laughing and whooping.

"Let him go," the captain barked, as two lieutenants made to peel away and chase him. "Not yet."

Titus stopped before the crowd and sent up a cry, the ancient ululation of the Nvengarian people, used in times of war or drunken revelry—it never truly mattered which.

The noise of it was taken up here and there throughout the crowd, along with whoops and screams that rose to engulf the city. Damien, on the last bend, turned in his saddle and saluted. The crowd screamed louder, waving hands and flags of Nvengarian blue and gold, banners that had not been *all* torn down at Midsummer.

"Greet them," Damien said quietly to Penelope. "They need you."

Penelope glanced at Damien in quiet trepidation, then she drew a breath, smiled, and raised her hand in a very pretty wave.

A wall of sound hammered at them. The horses moved restlessly, ears flicking. Down below, people filled every street, a riot of color and noise and banners waving back and forth. They cheered and screamed, and when Penelope waved again, the sound pulsed forward, every throat shouting for the princess.

The captain was wise enough not to do anything to Damien and Penelope. He merely rode on, as though he and his men guided them, until they reached the elaborate arch of the castle entrance.

They rode through the ancient arched tunnel, where several enemies of the realm had met their death, and into the bright but quiet courtyard of the castle. The captain ordered his men to dismount, and the portcullis clanged closed behind them. They could hear the shouting of the crowd below, but faintly, behind thick walls.

The troop led Damien and Penelope, on foot now, into the castle proper. Damien walked close to her, their hands entwined. Sasha walked close to Damien's other side, bumping into him from time to time, his breathing ragged. Damien sensed his terror but his equal determination to see this through.

Petri walked on Penelope's other side, placing himself between her and the officer who tried to escort her. Egan hulked behind them. Titus, he knew, was still below, stirring up the crowd.

They went through ground-floor halls plain and utilitarian, then up stairs into halls more lavish. Cathedral-like ceilings soared above them, stained glass filled windows, gilded moldings glittered in the sunshine, and tapestries adorned walls alongside Dutch paintings from the sixteenth and seventeenth centuries.

The hall that led to the throne room was more elaborate still, huge black and white squares running diagonally, niches in the walls filled with man-sized marble chess pieces. Bored princes of old had ordered sweating lackeys to push the carved pieces about on the squares of the floor to entertain foreign ambassadors. Damien's father, once wanting to rid himself of a troublesome duke in the Council, made the duke play the game for his life, and was pleased when the duke lost.

Tall, gilded double doors opened into the throne room, which was a patchwork of red and blue glass windows, gleaming marble floor and walls, twisted ropes of gilding on pink marble columns, huge gold-cloth banners of the Princes of Nvengaria, more tapestries, paintings, gilded chairs set along the aisle for the lucky who made it this far, and at the far end on a marble dais, the Imperial throne of Nvengaria.

The chair itself, gold-leafed, padded in blue cushions, was uncomfortable as hell, but it looked impressive. It sat alone under a cloth-of-gold awning, and behind it hung the snarling wolf banner of the Princes of Nvengaria.

Alexander, Damien saw as they entered, had not deigned to use the throne. A simple mahogany desk with a chair that looked more comfortable reposed near the steps of the dais. The outside light sent rose and blue patterns on the white floor beneath it, but none seemed to touch the desk.

Efficiency, it said, rather than ornate foolery.

Alexander rose from behind the desk as they approached, looking very much at ease. He even bowed. "Damien."

"Alexander." He held up Penelope's hand, which was still entwined in his. "May I present my wife, Princess Penelope of Nvengaria."

Alexander's edged blue gaze flicked over her from head to foot. "Charming." He turned back to Damien and studied him with the same chilling scrutiny. "Against all odds, you have arrived." He smiled thinly. "But too late."

"You have been a worthy opponent," Damien said, suppressing his growing rage. He wanted nothing more than to throw the man through the nearest stained-glass window, and have done. The windows, however, were thick against winter storms and too well made. Likely Alexander would simply bounce off them and still be there. "What is your next move in this game?"

"Arrest you and your men." He slid his glance over the rest of them, then back to Damien again, as though he could not look away from him. "McDonald can return to his native Scotland; he has no part in this. Miss Trask, as well, may go home. I have no quarrel with her and will arrange her safe passage to England."

"Damien and I married," Penelope interrupted, her voice tight. "In an English church, so therefore, I am no longer Miss Trask. I do not know what the protocol is regarding my official title, but I know that I am Princess of Nvengaria."

Alexander turned his gaze to her, his eyes going sharp and delighted. "No," he said, his voice soft. "You are not."

Chapter Twenty-three

Penelope blinked. Alexander was smiling a smile she did not like, and the light in his eyes was knowing.

The duke was quite a handsome man, nearly as attractive as Damien. They were of an age, he and Damien, and Alexander had the same black hair and deep blue eyes, his skin slightly browner than an Englishman's. His Nvengarian blue coat with its many medals stretched tightly over a well-muscled torso, and the blue and gold sash of the Grand Duke crossed his chest from broad shoulder to firm, tapered waist.

He wore trousers tight enough for Meagan's approval, hugging muscular thighs and disappearing into high black leather boots. His hands, ungloved, sported only one ring, a ruby that matched the glittering red stone that hung from his ear.

"I am," she said, her voice growing fainter. "I did not believe it at first, but I inherited the ring, and I felt the prophecy, and I believe now."

She glanced sideways at Damien, who stood with his shoulders relaxed, his stance one of a man who has the upper hand. She knew, however, that although the mob hemmed in the gates below the castle, Alexander ruled inside, and he could easily have Damien shot and his body unceremoniously flushed out with the sewage.

"I thought you might," Alexander said. He spoke in a deep baritone, his voice almost sensuous. Women must swoon at his feet.

He beckoned her to the desk and slid out the chair. "Come and sit, Miss Trask. I have something to show you."

Damien remained where he was. When she looked to him for guidance, he gave her a barely perceptible nod.

She unclasped his hand and walked quickly to the desk, her muddy boots clicking on the floor. She knew she looked a mess in the old traveling dress with her hair coming down and bits of earth falling from her skirt, but she held her head up and met Alexander's eye without flinching.

She sat down as though he'd invited her to a supper in Grosvenor Square, and allowed him to push in the chair. He opened a drawer of the desk and removed a long scroll, looking rather like a rolled-up map, and several small silver disks.

He spread the paper across the desk, using the disks to hold each of the four corners so the page would not roll up onto itself. The paper was not a map. Spidery writing covered it, along with scrolling lines running every which way.

"You read Nvengarian?" he asked her. He spoke English perfectly, with only the faintest accent, unlike Damien who always allowed an accent through.

"A little," she said.

"It does not matter; these are mostly names." He pointed with a broad finger to the top of one column, to a single name, Augustus Adolphus Aurelius Laurent.

"This, my dear, is the first prince of Nvengaria, joint ruler with Prince Damien's ancestor."

"Yes, I know all about it. I descended from him, through his daughter."

She sensed Sasha craning eagerly from behind Damien, trying to see the paper. The opportunity to gaze at another document of the family tree was enough to drive away his fear.

"No," Alexander said, his voice almost kind, "you did not. You see here?" He drew his finger down the column, ruby ring winking. "The line flows quite easily all the way to 1567, where it ends with Princess Elisabeth Amata Anastasia Renee. And here it says, 'she died childless.'"

Penelope peered at the just-legible writing and agreed, reluctantly, that the Nvengarian words said just that.

"Now here . . ." He gestured to the other column with the name "Elisabeth Bevridge" at the top. "Here is as far back as I traced your family tree, beginning with your mother, Simone Trask, nee Bradshaw. The lineage is not a low one; you have quite a few daughters of earls and viscounts in your past. Elisabeth Bevridge is your ancestor, the record of her appearing in Oxfordshire in 1560." He gave her a look of near sympathy. "It was an easy mistake for Sasha to make. The name of the man the last daughter of Prince Augustus married was Bevridge, but it was a different family altogether. The Elisabeth Bevridge from whom you descend was born in the north of England, married one Thomas Bevridge there, and moved with him to Oxfordshire. Princess Elisabeth married a Jeremiah Bevridge, a native of Oxford."

Penelope stared at the lines and curlicues in silence. No magic, no rings, no spells, no prophecy, just simple history, carefully researched and written in black ink on parchment. The fairy tale dissolved and fell away.

She lifted her hand, willing her fingers not to tremble.

Light flashed on silver. "I have the ring, passed down through my family. It matches Damien's."

Her voice grew firmer with each word. The ring was tangible, too, a talisman passed from person to person for centuries. The lines of its crest were blurred, like the lines on the Roman tablet marking the ancient crossing of the Danube.

"Purchased from a shop in Oxford in 1662," Alexander said. "By one of your forbears. The proprietor told her it belonged in your family."

Penelope sat, silent. She did not entirely believe Alexander, but she had to agree that all he said was plausible.

And more than likely probable. How ridiculous to think she was the long-lost princess of a fairy-tale kingdom, needed to save a people. She was Penelope Trask, spinster, of Little Marching, Oxfordshire, collecting folk tales that she translated and copied.

The truth was, she'd loved the tales because she'd wanted to live one, she'd wanted to believe that one day a prince would come for her, would love her for herself, in the way Reuben White and Magnus never would. And when Damien had turned up, she'd not tried very hard to resist him.

Her eyes misting, she looked over at Damien. He was her husband, and she carried his child. That was real.

She noticed, through her tears, that Damien looked neither surprised nor outraged at Alexander's revelations. She rose to her feet, limbs trembling. "You knew this," she breathed to Damien. "You knew I was not truly . . ."

His eyes were sad. "I knew Alexander had these papers. I also knew Sasha's notes said differently. He believes the line unbroken."

"He is wrong," Alexander said.

"I hardly care," Damien answered. "I know what I felt when I saw her."

"But you did not know when you set off," Penelope said, realizing. "You did not know which I'd turn out to be."

She saw him swallow, but his eyes never wavered. "I had to take the gamble. The stakes were worth it."

"Would you have told me if you discovered I was not the princess?"

He hesitated a long moment. "I do not know."

"Because you needed me for Nvengaria."

"Yes."

Tears dripped down her face. "I only wanted a husband," she whispered, "and to be in love."

Alexander gently slid aside the weights and removed the paper. "I regret to have caused you pain," he said. He sounded like he did regret it, a polite host not wanting to cause a guest discomfort. "But my interpretation is the correct one."

"When I saw you, Penelope," Damien interrupted, "I knew Alexander was wrong."

Alexander shot him a glance that was almost puzzled. The Grand Duke was a very intelligent man, Penelope sensed, and Sasha was driven by fanaticism. They were like the two sides of Nvengaria, Alexander's steely intelligence and Sasha's passionate emotion.

Damien had been forced to choose which he would believe. She wanted to tell him she understood, that she knew he had deliberately chosen love over cool reason, both for Nvengaria and himself. And that the choice had been difficult.

"We can never truly know," she said softly. She glanced at Alexander. "But I can choose which one to be."

"You would be a fool not to choose to return to England," Alexander said.

She gave him a little smile. "I am a fool then. But Damien needs me here."

Sasha made an exasperated noise. "Why do you argue? It matters not what is on your paper, Your Grace. She *is* the true princess. She follows the prophecy. She loves the prince, she tamed the logosh, she heals wounds. She healed me. Look." He began hastily unbuttoning his coat, ready to show the closed knife wound in his back.

"Sasha," Damien said sternly. "Not now."

"But she healed me. We found her, just as was prophesied. She is the true princess."

Alexander gave him a cold smile. "A man may recover from a wound without being healed by a princess."

Sasha pointed at him. "You were not there. I was nearly dead. She brought me to life. She will bring life back to Nvengaria. She carries the prince's child."

"*Sasha.*" Damien swung around, his eyes filled with anger and fear.

"Shut your gob, you stupid man," Egan said at the same time.

Alexander's expression changed instantly from polite urbanity to the ruthlessness of a sword's edge. He turned glittering eyes to Penelope. "Is this true? Do not lie."

Penelope nodded once. The tension in the room rose swiftly, Alexander poised and ready like an executioner's knife.

"I hoped the prince would not touch you," he said. "But he could not resist, could he, a beautiful woman, the rituals, the famous Nvengarian lust? I cannot let you go, Miss Trask. Not while you carry the prince's son."

"You can," Damien said in a hard voice. "Let her live as a widow in Oxfordshire. It might be a daughter."

"That does not matter, and you know it. A boy prince will want his kingdom, a girl princess will claim descent from Augustus, no matter the line is broken."

"Leave her alone, God damn you."

"There is a way," Alexander said thoughtfully. He let the paper roll in his hands and laid it back on the desk. "Marry me, Penelope, when he is dead, and claim the child is mine."

Eyes wide, she shook her head. Alexander let his tone grow patient. "'Tis better than going on the execution block next to him. I will save your life, but I swear there will be no more princes of Nvengaria."

"Damien is nothing like his father," Penelope cried. "He is gentle and kind and would never think to execute a woman."

"No, but he would trick one into marrying him and lie to get her into his bed." Alexander moved close to her. "Do you not see, Miss Trask? If you look at him sometimes, you see the madman inside him. It is like a trick of the light, and then you realize that the madness is truly there."

Penelope wanted to draw a breath and tell him he was wrong, but it died on her lips. She thought of the times Damien had looked at her, his eyes cold as ice, remembered how he'd held her in the bath in Little Marching, begging her to not let his father take him over.

"You see it, too," Alexander breathed. "Do you not?"

Penelope said nothing.

"It does not matter," Damien broke in. "You want to rule Nvengaria like it was a shipping company, with neat returns. You want it to be clean and free of corruption, running along with all parts oiled. But it is not what the Nvengarians want." He gestured to the stained-glass windows. "They want the fairy tale, the prince and princess. They want love and hate and lust and rage; they do not want oiled machines. Open the windows, Alexander. Listen to what they want."

Alexander looked as though he wanted to shoot them all then and there, but he gestured for one of the lackeys to pull back the casement of one of the arched windows on the stone wall.

Sound poured through the window from the city below. Faintly she could hear Titus's cries, but over that was pulsing sound, like a heartbeat, a chant from thousands of throats.

Damien, Damien, Damien, Damien.

"I inherited the title of Imperial Prince," Damien said softly. "But I rule only by will of the people."

"I will not let you have it," Alexander said tightly.

"If you kill me, if you harm Penelope, they will rip you to pieces."

Alexander looked toward the windows, his eyes glittering. Penelope saw his chest rise with a sharp breath. He was angry, but his anger was not mad or mindless. The anger was clear and intelligent. He saw exactly what was wrong, and sought only to put it right.

"Perhaps if—" Penelope began, but broke off when the soldier at the window suddenly screamed and fell backward, his face covered in blood.

"What the hell?" Egan rumbled and drew his knife.

They poured in through the window, at least twenty of them, fast and dark and snakelike, moving with speed that the eye could not match. One moment they were not there, the next they simply were, surrounding the soldiers in a perfect ring, trapping the men, Alexander and Penelope, and Damien and his friends.

They were men, tall and hugely muscled, but they hadn't been men a moment ago. Each had a mane of thick black hair cascading to shoulders, each was covered only in an animal skin slung across his hips. Their faces were man-shaped, but slightly narrower in the jaw, and their eyes were odd, wide and dark blue.

"Logosh," Penelope exclaimed. "They're logosh."

Damien stood silently, but Egan broke into a harsh laugh. "I'll be damned. Wulf didn't fetch his mum, he fetched his dad, and all his dad's friends." He clapped both hands on Damien's shoulders. "Damien, lad, you are one lucky son."

"It was not luck," he returned.

Penelope gasped. "You told Wulf to find them."

Damien nodded once. "I thought I might need an army of my own."

The soldiers stared at the logosh, faces white. They might never have seen logosh before, but they knew what they were, and of what logosh were capable.

The logosh by the window said, in thick Nvengarian, "We serve the princess."

Damien threw open his hands, smiled at Alexander with his old charm. "I would think hard before hurting Penelope in any way. These are her retainers. The princess and the logosh. You know the legend?"

Alexander spoke as though he watched something from far away. "The princess healed the logosh, and won his undying loyalty, and that of his tribe."

"You do read fairy tales," Damien said. "That is what our people want, the legends. The reforms will get done. But the legends are forever."

"But she is not really the princess," Alexander said. "She is a sham."

"Do you think that really matters? There was a story, and now it's come true. They need that. They need *her*."

"They need me," Alexander snarled.

"Penelope, go to the window. Greet your people. See."

Grasping her skirts in her shaking hands, Penelope clicked to the window, passing between two of the scantily clad, very muscled logosh. They did not bow to her or smile, they simply turned as she passed, fixing their strange eyes on her.

She pulled back the half-open casement and looked out.

The wall of the castle here dropped straight down to the city, unimpeded by any curtain walls. The drop was sheer, fifty feet or so—the logosh had climbed straight up it. In the town, at the bottom of the wall, were the people, a mass of color and noise.

When they saw Penelope, they nearly went insane. The chanting of Damien's name faded, to be replaced by a tumult of cheering, a wave of joy that swamped her. She lifted her hand to them, and the cheering, if anything, increased.

She looked back into the room and held out her hand. "Damien."

He came to her, his Nvengarian medals clinking, his dark hair dusty, his chin unshaven. He looked much as he had when she'd first met him, a charming, handsome man who swept her from her feet and began to make love to her in Holden's meadow.

He stepped to the window. Screams and cheers floated to them, banners waved. Damien cupped Penelope's face in his hand, leaned down, and kissed her.

She heard Titus's cry and the crowd's response, but she felt only Damien's hungry kiss. She laced one hand around his neck, rising to his mouth.

Inside the room, Egan swore. Penelope broke the kiss and looked around in time to see one of the soldiers draw his pistol and level it at Damien.

The pistol flashed, powder exploding. Damien flung Penelope to the floor and landed on her as the bullet crashed into the glass. The logosh attacked.

She heard men screaming and the high-keening shrieks of the logosh. Another logosh skimmed up the wall and in through the open window, a very small one.

"Wulf," she shouted as he leapt over her and straight onto Alexander.

Damien sprang to his feet, running for him. Penelope scrambled up, wrestling with her skirts, dashing after him. She noted that Petri had pulled Sasha out of the way, while Egan ran to help Damien. The two men yanked the maddened logosh from Alexander and tossed him aside.

Alexander lay on the floor, his beautiful blue coat in

shreds, the Grand Duke's sash of office slashed to ribbons. Alexander's face was pasty white, blood streaming from wounds in his stomach. He struggled to breathe.

Wulf landed against Penelope and became a boy before he hit the floor. His fingers and mouth bloody, he threw his child's arms about her waist.

She gently pressed him aside, and sank to her knees beside Alexander. Petri pulled open what remained of the coat. "That is a death wound," he announced.

Damien looked grim. Penelope smoothed Alexander's hair from his cold forehead.

His eyes, filled with pain, swiveled to her but did not focus, as though he struggled to see but could not. "I'll not let him win," he said.

"Do not move too much," she begged.

"No." He groped for her hand. "Miss Trask, you must promise me you will not let the monster out."

Penelope took Alexander's ice-cold hand between hers. "I will watch him," she said softly. "I promise."

Behind her, the logosh had stopped. The soldiers, terrified, had surrendered. The logosh, men once more, stood over them, looking as calm as they had before the fight began.

"Tell my son." Alexander broke off and gasped, blood trickling from his mouth.

"You have a son?" Penelope asked, her voice gentle.

"Tell him I love him," Alexander whispered. "Tell him not to be ashamed of me."

"I will take care of him," Damien said, on one knee next to him. "I swear that."

"Not you," Alexander said, seeking Penelope with sightless eyes. "Her."

She squeezed his hand. "I'll not let you die."

Sasha made his way to Penelope. "She is the true princess," he told Alexander, standing over him. "She can heal you."

Alexander gave him an ironic smile, although it was clear he could see nothing. "I am not reassured."

"Bring me water and a sponge and bandages," Penelope commanded. "And herbs—lavender and chamomile."

Petri looked troubled. " 'Tis mortal, Your Highness. His stomach's cut."

"Bring them," she said sternly.

Petri creaked to his feet, resigned, and departed.

Damien helped her move aside the coat and shirt and the slashed waistband of Alexander's trousers. Penelope put her hands to the bloody mess of Alexander's stomach. His blood pulsed around her fingers, and she felt his heartbeat, strange and erratic.

She had no idea what to do. She only knew she could do it.

She closed her eyes, letting her thoughts slide away, comforting darkness taking their place. She saw, not his bones and muscle, but lines and crosses that had to be arranged in a certain way. It gave her pleasure to straighten them in her mind, to cross one over the other, to align this one with that one. Everything untangled to become smooth and straight and neat. The finished pattern made her smile, sending a warmth like joy over her body.

Alexander gasped, and she opened her eyes.

He was staring at her, his focus sharp, his lips parted in shock. But color had returned to his face; his breathing and heartbeat were as normal. Every wound on his torso had dried and closed, dark red streaks the only evidence he'd ever been hurt.

Petri stood beside her, a dripping bowl of water in his hands, and Egan looked over Damien's shoulder, his mouth open. Damien looked at her with eyes full of astonishment, but behind that pride and love.

"You see," Sasha said, shrugging as though nothing extraordinary had happened. "She is the true princess, as I said."

* * *

The royal wedding was scheduled to take place in a week. When the duchess who would be in charge of protocol heard the news, she had hysterics. "A week? I cannot organize a royal wedding in a week! There is a banquet, and invitations, and . . ."

Damien soothed her by telling her that while the wedding would be a simple affair, the coronation, which she had months to plan, could be the most opulent in the history of Nvengaria.

She went away, shaking her head, and Sasha, looking aggrieved, went with her, no doubt to explain that Damien was an eccentric.

There remained the question of what to do with Alexander. Damien had placed him under house arrest—no more dungeons, he'd said sternly—but he had to end it sometime. He had the jailors, retainers from the new palace guard, handpicked by Petri, bring Alexander to see him in Damien's small study a week after Alexander had surrendered.

Alexander sat in a comfortable wing chair facing Damien. Damien had chosen this room to be part of his suite because it had the least amount of gilding, marble, wall hangings, and garish furniture. It looked like the large study of a simpler country house, and Damien wanted simplicity.

Alexander waited, fingers steepled, for Damien to pronounce his sentence. He might be waiting to learn the outcome of a horse race he had only passing interest in.

Damien began without preliminaries. "Your reforms are sensible, you know. I went through all your notebooks, all your schemes. They make much sense given Nvengaria's need to compete with the rest of Europe in industry, and yet to keep us from being swallowed by the larger fish."

"I am pleased you approve," Alexander said.

"I more than approve, I will adopt most of them; they match my own ideas. Your outline for the restructuring of government, on the other hand, will have to go."

"The restructuring is not implausible. Our system was out of date a century after it was initiated."

"Maybe," Damien conceded. "It is unwieldy and divides power too unevenly, but it will have to do. The only way I could instigate a complete restructuring is to force it on the people, by sword if necessary, and that I refuse. Gradual change is better. I recalled the Council of Mages."

"So I heard." Alexander's eyes darkened with anger. "Most of them were loyal to your father and will fight you on anything you want to change."

"I know that."

"Many in the Council of Dukes bear hatred for you as well. They did not like me, but they simply did not like *me*. They loathe the Imperial Prince with a hatred that has run deep for centuries. It is a different thing."

Damien nodded, twisting the heavy silver ring on his finger. "I will handle each problem as it occurs. I never thought that being Imperial Prince of Nvengaria would be a particularly safe occupation."

"Why did you come back?" Alexander asked softly. He let his hands hang from the chair's arms. "The first time, I mean, when Misk brought you the ring. You could have fled to the other side of the world and said to hell with Nvengaria. You have your own money and your popularity in Europe is enviable."

Damien had wondered the same thing many, many times. He remembered the evening when Misk had come to his chamber in Paris, and the lackeys had knelt to him. He'd stood poised between two lives, the difficult one of Imperial Prince, and the lonely one of playboy Damien, rich and carefree and admired.

"It called to me," he said. "That is the only way I can explain it. Nvengaria called to me, and I believe the prophecy did, too. I cannot now imagine a life that does not have Penelope in it."

Alexander watched him closely. "When you look at her, the monster goes away. You look besotted, but like a man who will never let anything hurt her, least of all yourself."

The trouble with Alexander, Damien had always thought, was that the man was too perceptive for his own good.

"I intend to keep watching her," he said. He felt his lips move into a smile. "Try falling in love, Alexander. 'Twill make your life—interesting."

"No, thank you. I find it interesting enough."

"Words of a man who has never swum those waters. You will happily drown."

Alexander gave him a cool stare. "I much doubt it." He touched his stomach, where the wounds had healed. Petri had made certain that his blue and gold sash of office was mended, as well. "However, I have learned never to argue with magic."

"When magic touches you, I will be first to congratulate you. But we must return to the problem of what to do with you."

His dark brows flicked upward. "I confess, I had thought to finding myself facing a firing squad at any moment."

Damien's amusement fled. "I am not my father. I will not execute every person who annoys me. One loses one's friends as well as enemies when that happens."

"But if you spare every person," Alexander pointed out, "then your enemies will begin to take advantage of you. They will move against you, knowing you will not stop them."

"I never said I would not stop them. I simply said I do not believe in random execution. I intend to have trials and juries and councils and so forth. No stealing people away in the middle of the night. No dungeons, no arbitrary firing squads."

Alexander laughed mirthlessly. "You'll not last a week."

"We shall see." Damien narrowed his eyes. "As for you—you do have many supporters. There are plenty of reformers in this country who admire you. If I put you to death, you might become a martyr to our volatile people, who will move against me. The best thing to do is have you work for me."

Alexander stilled, the ruby in his ear glinting against his dark hair. "You could never trust me by your side."

"No, I do not." He turned the ring. "What I want is for you to work for me elsewhere, in the courts of Europe, especially that of England. You do not want the Hapsburgs or the Ottomans to swallow Nvengaria, and neither do I. You have done much to help keep them out, but you need to go out into the world and discover exactly what they are up to. Anastasia does much, but she is rather fanatical in her hatred for Austria, which makes her miss things. I need someone more neutral, who is for Nvengaria, but not necessarily against everyone else."

"And you would trust me to do this?"

"Yes." He smiled faintly. "Because you would never raise an army of Germans or Prussians or Austrians to march here and overthrow me. You bring in German soldiers, they might decide to stay and invite their leaders to follow. Mercenaries need a great deal of money to be placated. I would trust you because you love Nvengaria as much as I do. More, probably."

Alexander considered. "So you wish to exile me. A punishment that will hurt me more than death."

"I cannot trust you here. I need you out there. It is not exile, unless you want it to be. You may come home anytime." He paused. "I really do need you, Alexander. I do not trust you against me, but I do trust you to want what is best for Nvengaria."

He sat back, his bearing as imperious as ever. "What of my son?"

"What of him?"

"Is he free to accompany me? Or will he be held here as a hostage for my good behavior?"

Damien gave him a long look. "You expect so much cruelty from me. Penelope would never allow me to use the boy as a hostage, you must know that. Take him or leave him, as you wish. If he stays, Penelope will look after him and see to his schooling and all those other things women like to do."

"His own mother had little to do with him," Alexander observed. "Although that does not mean she did not care for him."

Damien softened his voice. "I am sorry for Sephronia's death."

Alexander shrugged, as though it meant nothing, but Damien saw true grief in his eyes. "It was quick, in the end."

"Do this for me, Alexander," Damien said. "I need you in England. I need the Regent's help against Russia and Austria and the Ottomans if necessary, but I do not trust him, either. I need someone strong to keep him and his advisors tame. I need someone who they will know can be ruthless if necessary. I need you to be my sword."

His brows lifted. "You want me to intimidate them, in other words."

"Yes. I can cajole them, but the Regent still thinks of me as the dilettante prince. His only thoughts about me are to compare horses or suits or mistresses. He will not know quite what to do with you. You will terrify him." He smiled at the prospect.

"You do have cruelty, Damien," Alexander said. He

was silent a moment, then gave Damien an unreadable look. "Very well, I will help you."

Damien looked at him, slightly surprised. "You agree?"

"As you said, I want a strong Nvengaria. I do not trust you, but I will work for it any way I can. This is much like what I wanted at first, you know—a figurehead for the people to love and worship while I worked for an efficient state. I want Nvengaria, not adoration."

Damien did not trust Alexander either, but knew he'd be fool to throw away such an asset. Alexander was definitely a man he wanted on his side, and he imagined the Regent's trepidation when Alexander began to negotiate. Alexander would have the Regent begging for mercy. He was almost sorry he'd miss it.

Damien likewise knew that Alexander would always be watching, waiting for Damien to show signs of becoming his father. Alexander, for all his ruthlessness, truly did love Nvengaria. Damien knew the man would fight to the death to keep it free.

He let none of these thoughts show on his face. "Excellent," he answered. He rose and took up a flask of Nvengarian brandy. "Let us drink to it. Then I must see to preparations for my wedding."

He brought the flask and glasses back to Alexander. They each poured their own and examined the glass and fluid closely before they took the first sip, at exactly the same time.

They could never be too careful.

Chapter Twenty-four

The royal wedding took place on a fine and fair day, in the royal chapel high in the castle of the princes of Nvengaria. A bishop joined the couple in matrimony for the second time—third if Penelope believed the Nvengarian betrothal ceremony was truly a wedding.

Penelope stood in a gown of white silk satin covered with a filmy net of white tulle, Damien distractingly handsome in Nvengarian blue. His medals gleamed, and he wore a slight smile, happy that his plans had at last come to fruition. Prince Charming had won.

Sasha had stood in for the father of the bride, beaming with pride as he gave her away. Egan hovered at Damien's side as best man, looking a bit shaky from revelry the night before. Damien seemed none the worse for wear, but Egan and Petri had red eyes and white faces and wore expressions of pain.

Penelope reflected that her very low-church father would have fainted to see his daughter marry in this papist ceremony, with the bishop in his miter and cloth of gold robes, chanting over the host, and leading her and Damien to kneel to a statue of the Virgin.

Trappings, Damien had said. A thin layer of Catholicism over the roiling paganism of Nvengaria.

The logosh had vanished as quickly as they'd come. The leader, who called himself Myn, had gazed at Penelope with his strange blue eyes and vowed that if she ever had need again, he and his band would be at her side in an instant.

She was touched, but slightly unnerved by this devotion and Myn's claim that he could produce a thousand logosh whenever she called. They would respond only to her, he said, not the prince. Then they'd flowed away, and were gone.

Wulf, on the other hand, stayed with Penelope. He had refused to leave with the other logosh, and Penelope was happy to let him stay. She had grown fond of the boy. Damien was more reluctant, but agreed that he had saved her life more than once, for which he'd be eternally grateful. Wulf was given the uniform of a page, but no duties except to follow Penelope and keep her from danger. He attended the wedding today, crouched in front of the pews, watching the proceedings with fascination.

Alexander also attended the wedding. He sat in the front row, his status as Grand Duke of the Council of Dukes unchanged. His small son, a dark-haired, fine-looking lad who smiled more readily than his father, sat beside him.

Alexander would be leaving for England the next week. Damien knew that he, like Lady Anastasia, would work for the good of Nvengaria, not Damien himself.

"He'll enjoy playing spy," he told Penelope. "I imagine he'll be very, very good at it. And he will keep his eyes on me at the same time. If he ever believes my father has returned through me, he will be back."

Penelope knew, however, that Damien had somehow turned Alexander to his side. She'd begun to believe Damien's ability to handle people was nearly magical.

On the subject of magic—she glanced back at Sasha. The night before, while at a banquet dinner with both Council of Dukes and Council of Mages, Damien had commented under his breath that he'd like his councils to disappear so he could spend the time alone with Penelope. Sasha had said brightly, "I could send everyone to sleep if you like. Except—ah—it might send you and Her Highness to sleep as well."

Damien had turned to him, gaze intent. "You set that enchanted sleep back in Little Marching?"

Sasha had turned bright red under his beard. "I did."

"You are a mage? Why the devil haven't you told me?"

He looked modest. "A humble one only, Highness. I could never, ever be strong enough for the Council of Mages. It was a minor spell, simple. Only—I miscalculated."

Penelope leaned around Damien, interested. "What do you mean, miscalculated?" she asked.

"It was meant to send the logosh to sleep," Sasha confessed. "He crept back to the house, and I feared he'd hurt the princess. I meant to do a sleep spell, then alert the guards so they could creep up on him and kill him." His flush deepened. "But the entire household went to sleep, not only the logosh. Being asleep myself, I could not undo the spell."

"Sasha," Damien rumbled.

The small man bowed his head. "I am deeply sorry, Your Highness. You may punish me as you see fit."

"You old fool," Damien's voice softened. "If you ever want to use a spell to protect me again—tell me first."

"Yes, Your Highness," Sasha said. Then he smiled, knowing he'd been forgiven.

* * *

After the wedding ceremony came another long banquet, then a ball. Damien smiled and talked and charmed his way through it, though Penelope's feet hurt, her head ached, and she could not remember by the end of the evening what she'd said to whom. She'd danced with Damien—the first dance—and then had been passed around through the entire Council of Dukes and Council of Mages, at least those who could stand up long enough to dance.

Egan McDonald had lapsed into playing the Mad Highlander, regaling people with harrowing stories of life in the Highlands and life on the Peninsula during the war, and hopping up and down and kicking his feet wildly when someone demanded to see a traditional Highland dance. The Nvengarians loved him.

As the evening progressed, the resemblance to a cultured ball at a Mayfair home diminished, and the Nvengarian characteristic took over. Wine flowed, the dancing moved from constrained waltzes to free-for-all wildness, and the music became more and more frenzied.

Even the most staid matrons and gentlemen joined in the circle dances, where circles wove inside circles, and lines of people, linking hands, pulled each other in sinuous waves through the huge ballroom.

Those not dancing clapped, including Penelope and Damien standing on the dais together, the sound growing louder and faster as the dancers frantically tried to keep up with the time.

The laughter gave way to whoops and ululations as the ancient madness that lay buried inside every Nvengarian rose to the surface. Penelope's heart beat faster, feeling the stirrings inside herself, dark needs that told her, more than Alexander's pieces of paper, that she was truly one of them.

She felt Nvengaria's magic and its wildness and its barely suppressed barbarism seeping from the bones of the land itself. No matter how many elegant palaces and estates adorned the hills, they were at heart a very basic people, as primitive as the logosh. There was probably more link to the logosh in Nvengarians than they knew themselves.

As the ballroom grew darker, the red light of braziers taking over the light of candles burned to the nubs, Damien came to Penelope's side. His fingers hard on her arm, he said, "Let us adjourn."

"Should we?" she asked, glancing about. "We are the guests of honor."

"We should." His face was flushed, his eyes, like those of his people, deep blue and glittering. "Else I'll drag you under the table and ravish you."

"Then we should go," she said quickly.

They made no formal good-byes. Damien simply led her to a small door in the back of the room, and out.

He hastened her through dark narrow servants' halls and up winding staircases until they reached the bedchamber they were to share. Damien's huge bed of state, nearly twice the size of the one they'd been given in Carleton House, dominated the room. A canopy of red and gold hung from the high ceiling above it.

"Goodness," Penelope said. "Seven or eight people could sleep in that."

Damien kicked the door closed. "Tonight, only two." He stood near the door, looking more like one of the logosh of the mountains than an Imperial Prince. "Take off the dress if you want to save it from me."

She touched the fine silk of her white gown. "It is rather splendid."

"Take it off," he repeated. "Else I'll rip it from you."

She remembered how he'd asked her to slowly undress for him the night at Carleton House, but she sensed that tonight, he had no such patience. Under his intense gaze, she quickly stripped off the gown and laid it across a chair.

He came to her, strong fingers unhooking the stays and skirts she wore under it. "Everything off. I want you bare for me."

He unlaced and yanked the chemise from her, then pulled her naked against his Imperial Prince's uniform.

"Mine," he said. "Beautiful, beautiful, and mine."

His kiss was more like an assault, teeth and tongue probing her mouth, his civilized behavior completely gone. Prince Charming had vanished, the real Damien taking his place.

He scooped her up and carried her to the bed, throwing her to the middle. She raised herself on her elbows to watch him quickly get out of his clothes, leaving them all over the floor. "Petri will scold," she said.

He growled. No, more of a snarl of some ancient beast. Naked, he got on the bed, moving with sinuous grace to the middle of it.

"I want you," he said. "I want you hard and fast and I do not intend to be gentle about it."

Her heart beat faster, a dark shiver trailing down her spine. "Do your worst, Prince of Nvengaria," she said coyly.

That had been a mistake. His eyes grew dark with a kind of delirium, desire overtaking his senses.

He flipped her over, then pinned her outstretched arms with one hand holding both her wrists. He spread her thighs with his knee, then lifted her hips and entered her swiftly.

She screamed. She thought she'd experienced so much with him, but this went beyond it. His powerful thrusts touched places she'd never been touched, awoke feelings she'd never known existed. She screamed and screamed and he rode her until he peaked with his own climax, then he rolled her over and, still aroused, entered her again.

He took her three times before he finally collapsed beside her. Exhausted, she kissed him, her lips swollen, scraped by his teeth and tongue. She had the feeling that he could have gone on a few more times; he was simply being kind and letting her rest.

"Damien," she said sometime later, when her voice returned.

"Yes, love?" His voice, too, was broken.

"On Midsummer's Day, when we were snowed in up in the mountains, the prophecy ended."

"Yes." He kissed her brow with gentle lips.

"Yet I still loved you. I felt the prophecy go, but I still loved you more than my own life."

He smoothed her hair. In the shadows of the canopy, his eyes were dark, almost black. "And now?"

"Yes. Still."

He looked at her a long time. "I felt the prophecy die, too. But I knew, I've always known, that it made no difference." He kissed her. "I love you madly, Penelope."

"When we arrived in Nvengaria, three days late, when it was all for nothing, they still wanted you," she said. "You did not fulfill the prophecy in time, you failed, and they still wanted you."

He smiled, his charm and arrogant assurance returning. "That is what Alexander did not understand. Some things are more powerful than prophecy or magic."

"Love," she said.

He nodded. "The most powerful of all." He smiled. "I ought to write a ballad."

She touched his cheek and smiled sleepily. "Tell me another Nvengarian fairy tale instead."

He chuckled. She snuggled against him, liking the warm vibration of laughter on his chest.

"Once upon a time," he said, drifting his hand through

her hair, "there was a beautiful princess. One day, a very handsome, very charming prince came along and carried her off to his kingdom, far, far away."

"Mmm, I like that." She traced the ridges of his abdomen. "Did they live happily ever after?"

He kissed her, his voice roughening. "They will, Penelope. They will. This I swear to you with all my heart."

Epilogue

His Imperial Highness, Prince Damien Augustus Frederic Michel of Nvengaria, and her Imperial Highness, the Princess Penelope, announce the birth of a prince on the Seventh Day of March, the year of our lord Eighteen Hundred and Twenty. The child shall be christened his most royal Prince Damien Sasha Egan Augustus on the Tenth Day of March, Eighteen Hundred and Twenty, in the Royal Chapel at the castle of the Imperial Princes in Narato.

The invitations were written in gold ink on gilt-edged parchment and delivered throughout every country in Europe. One special announcement went to the London house of Mr. and Mrs. Michael Tavistock, number 32 Stratford Street, near Portman Square.

"Fancy," Simone said, when she opened the announcement at the breakfast table, "I am a grandmother.

Michael, that means you are a grandpapa. A stepgrand-papa, anyway."

Michael Tavistock smiled at his wife. "Excellent news. We must send a gift."

"What do you send an infant prince?" Simone mused. "Goodness, he must be surrounded by silver plate from every king in the world."

"I intend to knit him a cap," Meagan declared on the other side of the table. She licked jam from her spoon, eyes happy. "After all, I am his auntie, and the poor little thing will need to keep his head warm."

"I imagine he'll have dozens of caps," Simone pointed out. "All of velvet and silk, I shouldn't wonder."

"But not one knitted in good English wool by his stepauntie."

Michael set down his coffee cup, enjoying the sight of morning sunlight on his wife's golden head and his daughter's shining red one. "An excellent idea, Meagan. Penelope would enjoy receiving such a thing from you."

"Penelope will, yes," Simone said. She sipped her coffee, looking momentarily mournful. She sighed. "The dear girl is so *practical.*"

A month later, in the castle of the Imperial Princes in Nvengaria, Penelope, sitting on a small red-upholstered throne next to the prince's larger one, received a package from England from a liveried messenger. She thanked the man and opened it with eager fingers.

When she saw the tiny fitted cap in blue and red striped wool, her eyes filled with happy tears. "Oh, Damien, come and see."

The Imperial Prince of Nvengaria lay on his back on the polished floor before the double throne, his small son on his chest. One large hand cradled the boy, who slept in the relaxed way of infants, his small hands curled to fists on his father's waistcoat. "I cannot rise at present, love," Damien said softly. "I'll wake him."

Penelope pushed the wrappings aside, rose, and seated herself gracefully on the floor, her Nvengarian silk gown spilling to the floor. "Auntie Meagan knitted a cap. Is that not a fine thing for a princeling's head?"

Damien examined it. "Indeed, he shall wear it when the next diplomats come to ogle him."

"She knew exactly what to send, bless her."

Damien studied her a moment, stroking his son's tiny back. "You miss them."

"Oh, yes. Every day. But I can see them through Nedrak's scrying crystal, and Sasha said he is working on a spell that will let me write on a paper, and the words will appear on a paper in front of Meagan almost immediately. Would that not be splendid?"

Damien snorted. "Sasha's spells do blunder, you know."

"Yes, that is why I have encouraged him to do much research first."

Damien laughed, shaking the baby, but he did not wake.

Penelope laid her hand on Damien's, brushing fingers over her child's fine black hair. "I do miss them. But I would not trade this for the world. You and he are my family now."

Damien bent a smile on her, warm and full of promise. "I am pleased, my princess."

"This is our happily ever after, isn't it?" she asked dreamily. "A family, and love."

His eyes darkened. "Yes."

"It is what the prophecy wanted, I think," she said. "To reunite the line, but to do it in love. Your father mired everything in hate, and Alexander continued it, even if he did not mean to. The prophecy wanted love."

Damien pulled her down to lie against him. Baby

Damien yawned, opened his dark blue eyes, focused them on Penelope a moment, then went back to sleep.

"I am damn pleased it did," Damien said, his voice low.

"It is not really the end of the story, is it?" Penelope said. "But the beginning."

Damien turned his head and kissed her lips. She felt now-familiar fires stir that nearly a year with Damien had not quenched.

"I hope our story goes on forever, Penelope."

"So do I."

He smiled against her lips. "We will have to tell it to our boy one day. The real story, not Sasha's wild embellishments."

She laughed. "The real story. About how you swept into my life and turned everything upside-down and charmed me into loving you."

His smile went wicked. "Perhaps later today we can again remember some of the details?"

She had learned how to be as wicked and teasing as he. She nibbled the lobe of his ear. "I would be most pleased, my prince."

Damien kissed her again, a long, deep kiss. "I love you," he said, his blue eyes warm.

"I love you."

He stroked the baby's back with his thumb, and Penelope smiled. "Now I have two Prince Charmings in my life," she said. "Can any girl in the entire world be as lucky as me?"

The Care & Feeding of Pirates

Jennifer Ashley

Honoria Ardmore is as prim and proper as they come. Her sole moment of indiscretion was when she fell for a roguish pirate. But he died, or at least, that's what she assumed—until the night he showed up eager to pick up where they had left off….

Christopher Raine cheated death, and he believes life owes him his just rewards. So he sets out to reclaim the woman of his dreams. And this insatiable pirate is not one to let trivial details get in his way.

JENNIFER ASHLEY
CONFESSIONS
of a
LINGERIE ADDICT

The fixation began on New Year's Day: Silky, expensive slips from New York and Italy. Camisoles and thongs from Beverly Hills. Before, Brenda Scott would have blushed to be caught dead in them. Now, she's ditched the shy and mousy persona that got her dumped by her rich and perfect fiancé, and she is sexy. Underneath her sensible clothes, Brenda is the woman she wants to be.

After all, why can't she be wild and crazy? Nick, the sexy stranger she met on New Year's, already seems to think she is. Of course, he didn't know the old Brenda. How long before Nick strips it all away and finds the truth beneath? And would that be a bad thing?

- -